SHATTER

by
Justine Dodge

ISBN 9780692620168
LCCN 2016901107

Printed in the United States.

for Nana, my first reader.

Peter

Scout bullets ricochet off the log walls of the trader's shop between the shooters and my position, narrowly missing my face. I duck, covering my head and crouching low in the snow. When the gunfire pauses, I lean out from cover to fire back at the Scouts, but the wind drives freezing flakes into my face and makes it difficult to aim.

"Filthy buggers," I shout. Beside me, Felix yanks me back by the collar of my fur coat.

"Keep your bloody head down!" He orders, peering up at the Glass City hovering overhead to make sure no more hovercrafts are coming.

I fire off another shot, then duck back down behind our meager cover of the rust-pitted steel wagon that leans against the back wall of the butcher's shop—a squat building made of mismatched lengths of weather-grayed wood. "You bastards are messin' with the wrong brothers!"

"Ah, language." Felix backhands my shoulder before leaning around the edge of the wagon and firing his pistol. The Scouts dive behind the opposite corner of the building.

The people of Colfer are hiding inside, like they always do.

A bullet whizzes past my ear, and I duck further down, my heart pounding. There's got to be only two or three of them, but there are so many bullets it's hard to tell for sure. "Bloody hell! They just keep shootin'."

My brother hits me again. "Watch your language!"

"Are you really givin' me crap about that now?"

"Well ya weren't cursin' earlier!"

"I wasn't gettin' shot at earlier!" I crawl toward the butcher's shop and peek around the corner. The village of Colfer is more like a disorderly cluster of buildings than a proper village; a couple shops and a bunch of houses, mostly belonging to hunters.

A Scout breaks cover, firing repeatedly at the spot I just crawled from. I slide down the wall and press my shoulder against the wood, leaning around the corner. Taking aim, I send a bullet through his skull. I drop back behind cover at the same time he hits the ground.

Felix's eyebrows go up. "Nice shot."

I feel sick every time I have to take one of these guys out. My brother and I are hunters, but these are people, not animals. Or at least they're supposed to be. The sound of gunfire ceases, and Felix and I both peer around our cover in time to see the remaining Scout disappear between the trader's shop and the old hunter's home with the boarded up windows.

"The last one's on the run."

Felix huffs a sigh, his dark red hair plastered to his forehead with sweat and melted snow. "We'll have to chase him down. He'll bring more."

I rub my eye. "I wish we could just go back to huntin' animals."

"Don't we all?" Felix reloads his gun before starting after the Scout at a jog, stumbling through the snow. My chest feels heavy, and I follow after him without another word.

Felix picks up his pace, and I do the same, tripping and rolling in the snow.

"On your feet you idiot."

"Shut up." I hurl a handful of snow at him before lurching to my feet.

"Where's their hovercraft? Did you see it land? Or was it cloaked with their bloody invisibility tech?"

"Well we won't find it if it's invisible." I glance toward the outskirts of town, but see nothing. The thought of getting shot by invisible turrets makes me move closer to the buildings. "We won't find him either if he's reached it—if he hasn't already got to it then we need to make sure he never does."

The Scout reappears suddenly behind us, a flash of red dashing out from between two buildings that are leaning together so that their rooftops are touching.

"Stop!" Felix lunges after him, and the Scout glances over his shoulder, face twisting with panic. He turns and fires twice, sending my brother diving behind a house. A woman screams at the sound of the Scout's gunshots. I flatten against a wall to avoid getting hit, praying the Scout doesn't find the woman before Felix does.

But Felix is too slow. The Scout finds her first, and he reaches beneath the porch attached to the trader's shop. He drags a woman out by her hair. The Scout holds her in front of him with his gun to her head. Aileen, the butcher's wife.

Felix steps out into the open ahead of me, his gun trained on the Scout. He's unable to get a clear shot.

The door to the butcher shop opens and Castor steps out, animal blood all over his apron. "Aileen!"

The Scout shoves his gun against her temple, the muzzle of the weapon disappearing in the mess of frizzy white-blonde hair. "Don't you take a step closer!"

Felix waves Castor back inside. The butcher swallows and closes the door slowly. Felix and I never miss—the Scout is as good as dead. Felix stays where he is, keeping his gun trained on the would-be abductor.

"You don't have to do this." Felix says it calmly, but I know he hates the words. "We're all just people, tryin' to survive."

While Felix distracts him, I slink back toward the butcher's shop behind the Scout, ducking between buildings and looking for a better shot.

"You're not people! You're monsters!" The Scout hisses the last word through bared teeth. His brown hair is stuck to his forehead, and the whites of his eyes are showing.

I swear under my breath at the man's audacity, and Felix snaps. "*We're* the monsters? You abduct us from our bloody homes!"

I pull my rifle off my back and prop myself against the wall of a house behind the Scout, scoping down the barrel and fixing my sights on his head. I'm at the perfect angle now, I don't risk hitting Aileen, but the thought of shooting another human being makes me hesitate before pulling the trigger.

"Do it!" Felix shouts.

Before the Scout can turn, I take the shot.

The Scout's head snaps to the side and he drops without a sound, and Castor runs out of his shop. He pulls his wife into an embrace, holding her as she sobs hysterically. I step back out into the open. Felix crunches through the snow and claps his hand on my shoulder, staring down at the Scout's corpse with a mixed expression. "Well. That's one way to start the day."

"Were there more?" I ask. It had seemed like an awful lot of bullets flying for just two Scouts.

Felix grunts. "We better hope not."

I reach out and touch Aileen's shoulder. "Are you okay?"

Blood spatter paints one side of her face and I cringe, reluctant to point it out. Castor has turned her away from the dead Scout, and her hysterics are finally starting to calm down. She takes a shuddering breath and nods.

"Thank you," Castor tells us, swallowing hard. "If you need anythin' from me just ask. Ya boys comin' in today?"

Felix stoops and starts picking through the snow for shell casings, and I nod. "Aye. We were comin' to see you when these jackals ambushed us on our way from Addy's."

Castor loosens his hold on his wife, and she pulls away from him. "Go on in the house and clean up, love. I will just be a moment."

A few men dressed in heavy wolf furs file into the streets as life in Colfer returns to normal. The Dead Handlers hover quietly nearby until Felix steps away from the body of the Scout. Their hoods are pulled down over their foreheads against the cold; the black skin of their polar bear fur clothes make them look like grim reapers—a fitting appearance, I suppose. They pick up the body and carry it toward the old burnt out gym. The other Scout's body has already been cleared away.

The clothes and weaponry on the bodies will be stripped away and sold for a high price. Part of me wants to protest that we were the ones who did the killing, we should at least be able to get a new pair of boots out of it, but the Dead Handlers have made it clear that what comes off the dead goes to them—a fair price to pay for the job they do.

"So are ya gonna stick around for long then?" Castor watches the Dead Handlers haul the body away.

"No. We've got another hunt today. Addy's runts have eaten all our stores," Felix says.

We start walking slowly toward the butcher's shop.

"Remind me again why you are still livin' with that woman? You Gerrethson boys are all old enough now to live on your own. Take one of the empty shacks. Move out on your own."

"Because this idiot doesn't want to leave," I say, not bothering to hide the growl in my voice.

"That's because she's family." Felix gives me a look. "I promised Mum I would take care of her and her kids."

"Was that before or after she became a whore?"

"Peter!"

"What? I'm sick of her! I don't care that she's family, she's just takin' advantage of us and addin' more bastard mouths to feed!"

"Watch your bloody language!"

I throw my hands up. "Why are you constantly ridin' my arse about language! Nobody out here cares!"

Felix grits his teeth. "Mum would."

"Well Mum is dead, she's not goin' to care what—"

Felix catches me by the front of my coat and slams me against the wall of Castor's shop.

"You listen to me you little *brat*," he spits, and I flinch. "I am doin' the best I can out here. Mum wanted us to grow up *decent* and *respectable*—" He shoves my chest for emphasis—"and your cursin' all the time makes you sound crude and stupid. I thought I taught you a wider vocabulary! Just because you never knew Mum doesn't mean you can just piss all over the promises I made her."

I don't meet his gaze, shame flushing my face and forcing my eyes to the ground. "I'm sorry," I whisper.

Felix lets go of me, and I drop back to the ground.

"So am I," he hisses. He shoves through the door of the butcher's shop and slams it shut behind him.

Castor just shakes his shaggy blond head, staring after Felix with wide blue eyes.

I straighten my fur coat, my hands shaking from rage. I'm nineteen and my brother is thirty-five, but that doesn't make him my father. Most of my anger is directed to Felix, but some of it is for myself, and that only makes me angrier.

Castor catches my arm before I go inside. "Oi, listen." He makes me face him. "Your mother was a good woman, and your father was one of the more respectable men down here."

I scoff. "He was a violent angry drunk."

"He *was*. But your mother's naggin' changed that. He gave up drinkin' because it was destroyin' his family. He learned to keep his head. Sometimes it's better to calm the situation rather than inflame it by effin' and blindin' at everyone around you. Your brother's just tryin' to keep you from gettin' yourself into trouble."

Castor gestures for me to follow him into the butcher shop. Inside, I sit quietly on the barstool next to Felix, who is turning his knife over in his hands.

"So….is Addy still poppin' out babies then?" Castor asks.

I cringe. "That is not the image I needed right now."

Felix shakes his head, not looking up. "Not since last year. No one new in town who doesn't know better than to stay far away from her bed."

Addalynn's kids are as spoiled as one can get on the Surface. Orphans never lasted long—the asteroids threw everyone back to the dark ages, when children were just another mouth to feed. But our cousins still have their mother—and Felix, who's such an 'honorable' sap that he allows them to take the better cut of what we catch. The only reason I'm still alive is because when our parents died, Felix had been old enough to hunt, and our aunt had just lost her husband. I don't think the fact that we're family had anything to do with it, but Felix likes to think so. If Addy cared that we were family, she wouldn't constantly take advantage of us, and her brats would be helping us hunt.

Castor stands behind the bar; Castor is the butcher, but his shop doubles as the tavern. Shelves line the back wall stacked with chipped glassware, and a few paltry bottles of liquor. About five other hunters sit at the rickety old tables, talking about where they plan to hunt today—hunters who'd probably been hiding and pissing themselves while we were outside dealing with the Scouts. Then again, no one wants to be hauled off by Scouts to the Glass City to be a slave.

"Freezin' out there," Felix mutters, puffing vapor into the chilly air with every exhale.

"When is it not?" I grunt. I'm not sure which has contributed more grumpy mood, being woken up at four thirty by Addy's three-year-old, getting ambushed by Scouts, or Felix and his stupid promises.

Felix reaches over and rubs the top of my head roughly. "Quit your blubberin', kid."

I jerk away, scowling as I pull my gloves off. Kid. Unless he's being serious, I'm always 'kid'. It used to infuriate me, but it doesn't bother me so much now—even though I'm still pissed at him—because he's trying to take my mind off killing people.

Our difference in age almost makes Felix old enough to be my father, but he's never been a father, always a brother. A brother who fights by my side, and follows me into whatever trouble I get into; always dragging my sorry butt out of it.

Castor pulls down a pair of chipped mugs. He nods to each of us as if it's just a normal day. "The usual?"

"You know us so well." Felix almost smiles.

"Come on. You just saved my wife from whatever happens to people up there in the Glass City." He is smiling, but a darkness passes over his face. "Whatever you want. It's on the house."

"You know what alcohol did to Da. Mum wouldn't stand for it if she were here," Felix tells Castor.

"There he goes on about Mum again."

"Don't you start," Felix warns.

"Just get us the bloody drink," I mumble, irritated. All this talk about how honorable our father was and Felix can't even say he was an angry drunk. Even if he gave up drinking, that doesn't change what he did before that. I might not have known my father, but if Felix won't drink because he thinks alcohol will have the same effect on us, then Da must've been pretty bad before Mum got to him.

"Touchy touchy." Castor scolds, but I can hear the humor in his voice, and he turns away and bustles off.

Behind us, the door squeaks open; heavy footsteps clomp into the building. Felix and I pay the newcomer no mind, gladly accepting the chipped mugs from Castor as he returns with our water, which is still hot.

"What a racket," a man grumbles behind us. Garret pulls out a stool and sits next to me. He's scruffy, but because he's a Dead Handler, he's got a strong build.

"Mornin', Garret," Felix says over my shoulder.

"Mornin'." He nudges me roughly with his elbow. "Did ya see it? Some Scout got his head blown off just a few minutes ago. Stupid. The shooter will only attract more of them to us. They're like ants. Kill one and the whole hive comes lookin' to find out what happened."

I resist the urge to roll my eyes. There haven't been any ants in forty years—the eternal winter that froze the planet after the asteroids hit wiped out most life on this planet. Before then, they say it could get as warm as a stove and that the sky could be crystal blue. Sometimes I think it's all a fairytale; the sun, the moon, the stars—a world where you didn't have to fight to live every single day.

Garret never saw any of that—wasn't even alive then—but he sits beside me spouting off like he knows everything about the old world, when he's barely older than Felix. Must be drunk again. I don't say anything, taking a gulp of water and letting it wash out the nasty taste of the morning.

Felix snorts. "Ants didn't live in hives, that was bees."

I snicker, adjusting the strap on my rifle.

Garret glares at us, close enough that his hot breath breezes in my face. He grasps my arm. "'Twas you, wasn't it. You were the ones who killed the Scouts"

I slowly set my mug down, tensing. "Aye, it was." I keep my voice smooth and calm. No point in denying it. Beside me, Felix glances sidelong at Garret, his elbows resting on the bar and his mug clasped in both hands. Castor slows as he walks by, a worried expression pulling at his face before he hurries off toward one of the few other people here, the hunter that lives next to the trader's shop.

"Do you know what kind of hellfire you could bring down on this town?" Garret growls, and I close my eyes to keep them from rolling.

"I saved a woman—who happened to be your aunt, by the way. I didn't see anyone else steppin' up to do it. Even though there was a room full of armed men right here." I say the last bit a little loud and then feel bad. The other hunters don't deserve to be called out, just because this man is acting like a fool. If I had been inside the butcher's tavern when the Scouts had come, I probably would have stayed hidden too.

"You're a fool. You might've saved one woman, but you've killed the rest of us!" He definitely smells like he's plastered, and part of me wants to snap at him.

Instead, I remind myself of what Castor had told me, and in attempt to keep Garret talking rather than fighting, I ask, "So you don't care that your aunt was almost murdered a wee bit ago?"

"They always take someone," Garret says, with a little less force.

"So, as long as there are sacrifices from Colfer to the glass gods in the sky, you don't care who it is? Just so long as it's not you."

"Peter." Felix's voice is flat and warning.

"Where have you been?" I ask, before Garret can explode. It's usually easy to change the subject with him when he's drunk. "I haven't seen you around lately. Did Jimmy send ya somewhere to get some more supplies for the shop?"

Garret lets go of my arm to accept a glass stein from Castor, who looks nervous as hell. "Brimstone. Someone told Da that their Dead Handlers had found his sister. She's been missin' for eight years."

I've heard of Brimstone and other places like it; they're almost cities, built in and around ancient castles that have been around since before the asteroids struck, and probably will be forever, but with so many people crammed into a little space disease tends to build up quickly. "Was it her?"

"Aye. Or what was left of her." Garret glares at me. "She never stood a chance. None of us do. The Glass City has everythin' up there. Technology, weapons, medicine. I can barely get enough light out of my blubber oil lamp to see by if I have to go to the jacks in the middle of the night. You pissed them off, Peter. They'll kill us all for what you've done."

I finally roll my eyes at the drama. He sees me, and his face turns red. "What, ya think I'm crazy? Think I don't know what I'm talkin' about?"

"No." *Yes.* "If it makes ya feel any better, I'll just let the Scout kill your aunt next time, alright? I'll just let him run around shootin' everyone he sees so that I don't upset his friends."

"You think this is funny?!"

"Am I laughin'?"

He lurches to his feet. Felix's body goes rigid, but he remains seated. "Get up and face me like a man."

I sigh. People are watching us. They know of Felix's reputation, and mine. Felix has decided we are the police of Colfer, and we should make sure people get along or get out. If someone starts a fight, we finish it.

I'm sure the other hunters would enjoy a little entertainment, but I don't want to deal with every problem I face with my fists. That would just give Felix another reason to nag at me. "Look, I meant no offense. Just sit down and let's talk it through like civilized gentlemen."

"The act of bein' civilized died out with half the planet forty years ago. Stand up and put 'em up," the man growls, raising his fists.

"Ya don't want to do this."

"Aye, I do you son of a whore—" Before he can finish, I'm on my feet and swinging my left fist. I catch him in the jaw and he hits the floor. Garret gasps, holding his jaw and blinking rapidly as I sit back down, flexing my sore fingers and mumbling into my glass.

"Now what did I tell ya?"

"You stupid—ya think you can just treat your elders that way!? That's just filfy, you dirty rotten-"

"I thought bein' civilized died out."

Garret scrambles to his feet, his lower lip bleeding, but before he can take a swing at the back of my head, Castor speaks up, "I wouldn't do that, Garret. Perhaps you should lay off the drink a wee bit? You know their reputation for finishin' fights."

"Well there's a first time for everythin'," Garret growls, grabbing the back of my shirt and yanking me off my stool.

I let him pull me away, and when he tries to pin me against one of the rickety old tables, I jerk my knee up and kick him hard in the stomach. I lean my elbows on the table as he stumbles back and falls. He gets up, and plows toward me again, tripping on a crooked floorboard.

Felix sighs, glancing nonchalantly over his shoulder as the man sprawls on his face. He gives me a warning look, but I ignore him.

I cross my ankles, smirking as Garret scrambles to his feet.

He jabs his finger at the air. "I'm gonna make ya pay, boy."

I shrug. "I would suggest ya don't."

Garret narrows his eyes, shaking his head. "You stupid, arrogant little pest."

I am being arrogant, I know, but right now it's feeling good. Garret lunges at me, but I dodge his blow with ease as he whirls his fists through the air. The other hunters in the bar guffaw, and I wonder how many of them are just as drunk as Garret.

Finally, the man hollers and barrels into my chest, slamming me against the wall and ramming his fist into my ribs. There's a collective "oooh" as the other men grimace.

I gasp, more surprised than hurt, and I jam my elbow against his spine.

Felix downs the last of his water and slams the mug onto the table, wiping his mouth as he gets up and stomps over to where Garret is struggling to hit me. He grabs the back of Garret's shirt and yanks him back, slamming his knuckles into the man's face so hard that I can hear the cartilage pop in his nose.

Without a word, my brother steps over Garret and sits back down at the bar. I sit next to him, grimacing at my sore ribs.

Garret gets up, but he doesn't come after us again, and instead moves to the other end of the bar and contents himself with giving us dirty looks. It's not the first time he's picked a fight with us, but he seems to forget every time he gets drunk—which is a lot. We don't usually get along unless he's sober, but given his job as a Dead Handler, I guess I can't blame him for wanting to drown himself in booze.

"Can't believe ya started a bar fight," Felix mutters, glancing at me sidelong.

"I didn't start it; he did," I say, quiet enough for only Felix to hear.

"You're the one who hit him first," Felix says, as if its logic. "Da would be pissed."

I clench my fists. "Unless he were drunk, then he probably would've helped more than you did."

"Except he gave up drinkin'. And for exactly this reason." Felix drums his fingers on the table as Castor walks by. "Hey Castor, before we get outta your hair, we were supposed to be comin' here to get our knives sharpened." Felix pulls out his knife and then slides mine out of its sheath at my belt. He slaps them down on the bar and then gives Garret a meaningful look.

"Sure, Felix," Castor says, wiping out a glass with a towel as though the fight had never happened. "On the house today. It's the least I can do for the men who saved Aileen's life."

Felix nods, smiling a little. "Thanks."

Castor winks. "Don't get used to it though, I still gotta survive."

"Sure." Felix stands. He looks down at me. "Ya gonna sit here all day or are ya comin' with me?"

I scowl at my mug for a second, then drink the rest of my water, getting to my feet. I drum my fingers on the table, cringing at the sound of metal on stone as Castor sharpens our blades. When he's finished, he hands us our knives back, as well as some flares. Without a word, I follow Felix back outside to go hunting.

Rachel

"I'm not sure this is a good idea…." Clayton's green eyes flick from the ground to the door to my feet—everywhere but to my face. He pushes his fingers through his short blond hair, chewing on his lower lip.

I give him a look that says *'seriously?'*, and he shifts his feet.

"I'm just saying, Rachel, I don't think your father would approve."

"Oh come on, he's not a monster." I take his hand, pulling him out the front door of my Hybrid-Glass mansion and tugging him down the steps of the porch. He catches one of the pillars as he goes by, but lets go when I give an exasperated sigh.

"No, we're going to walk," I say as he edges toward the hovercar parked in the crystal driveway. "Exercise is good for you. You need it." I adjust the strap of my bag on my shoulder, glancing inside to make sure my touch-pad is there.

I had decided to bring Clayton with me to meet Malcolm at Greenhouse Park as a sort of apology for getting him into trouble; it is kind of my fault that my father had punished him, as I did kind of encourage him to call me his sister. Though, I had warned him not to say it in public.

Clayton's hand trembles in mine as I lead him down the street to the base of the massive dome that encases the city. There are a lot of tropical plants in Greenhouse Park, so in order to reduce energy required to heat the gardens, the park is on the exterior of the dome, encased in its own tube of glass that encircles the entire city. There are several entrances to the garden, but the one closest to my house is the East Gate. I press my palm against a scanner built into the glass, laughing as Clayton flinches at the opening of the sliding glass door. "It's not going to eat you."

He follows me into the park, glancing around at all the colorful plants. The sunlight glares through the leaves, making his blond hair look like it's glowing.

Off a ways to the right of the East Gate, Malcolm is lying in a small patch of grass next to the dirt path, his thick arms behind his head as he squints up at the blue sky through the dome. His backpack and its contents are strewn across the ground beside him. If there are still jocks in high-school, Malcolm definitely looks like one: tall, strong, and ridiculously attractive, with black hair and blue eyes.

"Hey!" I call, running ahead of Clayton and cartwheeling over Malcolm. Malcolm jumps, sitting up in surprise. I trip on his legs, and he laughs as I fall on my butt.

"Smooth." His blue eyes sparkle, and he winks at me.

"Shut up." I punch his arm, my face burning. Clayton approaches, hesitating before sitting down next to me. I notice him wince and I scowl. "I don't get what's so wrong with Clayton calling me his sister. I mean seriously, we grew up together, we're basically siblings."

Malcolm had been there, so he knows what I'm talking about. He glances sidelong at Clayton. "Maybe your father doesn't like you relating so closely with animals."

I punch him again. "Clayton is not an animal," I hiss. "He's my best friend."

"Rachel." Clayton's eyes shift to Malcolm and then back to me, his gaze is pleading.

"What? You are! Dad isn't going to find out." I give Malcolm a pointed look.

Malcolm holds up his hands. "Whoa, I was just joking Rachel. Your father's nuts, I don't actually think Clayton is an animal. And—it's not like I'm going to tell your dad that he's your best friend."

I cross my arms. "You'd better not."

Malcolm leans back on his elbows, working his jaw for a second. "Well, he's not smart enough to do your homework, or you wouldn't have needed to ask for my help."

I gasp dramatically, covering Clayton's ears. "He's right here!"

Clayton pulls away. "Don't."

"What? Don't worry about your feelings?" I catch him around the shoulders before he can scoot away, pulling him closer and rubbing my knuckles in his blond hair. "Stop being so serious, bro. If I don't worry about your feelings who will? We don't need poor baby Clayton feeling all alone in the world."

"Stop." Clayton shoves me away. "I'm not your pet."

"Aw, but you're so adorable when you're mad," I tease.

"Shut up." Clayton narrows his eyes at me, but when he glances at Malcolm, his glare vanishes.

I push him over. "Oh come on, lighten up." I pull out my touch-screen, pulling up a picture I had taken. "Malcolm, you promised you'd help me."

"I did, but only because you have no one else to turn to." Malcolm rolls onto his stomach, propping himself up on his forearms and peering at the screen. "Still happy you're home-schooled?"

"Shut up. I still get to sleep in longer than you."

Malcolm rubs his eyes. "Okay, what did you need help on?"

I point to the picture of a small, rectangular device. "So I know that these heal wounds and stuff, but I don't know how, and my mom says I have to write a paper on it and give it to her in two days."

"Well, you came to the right person. I happen to be an expert."

"An expert? Psht, go soak your head."

"So, there are two different kinds—those that heal bones and the ones that heal flesh and skin and other tissues—"

"I *know* that, but how do they work?"

Malcolm runs his hand over his short dark hair. "They use stem cells."

"Which are….?"

He gives me a look like '*really?*'.

I raise my hands. "What, my mom doesn't tell me all these things, she wants me to look it up in the library database or something."

"Stem cells are undifferentiated cells that can pretty much produce any other kind of cell, kind of like the building blocks for all the cells in your body. Almost a century ago, our scientists found a way to harness their ability to promote cellular regeneration and control it using nanotechnology."

I blink. "You wanna explain that in English?"

Malcolm laughs. "Basically these microscopic computer bugs carry stem cells to the site of the wound and deliver messages from the computer in the device. The device itself tells the cells what to do once they get there, which is why you have to wait until the wound is healed before you take the device away."

"Oh. Creepy." I peer closer at the picture.

"What happens if you take the device away before it's finished?" Clayton speaks up. He's always been curious, and lately I've been sneaking him into lessons with my mom.

Malcolm raises a dark eyebrow. "Why do you need to know?"

"Sorry." Clayton flicks his eyes to the ground.

"You don't have to apologize, Malcolm won't bite."

"I might." Malcolm clacks his teeth, and Clayton flinches.

"Knock it off Malcolm." I laugh. "You guys need to get along. You're lucky I don't have any other friends."

"Ouch." Malcolm clutches his chest like he's been stabbed in the heart. "But what would you do without me?"

"Eat your heart out Malcolm." I tell him.

His jaw drops dramatically, and he rolls over in the grass, covering his face with his hands. "Ah—my ego! It's damaged!"

"Considering the size of it, that's probably a good thing."

"It burns!"

Clayton's smiles, relaxing a bit.

I lean back on my hands and cross my ankles. "Why can't you pull the device away before it's finished?"

"Maybe you should ask Clayton." Malcolm pretends to pout.

"So... could it be that the stem cells wouldn't know what to do without the computer in the device givin' them orders?" Clayton asks hesitantly.

Malcolm gives him a funny look. "Well at least someone can figure things out on his own. That's part of it, yeah. Unless you were to use direct injection with a syringe or something, the stem cells won't be following specific orders. Either the stem cells will die off, or they'll take the form of whatever tissue they're touching and reproduce indefinitely, which can be a big problem."

"Psht. Maybe I should've just asked Clayton to help me with my homework then."

"Aye, since I'm the only one who listens when your mum is teaching." Clayton's eyes twinkle.

Malcolm pulls a face, and I change the subject quickly. "Your Irish is showing."

Clayton frowns. "What?"

"'Aye'?" I nudge him. "It's faded, but you definitely have an accent."

Clayton shrugs. "Well, I was four when I came up here, remember?" He looks sad for a moment, then plasters on a smile. "So of course it's faded."

"Well, I'm not gonna lie, it would be pretty awesome if you still had a really thick Irish accent," I say, poking him. "Then you could help me practice."

"Well I guess that sucks for you."

There's the Clayton I know. I scoff. "And for you."

Clayton grins. "Nah, I don't really care that much. And besides, I don't think ya really need me for that. Your accent sounds almost perfect."

"Why thank you," I say, trying to mimic the accents I've heard from the movies.

"Ok!" Malcolm cuts in, sitting up and crossing his legs. Clayton flinches, shutting his mouth tight. He flicks his gaze toward the ground, the humor gone.

I frown, but before I can comment, Malcolm drags his backpack between us. "So we had this weird experiment in school today." He takes out a small box, opening it and pulling out a glittering diamond necklace. "We learned how to compress coal into diamonds—I wasn't really paying attention, but I got this." He hands me the jewelry, and my eyebrows shoot up.

"Malcolm—I can't take this."

He raises an eyebrow. "Why? You think I'm gonna wear it?"

"I...no but—your mom might—"

"She has enough jewelry for an army, she's not going to care. And besides, I want to give it to you." He scoots behind me on his knees, fastening the clasp of the necklace behind my neck.

"I…. don't know what to say." I can feel my face burning, and I shake my head, twisting the end of my blonde ponytail around my finger. "Dang, I wish I could do experiments like this. Mom thinks I'll burn the house down or something."

"You probably would." His fingers find the knotted yarn of the necklace I was already wearing. He yanks it up so he can see it. "What's this?"

"Oh—Clayton made it for me." I take it off and show it to Malcolm. Clayton seems to shrink into the ground. "Oh don't be shy, it's awesome!"

"Only because you showed me how." Clayton's green eyes flicker to Malcolm and back to the ground.

"You helped him make this?"

I put the necklace back on. "We were really bored, and we had nothing else to do." I grab Clayton's wrist—despite his horrified expression—and I show Malcolm the bracelet I had made. "We homeschoolers know how to *really* party."

Malcolm's fingers dig into the grass as he sits back, and he gives me a weird look, shaking his head. "What next, you gonna braid each other's hair?"

"Maybe we will!" I nudge Clayton, who forces a smile. "Hey are you okay?"

"You made him wear a bracelet, of course he's not okay." Malcolm kicks my foot, uncrossing my ankles.

"I wasn't asking you." I cross my ankles again. "And besides, you like my bracelet, right Clayton?" I lean against Clayton's shoulder, bumping the side of his head with my own. He nods slowly, glancing down at me. "See? This guy's learned to just go with the flow. I have sucked him into my wacky world of homeschooling and now he can't escape."

Malcolm raises an eyebrow, and his eyes harden. "Is that so?"

"Yup. And you're next."

"Ha. No. You guys can make all the charm bracelets you want, but I happen to like having the upper hand."

I snort. "What upper hand?"

Malcolm taps my touchpad. "You have no one else to help you with your homework. Speaking of—was that all you needed?"

"Oh." I slap my forehead. "That's right. Homework." I hesitate, then give Malcolm my best puppy-dog face. "I still have more…."

"That's what I thought." Malcolm smirks.

"Just…." I dip my head. "Can you like, explain these devices in detail while I take notes? I don't feel like going to the library today."

"I can, but you're going to owe me."

"Owe you what?"

Malcolm rubs his chin, squinting his eyes. "Hmm. I will think of your payment later. For now, prepare your ears, or Clayton will have to repeat everything for you."

I wince; he wasn't supposed to remember Clayton saying that he listened in on my lessons. Servants aren't allowed to have lessons in anything but housekeeping or cooking. I pick up my touchpad, opening the notepad app and tapping my thumbs on the screen. "Don't talk too fast. I need to take notes."

Malcolm clears his throat, then rattles off a lecture about the science behind nanotechnology and stem cells, and I type frantically to keep up, occasionally stopping him to ask for clarification. I can tell Clayton is listening intently, even though he pretends not to by closely examining a row of snapdragons growing at the edge of the grass. Malcolm finishes with a flourish, rising to his knees and bowing dramatically. "And that is exactly how healing devices came to be."

I save my notes, smirking. "You pretty much just wrote my paper for me. I need to ask you for help more often."

"That's fine with me." Malcolm winks, and I punch him. "Ow! Don't forget—you owe me."

"Sure." I put my touchpad back into my bag. "It's not like I have anything worth giving you. Clayton and I could make you some bracelets."

"How about no."

I snicker. "Then what do you want?"

Malcolm studies me for a moment. "Well. The sink in my kitchen has stopped working."

"Pft, I can't fix that."

"Obviously. But Clayton can."

Out of the corner of my eye, I see Clayton stiffen. I frown. "Why can't your servant fix it?"

"His hands are burned."

"....How?"

Malcolm shrugs. "He did something stupid—it doesn't matter. My point is, I need my sink fixed, and you happen to have one of the best servants, so...." He wiggles his eyebrows.

"Well...." I start, but Clayton's hand clamps around my wrist.

"I don't think that's a good idea." He looks me in the eye, shaking his head.

"Why not?" I frown, looking at his knuckles as they turn white. "Dude, chill, it's not like you don't have some free time. My father won't mind, I'll just tell him I sent you on an errand—which isn't a lie." He's probably still jumpy from last night. Not for the first time, I wonder just how severe my father's punishments are.

"Rachel, I don't think—"

Malcolm clears his throat, and Clayton stops talking. "I'm sure Mr. Brown won't mind. You won't get in trouble. Besides, Rachel owes me, and it's not like she can do anything."

My jaw drops. "Hey!"

"Well, can you fix a sink?"

I glare at him. "Can you?"

Malcolm opens his mouth, then shuts it again, defeated. "Yeah, that's what I thought." I turn to Clayton. "And—you're like the best servant in the whole City, you can fix a leaky sink in no time."

"Yeah, if I were you I'd jump at the opportunity to prove that," Malcolm says matter-of-factly.

"That's because you're so full of yourself you have no room for humility," I joke.

Clayton doesn't say anything more, his green eyes fixed on the snapdragons.

"So when did you want your sink fixed?" I ask Malcolm.

Malcolm checks his watch. "Well, my mom doesn't get home for another hour, so maybe now?" He winks at Clayton. "She's been complaining about the sink all week. We'll make it a surprise for her."

"Sounds good, I'm sure that'll make her happy." I grin. "What do you think, Clayton?"

Clayton nods his head sullenly, his eyes still on the flowers. I slide my arm around his shoulders. "Hey, it'll be okay bro. Dad won't bother you, I promise. "

Clayton doesn't look at me, however, and Malcolm grabs his arm, hauling him to his feet. "Come on man, we've only got an hour."

"See ya later Clayton." I wave, but Clayton doesn't wave back, casting me a sad look over his shoulder before disappearing through the exit from Greenhouse Park.

Peter

"Bloody cold. Can't feel my fingers," I grumble.

"Hmm. One day, this will all change," Felix says. We're sitting on an outcropping of rock that juts out above the icy water, where the penguins are diving for fish and huddling in masses of blubber on chunks of floating ice. It's hard to imagine that penguins didn't used to live in Ireland, but since the asteroids hit, they've moved way up from the south pole.

Our legs hang over the edge, and below us the rock is undercut all the way down to the water. This morning's storm has passed, and above us, the slate grey sky stretches out endlessly in all directions, stark in contrast to the dark blue waters of the Atlantic Ocean. Behind us, the rock we're sitting on slopes back down to the level ground, a frozen white plain that reaches all the way to the edge of the sea in one direction and rises slowly up to the hill before Colfer in the other—the land changed a lot after the asteroids struck.

It's peaceful out here, and despite the cold, I like it. This frozen wasteland isn't too bad when nothing's trying to kill us. Felix and I always hunt here, just because we can be alone in the quiet, away from the gloom and starvation of the streets of Colfer.

"One day, the Glass City will fall, and they will be forced to cooperate with us. They'll have to share their technology, in exchange for our skill. But now, they're nothin' but pampered…." He trails off, his face twisting as he tries to find the right word.

"Pompous arses?" I suggest.

"Ah, language," Felix warns. I roll my eyes, and he smirks. "But aye. They know nothin' of survival, but we do. We could work together. With their technology, and our skill…. maybe the human race would thrive again, the way it used to."

"You really want to work together with them?" I wrinkle my nose.

"Can't keep fightin' forever. We're all human Peter. Someday they'll figure that out." He pulls something from his pocket; a photograph, creased from being folded several times in the same place, the edges worn and fragile. "I've been meanin' to give this to ya for a very long time, but I couldn't seem to let go of it. I know your birthday's still four days away, but take it now before I lose the guts to part with it." He hands it to me.

I take it carefully, handling it as though it were made of the thinnest of ice. Our birthdays were always a private thing, something we kept from Addy and her kids. Gifts were rare, but we always found something to give each other. The photograph is that of a young man and a woman standing with their arms around each other in front of a bright sunset. The colors are faded with age, but the red and orange and yellow are amazing, strange trees hunching over the smiling couple. Before I can ask, Felix explains. "That's our parents. Two years before the asteroid struck. They were both fifteen. Grew up together."

I don't respond right away, taking in every line of their faces, the light in their eyes, the complete and genuine joy in their smiles. I've seen pictures before, but they're rare, and never like this. Never of my parents. I brush my thumb lightly over the face of my mother, seeing the resemblance to my brother and I in both parents. Felix and I have the same dark red hair as our mum. I look up at my brother, at the hard features and icy blue irises, and smirk slightly to keep myself from getting misty-eyed. "You have Mum's eyes," I tease.

Felix shoves me, his face turning red and his teeth digging into his lower lip to stop a smile. "Shut up."

I stare at the picture for another minute, then give my brother a hug. "Thank you," I whisper, letting some of the anger from this morning fade from my mind.

Felix thumps my back roughly, chuckling. "Alright, don't get all sappy on me kid. You're welcome."

I fold the photograph and place it in my own pocket, huffing a sigh as I lift my sniper rifle onto my lap. Weapons are hard to find, but there are lots of them if you know where to look. When the asteroid first struck, and all the riots broke out, violence was explosive, and pretty soon everyone just killed each other off, leaving weapons lying around the streets of ghost towns. There's an empty city right next to Colfer, but massive wolf packs keep most people out of it. Ammunition is harder to get a hold of—unless, of course, you happen to be me or my brother. We pick up ammunition in the same places we get our guns, as well as empty shells that we refill and reuse.

"We should probably start huntin', or we won't be back before dark," I say quietly, and we both stand.

"Let's get somethin' a little more than penguin. I'm starvin'."

I nod my agreement, my stomach twisting in knots to remind me that it's empty. We haven't been able to get as much food as usual—it's not as safe as it is in the summer, as it's colder and it gets darker sooner, so most of the food goes to Addy and her kids. Felix and I get the scraps, despite the fact that we were the ones that got the food in the first place, whereas they never do anything. We try to get as much as we can, but with all the nocturnal predators out here, no sane hunter stayed outside after dark.

As we trudge through snow, my brother stops me with a hand on my chest, startling me from my thoughts. Without a word, he points, and I follow the line of his finger to a small white polar bear pawing at the water, her nose twitching as she searches for the fish she knows is down there somewhere. Felix and I raise our guns, scoping down the barrel with both our sights on the beast's head, but the appearance of two cubs stops us short. Having no parents ourselves, we've always had a soft-spot for abandon kids, whether human or animal.

"We are such saps," I mumble.

Felix snorts, lowering his gun and heaving a sigh. "I hate that about us."

"Aye." I turn away, squinting across the white landscape. "But we need to find somethin' soon. It's gettin' late."

"Perhaps there's a male somewhere nearby."

I shake my head. "We'd never be able to haul that all the way back home."

Felix heaves another sigh, wrinkling his nose. "We could get a few more penguins than usual. They don't have much for meat on them, but maybe we could clean them here, that way we could carry more."

"Maybe." I shrug. "Either way, my stomach is killin' me. If I don't get somethin' soon, my stomach's goin' to take a knife to my intestines."

"So graphic." Felix grimaces.

"So true."

"Too true. What's that?" Felix frowns. The visibility around us is starting to shrink with the snow that's starting to fall. I can't see the horizon any more, just a gray-white blur between clouds and snow drifts. Three black dots hover above the snow in the direction Felix is pointing. They don't move even though the snow swirls in the wind.

"I…. have no idea, but I don't think I want to find out." I take a step back.

"Could they be people?" Felix ignores me. For a grown man, my brother can be such an idiot.

"I don't think so. They'd be movin'. We should just get a few penguins and go."

"Well what if they are people, and they're just far away?" Felix gives me a look. "What if they're hurt?"

"Then that's their problem. We can't afford to be stuck out here at night, it's already four o'clock. It's gettin' dark. And it's not that I don't care," I add when Felix's expression darkens, "I just don't think that those are people."

"Then what do you think they are?" Felix challenges.

I look back, swallowing. "Eyes and a nose." No sooner than I say it do the three black dots disappear.

Felix falls silent, both of us staring at the place where the spots had been. Felix looks through the scope of his gun, then lowers it again, apparently seeing nothing. "You're right kid. We should get a few penguins and get the heck out of here." We both back toward the water, slowly turning around with our ears strained and our eyes peeled. The crunch of the snow beneath our boots suddenly seems too loud. Even as we near the water of the Atlantic, where the splashes of the penguins fill the air, everything seems too quiet, as if the world is holding its breath.

Felix and I crouch in the snow, scoping down our rifles and firing at the same time. Two penguins keel over where they had just climbed out of the water, the fish from their beaks flopping on the ice beside them. The other penguins scatter, diving into the water and disappearing under the ice. It's not much, really, which makes it certain that Felix and I will go another day without food—my stomach snarls its complaint—but my spine tingles as though the fingers of winter are reaching through my coat and drumming on it.

Felix and I scramble down the slope to the water's edge.

Out of the corner of my eye I see a flash of white, and when I turn to look, my throat constricts. I stop Felix, pointing at the floating body. "Another one."

Felix looks, then turns his face to the sky, his upper lip curling. "Blasted City."

"Should we take him back?"

Felix shakes his head, his voice strained with contained rage. "No, we can't carry him all the way home right now. Let's just get him out of the water so he doesn't get washed out again. We'll let the Dead Handlers know he's here." We both drag our feet to the edge of the ice, reaching over the edge and grabbing the arms of the body as the waves push it closer to shore. Grunting with effort, we heave him out of the water, rolling him onto his back. Pale green eyes stare up at the sky, and ice frosts his blond hair. There are dark bruises around his throat and on the side of his face, and his chest is all but collapsed. I crack a flare, planting it in the snow next to the body. Hopefully it'll scare off any polar bears.

Felix swallows, then turns away. "Let's get our catch."

I slide to a stop next to the penguin I shot and haul it over my shoulder, catching the flopping fish and shoving it into my bag. Felix hands me the other fish, picking up his own penguin and turning back toward home as a snow starts to fall again. We need to get back while we can still see. The only way to navigate out here is by landmarks, like the hill before Colfer. Compasses don't work too good since the asteroids hit, and nobody on the surface has seen the stars in decades.

We've barely started walking when a long, low wail drifts across the snow, rising and falling like the melody of some dark lullaby. Felix and I freeze, looking at each other with huge eyes. "No," Felix breathes, "No way."

There are wolves, and then there are Sirens, and a whole pack of wolves is not nearly as deadly as a single Siren.

The wail ends, then starts up again, closer. We both drop to our bellies in the snow, tense and ready with the butts of our rifles pressed firmly against our shoulders. Felix turns in the snow so that we're facing in opposite directions, so we can see both ways, and we remain like that, still and tense, listening as the Siren's song draws closer to where we're laying in the snow, the sound coming from all around us.

I peer down the scope, but all I see is white, and suddenly, the wails stop.

I feel Felix tense, his elbows digging into the back of my knees, and I scan the flat plain for anything—*anything*—that could be the source of the sound, but nothing catches my eye. I slowly roll over onto my back, glancing briefly in Felix's direction.

I hear him gasp before I see it coming. The massive white canine seems to melt from the snow, lunging toward us with fangs bared and paws reaching forward. I jerk my gun up, firing.

Its body jerks under the impact of the bullet, but doesn't seem affected at all, and it slams into my chest full force. I cry out as the beast's fangs snap at my throat, drool splattering my face and dripping onto my neck. I barely manage to catch its jaws before they close around my neck. The Siren's jagged teeth jutting out from its mouth cut at my fingers, my left hand on the end of its wet nose and my right prying at its lower jaw, but its mouth still opens and closes, struggling to tear out my throat and only more driven by my blood that coats its tongue.

I slip, and its jaws slam against my chest, its sharp fangs digging into my skin, and I scream. Felix hollers at it, but he's pinned against my legs, the Siren's hind paw heavy on his back and limiting his mobility.

I struggle to push the Siren away, but it's far too strong, its fangs tearing at my collar bone and its claws digging into my ribs. Felix shifts on my legs, straining to crawl out from under the massive beast, but it's too heavy. I see him start to reach for his gun which had been knocked out of his hand by a giant paw.

Gritting my teeth, I bend my knees just enough to give him a little bit of space, and he snatches up his rifle with his right hand and twists so that the barrel of the gun is aimed at the Siren's head.

With a yell, he pulls the trigger, sending a bullet through the back of the Siren's head and blasting off its left ear.

But instead of collapsing, the beast howls it's eerie howl, pushing off of me with such force that my chest feels like it's caving in. It whirls on Felix, shuddering and snarling, blood dripping down its face and neck.

With lighting speed, the Siren pounces at my brother, who just barely manages to roll out of the way, only to have to keep rolling as the beast springs at him over and over, missing his body by fewer and fewer inches.

Gasping for breath, I grab my own gun and try to aim it at the Siren, but it moves so bloody fast, and every time I get my sight on its head, it moves out of the way.

"Hold it still!" I yell, my hands shaking. Felix gets stuck in the snow, and the Siren finally lands on his back, its teeth tearing at his thick fur coat but not yet getting flesh.

Yelling, I lunge forward and grab the canine by its tail, at the same time dropping my gun and pulling my knife from my belt. With a powerful blow, I hack off its tail right at its base. The Siren squeals, its hind legs giving out and its jaws opening long enough for Felix to squirm away. I reach for my gun, but when I raise it to fire, the Siren has already taken off, half running half stumbling toward the water. Its wails echo behind it.

"Felix!"

"I'm fine." Felix pants, staring in the direction the Siren went. He relaxes slightly, then sees me, and his eyes grow big again.

I frown, glancing down at myself, and the sight of my bloodied chest reminds me of the pain. I fall backwards, gasping and blinking back tears, and Felix leans over me. "Peter, you're gonna be okay, ya hear me? I'm gonna get ya out of here." But I know he can't carry me all the way back home. Not in this weather, not with it getting later and later by the second. I shake my head, taking a deep breath and slowly climbing to my feet.

"I'll be fine." I glance at the fluffy white tail in the snow, swaying. "That thing is worth a fortune."

Felix snatches it off the ground, wrinkling his nose at the bloody stump. "You sure showed her."

"Her?"

"While you got her pearly whites, I got the other end."

"That's nice Felix." I stoop to pick up the penguin I'd dropped, but Felix stops me.

"You can't haul that thing all the way home. You need medical attention, kid."

"We can't afford it." I remind him, swallowing hard. "Addy wouldn't pay for it, even if she could."

"That doesn't change the fact that ya need it." Felix takes my arm when I start to fall forward, shuddering. "Peter, we need to get ya home."

I hesitate, taking a breath. "We've only got the Siren's tail. It might be enough for just us two, but it won't be enough to satisfy Addy and all her brats."

Felix looks uncertain. "Fine. But if ya can't carry it, then just drop it. Plenty of hungry wolves out there, it won't go to waste." He glances worriedly at my chest. "We'd better hurry, before ya bleed out like a stuck pig."

I cringe. "I don't think it's that deep. It just *hurts*." I breathe the last part, closing my eyes tight and dropping to my knees.

Felix crouches next to me, helping me lift the smaller of the two penguins over my shoulder. My head is swimming. Felix stands, looking at me with a concerned expression. "You're a bloody mess." He tells me, tucking the Siren tail through one of his belt loops.

"Thanks," I grumble, trembling. It *burns*.

"We don't have to go back to Addy's, ya know." I tell him, breathing more heavily as we start to trudge back to Colfer. "With just this tail, we could afford to finally get away from her. That cave by the Atlantic? We could live there, we've already got quite a bit of our belongin's down there, we'd only need to find some way to make a door or somethin' to cover the entrance." A few weeks back, we had found a large cave with three separate spaces connected by tunnels. Since then, we had been moving our stuff—guns, ammo, knives—from Addy's house and hiding it in our cave; her kids like to get into what belongs to Felix and I.

Felix smiles slightly. "We could."

Excitement fills my burning chest, giving me strength to keep from collapsing in the snow. "I hope so. I was on the verge of stranglin' Cole the other day." Cole was Addy's eleven-year-old son.

"Careful now kid, if we kill someone we'll never get anywhere without people tryin' to get justice, and anythin' we get from this tail would go to Addy."

I cringe. "No way in hell I'd let that happen."

Felix gives me one of his rare smiles, this one full and unrestrained. "We get back to Colfer, and we're rich. We can't just ditch them, though. They're family, and I—"

"Made a promise, I know." I'm too excited to argue: this is the first time Felix has ever considered leaving, I don't want to push it.

"Aye." He gives me a look. "And I—"

"Intend to keep it, aye." I shake my head. "No need to repeat yourself. If you want to stay and deal with them, fine, but I'm leavin'. Or at least not doin' anythin' for them anymore." I add quickly.

Felix considers this. "They'll have to get their own food. They'll actually have to get off their fat bottoms and do somethin'," he says at length. "We can relax for the first time in forever, livin' off whatever we get from this. We won't need to hunt, and our idiot cousins would be forced to learn how to catch their own food."

I return his smile, stumbling in the snow. *Have to keep walking until we trade the tail.* "No one ever taught us how to hunt." I point out.

Felix shrugs. "Aye, but they did give us a roof for nineteen years."

I nod my agreement. "Then we'll teach them to hunt, but they'll only get to bring back their own kills."

"Perfect. We'll have to stay there, though, to make sure nothin' happens to them."

I bite my tongue, exhaling through my nose. "Fine."

Felix laughs, full and loud. "I can't believe we survived a Siren attack. Good thing you thought of bringin' the tail, or else no one would believe us."

"And we'd still have to hunt every mornin'," I breathe, stopping to catch my breath.

Felix stops as well, the smile dropping from his face. "Peter?"

"I'm fine."

"Maybe we should-"

"No. I'm fine. I'll.... I'll be fine." I straighten, shifting the penguin over my shoulder. "Let's get movin'. I'm freezin' my butt off."

"Here—give me that," Felix says worriedly, taking the heavy penguin from me and heaving it over his own broad shoulders. He hesitates, then turns away again, giving me the opportunity to wince without fear of being seen. *Gotta keep moving.*

By the time Colfer becomes visible through the drifting snow— ramshackle grey buildings melting from the white plain and shadowy mountains in the distance—I'm drenched in a cold sweat, my own blood soaking my torn shirt and coat all the way down to my belt. My gun drops from my numb fingers, and I pause, stooping to pick it up. I only make it halfway down before I have to stop, my hands on my knees as I try to regain my breath again. I shudder involuntarily, pain spiking across my chest, and Felix realizes that I've stopped. He hurries back to me, placing one hand on my shoulder as he picks up my gun. "Peter? Peter can you hear me?"

"Of course I can, I'm not deaf," I say, but my words are slurred.

"Come on, now," he says quietly, sliding his arm across my back and half lifting me so that my weight is leaned against him. We make it the rest of the way back, me limping heavily and kept on my feet only by my brother's strength. Even Felix, though, is breathing heavily by the time we reach the trader's shop, which squats between a lopsided building made of mismatched lengths of grey wood—the butcher's shop—and another, smaller structure with a crumbling roof and boarded up windows; the house belongs to a hunter and his family. Across the street are about six other houses all packed together, some of the walls leaning against the buildings beside them. Altogether, Colfer has maybe twenty poorly built buildings in the main part of town, either scattered about or in some sort of 'orderly' cluster.

The trader's shop is nothing special, just a long log cabin with a patched up roof, the porch running around the front of it, recently cleared of snow. We stumble in through the front door, and Felix lets me lean against the counter. The shopkeeper's eyes widen as Felix drops the Siren tail. "How much?" He asks.

The shopkeeper—Jimmy—stares at it for a moment. There's no mistaking it for a wolf's tail: the Siren's tail is about four feet long. My brother grits his teeth impatiently. "In case you haven't noticed, he hasn't got much time right now." He jabs his thumb at me.

The Jimmy blinks, then heads to the back of the shop. We hear him rummaging around, then he comes back with an armful of stuff, which he lays out on the counter. "Four boxes of ammunition and gunpowder, two wool blankets, and two huntin' knives of your choice." He gestures at the cracked glass case at the end of the counter. "Along with," he stoops and lifts from under the count two heavy bags of rice, "fifty pounds of rice and free access to the butcher's shop for six months." Jimmy's brother is the butcher.

"Jimmy, my brother's bleedin' out, do you know how hard it was to get away from that thing? It would be nice if you threw in somethin' that might help him."

Jimmy hesitates, then digs underneath the counter again, lifting up a heavy looking black bag, probably from a Scout hovercraft. "Medicinal alcohol, gauze, needles, matches, scalpels-" I grimace "-and even some Neosporin. Fully equipped, nothin' missin'."

I look up at my brother, who pauses, then nods, pushing the Siren tail toward Jimmy. "And I want it known that it was my brother and I who scared it off."

Jimmy nods. "Of course. No one would believe me if I took the credit, I don't do nothin' excitin'."

Felix rolls his eyes. "Could I borrow a cart? I'll bring it back as soon as I can."

Jimmy points out the front door. "I have one outside around the corner. Keep it. I can't believe you survived an encounter with one of these things." He examines the tail, but his voice sounds oddly quiet.

"Oh, and….we've got another body in the Atlantic. Tell the Dead Handlers it's on the shore."

Jimmy closes his eyes, shaking his head, but I don't quite understand what he says. I blink, feeling dizzy, and my vision is fuzzy at the edges. I pull the front of my shirt open, blinking at the bloody gashes, which are much deeper than I thought. "Felix?" I mumble, frowning at my chest.

Felix turns to me, his eyes widening and his mouth forming words, but I don't hear him. I feel my eyes roll back and my knees buckle, and then there's nothing.

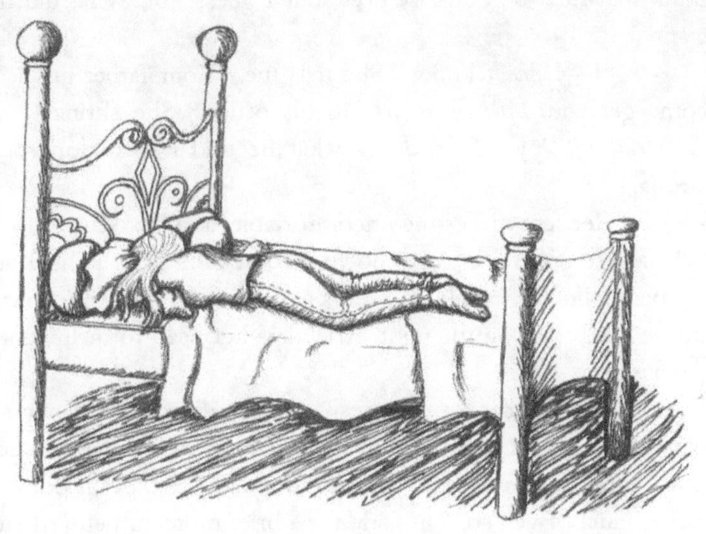

Rachel

It's late when a knock sounds at my bedroom door. I'm just back from a run in the park, so I'm not asleep, but I don't answer right away, focused on the book my mom told me to read. It's different than my regular school books, mainly because it's fiction, but it's crazy how some of this stuff is true today, even though it was written almost two centuries ago. The technology is especially accurate. The knock sounds again, and I sigh. "Come in."

There's a pause, and then the door opens to a small, thin woman. I frown. "Who are you?"

"My name is Arial. Your father sent me."

My frown only deepens. "What? I've never seen you before. If he wants me, he always sends Clayton."

Arial shifts her gaze away. "He's—out."

"'Out'? Oh, you mean he's not done fixing Malcolm's sink?"

"I....what?"

"He went to fix Malcolm's kitchen sink earlier today. I would think that he'd be done by now, but I guess not. What did my father want?"

"I—I don't know." She tells me. "Your father just told me to come get you. He wants you in his office." She shrinks against the doorframe. "I'm just…. doing what he told me to do. Is…. is that wrong?"

Her fear makes me uncomfortable, and it's difficult to ignore it. "Of course not. I'll be right down." Something's not right. I get up off my bed, following Ariel downstairs and to the left, walking down the hall to the third door on the right. Ariel dips her head formally, opening the door for me.

My father is a very decisive man, with a strong jaw and intense blue eyes. I used to be afraid of him when I was little, simply because of how intimidating he could be, but now that I'm older it doesn't bother me so much. Even so, I hesitate for a brief moment before I step inside his office

He sits at his desk, a fancy piece of furniture he salvaged from some city on the Surface. The cherry wood is worn and ancient, stark in contrast to his pale skin—my father has always been rather white. He glances up from the holographic document, brushing it aside when he notices me. My father hesitates, which is unlike him. "Rachel…. you might want to sit down." He gestures to the chair in front of his desk.

I give him an inquiring look, doing as I'm told. "What's wrong?"

Dad is quiet for a long time, examining my face with a hard expression. "Clayton is dead."

I blink, stunned. "I—what?"

"He was hit by an activity bus on his way home."

"I—how is that even—" I can't think straight, my head spinning. "That doesn't even make sense."

"The sidewalks hadn't lit up yet, it was twilight, and the school bus driver was yelling at a student. Clayton was crossing the street and was hit."

I just look at him, opening and closing my mouth like a fish out of water. The way he talks makes me think it isn't true, like maybe this is some sort of cruel joke, but my father isn't like that. He's too serious. He wouldn't do that, would he? But what else could it be? He couldn't be telling the truth. No way. There's no way he could be dead, no way. How is that even possible?

My father folds his hands on his desk. "The question is, what was he doing out so late anyways?"

"I…. he was fixing Malcolm's sink…." I can't seem to breathe properly. "How could this have happened? He was my best friend. He was like my big brother. He was the closest thing I had to a sibling." I say it without thinking, and my father's expression darkens. I shut my eyes, cursing myself.

"I didn't know he meant that much to you."

I look up at him, incredulous. "Would you have approved if I'd told you sooner? We did everything together, I don't even…. I can't…." I don't even know what I'm trying to say. "I was just talking to him earlier," I whisper. "What about the driver? And the kids?"

"The driver will be fired and fined, and her servants will be removed from her custody for a month. The passengers are fine."

"I can't believe this."

My father brings up the hologram again, scrolling through images. "Well, maybe you shouldn't have gotten so attached."

"*What?*"

He looks at me over an image of the city's basement level. "Your servants are just animals, not friends. There are millions of Surface Dwellers, I'll get you a new one tomorrow."

My jaw drops. "How can you say that?"

"They are a lesser species, Rachel. Like the apes before them, they are less evolved than we are. Whatever you might have felt for Clayton he was incapable of feeling for you."

"Are you kidding me? Less *evolved?* So what, over the past forty years we suddenly grew extra brain cells and they all lost theirs? Are you forgetting that half the city was born before the asteroids struck? You were born then too, remember? Are you less evolved?"

"That's not how evolution works—"

"Because it doesn't work!" I stand up suddenly, knocking the chair over. "It has never worked! People are *people* Dad! The Surface Dwellers aren't 'less evolved' just because they don't have our technology that doesn't even make sense! How can you even—"

"Sit down!" My father's voice overrides mine, and I close my mouth. My eyes blur with tears, but I don't sit down. Dad's face twists. "I don't know what kind of garbage your mother is teaching you, but I am getting real tired of it. While she teaches you all this crap about love and life she forgets to mention the horrors those monsters unleashed on us in the beginning. They sabotaged our city, Rachel, after they slaughtered half their own on the Surface. Do not tell me we are the same!"

I just stare at him, my throat constricting. "You're right," I whisper. "You're worse." I turn and run from his office, shoving out the front door of my house and racing down the street toward Greenhouse Park. The brown crystal path glows as I run down it, and I follow it until I reach the small trail that turns off to the left, toward the edge of the dome.

I stop at the glass, the skydeck stretching over open air on the other side, and I barely remember to take an oxygen mask off the hook by the door and check my parachute to be sure that it still works before pressing my palm against the scanner. There's a hiss, and a door slides open. The cold presses down on me from all around, and I dash across the open catwalk, opening the door of the smaller dome that encases my private garden. I glance over my shoulder at the massive dome behind me, making sure that no one has followed me before I let the door slide shut.

Inside is filled with flowers of all kinds that had been saved from the asteroids, and I push through the leaves to the tiny crystal fountain in the center of a glass circle, dropping to my knees next to it and screaming into the water. How could this have happened? How is this even possible? No one *ever* gets hit by hovercars up here, it's unheard of!

I curl up into a ball, bracing my head between my knees and sobbing. Just a few hours ago Clayton and I had been talking and laughing, how can he suddenly be gone? Through the glass floor beneath me, the clouds part for a few brief moments, allowing me to see all the way down to the scarred and broken Surface, stark white against the dark ocean. I stare at it intently, trying to calm myself, to think of anything but Clayton. The closest land is Ireland, which is just below me and a little to the east. Clifden Bay is much smaller than the textbook maps portray it to be, as most of Ireland's west coast crumbled during the catastrophe, sloughing off into the sea with most of the smaller islands surrounding it. It took me a few years to realize why the coast on my maps looked so different.

The Surface is always under ice and snow, but there is a massive canyon that splits Ireland almost all the way across from east to west, which was made by one of the smaller meteorites that had been caught in the asteroid's tail. Even from way up here, I can see the glow of lava in the ravine, and several other cracks in the earth all split away from the bigger one at jagged angles

I don't know how long I stay like this, staring down through the hole in the clouds and turning the necklace Clayton had made for me over in my fingers, but I know it's been a while when I hear the door to my garden slide open and shut. Strong arms slide around me, and Malcolm's voice whispers, "I'm sorry."

Part of me wants to recoil, to scream at him that this is all his fault, but the rest of me knows that I can't blame him for something he didn't do. Instead I just lean into him and breathe, trying to stop crying, to calm down, but it's a long time before I finally fall quiet. "How did you find me?" I mumble into Malcolm's shoulder.

"Your father." He lets go of me as I pull away and sit up straighter.

"I don't understand how he could be gone. Just earlier today…."

"I know."

"He was right here." My eyes start tearing up again. "I was just talking to him, I can't believe this I have to be dreaming I—I don't—understand."

"I know."

I bury my face in my knees again. "How could you let this happen?" I whisper.

"I'm sorry."

"No you're not!" I snap, gritting my teeth. "Why didn't you walk him home!?"

Malcolm opens his mouth, but nothing comes out. I suddenly feel guilty, and I swallow another sob. "I'm sorry," I choke. "I don't even…. I know it's not your fault. I'm sorry."

Malcolm doesn't respond, watching the fountain with his blue eyes. At length, he says, "What is this place?"

I want to yell at him for changing the subject, but instead I let out a shuddering breath. "My grandfather had it built as his own private garden when he was designing the city. It was supposed to be a place for him to be alone with his thoughts, and when I was born, he'd take me here all the time. He died of a heart attack, and our greenhouse is where I go when I miss him or when I just want to be alone. I don't remember him very well anymore, but I do remember his stories." I point to a bench on the other side of the fountain. "He'd put me on his lap and tell me all sorts of things about the Surface before the asteroids struck."

"Sounds like pleasant memories."

I nod, sniffing. "What about your grandpa?" Anything to get my mind off of Clayton.

Malcolm gives me a funny look. "He died before I was born. You should know this, I'm pretty sure I've told you."

"Oh….yeah." Jasper Crysis had been part of Plan A; find a new planet before the asteroids struck. He had never returned. Malcolm gets to his feet, holding his hand out.

"Show me around?"

I hesitate, then take his hand, wiping my eyes with my sleeve. I lead Malcolm around the entire circumference of the dome, turning on the sprinklers as I go. Our water is both recycled and brought up from the Atlantic Ocean, where it's desalinated in the basement level of the city, where the generators are. Malcolm looks around in awe. "This is all yours?"

I nod. "Yeah. I take care of them. Most of them are grown by hydroponics, like in Greenhouse Park, but a lot are in flower pots with dirt from the Surface. My grandpa told me to take care of it. Guess he was lucky I turned out to be a girl who likes taking care of flowers."

Malcolm flashes me one of his ridiculously adorable grins, his light blue eyes sparkling. "Yup. Lucky."

I try not to, but I smile. "Shut up you creeper."

"This place is amazing." He tells me, looking around at all the different plants. He looks sad for a moment. "It's…. I don't know, I'm starting to wish I was the mayor's daughter."

"I did not need that image in my head."

Malcolm shakes his head, cringing. "Neither did I." He snickers. "Man, I don't think I could ever bring myself to wear a dress or a skirt, even for a prank."

I squint at him with a sort of choking laugh. "It freaks me out to think that you would even think of that."

"What? I think I'd look cute in a dress, what about you?"

"I think I just threw up a little."

Malcolm bursts out laughing again. I chew my lip, twisting at the end of my pony-tail. Should I be laughing right now?

"Oh, yup. That's a great image."

"No," I say, trying not to laugh. "It's bad."

"Well, it seems to be making you feel better, at least."

The smile drops from my face, and I feel guilty again. "I don't think I should be feeling better."

"Hey, I don't think Clayton would want you to be too sad about him. I'm sure he liked it when you were happy."

I sniffle, feeling another sobbing fit coming on as the weight of Clayton's death starts creeping up on me again. "Maybe I should go home."

Malcolm slips his arm across my shoulders. "Aww, but you were just starting to be you again."

"I just…." Don't want to laugh. Don't want to feel happy. Don't want to be myself. "….want to go home."

"Okay. I'll take you home," Malcolm says, putting his oxygen mask over his mouth and nose. I do the same, and we step outside. The wind has picked up a bit, blasting through my hair, and I press against Malcolm as we make our way across the catwalk.

Once again in Greenhouse Park, I take my oxygen mask off, my lungs filling with clean air as I breathe in deeply. Malcolm leads me through the park and into the city, remaining quiet all the way to my mansion. He stops me on the front porch. "Hey—look Rachel, I…." He closes his eyes. "I'm sorry. I should've walked with him or something."

"So you could get hit too?" I shake my head. "Malcolm this isn't your fault. I'm…. I'm not mad at you." I tell him, even though that's not entirely true. I don't want to be mad at him, but part of me can't help but blame him, if only a little bit.

He takes both of my hands, forcing me to look him in the eye. "I promise to find some way to make it up to you, okay? I'll always be here, whenever you need me."

"Uhm, okay."

I see him hesitate, then he leans forward and kisses my cheek, letting go of my hands and walking quickly down the steps and down the sidewalk before I can say anything. I stare after him, wondering what exactly happened.

I take a shuddering breath, then open the front door, taking the stairs two at a time up to my room. I jump onto my bed and bury my face in my pillow, unwilling to cry but unable to stop as my emotions come crashing back down on me now that I'm alone again. *Why? Why?*

I hear the door open, feel my mother sit down next to me and start rubbing my back. "I'm so sorry, sweetie."

"Why him? Why couldn't it have been someone else?" I feel selfish even as I say it, but Clayton was like my brother, my bestest friend in the whole wide world. My father had never let me go to the public school—ever. I don't really have any real friends, only Clayton.

"Honey, don't say that. I know you're hurt, and I'm sorry. If there was anything I could've done…." She trails off, leaning over to give me a weird sort of hug. Her brown hair tickles the back of my neck. "I'm so sorry, sweetheart. I wish I could've done something."

I sniff. "It's not your fault," I croak, even though I really don't feel like trying to comfort her right now. But my mother has always been more sensitive than me. "It's not your fault."

"I know how much you cared about him. And I know he cared about you, too. He called you his sister yesterday, by accident. Remember?"

Of course I do, but it only hurts to think about it, and I start blubbering like a baby again. "That was just yesterday." I sob. I had thought it was awesome, but my father had seemed irritated for the rest of the dinner, as were our guests.

"I know sweetie." Her voice cracks.

I want to speak, to ask more questions, but the sobs make it impossible to form words. I wish I could just stop crying, it's not like my tears will bring him back. But, thinking like that only makes me cry harder, and I pound my fists against my pillows.

After a while, my mother gets up and leaves the room, my tears just too much for her. I eventually stop crying and start thinking of Malcolm. My cheek burns where his lips brushed my skin, and even though I'm alone, I feel my face turn red.

After all this time, how come Malcolm didn't make his intentions clear until now? Do I like him like that? Why wouldn't I? Clayton used to tease me about him all the time. He is smart. Good looking. His family is close to mine. He is the only person I know that's my age other than Clayton. My eyes fill with fresh tears. I don't even know what I'm supposed to feel.

Peter

I wake up feeling sore and sick, the heat of fever drenching me in a cold sweat. My chest is bare, save for the bandages over and beneath my collar bone. A wool blanket covers me from the waist down, and my jeans are plastered to the backs of my knees with icy sweat. I keep my eyes closed as my other senses sharpen. A door slams, and muffled voices sound in the other room. Slowly they become clearer, and I can hear Addalynn say, "I can't afford this."

"Well it's a good thing you're not payin' for it." Felix's response is gruff.

Addy scoffs. "What are you talkin' about? This is *my* home!"

"I am failin' to see your point."

"I am the head of this household, and I am tellin' you that we can't afford to pay for all this medical supplies!"

"And I am tellin' you that you don't pay for anythin' around here, so you wouldn't know!"

Addy sighs. "We need to prioritize—"

"Prioritize!? That's my brother you're talkin' about! Your nephew!"

"So what? You're certainly not gettin' enough to feed the rest of us, all the food is goin' toward medical supplies!"

"Well what do ya want me to do, let him die?"

"Aye, and then the rest of us can live!"

There's a crash, and something hits the door to my right. Felix's voice is low and threatening, right outside my room. "Who do you think you are, decidin' who lives and who dies? You think you're so high and mighty that you get to play God?"

"You owe me—" Addy starts, but Felix cuts her off, the door thumping again.

"And we have more than paid you back. We're your family, Addalynn, we shouldn't have had to owe you in the first place. All you've done is take advantage of us, and now ya think I'll let my brother die for you? You're out of your bloody mind woman." There's a pause, then, "As soon as Peter gets better we're leavin'."

Addy tries to argue, but when Felix is done talking, the conversation is over. Addy might think she's the head of the house, but Felix has always been the one to give the final word. The door to my room opens and shuts, and I hear Felix sit next to me. A cool cloth presses against my forehead, and I flinch, my eyes flickering open. Felix is hunched over me. He grimaces when he sees I'm awake. "Where are we?" I mumble.

"Addy's," Felix says it shortly, and I know something's wrong.

"Why?"

"There was no way I could get ya all the way back to the cave. But don't worry. I dropped you off here, then took everythin' to the cave. I managed to seal off the entrance with rocks, so that it's not so damp in that one room."

"Then what's wrong?"

Felix scratches at the thin line of stubble along his jaw. "You, kid. You have a fever, a high one. I can't get you out of here without gettin' ya killed. You've lost a lot of blood, Peter, why didn't ya tell me how deep those bites were?"

"I didn't know," I murmur, wanting to go back to sleep, but hurting too bad. And it's not just my chest; my entire body throbs with pain, especially my throat, which is dry and scratchy. I think there might be something stuck in it, but I can't cough it up, and coughing only hurts. My brother shushes me, scowling.

"Addy doesn't know about the Siren, but it will only be so long before word reaches her or one of her kids. You'd better get well soon, or we might have to share most of what we have."

"That would suck. What does she think happened to me?"

"Wolf." He shrugs. "She's pretty satisfied with the penguins and the fish, but she's only willin' to share if all her kids have enough to eat. Which won't help you at all."

My stomach tells me that that's not okay, but I can't do anything about it. "That's not good."

"No, of course it's not. Sometimes I want to kill that woman." Felix bares his teeth. "After all we've done for her, after everythin' we've given her, she treats ya like this. It's infuriatin'! As soon as you can walk, we're leavin', and we're not comin' back."

"I know. I heard," I croak, shuddering as the pain in my chest flares. "It's about bloody time you figured it out."

"She's never been this bad. This time she crossed the line."

"I'm pretty sure she's done that several times. We should've left sooner."

Felix sighs. "No. I made a promise. They're family, Peter, and no matter how horrible they are, that won't change. I stayed because I gave Mum my word, aye, but I also because I didn't want us to sink to Addy's level. Just because she would let us starve to death doesn't mean we should do the same to her. That's what I've been tryin' to tell you all these years. We're better than that. *You're* better than that."

"Until now."

Felix rubs his face. "Until now. But that's different. Things can only get so bad before it becomes stupid not to leave—"

"I think that was a long time ago."

"In which case you have to put your foot down." Felix finishes, glaring at me. "We're not goin' to let them starve. But we're not stayin' here either. We're not givin' them the majority of what we get anymore. They're goin' to have to start earnin' things on their own. And if they don't like it, *then* they can starve."

"Aye. Careful what ya say, though. If ya keep givin' speeches, they might kick us out of the house early. Or else have ya hauled off to the pits 'cause you're a crazy old man."

Felix snorts, rolling his eyes, but he doesn't smile. "Whatever. If I go, you go, and don't be forgetin' that."

"I haven't. That's why I told ya to watch your words." I try for a grin, but it probably looks more like a grimace.

That's when Felix cracks a small smile. "And there's my wee little brother."

"And there's my grandpa." I chuckle, then wince.

"Hey, I'm not that old."

"So? You're still an old man. I'm surprised Addy still lets us stay here."

"Alright, you bum, shape up before *I* kick your butt out of the house." My brother smirks, but only slightly now, and I'm not sure how real it is. He reaches over and tousles my hair. I wrinkle my nose, pushing his hand away.

"Shut up." I almost laugh, but it doesn't come out. Instead I just grin, glad to see that my brother has lightened up a bit.

Felix shakes his head. "Whatever. Good to see that you're not dyin'."

"What makes you think I was dyin'?"

Felix just sighs and rubs his face with his hands, the smile dropping away and weariness taking over his expression again. "Just…. get some sleep kid. I need to go huntin'."

"We just went huntin'." I'm confused.

Felix shakes his head. "That was two days ago. It's about time you woke up, ya gave me a bloody heart attack."

I frown, feeling sick. "Then…. don't get yourself killed. Love you." It just comes out before I can stop it.

The corner of his mouth twitches up slightly. "Dork. Love you too kid. Don't die on me."

"Wouldn't dream of it."

He smiles slightly and gets up, pausing at the door. "I'll be back soon. Try not to kill the monsters, I can't stop them from comin' in here when I'm gone."

I groan, and he leaves, shutting the door quietly behind him. It must be early in the morning, because Felix is only just leaving to hunt, so maybe Addy's kids are still asleep. Maybe I can get more rest.

It's much later when sleep finally decides to come back. My eyes have just closed when a flash of pain explodes across my chest, and I flinch, sucking in a breath. My eyes fly open and fall instantly on the small, dark haired form standing next to my cot, his arms crossed over his chest. I let my head drop back onto my pillow, letting my breath out slowly and fighting every urge to get up and beat the crap out of him. Not that I could right now anyways. Cole smirks. "What happened to you?"

"Wolf," I growl, trying to relax.

"I'm sure."

I open one eye, glaring up at him. "What do ya want?"

"I think there's somethin' you're not tellin' me."

"Oh?"

"Aye." Cole narrows his brown eyes. "It wasn't a wolf, was it?"

I look at him, confused. "What? Of course it was a bloody wolf, what else would it be?"

Cole shrugs. "No idea. Guess I just wanted to pester you."

I groan, closing my eyes. "Please just let me sleep."

"You slept for two days." He points out.

"I don't care," I moan. "Just go." I feel the heaviness of sleep tugging at my limbs, trying to pull me under, but before I can give into it, I'm once again blinded by pain as Cole pokes at my chest.

"Mum says we need food."

"Felix left a while ago. He'll bring back somethin' to eat soon." *Please let me sleep.*

"I don't want penguin." Cole pouts.

I let out an exasperated sigh. "You're what, eleven now? Why don't you go huntin' for once? If ya don't want penguin, go out and find somethin' better."

"Maybe I will."

I snort. "Not likely. Ya don't know the first thing about huntin'. Hell, ya don't even know how to fire a gun."

Cole scowls. "So?"

"So go away. Felix will find somethin' to eat. Maybe he'll get some more fish."

"I don't want fish."

"Ugh, then starve." I roll over, stiff and sore, and stuff my head under my pillow, my back to the boy.

"No."

I don't respond, letting myself relax, but just as I'm about to pass out, Cole starts shaking me violently until I cry out. "*What do you want!?*"

Cole flinches back.

I glare at him over my shoulder, my teeth bared and my entire body tense.

"Nothin'."

I drop my head back on the pillow. "Then go *away. Please.*"

"My house."

I just moan, covering my head with my pillow again. "Once I'm outta here, I'm never comin' back," I growl at him. "You can starve, for all I care, but I'm never comin' back."

"Well, I don't care about you either." Cole sounds defensive, but I don't look at him.

"Good, then ya won't miss me."

Cole snorts. "As if ya have anywhere to go."

I slowly roll over to look at him, my eyes narrowed. I open my mouth to tell him he's wrong, but I stop, jerking my head toward the door and freezing, my ears straining.

"What now-" Cole starts, but I shush him, sitting up fast and swallowing a yell as the gashes on my chest reopen.

Outside, the sound of a powerful motor rumbles, vibrating the air around the old shack. The EMP's, which happened after the asteroids hit, destroyed every engine on the surface, so the grumbles coming from outside mean only one thing: Glass City Scouts.

Without even thinking, I'm on my feet and hooking my arm around Cole's waist, hauling him into the other room. I snatch my coat—the one with the picture of my parents in the pocket—off the end of Felix's cot as I go, pulling it on quickly.

Addy and her kids are already tromping down the stairs to the cellar through the hatch in the floor, Addy yelling at them to hurry up.

She sees me, her face twisting with uncertainty when she sees her son doubled around my arm. Cole hollers at me, his eyes huge with fear, and I half throw, half shove him toward the hatch. Behind me, the door slams open, the rumble of the motor roaring louder with every second.

Felix stumbles in, dropping the penguins he'd had over his shoulder and charging toward me. Cole jumps down the stairs, glancing back at us briefly.

Around us, the walls start to crack, the entire shack rumbling.

There's no time.

Felix will never make it, and it would be too easy for the Scouts to find Addy and her kids if the hatch isn't covered. I leap the last of the distance to the hatch and land just behind it, flipping it shut and covering it with the fur rug just as the entire shack is torn away, the roof thrown yards down the street and the walls collapsing around us.

Felix shoves my rifle into my hands, firing his own up at the massive hovercraft that materializes out of the sky above us. The heat from the hovertech blasts us like a hot wind, but we stand together side by side to face it.

Ropes drop from either side of it, Scouts in their red uniforms sliding down them and starting toward us. Felix and I fire at them repeatedly, ducking behind the overturned table as shots ring around us.

Pounding feet sound all around us. We peek over the edge of the table, shooting the few Scouts who dare to approach, ducking again as the Scouts fire back.

Suddenly, the gunfire ceases, the roaring of the hovercraft the only thing that keeps the silence at bay. Then, above that, the barely audible sound of something clanking across the floorboards.

Felix and I peek around the edge of the table, our eyes falling on a small, cylindrical case of metal. I frown, and Felix's body crashes over mine, covering my head just seconds before a massive explosion. The floor falls away. My back hits the edge of the table and knocks it over again. And then it's just quiet.

I blink, dazed. My ears ring; all sound is faded, distant.

"Felix," I mumble. My entire left side feels like it's on fire, but it's a detached feeling, as though it's not really me who feels it. I crawl toward the edge of the hole, peeking blearily over the broken and shattered floorboards.

I see my brother's twisted body in the basement, and my heart stops. "*Felix!*"

Crunching boots sound behind me. I glance over my shoulder, then choke a cry, reaching for my gun only to realize that it's nowhere near me. I cough heavily, pushing myself further off the edge, toward my brother. Before I can fall, however, two pairs of strong hands catch me under the arms, hauling me back despite my screams of pain. I struggle, ignoring how much everything hurts and kicking out at the knees of the Scouts trying to haul me off. "Felix!" I yell again. I need to get to him. He's hurt, he needs help. "No—get off me!" I snarl.

I cry out again, finally managing to wrench away from my captors and lunge back toward the edge, struggling to get back to my brother. "I'll come back!" I yell at him, unsure if he can hear me or not. "I promise!"

Rachel

I wake up in the morning around ten o'clock, expecting the sound of Clayton's vacuuming, but the room is silent. My eyes are crusted shut by the salt from my tears, and I keep them closed. The memory of everything that happened last night swirls through my head, but it feels like a dream. I know Clayton's dead, but for some reason, it doesn't hurt as bad as before. At least he's in a better place, I guess. And then there's Malcolm's kiss.

I drag myself out of bed, yawning and stretching before getting to my hands and toes and hammering out about fifty push-ups. I roll over and do half as many sit-ups, then relax, feeling refreshed. If I'm ever going to the Surface, I need to be in good shape.

I spend a few minutes putting on my makeup, covering up my puffy eyes with mascara and eyeliner. Why would Malcolm do that? I know he's had a crush on me for a while now—woman's intuition—but why would he just now start to make it obvious? Does he expect the feeling to be mutual so soon after Clayton died? *Well.... Who else is there?* I scowl at the thin, rather fit girl the vanity mirror. Now is not the time to be thinking of this. "Stop being such a stupid girl." I scold her, then pull a TRRD out of the dresser drawer.

I lay it flat in front of me, staring at it intently. This one is about the size of my palm, flat and rectangular with a ridge on the back for a handle. Two little buttons sit one above the other on the handle, one for healing and the other to activate the nanobots.

I recall Malcolm telling me about them, but then I remember how Clayton had asked questions about them, and I shove the device back in the drawer. I take a deep breath, then let it out slowly, blinking rapidly to keep the tears from coming. There'll be time to study the device later.

I unlock my bedroom door and tromp down the stairs, wearing skinny jeans and a baggy T-shirt the Suppliers had salvaged from the Surface.

Instead of heading out to go on my usual morning run, I make my way through the foyer toward the kitchen to get myself some eggs.

All of a sudden, the front doors burst open. My father storms through, followed by three doctors pushing a stretcher. Lying unconscious on the stretcher is someone I can't really see, but I do catch sight of blood—lots of blood—and then they're gone, hurrying off down the hall and toward the medical room.

I wonder who it could be—certainly someone important enough to be brought to the mayor's house—and then I see the Suppliers in their red uniforms march in after them, not giving me a second glance. I forget about breakfast, and follow them.

I slip into the medical room behind one of the Suppliers, peering around them to where the stretcher is. There are enough people in the room that my presence goes unnoticed. The doctors hunch over a patient with an oxygen mask covering his mouth and nose. My father stands by the head of the stretcher, watching as the doctor's cut off the patient's clothes, revealing charred skin and burnt flesh beneath. I swallow a gasp, getting the feeling that I'm not supposed to be here.

"How bad is it?" My father asks of one of the doctors.

"Bad, but not as bad as it could've been. The other one shielded him from most of the blast. There's still quite a bit of shrapnel stuck in him, though, it'll take a while to get it all out."

"How long till' he'll be able to work?"

The doctor—a short, pudgy blonde man with a baby face and big glasses—shrugs. "A few hours, maybe? Possibly all day. Really, it's surprising that he survived this at all." Behind him, the other doctors slowly sweep TRRDs over the patient's burns, leaving behind smooth, bare skin across a well-muscled chest.

"Hmm. Make it quick." Is all my father says in response, starting toward the door. I squeeze out the door and run down the hall, sitting on the bottom step of the staircase as if I've been there for a while. My father strides out into the hall less than a minute later, and I get up when he sees me.

"Who was that?" I ask.

"Who?"

"Dad, I'm not blind. I was coming downstairs to get some breakfast when you guys suddenly burst through the doors with someone on a stretcher. What happened? Is he a Surface Dweller?"

"You've always been a nosy little bugger. Just like your mother, eh?" My father shakes his head, smiling and messing up my hair.

"I suppose I shouldn't tell her you said that." I'm still mad at him, but some of that anger starts to fade. Everyone makes mistakes now and then, and everyone needs forgiveness.

My father grins. "Not if you want to see me again."

I laugh, walking over so that I'm standing in front of him. "So? Who was that?"

"Just some Surface Dweller. He was injured in a gang fight, so we brought him up here."

I frown—it's been a long time since we've brought a Surface Dweller to *our* house. "You can't replace Clayton."

My father sighs. "We need another servant to do Clayton's job, Rachel. I'm sorry if that upsets you. I was going to wait, but then this kid showed up, and…." My father trails off. "Anyways, he needed help. Don't get so attached to this one, okay?"

"Don't get too attached?" I hiss.

"You know what I mean, Rachel. And besides, I don't want you to get hurt again. Please don't argue with me right now." He adds when I open my mouth to protest.

I want to be mad, I want to yell at him, accuse him of moving things along too fast, but I don't. I'm not stupid, I know that what he did was not only smart, but also the right thing. I take a breath. "Can I see him?" I ask, pretending that I haven't already. I mean, of course I did, but I didn't see the extent of the damage.

"Honey…. I don't think that's a good idea."

"It's not like I can't handle a little blood." I roll my eyes.

My father shakes his head and starts to leave, "No, let's just let the doctors do their work first. Give him some time to rest."

I remain where I am for a moment longer, watching him go, then head through the dining room and into the kitchen like I had planned to earlier. My mother is sitting at the end of the window booth that wraps around half the kitchen table, reading a copy of an ancient newspaper from the library. My mother loves the newspapers, and the one she has right now is from 2016. "That's a loooooooong time ago," I tell her, and she looks up as though she hadn't realized I had sat down across from her. She gets like that when she's reading.

"Yeah." She smiles, and the day seems to brighten a little. My mom can always cheer me up. "The world was falling to pieces for a while there. Especially Germany. Nazis started crawling out of their holes again. Germany for Germans." She puts down the newspaper. "Strange how history repeats itself so quickly."

"Well—that hasn't repeated for a while now."

"Hmm. I guess a second ice-age puts a hold on the cycle. Or at least parts of it."

"Parts of it? What parts have repeated?"

She gives me a sad look, asking a question instead of answering mine. "How are you feeling honey?"

"Fine," I say at length.

"Rachel…."

My eyes burn, and I explode. "He told me that I shouldn't have gotten so attached!"

"Who?"

"Dad! He told me that Clayton was just an animal, that he wasn't really my friend! How could he say that?"

Mom takes a deep breath, rubbing her face wearily. "I don't know honey. Your father…. When you put a higher value on the lives of certain people rather than considering us all equal, you say stupid things." There's a bitterness in her voice that makes me frown. She studies her hands for a moment, then changes the subject. "I suppose I should feed you, huh?"

I slump, nodding. "Sure."

"Alright." She gets up, but so do I, and we make breakfast together, her with the eggs and me kneading the dough and sticking it in the minute-oven. All our kitchen appliances are lined up against the wall opposite the window, behind the island that sits between the counter and the window booth. In a few minutes, the eggs are done, and I slice up the fresh bread and pop the slices in the toaster. Soon enough, my mother and I are sitting in silence at the table again, eating eggs and toast. I love spending time with my mother, even if we don't say anything. Besides, I don't really feel like talking anyway. All I can think of is my father. If all men were created equal, then why can one man own another? *No, this is different. The Surface Dwellers work to earn their own home. We don't own them, we give them opportunity.*

"So…. I saw you with Malcolm last night." My mother's voice startles me from my thoughts.

I involuntarily jump. "What?"

"I saw him kiss you. It's about time too. His mother and I have planned this since you two were born."

I jump again. "What? No!" Not that I actually know anyone else in this stupid city.

She laughs. "Too late, it's already been decided. You two were destined for each other from the start."

"Mooom," I say, exasperated. I can feel my face burning, and I twist my pony-tail around my forefinger. "It's not like you gave me many options anyway."

"Hey, we didn't want you growing up getting special treatment from all those public school kids and becoming a spoiled brat. Being the mayor's daughter isn't easy, people will either suck up to you all the time or make fun of you. Trust me, I'm his wife, I have to deal with the same problem."

I roll my eyes. "That's a really stupid reason Mom. I can handle it."

"Well, when you turn eighteen, you can do whatever you want, but until then, you're still my baby."

"Ugh Mom. Just keep your mouth shut about Malcolm."

"Alright, alright. I won't tell anyone." She giggles like a teenage girl, her face just as red as mine. She stares at me a little bit, beaming while I hold her gaze and wait for her to react. After a second, she squeals, shoving her hands against her mouth. "You guys are gonna be sooo adorable!"

"Mom shut up!" I laugh, pushing her shoulder. "It's not like we're dating or anything." As soon as I say it, I feel my face burn impossibly hotter.

"Well. They're coming over today for lunch. Mr. Crysis and your father have business or something to discuss, and Marilynn decided she didn't want to be left alone at the house so…." She glances out the large window looking out over the front yard, and her smile grows. "There they are now."

"What?" I look out the window as well. Malcolm and his family are walking down the street, heading toward our house. "Oh." That's all I need.

"You do like him, right?" My mom asks.

"I don't know. I mean, I do, but right now it's just….I don't know." Malcolm's a nice guy, but I don't think he picked the right time to express his feelings. "Don't...Say...Anything!" I hiss, and Mom pretends to zip her lips, even though she's still smiling and trying to hide it.

"They're staying until lunch, then leaving after we eat." Mom winks, and I scowl trying to hide my embarrassed smile, pulling my finger out of my hair.

"Just don't," I say, then get up, rushing back through the dining room and into the foyer. I open the black crystal door just as Mr. Crysis rings the doorbell. He raises a dark eyebrow, his steely brown eyes staring me down.

"Where's your father?"

Malcolm's father has always sort of scared me. He's very serious all the time, and I don't think I've ever seen him smile. I don't even think he can anymore, judging by how often the corners of his mouth are turned down. "I don't know. I saw him heading toward his study."

Mr. Crysis nods curtly, glancing down at Malcolm. "Don't do anything stupid," he says before stepping past me and heading down the hall.

"And your mother?" Mrs. Crysis wants to know.

I swallow, knowing how gossipy her and my mother get. No doubt the fact that I like Malcolm will turn up sooner or later—likely sooner—despite Mom's promise. "My mom's in the kitchen." Mrs. Crysis is a lot older than my mother, but it's clear she doesn't want to accept that: every time I see her, she's got a ridiculous amount of makeup on, most of it to cover up the tiny creases around her eyes and mouth. Really, I think she would look better without all that makeup—or at least, more human. I shouldn't make fun of her, though. She's still a nice person, and pretty much my mom's best friend.

Malcolm remains in the doorway, his face just as red as mine.. "How are you feeling?"

I hesitate, then shake my head. "I don't know. Like I shouldn't be laughing, like I should be crying. But…. you're right. Clayton would want me to be happy." Malcolm just nods, not meeting my eyes. I glance over my shoulder toward our moms. "We should get out of the house. Mom's been pestering me about you." Of course, I think of how weird that sounds after I say it.

Malcolm raises an eyebrow. "Oh? Why?"

I suck in my lower lip, twisting at the end of my ponytail. "No reason."

"Uh-huh." Malcolm grins, but he doesn't say anything else about it. Instead, he takes my hand, and sorrow flees from my mind. "Shall we?"

All I can do is nod, and he leads me off down the street toward one of the entrances to Greenhouse Park. "What was that all about?" I ask as we walk.

"What?"

"'Don't do anything stupid'." I mimic his father's monotonous tone.

Malcolm doesn't respond right away, staring off down the road. "He's just his normal grumpy self."

"What's his problem?"

"I don't know. Probably some troublesome Surface Dweller in the desalinization plants or something. Got some new hands the other day, and there's no doubt a few that are causing problems."

"Hmm." I purse my lips. "But he's always like that."

"Yeah well….there's always something pissing him off."

Peter

The room blurs in and out of focus for several minutes before I can finally make out specific objects. Everything around me is white or silver, shiny and pristine—unlike anything on the Surface. The pain of burnt flesh has faded. All that remains is a distant throb. I look down at my bare chest, expecting to see bandages, but all I see is smooth, unblemished skin. Even the wounds from the Siren are gone, and I frown, touching my collar bone with my fingers. I look around blearily.

On a small table to my left, a few healing devices are piled on on top of the other, and I assume they're empty. The cleanliness of the room around me and the fact that I still have skin can only mean one thing: I'm in the Glass City.

No.

I have to get back, I have to get home to Felix.

Felix. If I'm in the Glass City, there's no way I can get to him right now. I'm breathing heavily. I try to slow down, try to keep from panicking, try to keep the images of Felix's broken body from my mind. *No. No, he's okay. He's gonna be okay,* I tell myself, even though I know there's no way for me to be sure of that. . *I have to get out of here.* I half fall, half climb out of the hospital bed, shocked at how cold it is, and I realize I'm not wearing anything. My old clothes are in a blackened, shredded heap on the floor by my bed, and I clench my fists, feeling violated.

A line of green uniforms are hung up along the wall next to my bed, and I grab one, tugging the pants on just as the door rattles. Panicking, I hide the shirt and the hanger underneath the pillow, jump back into bed and cover my legs with the sheets. A short, baby-faced doctor bustles in, pulling up short when he sees that I'm awake. He clutches his clipboard to his chest, then lets out a breath, scowling as if I had intentionally scared the crap out of him.

"Let me go home," I growl as he draws closer. He doesn't even acknowledge that I said anything. He just pins my wrist and—before I can resist—presses a cylinder against the crook of my arm, the metal tip heating up as the glass tube fills rapidly with blood. Panic floods my chest, and I want to shove the man away, but what will happen if I move too soon? Will the cylinder damage an artery? Will I bleed out?

Before I can decide if it's worth the risk, he takes the cylinder with my blood and turns his back to me, sticking the tube under a strange device with a bright light on the bottom. He presses his face against some kind of eye-piece at the top of the device, giving me a clear shot to the door.

I slowly slide out of bed, creeping toward the door and quietly turning the handle. I slip out just as the doctor turns around. He yells behind me, and I take off running down the long hall that stretches out in front of me.

I hear footsteps behind me, and I jiggle a few locked door handles in search of a weapon—anything that can help me escape. The doctor grabs my shoulders from behind, but I jerk my head back, hitting his face hard and knocking him down. I give up on the doors and start running again. My feet stick on the crystal floor and I catch myself on the railing at the base of a huge, grand staircase, gaping at the massive foyer before me. To my left, the wall opens up into what looks like a sitting room, but there's no one in it—which means there's no one standing between me and the front door across the foyer.

Without hesitation, I lunge across the foyer. I reach the door as it opens to a dark haired young man and a young woman, both staring with wide blue eyes. They blink in surprise when I slide to a stop in front of them, gasping for breath. The woman pulls her finger from her blonde ponytail, standing on her toes to peer around me.

"Stop him!" The doctor yells. I glance over my shoulder, then back at the couple in front of me. The man dives at me, trying to tackle me to the ground. I stumble under the impact, but recover enough to use his own momentum to throw him off me. He leaps on my back, hooking his arm around my throat.

I stagger in a circle, struggling to breathe. He squeezes harder, and I slam him hard against the wall, winding him.

"Malcolm!" The woman gasps.

Yelling, I pull him over my shoulder and throw him to the ground. Malcolm chokes, gasping like a fish out of water as he tries to pull air into his lungs.

I push past the young woman and out into the open—and then pain burns across my back, dragging me to my knees. A scream rips from my throat. I heard no gunfire, but it feels like I've been shot. I gasp, rolling onto my back and shuddering uncontrollably.

A man's face blocks my view of the strange blue sky overhead. He shakes his head, his hair—the same shade of blond as the young woman's—falling across his forehead. "Feels like you've been shot, huh?"

All I do is tremble, unable to form the words to yell at him or find the strength to wrap my hands around his throat.

"Dad?" I hear a woman's voice say.

"Not now, Rachel," the man mutters, taking ahold of my jaw and squeezing hard and speaking low enough that his daughter can't hear him. "It's what happens to people like you, boy. It's a special new device we invented to keep you in check, one that inflicts pain—and you're the lucky guinea pig. Now you have it, and I have control of it. The more you behave, the less I'll have to use it, do you understand?"

I finally manage speak. "Where's—my brother?" I croak, wincing as I try to get up. It still feels like I've been shot, but my back is dry; no blood.

"I don't know what you're talking about," he says, but his cold blue eyes say otherwise.

"Where's Felix?" The only thought on my mind now, aside from pain, is my brother. He's the only family I've ever had, I can't live without him, I can't leave him to die. "He's hurt."

The man looks sidelong at his daughter, hooking his hands under my arms and pulling me to my feet. I stumble against him, and the pain is gone, disappearing as though it had never been. Finally coming to my senses, I catch myself on the doorframe as the man tries to pull me inside.

"No—I need to get to my brother."

"You need rest. You still need time to recover." His voice is a little too loud, and the young woman behind him looks on in confusion.

"I'm *fine*," I spit. "Felix is the one who's hurt and he doesn't have any of your fancy healin' devices. Please just let me go to him."

The girl—Rachel—speaks up. "Dad, you can't just leave his brother to die."

"We'll go back for him later, I promise," the man says.

The tiniest bit of hope sparks in my chest, but it fizzles out quickly. He was just threatening me a second ago, why is he suddenly promising to save my brother? But if there's a chance he's telling the truth,

I'm sure as hell not going to let it slip by. "There's no time to wait. He's dyin' I need to get back there now."

"He doesn't look like he needs rest." Rachel adds, her face turning pink. "Maybe he could go back with you to the Surface. It's not like that gang could get to him with you guys there."

I squint at her. "What gang?"

Rachel blinks, and her father's grip tightens on my arm. "Look, I'm sure your brother will be okay for a little while longer, but you can't help him if you're dead. You need sleep-"

"I don't!" I insist, turning to Rachel and pleading with my eyes.

Rachel shifts uncertainly, twisting her blonde ponytail around the end of her forefinger. "Dad.... You saved him, you can't just leave his brother—"

"Saved me?" I look at the man, and it suddenly clicks: he's never going to save my brother. He's only saying he will to make himself look good for his daughter.

"From the gang," Rachel says it as if I should've already known.

I clench my fists. "Did he tell you it was a gang?" I refuse to play into whatever lie this man is telling his daughter. No amount of bullets will make me dance.

The man's eyes flash, and his hand goes to his pocket. My knees buckle and I gasp as pain explodes all across my back again. I slump against him, but he doesn't let me fall.

"What did I tell you?" He says, then looks at his daughter. "He needs rest."

"What about his brother?" Rachel asks.

"We'll send someone for him, I promise."

"*Liar*," I hiss, shuddering. I twist at his wrist, turning it as far as it can go in an attempt to break it, but then the pain in my back grows worse and suddenly my hands won't listen to me anymore.

The man hooks his arm around my chest and drags me back into the medical room, forcing me to lie back on the bed. The doctor hurries through the door—his nose still bleeding from where I'd hit him in the face—and the two men struggle to strap my wrists down.

I kick at Rachel's father, catching his jaw and knocking him back. With an angry snarl, he uses his weight to hold my leg down, tightening a strap around my ankle just as the doctor does the same to my other leg. Then they leave me alone in the room.

The pain in my back fades, and I tug at my restraints, infuriated. I need to get *home*.

After a while the door opens again, quietly, and I look up. Rachel slips in, shutting the door carefully behind her and looking at me curiously. When she doesn't say anything, I wrench at my restraints. "What do *you* want?"

"What did you mean when you said 'what gang'?" She asks after a second. She looks uncertain, her eyes drifting to the leather straps around my wrists.

"Exactly what it sounds like. What gang?" *What else would I mean?* I twist at the restraints again, but they're too strong.

She looks confused. "The one that attacked you, the reason you're here."

I narrow my eyes. "Is that what your father told you?"

Rachel crosses her arms, tilting her chin up. "It's what happened."

I groan, dropping my head onto the pillow. "You don't know anythin', do ya?"

"Of course I do," Rachel says defensively, scowling.

"No, ya don't. Ya think I got blown up by a gang?" I snort. "We don't have much for explosives on the Surface, Deary. Everyone owns a gun, there aren't many people who will risk gettin' shot over whatever a single person might or might not be carryin'. A gang won't attack a single person unless he's a trader, it's not worth it."

Rachel blinks. "What are you talking about?"

I shake my head, taking a breath. "What do ya know about the Surface?"

"I know that it's quite the place to live. I mean, it's dangerous, and kind of empty, but isn't it nice to have every day be an adventure? Where something new and exciting is happening every minute instead of being stuck up here doing the same thing day in day out? And if things get too rough we help you. You can even earn your way up here."

She sounds so certain that I can't hide the look of disgust on my face. "Is that what ya think? Is that what they tell you? Is that how you convince yourself that it's permissible to abduct and enslave us?" I scoff. "Ya think your father saved me? You're wrong. But you can make it right. You can help me, you can let me go. Just get these off of me, let me go."

Rachel's expression is an odd mix of confusion and shame, but before I can go on, the door behind her bursts open. "Rachel!" Her father barks, and Rachel jumps.

"Dad—I—"

"What are you doing in here? I told you to stay out!"

She swallows. "Why?"

"Because he's sick, and he needs to rest! How can he get any rest if you're in here pestering him? Out!" Rachel's father shoos her out the door, slamming it behind her and whirling on me.

"Looks like I've tested your wee little girl's faith in you." I smirk.

The man's eyes flash, and he jams his hand into his pocket. The pain this time is far worse than before, like my entire back is on fire.

I bite back a scream, straining against my restraints and baring my teeth with my eyes squeezed shut. I will *not* give him the satisfaction of seeing me cry.

"It looks like you need to learn a little lesson in *respect*." He unstraps my wrists and ankles, hauling me to my feet.

I hurt too much to fight back, leaning heavily against him and trying to get my feet to stay under me.

He drags me out of the room and down the hall—in the opposite direction of the front door. I try to struggle, but it just hurts too bad, and all I can do is groan as he pulls me down a set of stairs to the basement. He shoves me through another door at the base of the stairs. A wave of heat washes over me, the room hotter than the pits of hell. I can hardly lift my head to see a tall, thick man leaning against the wall opposite the door.

"Teach him what fear means." Rachel's father's upper lip curls, then he storms out of the room, the door slamming shut behind him.

I struggle to my feet as my eyes adjust to the dim red light. The pain slowly ebbs from my back, and I turn to face the Glass City pest still standing by the door. He turns to me, smiling and showing off his gapped teeth. I remember the bodies in the Atlantic, broken and crushed by years of abuse, and I snap.

Without warning, I pounce across the room and barrel into his middle, slamming him against the door and dragging him to the ground. The man grunts, managing to throw me off, but I'm on my feet before he is, drawing back my foot to kick him in the face. Before I can break his nose, strong arms hook around my waist from behind and lift me off my feet.

I kick and squirm, trying to get my arms unpinned from my sides, but whoever is holding me is too strong. I kick back, hitting his kneecap hard with my heel, but Gap Tooth is suddenly charging toward us. The man holding me moves his arms down, and Gap Tooth plants his foot hard in my stomach.

I double, coughing, and the man drops me. I land on my knees, catching myself with one hand. I wrap my other arm around my stomach as I try to regain my breath.

Gap Tooth growls, kicking me hard in the ribs and knocking me onto my side. Then they both take my arms, lifting me off the ground and throwing me face down on some sort of table. Before I can recover, they've tied my wrists and ankles down, a thick leather band tightening around my waist. I struggle, but am unable to break free, and Gap Tooth chuckles. "Stupid boy." He wags his finger in my face. "Even if you did escape, where would you go?"

"Anywhere but here." I wrench at the new straps, angry that I had let them pin me again.

The other man moves to a furnace yawning from the wall in front of me, the flames casting the room in an orange hue. He pulls from the glowing coals a long, red hot poker, and I freeze, every muscle in my body tensing and screaming at me to run, to move, to get out. But I can't. I can't even bloody *move*.

Gap Tooth takes the poker from his pal, holding it close to my face. "Got any rats on the Surface?"

I don't respond, staring cross-eyed at the glowing tip.

"Well, the thing about rats they learn quickly what to do and what not to do. Trial and error. They do the wrong thing and they suffer the consequences, and they learn not to make the same mistake again. That's all you are boy. A mangy Surface rat. You'll learn to do what you're told."

"Fat chance," I spit. Gap Tooth's grin drops from his face, and he turns and presses the hot metal across the small of my back. I scream, unable to hold it back, and the other man hands him another poker, taking the one Gap Tooth had just used and sticking it back in the coals.

"See? Trial, and error. Error and consequences." Gap Tooth leers, pressing the other poker against my shoulder blades. "If you don't fix that mouth of yours, this'll get worse." He finishes over my cry of pain. I twist at my restraints, but it's beyond pointless, and the poker burns into my back for a third time, and a fourth, and fifth and a sixth. I lose count after eleven and will myself to pass out, to escape through sleep, but I bloody well *can't*.

"You work here now," the other man says, shoving one of the pokers back into the fire. "Your life is serving those above you, and if you argue, if you talk back, if you disobey, we will make you suffer. We can bring you to the edge of death and back if we want to."

"Please," I choke as Gap Tooth lowers another poker to my back. Gap Tooth just grins, the glowing metal again burning into my back, just beneath my rib cage. I scream again.

Rachel

I'm silent all through lunch, quietly eating my sandwich and staring out the dining room window. I even ignore Malcolm, curling my finger in my ponytail as our parents talk. All I can think of is that guy who had come running down the hall in half a servant's uniform, of the strength it must've taken to throw Malcolm over his shoulder. Definitely not the strength of someone struggling to recover from high fever. I can't help but be amazed. Not very many people in the Glass City are that strong, and even with the Suppliers, there are only a few. They're the ones that bring up water and supplies from the Surface, hauling barrels full of salvaged parts and gadgets for our hovercars and such. They do a lot of heavy lifting, unlike the rest of us.

But this guy is younger than most of the Suppliers. Like, around my age. And he's got green eyes—not just green but cool, like pale green with dark green-black rims around the irises. I rest my cheek in my hand, absentmindedly taking a bite of my sandwich. And he's got dark red hair. And thick muscles across his bare back and chest and arms and—*whoa*. I stop chewing, staring at my sandwich. My face feels hot, and I glance around to make sure no one was reading my thoughts.

What about what he'd said, about the Surface Dwellers being abducted and enslaved? Do they really think we're enslaving them? Maybe it's just him, maybe he is just delirious, like Dad said. *It's not like we force them to work for us, right?* I chew my sandwich thoughtfully. *That* would *make them more like slaves.*

But being brought up here is a reward. They're not like the robots we used to have, before the EMPs on the Surface fried their circuits. Our servants have motivation to work hard, they aren't just programmed to do what they're told. The Surface Dwellers want to come up here, they're rewarded for good work. They're not held against their will. *Are they?*

Clayton pops up to the forefront of my mind, and I suddenly remember every time he flinched when my father walked into the room, every time he couldn't meet my eyes when I knew something was wrong, and he wouldn't tell me. That young man's words make a lot more sense than I want them to, now that I think about it.

But *no, dad wouldn't kidnap people*. He's the mayor, not a prison warden. Dad isn't a monster, he would never do something like that, especially because he used to warn me against kidnappers when I was little. My father helps the Surface Dwellers, he gives them the opportunity to earn their own home in the Glass City, even if he does think they're 'lower life forms'.

Malcolm sits across from me, also silent. I can tell his pride is seriously injured, so I don't say anything about it. I still can't fully process what happened, what that man had said with his thick Irish accent. It just doesn't fit what I know. Dad wouldn't lie to me like that, would he? I mean, what would be the point?

I can't ask my father about it. If only I could talk to that boy again, get him alone.

I finish lunch quickly and hurry upstairs to my room, leaving Malcolm at the table with our parents. I shut my door and lock it. The little button beside the doorframe glows a little, and I trace my finger around it. It's connected to a buzzer to Clayton's room in the basement, but it hadn't been lit last night. It's not lit unless there's someone in it.

I stiffen. It couldn't be that Irish guy, could it? *That guy* was Clayton's replacement? *Is this Dad's way of making sure I don't get 'too attached'? By bringing up the biggest jerk on the Surface?* I scowl, scuffing my toe in the plush circle carpet under and around my bed before crossing the room and sitting in the window seat.

If he is Clayton's replacement, then that means he is under my command—as well as my father's, of course—but he has to do whatever I tell him. I would never have used that against Clayton, but this guy isn't Clayton, not even close. I swallow back a sob, wiping my eyes quickly. I'm pissed that Dad would try to replace my best friend with some moron. And—why is he so hot? Does my father understand how annoying that is?

Focus. I tell myself, twisting the end of my ponytail around my finger. Why would Dad bring up someone who's so confused? That guy thought we were holding him prisoner or something. I'll have to talk to him again, ask him more about what he meant. About the Surface. And he'll have to tell me because he's my servant. But not until I see him again, not until the excitement of what happened earlier today dies down a bit, blows over.

I lean around the corner of the wall, stretching to pull a book out of the bookcase next to the window seat. I have nothing better to do, and I don't really want to hang out with Malcolm right now—not with thoughts of that stupid Irish guy's muscles still at the forefront of my mind. I cringe. *Gross. Stop that.*

I flip to the page I left off on last time, marked by my favorite bookmark: an adorable little Huskie puppy sitting in a bed of flowers. I've always wanted a puppy, but Dad always says absolutely not. I set the bookmark aside and start reading, learning about World War II for my history test. I get to a part describing the concentration camps and stop, chewing on my lower lip.

Maybe that's what the Irish guy is expecting it to be like up here? Maybe he thinks we're like the Nazis or something and we're going to force him to do hard labor and starve him and do all the horrible things the Nazis did to the Jews? If that's the case, then I need to let him know that the Glass City is nothing like a Nazi concentration camp. As much as I dislike him, I don't want him to be terrified of my city.

The thought of him freaking out in the medical room makes me close my book, but I still pause at the door of my bedroom. I could just let him figure it out on his own. Maybe he deserves to be freaked out for a while. *Nah.* I open the door. It's already been a few hours, the excitement has probably died down by now. He was probably being a jerk because he's scared.

I slide down the banister of the staircase, barely managing to catch myself when I fall off the end. I turn left down the hall and stop at the medical room. As quietly as I can, I turn the handle, pushing the door open just a crack and peeking through. The room is empty, and I frown, disappointed. That's right. The buzzer was lit—he's in the basement. Dad will never let me down there. I guess I'll have to talk to him later.

I'm about to leave when I see a pile of burnt clothes by the bed, and I pause. They're not like any clothes I've ever seen—at least, not in anything but history books: the remains of a thick, fluffy fur coat and a pair of pants that look like some sort of animal skin. I slip in the room and shut the door behind me. We have dogs up here, but this fur is thicker, and I crouch next to it, tentatively running my fingers through the gray fuzz. Part of me feels awkward that I'm touching some guys burnt clothes, but there's no one here to see me, so I flatten the coat out on the floor with my hands. The sulfurous scent of burnt fur floods my senses, and I wrinkle my nose, gagging. *Wow that's rancid.*

I dig my fingers through the pockets, just to see what kind of things Surface Dwellers carry, but I don't find what I would expect to find—like loose change. In fact, I don't find anything but a worn, folded piece of paper in the front right pocket of the pants. I unfold it carefully, the singed edges crumbling a bit in my fingers. A young couple smile out from the photograph, standing on the beaches of what looks like Hawaii—or maybe some Caribbean island. I recognize the palm trees and the white sand from some of my text books, although nothing on this frozen planet looks like that now. I hear the door jiggle behind me, and I fold the picture, quickly shoving it into the pocket of my own jeans and standing.

Malcolm stands in the doorway, giving me a funny look. "What are you doing in here?"

"I could ask you the same thing," I tell him, unsure of why my heart is pounding. It's not like Malcolm cares if I'm in here.

"I was looking for you. Our parents are still talking—I don't think they'll ever stop. I was wondering if you wanted to go for another walk in Greenhouse Park?"

I hesitate. But I don't want to hurt his feelings, and since the Surface Dweller is probably in the basement, I don't really have anything else to do. Besides, I'm starting to enjoy these walks with Malcolm more than I used to. Maybe Mom was right. "Sure."

"Awesome. But we can't let our parents see us though. Technically we're leaving, but you know how adults talk. Once they start they don't stop until they spot their kid." Malcolm winks. "Then they decide it's time to leave."

I snicker. "Too true."

We sneak through the foyer, careful to remain undetected. We slip out the front door and run down the street, laughing.

"They didn't suspect a thing." I snort.

"Yeah, but we can't be gone *too* long, or my dad will kill me."

"Why? He's the one who's still talking."

Malcolm shrugs. "Yeah, well. When it's time to go it's time to go. If I'm not there he'll get all grumpy and say they could've left hours ago— which I guess is true, but they're the ones who kept talking. Parents, right?"

I nod, smiling. "Yeah. Gotta love 'em. But you're eighteen now, why don't you move out or something?"

"I plan to after I graduate. Right now I'd have to talk to your dad and get a special note saying I could own one of the houses up here. But once I'm out of high-school, all I have to do is pick out an empty house and move in."

"Are you that afraid of my dad?"

"What? No! No, I just think he'd side with my dad and he wouldn't let me get a house, and then my dad would be pissed that I tried to leave against his permission and….ugh. It'll just be easier to wait until I graduate."

"Well what about your mom?"

Malcolm scoffs. "She doesn't care what I do. She's too busy freaking out over getting old. She's only like, forty-eight, but she's been pestering the scientists about an 'anti-wrinkle' machine of some kind." He shakes his head. "My mom is weird."

"Yeah, mine is too, but not that weird. She's thirty five and calls herself young. She's just obsessed with history. Her and Dad fight a lot, but they usually stop when I enter the room."

"Why do they fight?"

I sigh. "Well, my mom's Christian, and my dad is a hardcore evolution dude, and it's just awkward. I'm not sure how their relationship started, but Mom was really young and they had a thing. I don't think Dad was always into evolution. I think my grandpa got him into it."

"Hmm." Is all Malcolm says in response.

We're silent for a little while, walking into Greenhouse Park.

"Do you ever dream of visiting the Surface?" I ask.

He scowls, shaking his head. "No. Never."

I frown. "Why not?"

Malcolm considers for a long time, as if trying to find the right words. He keeps giving me sidelong glances, keeps biting his lower lip. Then, finally, he says; "Because it's so cold down there. There's pretty much nothing left. I like it up here. I like the gardens, the trees."

"But up here we're stuck doing the same thing every day! There's nowhere for us to go, nothing for us to do but run around in circles in this stupid park! There's nothing new to explore up here." I throw my hands out, gesturing around at the dome. "Don't you ever want to go somewhere other than here?"

Malcolm had wrinkled his nose. "Sometimes, but not down there. I dream of space, of another planet that's not ruined and scarred like ours. As childish as it sounds, I want to be an astronaut, like my grandpa was. He went to explore a whole different planet."

"I know that. But we can't launch a rocket from way up here. And—your grandpa never came back. We never heard from him or his crew again."

Malcolm thinks this over, sighing. "Yeah, I suppose you're right. But still, that's where I want to go. With all the stars and planets and—"

"Asteroid belts and supernovas and black holes." I finish his sentence, smirking.

"And you want to go to the Surface, with all the blizzards and ice and frostbite and wild animals and-"

"Alright alright, touché." I laugh, pushing him. I guess it is pretty cool that he wants to go to space. More exciting than my dreams of going to the Surface. I never knew Malcolm had an adventurous streak like me.

Malcolm grins smugly. "And besides, the people on the Surface are Savages."

"Surely not all of them are savages. Was Clayton a savage?"

Malcolm pales. "Well—that's—not what I meant. In space, there's no one who wants to kill you for your boots. Or for you meat." He grimaces.

"No one to hit you with a school bus either," I say quietly.

Malcolm tips his head back to look up at the Hybrid Glass roof of the tunnel. The sun has begun to set, even though it's only about five o'clock, and the sky fades from blue to black above. The colors of the sunset light up the base of the Glass City, sunlight filtering through the leaves of the plants around us from below. "Well. It's getting late. I should probably head back before my dad decides to hunt me down."

We turn and walk back to my house in silence, Malcolm slipping his hand into mine. This time, though, I don't feel so uncomfortable.

His parents are already getting into their hovercar when we get back. Mr. Crysis gives his son a dark look, and Malcolm lets go of my hand. "See ya later." He waves, climbing into the back of his hovercar. They pull out of the driveway and glide off down the road.

Mom is looking at me, her smile lighting up her face, but I hurry inside before she can interrogate me. I head upstairs to my room, locking the door behind me. I feel warm and fuzzy inside, and I smile to myself. I guess Malcolm is okay. Or—maybe a little more than okay.

I change into my pajamas, remembering the picture in the pocket of my jeans. I pull it out, my thoughts turn to the Surface Dweller again, and my curiosity comes slinking back like an obnoxious cat. He didn't sit around and read books or watch TV all day for a smidge of excitement. He probably hunted and climbed and explored. He's a true adventurer. Malcolm's adventure is just a dream.

Peter

The rooms in the basement are dingy compared to the opulence upstairs. The one I'm in now—'my room'—is just as awful as the first one: black crystal walls close in around me, and the floor covered with dust and old blood stains. The only difference is the lack of a furnace in this room, which makes it darker and colder. My 'lesson' is over and Gap Tooth and his friend have left me alone, locking the door behind them. I want to get up, to bust open the door or find some way to pick the lock, but my muscles are like jelly.

I grimace, sitting up stiffly and letting the scratchy blanket slide off me. I'm wearing the green uniform they gave me that's too tight across my chest and back. My burning back.

I groan and lay back down, careful to keep my back from touching the cot or the wall or anything. Just moving hurts, every movement pulling at the burns all across my back and sides and causing pain to explode across my vision in little white lights. I realize that I'm nineteen—for real now. Today is my birthday, unless I've been down here in the basement for longer than I thought. It did seem like they burned my back for an eternity, but it still feels like that red hot poker is pressed against my skin. I vaguely remember one of them saying 'good morning' when they threw the shirt for my uniform at me before they left, so it must be morning.

The door bursts open and I jump as the tall blond man, Rachel's father, strides into the room. He glares down at me, crossing his arms over his chest. "Up, it's time for you to get to work."

I'm about to tell him to go to hell when the man's hand moves to the pocket of his black pea coat, and pain spikes across my back for a brief moment.

"Get. Up."

I get slowly to my feet, hiding my winces and biting back my groans. I limp over to him, every fiber of my being hating him and the stupid device in his pocket. My fists clench, and I channel my hatred through my expression, wanting him to see exactly how much I despise him. He stops me with a hand on my chest. "Ah, is that how you treat your master?"

"I could skin you alive." I hiss through my teeth, tensing. I have at least three inches on him, and I'm probably twenty pounds heavier. Taking him down would be easy.

"But you won't. You know why?" His hand moves to his pocket again, and I catch him by the throat, shoving him against the wall.

I grab for his wrist, but I'm not fast enough, and the pain in my back intensifies, becoming more than just the pain from the burns. I grit my teeth, struggling to keep him pinned, to look him in the eyes and stare him down, but the pain only gets worse. I gasp, and the man shoves me off of him. Stumbling, I drop to my hands and knees.

"The thing is, I love a good challenge. There is any number of children on the Surface, an endless amount of weak and pathetic Surface Rats, but there's no fun in taking them. They're too easy to break." He leans over me, grabbing my jaw and forcing me to look up at his cold blue eyes. "There's always a certain amount of satisfaction gained from forcing a strong man to his knees."

I glare, but I don't say anything, shifting my gaze to the ground and straining to hide my pain.

"I need you to clean the house. Dust every room, vacuum the rooms and the halls, and clean the mirrors in the bathroom and bedrooms. The only good thing about you Surface Rats is that you don't eat up as much energy as robots." He shoves his hand in his pocket. "Oh, and my daughter likes to sleep in, so careful not to wake her. If you do, there will be hell to pay." He says it lightly, but I grimace all the same, the burns on my back reminding me of what will happen if I put one toe out of line. "From now on, you will call me Brown. My wife will be Mrs. Brown, and my daughter will be *Miss* Brown, and nothing more. Do you understand?"

I nod, then frown at the ground, still on all fours even though the pain has faded again. "Vacuum?"

"Liam will show you how." Brown steps out of the room, leaving me with the familiar face of Gap Tooth. *Great.*

"Come along now, rat," Liam tells me, even though he takes my arm in a firm grip and half drags me out of the room, leading me up a flight of stairs out of that God forsaken basement. He gives me a quick tour of the downstairs, showing me how everything works—the washer, the dryer, the dishwasher—all things that I've only ever heard about from the old timers in Colfer. Then he leads me down the hall and up the stairs, shoving me into a massive, empty bedroom.

"Make the beds, vacuum the floor, dust the furniture, and move on. Do the same in every room." He opens a closet door out in the hall and pulls something out of it. He carries a strange, three foot tall machine over to where I'm standing and presses the handle of it into my hand, pointing to a switch on the handle. "This is a vacuum cleaner, and this is the switch that turns it on." He flips the switch on the vacuum cleaner. The machine hums to life, lifting about an inch off the ground as lines of light along the cylindrical body start to glow. I try not to stare in awe, shocked at the tiny hovercraft-like machine. He turns it off, and it sinks back to the floor.

Liam taps the cylinder. "No need to empty it, that's already taken care of. All filth is burned." He gives me a pointed look, and I resist the urge to break his face. "All you need to do is make sure to charge it."

He shows me to what he calls an 'outlet', pulling a cord out from the handle of the vacuum cleaner and pushing the three prongs on the end into the wall. When he finishes, he slaps my already hurting back, the burns pulling open under his heavy palm. "From now on, it lives in your room. Now get to work," he orders, and leaves the room.

I blink back tears, gritting my teeth at the pain in my back, then start pushing the vacuum cleaner across the room. I can't help but be amazed by this strange device; first there's dirt in front of it, and then there's no dirt behind it. It hovers smoothly over the carpet: I don't have to do anything but push it across the floor. I've heard of electricity, but we don't have it down on the Surface. The EMPs wiped it all out, and no one on the Surface knew how to get it back.

I finish vacuuming the room, then make the bed and dust the furniture, all the while fuming to myself. I'm not some bloody maid.

I move into the next room after vacuuming the hall, my shoes sinking into the plush rug. After cleaning out a sitting room and a bathroom, I step into the last room upstairs, dragging the vacuum cleaner behind me, my back hurting too much for me to pick it up: it doesn't hover if it isn't turned on. I turn and stop, my face twisting.

The room is just like the others; cherry wood floors and elaborate decor. A plush purple circle carpet lies under and around the bed, and a large bookcase is pressed against the wall next to a window seat. I gape at the number of books stuffed onto the shelves: I've never seen so many in one place. Most books on the Surface were burned for fuel, and the rest were never in such good condition as these. Where does Rachel find the time to read all this?

Rachel is still asleep, her blonde hair splayed out on her light blue pillow like a halo. She is thin, but she's in very good shape, considering she lives in the City of luxury.

I plug in the vacuum cleaner and turn it on, hiding a smirk when she jumps awake. "Mornin' Miss Brown," I growl, and she gives me a startled look as I push the vacuum cleaner under her bed.

"What are you doing?"

"My job." My smirk drops from my face as I say it.

Rachel pulls her covers up higher as she sits up in bed. "Why would you wake me up?"

"Because it's eight o'clock, and it's about time you wake up."

It's Rachel's turn to scowl. "Are you kidding? I always wake up at ten o'clock, and that's never too late!"

"Well I always woke up at five o'clock, and that was never too early." I turn off the vacuum cleaner and start dusting the furniture.

"Why would you do that to yourself?" She grumbles under her breath, and she rolls onto her stomach, raising herself on her hands and toes. She lowers herself to the ground again, then pushes up. She does this about fifty times, and I watch her until she stops.

I raise my eyebrows. "What was that?"

"Push-ups. Gotta stay fit right?"

"You're ridiculous."

"You're the one who gets up at five in the morning." She sticks her tongue out at me.

"That's because huntin' is better durin' the wee hours of the mornin', when the sun's rays are first touchin' the sky. Predators are tired, not as ready to come after us, and the prey is just wakin' up."

"You hunt?"

"I did, before your blasted father dragged me up here," I mutter, then catch myself, wincing.

Rachel sits forward in her bed. "What was it like?"

I stop wiping down the window and look back over my shoulder at her, frowning. "Bloody miserable, that's what it was like. Freezin' your butt off for hours and hopin' to avoid wolves or bears or Sirens. Food is hard to find down there, and it's no joy tryin' to catch it. Stupid penguins are harder to catch than ya might think. Sure, you can shoot them, but once ya shoot one, the rest all scatter, and ya have to wait for them to resurface somewhere else in order to get enough to survive."

Rachel frowns. "But there are plenty of animals down there."

"Aye, but they're bloody well hard to get."

Brown gave me very clear orders not to talk to his daughter, and I don't particularly want to either. But the dreamy look in her eyes as she eagerly waits for more details bothers me. She seems to think going to the surface would make a nice holiday. I decide it is worth a little suffering to dash her dreams on the rocks. "And there're lots of wild animals that are huntin' you while you're huntin' somethin' else. It's dangerous, really, but it's life. You get used to it after a while. But a Glass City gobshite like you would not last one minute."

She ignores my jab and asks, "What's a Siren?"

I sigh, her curiosity starting to get on my nerves. If I keep talking to her it's going to get me killed. Or worse. "It's similar to a wolf but much bigger. 'Bout the size of a horse—at least, one that's just big enough for a grown man to ride. Some of them are bigger. They're all white, incredibly quiet, incredibly fast, and incredibly dangerous. My brother and I were attacked by one two days before I got here, I was recoverin' in our cabin on the Surface."

"So it wasn't a gang that hurt you—Dad saved you from a Siren."

"Sure." *Because Sirens explode in a ball of fire.* I roll my eyes.

"Is it rare that someone survives a Siren attack?" She leans forward, eyes alive with excitement.

I nod and finish cleaning the window. "Very rare. I'm surprised we made it." I huff another sigh at the memory, thinking of Felix. "My brother saved me. And now that he needs help, I'm stuck up here washin' windows rather than down there tryin' to keep him alive." My upper lip curls, then I stop myself, cursing under my breath. "But I'm sure your father will find him." I add quickly. I don't need her running to her father begging him to save Felix. Then Brown will know I was talking to her.

"You don't really believe that." She looks skeptical.

"Of course I do."

"Then what about what you said yesterday?"

"I…. your father was right. I was sick, I was…. delusional." I grimace at how stupid it sounds, grabbing the handle of the vacuum cleaner and dragging it out into the hall. "I've got to go."

"Wait," she says, and I stop in the doorway, gritting my teeth. "What's your name?"

"Peter." I'm surprised she'd want to know.

"Okay. Thank you, Peter." She gestures to the clean room, and I frown, backing out through the door and hauling the vacuum cleaner down the stairs. It takes at least two and a half hours to finish cleaning the entire house, and when I'm finally done, my back is killing me from lifting the vacuum cleaner down the stairs and bending over to clean under dressers and tables and cabinets. Every time I lean over, the burns across my back pull open, the fabric of my uniform chaffing against my burnt skin.

I find my way back to my own dusty room and clean that out as well, hoping that I don't get in trouble for it. Then I prop the vacuum cleaner against the wall and collapse on my cot, letting all my breath out at once. I don't know why I'm so tired. Even after a long hunt, I've never been this exhausted. Who knew cleaning would take this much energy? *Of course, if my back wasn't killing me, I'd probably be fine.* I close my eyes. Is this what Addalynn does every day? The house never looked much cleaner when Felix and I would get back from hunting, but it never looked any dirtier either. I wonder if she and my cousins survived.

Behind me, the door opens. "What do you think you're doing?" Comes Brown's voice, and I groan inwardly. "You think your job is done?" Brown chuckles. "Boy, you don't rest until I say you can rest. Get up."

I get up stiffly, rising to my full height and lifting my chin and staring him down.

"I have guests coming for dinner tonight at seven, make yourself busy preparing for it. I want the dining room to be spotless, and I want dinner ready before they get here."

"I just cleaned the dinin' room!" I say, incredulous. I see Brown's hand move to his pocket, and I involuntarily flinch, flicking my eyes to the ground.

"Clean it again. I'm sure you know how to cook, no?" Brown's voice is low and threatening, and I swallow.

"I can cook, but nothing fancy. We don't have many spices down on the Surface. I'm…. not sure I can be of much help in your kitchen." I try not to spit at him, but my upper lip curls despite how hard I try to stop it.

"That's fine, you will learn. The kitchen staff will help you. Come with me." He leads me back out into the hall and back to the kitchen. The room is through a small door in the dining room. To my immediate left is a table next to a large window overlooking the street, a window booth wrapping halfway around the table. On the opposite wall, a line of machines that I can't name are mounted above the counters.

A man and a woman shrink against the island in the middle of the room as we enter. The man has a stocky build, but he and the woman are both thin. They both have sunken, haunted eyes that seem to be looking at the world from behind the bars of a cage.

Brown shoves me toward them. "You take orders from him." He points at the man. "Unless my wife or I say otherwise. I want this place spotless, as well as the dining room and the living room. If I find one thing out of place, you're in a hell of a lot of trouble. I suggest you get to work."

He leaves, and I turn back to the two people. They both look at me like kicked puppies, and I wince, leaning against the wall and tipping my head back. I hate this. "Alright, look, I hate it here as much as you do, so-"

"No—ve love it here," the man croaks. His accent is thick, and he's slightly hard to understand, but I think maybe it's German. We don't get many travelers through Colfer, except for traders from the nearby towns.

I sigh. "You don't have to lie to me. I'm not gonna tell him."

The woman sighs, slumping as if relieved, but the man looks at me warily. I push off the wall. Already I can tell Glass City life is different: all the rooms are designed for comfort and elegance, rather than weighed down with furs to try and hold in heat. Aside from the tech, most of the stuff up here—like the elaborate furniture and embroidered drapes—is completely useless, serving no purpose but to look good.

"I am Joseph," the man says. "This is Arial."

The woman doesn't meet my eyes, her gaze fixed on the floor.

"I'm Peter."

"It is pleasure to meet you." Joseph holds out his hand, and I shake it.

"Well. You heard him." I pull away. "You're in charge."

Joseph nods to Arial.

Arial shows me where the supply closet is, and we start wiping down the windows that I had already washed earlier today, as well as the counters and tables and cabinets. We take the dirty dishes out of the sink, and Joseph shows me how the cleaning device works, even though Liam already did. I don't tell him this, though, thanking him instead.

"It burns food and bacteria off. Do not touch." He taps the flexible pad on the bottom, and I nod my understanding. "Just move slowly across the dish."

When we move to the dining room, it's been two hours, and my back is so stiff and sore that pain blinds me whenever I bend over. I can see Arial's and Joseph's pain too in their stiff movements and trembling hands, and I wonder what has been done to them, how long they've been here.

By the time we start cooking, we're all three worn and tired, especially Joseph and Arial. They show me certain spices that I had no idea existed—aside from salt—and I'm confronted by a mixture of scents that make my mouth water. I'm tempted to try them all, to see if they taste as wonderful as they smell, but Joseph seems to read my mind, and he warns me against it. "Too strong on their own," he says, shaking his head and wrinkling his nose.

The stove is not much different than the stove at Addy's, except the space underneath the stove top is covered by a door, and rather than wood for a fire inside, there are wire racks. There's no chimney either, but I guess there isn't need for one. Since it runs on electricity, I can't just leave it going to burn out, and I have complete control over the temperature.

Joseph doesn't really have to tell us what to do, and we finish making dinner much sooner than it took to clean the living room, dining room, and kitchen, partially because Mrs. Brown comes in and helps for a little while. She's a kind, chatty lady who loves to smile and laugh, and I wonder at how a woman like her ended up with a man like Brown. She seems to me the exact opposite of her husband. I want to ask what she was thinking when she married him—was she drunk? Was there a shotgun involved?—but I decide against it.

Once we're finished, I turn to head back to my room. Maybe I can sneak in some sleep while Brown is busy at dinner.

"You have to stay here," Joseph says quietly when we're finally finished, not meeting my eyes.

I frown. "Why?"

"You serve them."

I clench my fists. *So not only do I have to make their food, I have to feed it to them as well?* I'm silent for a moment, looking away over his head and working my jaw. "I wish I were servin' them poison," I mutter after making sure only he and Arial can hear.

Joseph gives me the slightest of smiles. "So do I."

"No." Arial shakes her head. "Rachel isn't as bad, and Mrs. Brown is kind to us."

"Ja, sure I guess. It's just Brown, und the Crysis's. Especially their arrogant son. That boy believes that he should get vhatever he vants exactly vhen he vants it. He's just as vicious as Brown."

Most of it I barely understand because of his thick accent, but I get the point. I swallow hard; the boy he's talking about is Malcolm, the young man who tried to stop me from leaving the house yesterday. I could kick his butt any day, but if the price I have to pay for beating his butt is having my back burned again, then it's not worth it.

I sigh, looking away. "One day, this blasted city will fall, and we'll be the ones in power."

Joseph touches my shoulder lightly. "I hope ve live to see that day."

I nod my agreement, thinking of Felix, of how we'd fantasize about destroying the Glass City. *Felix.* I have to get out of this bloody hell hole. I need to get back to him.

Joseph and Arial carry the food into the dining room, and I hear the doorbell ring in the foyer, bringing me back to the present. I heave another sigh, glancing at the meal that we prepared as it's spread over the dining room table. My stomach reminds me that I still haven't eaten in three days, and I swallow, my mouth watering. I've never seen so much food in my life, much less prepared it. If we had food like that on the

Surface, then my brother and I would never have to starve because of Addy's stupid kids. We'd never be hungry.

Thinking of Felix brings another wave of worry, but it's been over a day since I saw him crumpled in the basement through the hole in the cabin floor. Addy probably wouldn't waste her precious resources on him even if he survived the blast, and my hope of ever seeing my brother alive again begins to waver. *I have to get back.*

"Peter?" Rachel's voice startles me out of my thoughts, and I whirl, reaching for my gun. But my gun isn't hanging from its strap on my shoulder like it should be.

I scowl. "What?"

"Everybody's ready. You…. you're supposed to serve us." Her mouth twists. "Dad want's to show off his new 'prized specimen'."

I take a deep breath and let it out slowly to keep the sarcasm at the tip of my tongue rather than in her face. "Aye, Miss Brown."

Six people—including Rachel and Malcolm—sit around the long table, two of whom I assume to be Malcolm's parents, and Mrs. Brown at one end of the table. As they eat, I stand behind Brown at the head of the table, trying not to stare at their food. I hope no one hears how loud my stomach is complaining. I can only focus on hunger, which makes it difficult to make out what the dinner party is discussing. Their trivial dinner conversations don't hold any clues to escape anyway, so there is no sense listening.

All the while, Malcolm's eyes watch me, and even though I don't look at him, I can feel his gaze boring into me. I pour them their wine and serve them the food that they cannot reach, but I don't say anything, don't meet anyone's eyes. They're like a pack of wolves; eye contact can get you killed.

Then Rachel says something that makes my heart freeze. "Peter says that food is hard to catch."

Brown looks over at his daughter, eyebrows raised. "Who?"

I look at Rachel as well, trying to catch her eye, but she doesn't see me. "Peter." She points without looking.

I want to strangle her.

"Did he now?" Brown, however, casts a dark look over in my direction, and Rachel somehow doesn't see that either.

Rachel nods. "He says there's plenty to catch, but it's hard to get it, because there are other wild animals down there that hunted him as he hunted them. Maybe we could help them? I mean, some of our technology is perfect for hunting." She takes a bite of potatoes, talking around them as she chews. "That way we wouldn't have to bring so many of them up here. They could still be independent, and we'd just be giving them a hand up, not a hand out."

I'm not sure if I'm breathing, and I pour the wine into Mrs. Brown's glass without looking, accidentally spilling some on the white table cloth. I hurry to soak it up with the cloth that I have draped over my forearm, aware of Brown's eyes fixed on me.

Mrs. Brown moves her glass. "Oh dear, let me get something to help," she says, reaching around her plate and snatching up her cloth napkin. I can feel that my eyes are wide, and I try to relax, try to hide that I'm on the verge of running from the dining room to avoid Brown. Just the thought of the hot poker makes me want to run for the edge of this city and jump.

"Mr. Brown, may I have a word with your help?" Malcolm speaks up, after being almost silent all evening.

I slowly straighten, taking Mrs. Brown's wine-soaked napkin away from her.

Brown stops chewing, looking up at him and studying his face for a long moment. "Of course," he says, his eyes warning.

Mrs. Brown avoids looking at us as we exit the room. Rachel's eyes stare pointedly at Malcolm's back, a small frown creasing her brow.

Malcolm takes my arm, pulling me through the kitchen to the laundry room. "Start the dryer," Malcolm orders.

I can't help but smirk. I left the dining room willingly because Brown was there with his bloody pain device. But Malcolm has no such protection, and he is shorter than I am. I look him up and down, calculating how much I can hurt him without leaving an obvious injury that Brown could see. I wonder how much I'd get punished just on this boy's word alone, and decide it's worth it. "Why, so no one can hear me kick your butt?"

Malcolm grits his teeth. "You're the one who's going to be sore after this," he snarls, stepping closer.

"Aye, but I won't be the only one."

"Anything you do to me will be punished-"

My fist in his gut cuts him off, and he coughs. "I don't think ya want your lovely little bird in there to think you're weak, am I right?"

Malcolm gets in my face, his upper lip curled. "You stay away from Rachel."

I raise an eyebrow. "I have no interest in her."

Malcolm doesn't back away, narrowing his eyes. "Don't you lie to me, *slave*, you are nothing here, and I can do with you as I please."

I wrinkle my nose. "As you please? Don't think your wee little girlfriend's goin' to be very happy with *that*." The way I say it makes his face flare red, and he aims a punch to my ribs. I block the blow, catching his fist and holding it there. "After all, even I didn't make ya out to be a *poof*."

Malcolm bares his teeth and shoves me backwards into the wall, and my back flares with pain. Malcolm follows me, jabbing his finger in my face. "Maybe I'll stand in next time Brown beats your ass." He shoves me again, and I swat his hands away.

The burns across my back reopen at the sudden movement, and I let my breath hiss out through my teeth. Malcolm sees my pain and seizes his chance. He grabs my shoulders and slams his knee into my gut; I double, gasping, and he steps to the side, throwing me to the ground. I realize too late that I'm not recovered enough from the torture to fend him off the way I thought I could.

"I've killed one of you before," he says with a vicious kick. "But I don't want to put Mr. Brown through all the trouble of finding someone to take *your* place. "

He doesn't stop, repeatedly kicking me until I can hardly breathe. I feel my ribs crack and try to deflect his blows, but now that he has me on the ground, I am at his mercy.

Rachel

Malcolm comes back fifteen minutes later, but Peter doesn't follow him until a while after Malcolm sits down. He limps into the room with a clean cloth and hands a napkin to my mother, who accepts it with a strained smile. The look in her eyes tells me something is wrong, but I'm not sure what has happened. Peter hadn't been limping before, had he? Would Malcolm do something to one of the servants? Malcolm looks a little flushed and smug, and I get a cold feeling in the pit of my stomach.

Dinner finishes about a half hour later, during which Malcolm talks and laughs easily, his sullen mood seeming to have disappeared. Before they leave, I pull Malcolm aside, away from the ears of our parents, who are finishing their conversation in the foyer. "What was that?"

"What was what?" Malcolm smiles brilliantly, and I poke his chest.

"You know what I'm talking about. What did you do to Peter?"

"Do to him? I didn't do anything, I just wanted to apologize about what happened yesterday."

"*You* apologized?"

Malcolm shrugs.

I study him, not quite sure I believe him. "How noble. Next time don't apologize with your fists, okay?" Not that I care that much about Peter—I don't even know him—I just don't want Malcolm to be the kind of guy who beats up on people.

Malcolm's face twists at my words, and he scoffs incredulously.

Maybe I shouldn't have been so quick to jump to conclusions.... "Hey, see ya later?"

"Absolutely." He glances over his shoulder at our parents before pulling me into a quick hug. No one's really looking, but I'm sure that Mom somehow sees us. At least it wasn't a kiss this time, I'd never hear the end of that.

Once the Crysis family is gone, I get myself a glass chocolate milk from the kitchen. Peter is gone, so I can't hear his side of what happened between him and Malcolm. I head up to my room with my milk, shutting my door behind me.

I sip at my chocolate milk, trying to focus on the World War One textbook I'm reading, but really, I'm thinking of Peter. I mean, I don't want to think badly of Malcolm, but…. I scowl at my chocolate milk. "He's just some stupid Surface Dweller. I hardly know him, and I have known Malcolm all my life. Why should I doubt him," I say to the chocolate milk, but of course it doesn't respond.

I sigh, turning my attention back to the book and trying to focus, but even after a few hours, my mind keeps returning to the events of the evening, and the past few days.

I find myself picking up my chocolate milk and tipping it over the floor, letting it spill all over the hardwood. I stare at the puddle for a moment, then get up and push the small button by the door. The button is lit, which means he's in his room. He'll get my buzz and he'll have to come up here to clean up the mess. Then I can ask him what happened. I feel like I'm betraying Malcolm, but I guess I'll just have to live with the guilt—because I can't live with the questions gnawing at my thoughts all the time.

Sure enough, a few minutes later, Peter opens the door to my room and leans against the doorframe. He sees the mess, then looks at me. "Ya did that on purpose."

I shrug. "Maybe I did, maybe I didn't."

"It's past midnight."

Probably—it has been dark for hours. "Never been too late for me."

Peter narrows his eyes, but he doesn't argue, leaving the room and returning with a towel. He gets rigidly to his knees and starts wiping up the chocolate milk with it.

"So…. what happened with Malcolm?" I ask. Peter pauses. Only slightly, but I still see it.

"I just apologized."

"Did he apologize?"

Peter nods, not looking up. "Aye, he apologized first."

I'm pretty sure he's lying to me. "Wanna do something tomorrow?" I don't know why I ask, it just comes out of my mouth. Now I feel like I am betraying Clayton, but I miss having someone to do things with.

"What are you talkin' about?" Peter looks up at me at last, wearing a wary expression.

I shrug. "I don't know, like going for a walk or something. You still haven't seen the city."

Peter eyes me guardedly. "Why?"

"I used to go on walks with Clayton all the time." I try not to, but my voice breaks anyways. I swallow and go on. "He was your predecessor, you could say. You kind of replaced him, even though no one really could." I wince at how I worded that. "If I'm going to be stuck with you from now on we might as well be friends."

"I…. don't think I can."

"Don't be silly, of course you can. You're just as much my servant as you are my father's. I can take you places if I want."

Peter looks back down at the mess and continues to soak up the chocolate milk. "I don't know."

"Good, I'll send for you when you're done cleaning the house." I smile.

Peter jerks his head up, his expression incredulous, but he doesn't say anything. Instead he glares and gathers up the sopping wet towel, getting slowly to his feet. I frown, remembering how Clayton used to have the same strained expression whenever he had to stand up. I had never really given it much thought until it was too late, and I'm certainly not going to let it fly now. "Are you okay?"

Peter stops in the doorway. "I'm fine," he says without turning back, and then he's gone. I stare at the space he had occupied, then turn my attention out the window. My eyes fall on my empty glass of milk, and I sigh, wishing I had more. I wait a few minutes, then buzz for Peter again, not caring that it's almost one in the morning.

The door opens again to a very pissed off looking Peter. "What do ya want, Miss Brown?" I don't know why it's so cute when he calls me that.

I raise my eyebrows. "You can call me Rachel."

Peter just blinks slowly, and I hold up my glass. "Could you get me some more chocolate milk?"

Peter stalks across the room and takes the glass roughly, turning and leaving without a word. I watch him go, chewing on my lower lip. He's being a total jerk, for no reason at all—well, actually, I am waking him up at one in the morning. But still! It has to be easier up here than down on the surface. Down there polar bears probably woke him up at one in the morning.

Peter comes back with the glass full of chocolate milk, and he hands it to me. I take it carefully, setting it down beside me, but before he can leave, I say, "Sit."

Peter stops and slowly turns back, glowering at me. "I am not some bloody dog that you can order around."

"I didn't mean it like that." I promise, gesturing to the space beside me. Peter doesn't move. I give a sigh of exasperation. "I'm not going to bite you."

Peter scoffs. "As if that's the first thing that pops into my head when someone offers me a seat. 'Oh no, I can't sit next to her, she might bite!'"

"Then you don't have any reason not to sit down," I tell him, throwing his sarcasm back in his face. His accent is really thick—much thicker than Clayton's.

Peter hesitates a moment longer, then limps across the room and sits down beside me, his movements stiff. I turn so that I face him, but he doesn't look at me. "What was your brother like?" I ask.

Peter raises an eyebrow, keeping his green eyes fixed on his rough hands. "Why?"

I shrug. "Just curious."

Peter is silent for a moment, considering. "Strong. Brave. An idiot, sometimes, but he had his reasons. He's got an unusually high sense of morality—which I guess isn't a bad thing, considerin' our aunt is a *floozie*, but….well. It grates on my nerves now and then."

I smile, glad that I'm getting something out of him. "And your parents?"

Peter's silence stretches longer this time, until he finally says. "They're dead."

The smile drops from my face. "I—I'm sorry." I hesitate, then, "How?"

"They were eaten by a polar bears. Why is it any business of yours?"

At first I am horrified, but then I realize he made the polar bear thing up—or at least I hope he did. "I'm sorry, I was just trying to get to know you." I trail off, biting my lower lip and twisting the end of my ponytail around my finger.

Then Peter startles me by speaking without being spoken to. "Isn't it a bit stupid, bein' stuck up here in a city of glass? I mean, if it shatters, you're all dead."

I shake my head. "Everyone has parachutes." I hesitate, then lift up the hem of my shirt, just enough so that he can see part of the harness.

Peter frowns. "Seems bloody uncomfortable to me."

"You'll get used to it, and it's made of special material that is almost like a second skin, but really strong. It's a requirement, for safety reasons."

"I need sleep," he tells me. And I can see it, the dark circles under his eyes, the way he can hardly keep his eyes open.

I nod. "Okay you can go. But you're still coming on that walk with me tomorrow, whether you want to or not."

Peter

I pull my shirt over my head just as Brown leans against the door to my room in the basement. I grab the overcoat and button the front of it, but not before he sees the dark bruises all up my right side. "Ah, I see you had a little chat with Malcolm." He grins.

I don't respond, too exhausted from another sleepless night to retort. If Rachel hadn't opened her big mouth I wouldn't have had to pay for talking to her last night. I'm about to push past him when he shoves a bowl of lumpy gray goo against my chest. I catch it, startled.

"Eat."

I want to flip the bowl in his face, but my stomach tells me that's not a good idea. He watches me smugly as I take a tentative bite. I gag, barely managing to swallow without hurling. "You expect me to eat this?"

Brown shrugs. "Well we could shove it down your throat, but I think it would be easier for everyone if you just ate it. And make it quick. The house needs cleaning." He leaves the room before I can retort.

I wrinkle my nose, choking down the rest of the gruel and trying to imagine that I'm eating fish or penguin. It globs on to the roof of my mouth and my teeth, so that the bland taste lingers in my mouth even after I'm finished. I limp out of my room and drag myself up the stairs to the basement. Malcolm had kicked me a lot harder than I'd thought.

I clean the several rooms upstairs without complaint. I'm too bloody tired to complain. Rachel's still asleep when I get to her room, but I don't try to wake her up. If she wakes up she might try to talk to me, and as much as I hate to admit it to myself, I really don't want to get in trouble again. I don't turn the vacuum cleaner on right away, to give her more time to sleep. Instead I wipe down the cabinets and windows first, scrubbing fingerprints off the glass door frame in silence.

She seems naive, unlike her sadistic father. But she also seems childish. She sounded sincere when she was trying to convince Brown to go back for Felix, so maybe she's not a monster. She's only minimally brainwashed into thinking I'm her slave. I don't exactly feel like a pet when she orders me around, more like some doll being forced to have tea parties with her. When she talks to me I don't get the impression that she is intentionally trying to get me in trouble—more like she just wants a friend. She just doesn't seem to know how to be a friend.

I watch her, trying to discern how asleep she is. Her friendship might be useful, though. I don't have a parachute like she does, despite what she thinks. If I can find a way to get outside the dome, I am going to need a parachute. I could try to get close to her, to suffer through her ignorance until I can convince her to give me a parachute, but if I can find one in her room....

I shut the door, stepping into her closet and pushing through hanging clothes in search of a parachute, but there's nothing here. I dig through her drawers, careful to keep the clothes folded, but there's no parachute here either. I curse, checking under the sink in her bathroom. She's got to have an extra one, in case the one she's wearing breaks or something. Surely she washes the harness, which means there *has* to be another one somewhere for her to wear while the other one is being washed.

I jerk open the drawers of the vanity, clawing through notebooks and pencils, but still no parachute. I do, however, find an HD—if I get back to the Surface—when I get back to the Surface—Felix is going to need healing devices. They're hard to come by on the Surface, so I stuff this one in my pocket, glancing over my shoulder.

Rachel is still sound asleep, and I sigh. Looks like I have to suck up and be her doll. I rub the back of my neck, telling myself it'll all be worth it when I get my parachute, but the thought of letting her pull me around and tell me what to do still makes me cringe.

I finally turn the vacuum cleaner on. Rachel jumps awake, but I don't look at her, and I finish vacuuming the room without saying a word to her. I don't want to be too obvious by suddenly trying to be being friend.

I leave the room and clean the downstairs in silence. I finish in the kitchen, glancing across the foyer to the hall that leads to the basement, where my room is. I wish I could just go back to my room, get some more rest.

I look briefly over my shoulder in time to see Mrs. Brown glide through the door with a book in her hands, her nose buried between the pages. She's a small woman with short brown hair that's pulled back in a fluffy ponytail. Her brown eyes skim over the pages of the book faster than I could ever read. She's about to run into the island in the middle of the kitchen, but I stop her. Her book bumps against my chest and she recoils, sucking in a breath. She sees me and gives me a grimacing smile. "Sorry. I tend to lose my bearings when I'm reading a good book."

She moves past me and stands on her tiptoes, but the blue bag she reaches for is just out of reach of her thin fingers. She drops back onto her heels and sighs. "Could you grab that for me please?" She's far more polite than I thought she would be.

I don't argue as I reach up and effortlessly snatch the bag off the shelf. Raising my arm pulls at the burns across my back, but I hand it to her without complaint.

Mrs. Brown accepts it with a smile. "Marcus always puts it just out of my reach. I swear he thinks he gets it all to himself." She sees my inquiring look and smiles wider. "My husband loves pancakes more than any breakfast in the world. I think he has a serious addiction."

I give her a half smile, slightly lifted by her bouncy personality. Then the grin slides off her face and she leans a little closer. Her fingers gently touch my collarbone where my shirt doesn't hide the jagged red line of a burn. I flinch away, gripping the edge of the counter so hard that my knuckles creak. Before I can stop myself, I say quietly, "What is his problem?"

Mrs. Brown sighs, looking sad and ashamed. "He hates the Surface and all who inhabit it, his father gave him a reason to with all his ridiculous theories of evolution. And after the meteors hit, the people on the Surface did some awful things to survive—proving the point, or so he thinks."

"So because some Surface Dwellers did horrible things in the past, that makes it okay for him to do horrible things?" I say through gritted teeth.

"He seems to think so. To him, what the Surface Dwellers did showed that you are the lower life forms of a natural evolutionary cycle; we're the advanced versions of the human beings, and you're what's left over from the last 'human update'."

"You obviously disagree."

Mrs. Brown looks sad. "I believe all people are created equal in the eyes of God. Evolution is just a dead theory used to make people feel like they never have to answer what they do in this life."

I nod. "You sound like my brother."

She smirks. "Well, it's good to hear you have some kind of good influence."

"Aye." If Felix is still alive. I push the thought away. "If you're so opposed to the way Brown runs things, why don't you do somethin' about it? And why do you stay with him?"

Rachel's mother pours a white powder into a bowl and mixes water into it. "He didn't used to be this way." She wrinkles her nose as if she's smelled something bad, stirring the powder and water into a thick paste.

I lean over to sniff at the paste; it doesn't look like much, but it doesn't smell bad. I assume that her disgust is with her husband, not her cooking.

Mrs. Brown sighs again and goes on, pouring the paste into another pan on the other burner.. "Not everyone in the city is as violent and cruel as he is, but a good majority of them are. It's become part of their life. It's no longer wrong to them and I can't do anything about it. If I tried to speak out against it, the people would hate me for pointing out their flaws. But there's Rachel... I think she could make a difference, especially if she is mayor. I try to teach her history lessons that open her eyes and her mind. I make it clear that all life matters, all people are created equal. People used to believe that."

Rachel comes into the kitchen, and Mrs. Brown falls silent.

She finished cooking and stacks up a plate of flat, round, floppy objects that I assume are pancakes, then hands me one with a wink. "Don't tell Marcus."

"Thank you." I stuff it into my mouth and swallow it before I really can taste it. Whatever the flavor, my stomach is satisfied.

Mrs. Brown puts half her stack of pancakes on a plate for Rachel and they eat, making small talk as I stand by waiting to deal with their dishes—cringing as Rachel spills a sticky substance on the clean table.

"What about that paper?" Mrs. Brown asks Rachel.

"Oh yeah." Rachel gets up and races off. She's back in a few seconds, papers rustling in her hand. "I finished last night."

"Did you come up with a creative title?"

"Of course. Read it."

Mrs. Brown takes the paper from her daughter, squinting at the first page. "'Birds and Turds'?"

I raise an eyebrow, but I don't say anything.

Rachel bursts out laughing. "You said be creative."

"But where did you get birds and turds?"

"The acronyms. You know. B-R-R-D-s and T-R-R-D-s. BRRDs and TRRDs. Admit it, it's more fun than saying Bone or Tissue Repair and Reconstruction Device."

Mrs. Brown shakes her head. "You are a strange child."

Rachel scoffs. "You raised me."

"Touché." Mrs. Brown laughs, skimming over Rachel's paper. "Did you go to the library like I told you?"

"Maybe."

Mrs. Brown raises an eyebrow. "Really? And is the library's name Malcolm?"

"Maybe."

"That's what I thought."

"What? He's like a walking encyclopedia, he knows everything. Who needs the library when you have Malcolm Crysis?" Rachel giggles.

I marvel at their relationship. They talk like siblings, and it makes me wonder if that's what having a mother is like.

"Points for creativity, and points for being my adorable daughter. You get a…. B plus." Mrs. Brown sets the papers down, apparently done reading.

"What? B plus? That's not fair."

"Well, you were missing some of the history, as well as the fact that BRRDs and TRRDs are still manufactured in the Lab today." Mrs. Brown deliberately says each letter of the acronyms. "I guess the walking encyclopedia forgot to mention that?"

Rachel crosses her arms. "Pfft. Whatever."

"Hey, B plus is good."

"What about extra credit?"

"You're homeschooled, you don't get extra credit."

"Please?" Rachel makes a puppy dog face, reminding me of my obnoxious cousins.

"Uhh, okay." Mrs. Brown thinks for a moment, drumming her fingers on the wood table. She glances at me, then asks, "Where are the docking bays located?"

"Seriously?" Rachel looks confused.

"Do you want a harder question?" Mrs. Brown raises an eyebrow.

"Psht nah. Easy A." Rachel sticks her tongue out. "All around the outside edges of the City's basement level."

"Which is made mostly of?"

"Aluminum."

"Alright. Fine, you get an A." Mrs. Brown smiles. She finishes eating, kissing the top Rachel's head and casting me a meaningful look before leaving us alone. I stare wearily after her, leaning against the counter and absently watching Rachel eat with half lidded eyes. She shifts uncomfortably, but I don't really see it until she speaks. "You seem tired."

I suck in a breath as I snap back to reality. "Hmm?"

"Did you even sleep?"

No. "Aye." I can't let her know what Liam and Calvin did to me last night.

"You don't look like it."

"Well I did." I scowl, blinking slowly and almost forgetting to open my eyes again. I take another shallow breath, reminding myself that I need to stay awake, to keep breathing.

"Liar." Rachel gets up, and behind me, I can hear the sounds of her cooking something on the stove, but I'm too tired to turn around. I really didn't get any sleep at all last night—, too busy trying to breathe without killing myself, my broken ribs and my burns keeping me from getting comfortable in any way. That and Liam and his buddy reminded me of the price for talking to Rachel, burning most of the night away along with the flesh on my back.

A rich, mouthwatering aroma drifts from behind me, and I swallow. It's slightly nauseating, but at the same time it makes me wonder what on earth smells so good and how. The crackle and sizzle of cooking meat has never sounded so appealing, and it makes me long for home.

Rachel brushes past me, and I jump, realizing that my eyes were closed again. "Eat something. One pancake is hardly a breakfast."

"No—I'm fine. Really." I wince and try not to cry out when she moves behind me and presses her hands against my burning back, pushing me toward the table. She makes me sit down across from her, and scoots the plate in front of me, pressing a fork into my hand. The salty aroma is stronger now. Maybe I should just eat it.

"I wanted to say sorry. For the stupid chocolate milk stunt last night."

It was a stupid stunt, but at least it cut my 'lesson' short. I eat the bacon and eggs without saying anything, trying not to eat so fast this time. I don't think I've ever known good food until this moment. The bacon is crunchy and salty, but the eggs are smaller than the penguin eggs we usually get on the surface.

When I finish, she takes the plates before I can, putting them in the sink and gesturing for me to follow her outside. My body braces for the cold blast of winter, but the air outside the house isn't any colder than it is inside—in fact, it's warmer.

"I want to show you something. I don't really show very many people, though I really don't know very many people." Rachel grimaces.

I almost feel sorry for her if she doesn't have any friends aside from that Malcolm boy. He seems about my age, but his temper is like that of a jealous twelve-year-old.

"It's like my own personal garden," Rachel continues, "and I only let my bestest friends go there. Actually, Malcolm is pretty much it, him and Clayton—I don't really have very many people to share things with. I didn't want to think of you as replacing Clayton—I still don't! But it is nice to have someone else, now that he is gone, I guess. And you come from the Surface, I mean recently. As in you remember what it is like and must have a lot of stories, I can't wait to hear them."

I let her talk, taking in everything as we walk down the glass street toward the edge of the dome. I try to form a mental map in my mind, but the houses all look similar to one another: tall, straight, and unnecessarily elaborate—so unlike the rickety old shacks of Colfer. The houses are made of thick, opaque crystal of all different colors, and they line each side of the street. In front and behind the houses are large squares of grass and gardens. Off in the distance I can see the peaks of massive buildings, bigger than any I have ever seen, rising above the residential quarters.

There's so many turns, it's worse than being lost on a glacier, and way more claustrophobic. I only know which way is up, and even that looks strange. From the minute Rachel pulled me out the door, I could not keep my eyes off the sky. It's still the hazy blue-grey color I saw when I tried to escape the first day, and there's not a single cloud in the entire expanse. I can even see the sun, bright and white and glaring through the glass dome, whereas on the Surface it's always a fuzzy orb behind the clouds.

But I am most mesmerized by the blue. Could that really be the color of the sky? Or is it a trick of the dome's glass? People on the Surface who remember the time before the asteroids say the sky was blue, but I never imagined this. I always pictured something like the way snow in a crevasse has a bluish glow.

We reach the edge of the city, leaving the rows of glass houses behind. A small sliding door is built into the side of the dome. Rachel passes through, but what I see on the other side stops me in my tracks.

"Come on, it's this way," Rachel says from the doorway. Beyond the glass is not the outside of the dome. It seems like we are passing from the dome into a tunnel. Inside the tunnel is unlike anything I've ever seen before; a wall of green leaves and vines, full of colorful flowers of all kinds. The heat is startling, even when compared to the inside of the dome behind us.

I open my mouth to say something, but no words come out. I'm just too amazed, and I don't want to be.

Rachel laughs, grabbing my wrist and pulling me through the gardens. "Come on, you dork."

The gardens stretch off in both directions along the glass wall we just passed through; they must go around the entire diameter of the Glass City. Paths crisscross through the trees. Grass and plants cover the ground, and there's not a single snow drift in sight. I've never seen anything like it.

On the Surface, the trees are scarce, and they're nothing like these. These trees are tall and full, with lush green leaves of all different shapes and sizes. Rachel babbles on about all the different kinds of plants, but I'm only half paying attention.

Rachel points at the roof where lights are built into the glass. "Those bulbs give off a sort of artificial sunlight so the plants can grow better, because even up here we don't really get enough. But this isn't what I wanted to show you. Follow me." As if I wasn't already following her.

Rachel leads me through the gardens and to another door, this in the outside wall of the garden, and I wonder if there is yet another dome outside this one. How many domes make up the Glass City?

"This is *my* garden," she tells me, checking her parachute. I further take in my surroundings, overwhelmed by all the colors. Brown is going to kill me for this. I'm not even supposed to talk to Rachel, let alone go anywhere with her.

Rachel takes a folded square of yellow rubber from its hook next to the door, clipping it onto her belt. She takes an oxygen mask off the little rack next to the rubber squares, placing it over her nose and mouth—and holds one out for me.

"I—don't really need one," I say, not quite believing that we need that much preparation to exit the dome. It must be some trick to make slaves think they can't get out.

Rachel shrugs. "Suit yourself. It's pretty thin out there." Then she presses her palm against a scanner in the wall, and the door opens. Cold wind blasts my face, and she pulls me out with her, the door sliding shut behind us.

The instant the door closes the frigid air is perfectly still, and I gasp, struggling to breathe. I hide it when Rachel gives me a look, trying not to show how the labor of breathing is hurting my cracked ribs. I'm startled by how thin the air is, even though Rachel had said as much, and it makes me afraid to think of the disadvantage it puts me at.

We really are outside the dome now. But there's a skydeck in front of us, crossing the void between the dome of the city and a smaller bubble—a miniature dome stuck to the side of the glass city by only the crystal walkway. I follow Rachel across the long skydeck, my heart beating faster when I look through the crystal and see only clouds below.

I glance over my shoulder at the entrance to the tiny dome: across the skydeck, the dome of the Glass city curves off to the left and right, but I can't see around it. Greenhouse Park is, in fact, a tunnel, wrapping around the base of the city. From here I can see a lower level, beneath the Glass City. It looks like mostly metal, but occasionally a puff of steam blasts out from a vent, giving me the impression of a massive cylindrical machine attached to the bottom of the Glass City.

We step through another sliding door and into another garden full of much wilder plants. I gasp for air as I take in the riot of flowers and green all around us.

If I could catch my breath I would be gaping. I've only seen pictures of one or two flowers. There are countless splashes of greens and purples and pinks and blues and reds—more color than I have ever seen in one place. Taller plants curve against the dome of the glass roof so that the leaves cover the glass, and only patches of the hazy blue-grey sky shines through. Just as in Greenhouse Park, lights are embedded in the glass dome above, as well as in the curved walls around us.

An overwhelming array of smells flood my senses, the sweet aroma of flowers as well as the bitter scent of herbs, clashing together in a never-ending battle for dominance, so that the smell is sweet and pleasant in one place and sour in another. It's warmer in here than anywhere I've been, and humid too. A few trees reach up to the glass roof, just like the ones in the picture of my parents. *The picture*.... I feel my pocket, but of course, the picture Felix had given me isn't there. My heart sinks.

"These are palm trees," Rachel tells me, glancing over her shoulder to see my expression. She notices my hand on my pocket, and I can see her hesitate. She reaches into her own pocket, pulling out a singed piece of paper, unfolding it and holding it out for me. "I found this. It was in the medical room."

I snatch it from her fingers, running my eyes over my parent's faces, the sandy beach in the background, the palm trees. It's all intact, only the edges are blackened. I release a shallow breath, relieved that I haven't lost it forever, folding the picture and putting it into my shirt pocket. I don't want to say it, but I look at Rachel. "Thank you."

"Don't worry about it," she says, but she looks a little smug. She turns her back to me, listing off the names flowers as she walks by them.

My only escape route is the skydeck. But I need a parachute; if I jumped off at this height, hitting the water would be like hitting cement. But I'm so bloody *close*. Maybe I can steal a parachute? They can't be that well-hidden can they? Or maybe I can earn one? Rachel didn't seem to have any in her room, so maybe she doesn't have the authority to give them out. Maybe only Brown has that authority. The thought of sucking up to Brown and being a good servant makes me sick, but if I convince him that I'm broken and obedient, maybe he'll give me a parachute.

"And these here, they're gardenias, and these are tiger lilies, and chamomile, and thyme." She continues, twisting the end of her ponytail around her finger. I tune out her words, only half listening.

She still seems childish, naive, but she hasn't hurt me yet—hasn't even threatened to. Mrs. Brown had even said that Rachel could make a difference in the way things are up here. Maybe she could help me in some way, give me a parachute or something. I consider telling her, showing her my burned back, but what if I'm wrong? It could be that she's all sweet and friendly because I'm doing what I'm told, and the second I don't she'll go nuts. Maybe she even has one of those pain inflicting devices, like her father. I shudder. *No, it's not worth the risk.* She seems to think that servants have parachutes, so maybe they do, and I just need to earn mine. I'll do what I'm told, be the good slave. And I'll play along and be Rachel's pet, that way when I get my parachute, I can convince her to take me back out here.

Then all I have to do is jump.

Rachel

"So…. what's it really like? On the Surface?" I can tell Peter has lost interest in my flowers, and if I'm being honest, I'm getting a little tired of naming them. What I really want to know is what his life was like on the Surface.

"Exactly how ya think it is," Peter says, limping over to one of the Ginger flowers. He rubs the red petals gently with his thumb and forefinger. "Cold. Nasty weather. But plenty of food. Plenty of penguin and moose and caribou and such." He wrinkles his nose. "Sometimes it's a bit hard to catch, but your Scouts…help us, when we need it."

"Scouts?"

He searches for words. "Um, you know, your people. They come down to the Surface in their hovercrafts, and bring us up here."

"Oh, you mean the Suppliers. They do a lot more than bring up you guys. They also get food that we can't grow up here, and they bring up water twice a day from the ocean to be desalinated. I mean, we have two other domes that are dedicated to farming, with cows and pigs and chickens and stuff. They need a *lot* of water, more than we have to recycle, and the animals need to be fed too. Suppliers have *lots* of important jobs, they go all over the Surface. We'd probably be screwed without them." I pause, giving him a sheepish look. "I've always wanted to be a Supplier. I can't, because I'm the mayor's daughter. But, in a year or two, when I get my pilot's license, I'll become a Supplier whether my father wants me to or not. Then I can go explore the Surface whenever I want."

Peter gives me a look, and I get the impression that Supplier's aren't so important to the Surface Dwellers as they are to us. I search for another topic. "Are there many plants on the Surface?"

"No."

"Not even near the hotspots, where the magma is exposed?"

"Um. No. It's not warm enough to really grow anythin'. Only really hearty plants."

"Well, maybe when I'm a Supplier I'll bring seeds and stuff down to the Surface," I offer.

"Right." Peter doesn't look as excited as I feel, and I'm a little disappointed.

I'll be eighteen in one year—old enough to get my pilot's license. That's so close, and now I actually have a reason to go to the Surface that isn't selfish—but he doesn't care. So he can stay here then, while I go help the other Surface Dwellers.

"Have you gone to a hotspot before?" I ask, changing the subject again.

"Well, travel is dangerous. There are a lot of predators outside of the towns. The further from town you get, the more likely you are to get attacked by wolves or Sirens or somethin'. The only place I've been to other than Colfer is Hearthtown, and even that's a dangerous journey."

"Hearthtown?" I stop near the fountain in the center of my garden, looking down through the glass and through a tiny hole in the clouds at the giant, glowing crevasse splitting Ireland nearly in half. I wonder if Hearthtown is near that hotspot.

"It's a tradin' town. It's where we go when Jimmy—our trader— doesn't have what we need. There's lots of things in Hearthtown, includin' a few types of vegetables and fungi. Mushrooms, potatoes, sometimes carrots. It's risky, tryin' to grow things outside with so little sunlight, but they manage, because they're right on the *edge* of a hotspot, where the heat rises from beneath the earth. It's too bloody cold everywhere else, and even in the hotspots, it's only just warm enough to grow hearty things."

"You don't use artificial sunlight?" I point to the bulbs in the glass when Peter gives me a curious look.

"Um, well…. We don't have electricity on the Surface. We don't even know how to make it."

"Oh." I frown. Shouldn't the Suppliers be helping with that?

"Well, I could help with electricity too, when I'm a Supplier. And I can bring Malcolm—he knows how to build a generator. He can help the Surface Dwellers build one."

"If he doesn't freeze first."

The way Peter says it makes me take a step back. It's almost as if he wants Malcolm to freeze to death. I turn away from him, twisting my ponytail around my finger. The way he describes the Surface makes me appreciate the comfort of the Glass City. It also makes me wonder why on earth he would want to go back. What is up here that he doesn't like?

"Look, I probably should be gettin' back…." Peter looks uncertain. "I mean, I do have a job to do…. It's," he check his watch, "almost noon. I should probably be makin' lunch or….cleanin' those breakfast dishes."

"The other two can take care of that. You aren't the only servant we have."

"Rachel, we've been out here for hours. Maybe we should just go back. Your father-"

"What? My father what?" Rachel crosses her arms. "Are you afraid of him? Tell me!"

"No, of course not. Why would I be?"

"You seem pretty anxious to get back."

"Hmm" Peter says, wandering away from me slightly, toward the door.

"Do you ever smile?" I ask, put off by his indifference with our whole conversation. Has he been wanting to head back this entire time? Does he not want to be here?

He looks back over his shoulder at me, then looks away again when I raise my eyebrows expectantly.

"Of course. When I have reason to."

"Are you saying you have no reason to smile?"

"Aye, at the moment."

I gesture at the glory around us. "But you have all this! You have a whole new home where you're actually taken care of and warm and…."

Peter is suddenly in my face. "Which all means *nothing* because my brother is—" He stops himself, jerking head down and exhaling slowly through his nose. He opens his mouth again, but I speak before he does.

"I'm sorry," I say, "I—I didn't know."

Peter takes a breath, working his jaw. "No, I'm sorry. It's not somethin' you would understand, and…. I shouldn't have snapped at you." But his voice is taut.

"I don't understand because you're not *telling* me," I grumble, crossing my arms. "I don't think you believe what my father tells me. What *I* know to be true." Which doesn't make sense to me at all. Why would he believe differently? How can he not see the truth like I can?

"I…. don't know what you're talkin' about."

"If you really believed that the Suppliers—or Scouts, as you call them—help your people, then how come you're so afraid for your brother? Wouldn't your fear be eased by the knowledge that the Scouts would help him?"

I swallow. "Aye, but, you see…. there are so many people on the Surface. It's winter, and although it's always cold down there, it's even colder and more dangerous in the winter. There are several people who are sick, or who have frostbite, and…. durin' this time of year, your Suppliers might be too busy helpin' others to help my brother."

"Well, I could always remind my father to send someone specifically to help your brother. They could bring him up here," I offer. If my father saved Peter from that explosion, then he shouldn't have a problem with saving Peter's brother as well. *Unless Peter was right, and Dad was the one who hurt him….*

"No!" Peter blurts.

"No? Why not?"

"I wouldn't want to put him through that much trouble." He doesn't meet my eyes, but I can see the panic written all over his face.

I study him for a moment. There's something about my father that he's not telling me, and I'm not going to stop until I figure out what it is. "What really happens in the basement?"

Peter jumps. "What?"

"Do you think I'm stupid? I can see, you know. I have eyes. There's got to be a reason you wouldn't want your brother being brought up here."

"I…."

"I can see that you're hurt—I could see that Clayton was hurt too, and he did a better job of hiding it than you do. I didn't help Clayton, but I can help you. Let me help."

Peter stares at me, his face at war with itself. "I'm fine. It's nothin'."

I turn away, disappointed that his answer hasn't made me feel any better. It should have, though. It's what I wanted to hear. My father is still the great man I know he is. But the lie is clearly written all over Peter's face. I just don't understand why he would lie. He's safe here. "My father isn't a monster." It's meant for Peter, but maybe I say it more to convince myself than to convince him.

"Let's just go."

"Why?"

"I am hungry. Aye, again. We should go. I do appreciate your bringin' me here, it is…. amazin'." He looks reluctant to admit it.

Maybe I was just jumping to conclusions again, and Peter's urgency *is* just because he's hungry. Maybe when I finally become a Supplier, I'll take Peter with me. It'll probably be too late for his brother by then, but at least he'll be able to go home—he clearly hates it here. He can be like, my guide or something on the Surface.

I don't tell him this though. Not yet.

Peter

Outside Rachel's garden again, I grip the railing tight as I follow her across the skydeck toward the entrance to Greenhouse Park. Halfway across I glance back, my eyes falling on the skydeck that wraps around the entire miniature dome. Then we're back inside the gardens of the city, and I try not to gasp the fresh air inside. It's so bloody hard to breathe out there.

We make our way down the glass street in silence, and I wonder what's going on in her head. How far did I push her toward the truth about her father? Did she even fall for my lies? I doubt it. I didn't even know what to. I can only pray she doesn't put too much thought into what her father might be doing to me, but when I glance over at her, she has a blank expression on her face, like her mind is elsewhere. I swallow. If she asks her father about it, he'll hurt me.

I follow her up the front steps of her mansion, both of us stopping in the foyer. All I can think about is Arial and Joseph. Rachel had said they would take care of lunch, which makes me afraid that Brown will take out his anger on them. If it weren't for them, I wouldn't want to be back in this hellish mansion so soon.

Off to the right, Brown paces around the coffee table in the living room. I swallow hard, but Rachel leads me right to him. He smiles in relief when he sees us, but it doesn't quite reach his eyes. I feel my heart beat faster.

"Rachel, where've you been?"

Rachel rolls her eyes. "Oh, don't pretend to be worried, it's not like I don't go on walks all the time. I just decided to bring Peter with me this time."

I grimace, but only Brown sees it. "Alright, but next time let me know, okay? He has work to do in the basement."

I pale, and Rachel scowls. "Why?"

Brown is taken aback. "Because I said so," he says, giving me a dark look.

"He hasn't done anything wrong."

"That's not—"

"No! Why do you have to punish him? Is he not allowed to go outside? Am I not allowed to take him places? Is that why you would take Clayton to the basement before?" Rachel moves between me and her father, and I swallow again, tense. I want to tell Rachel to keep her trap shut. Even if she's just trying to help, she's only making Brown angrier. I know that whatever is waiting for me in that basement is going to be far worse than it has ever been before, thanks to her. I want to run back to her skydeck and jump.

"This has nothing to do with Clayton—"

"But it does! What happens in the basement? What do you do to the Surface Dwellers? How bad do you hurt them?"

Brown seems to get bigger, his face twisting and his fists clenching. "Rachel!"

Rachel flinches at the sudden raise of his voice, shock bringing tears to her eyes. Part of me wants to defend her, to tell Brown to back off, but I keep my mouth shut. If I'm going to earn my parachute, I can't go mouthing off to him in front of his daughter, especially right now.

As it is, Brown sees Rachel's tears, and his expression softens. He sighs. "Look, honey, I'm sorry. I didn't mean to yell. The sewage pipe came loose in the basement and is making a mess everywhere, I need someone with some muscle to fix it. The other two can't handle it. That's all, I promise."

Rachel looks back at me, uncertain.

"It'll be fine, Miss Brown. If I don't hurry the whole house will smell bloody awful." I hate that I'm playing along with Brown's lies, but maybe it'll take some of the weight off my punishment. And besides, the way he'd mentioned Arial and Joseph makes my blood run cold. The sooner I can be sure that the other servants are okay, the better. I don't want anyone else getting hurt because Rachel wanted to drag me to her stupid garden.

"See? Nothing to worry about." Brown doesn't look at me. "Your mother is in the kitchen. She said something about cookies, but that was a while ago, so if you want one you'd better hurry. You know how much Mom loves cookies."

Rachel smiles a little, but she still hesitates before running into the kitchen, leaving me alone in the foyer with her father.

Brown glares at me. "You're coming with me, rat," he growls, clamping his hand around my upper arm and dragging me down the hall to the basement door. It's not like I can't fight back; Felix taught me hand to hand combat, and it got to the point that I could kick his butt almost every time we fought. I just don't want him using that pain device he implanted in my back. That and my whole 'be a good slave' plan would be pointless then.

He hauls me down the stairs and down the narrow hall lined with doors—one of which leads to my room. But instead of my room, he shoves me through a different door, and what I see makes me suck in a sharp breath.

Joseph and Arial are shackled to the wall, cowering and trembling as Liam and the other man brandish whips and hot metal at them. I stop in shock, and Brown kicks me hard in the back, causing me to stumble in.

Liam looks up at me, smiling through the gap in his teeth. "About time you showed up. Got to punish someone when the idiot who disobeyed orders isn't around to punish."

"What are ya talkin' about?" I breathe, stunned. I can't take my eyes off of Arial and Joseph, off their bloodied backs and bruised arms. Joseph's shirt is in tatters, burn marks all up and down his blackened ribs.

"You idiot, what did I tell you? I said stay away from my daughter!" Brown kicks the back of my legs, bringing me to my knees. "Calvin!" He barks, and the second man pauses, the whip in his hand falling limply across his own back. He grins, then turns and grabs the back of my shirt, yanking it over my head before I know what's happening.

"So what do you do? You spend *hours* with her! You make her question me!" Brown snaps his fingers, and Calvin lashes me across my bare chest.

I fall back, catching myself with my hands and gritting my teeth as pain sears across my upper body. Brown kicks me again, knocking me over and stomping on my ribs.

"The mistakes you make never go unpunished, *slave*," Brown spits. "I told you to stay away from my daughter, and you ignored me. And if you're not here to receive your punishment, then someone else will." He gestures toward Arial, and Liam presses the red hot poker against her shoulder. She screams, and I snap.

"Stop!" I yell, but I keep myself on my hands and knees, trembling with the urge to pound Brown into dust.

Brown raises an eyebrow. "Is that any way to talk to your master?"

"Please." I grit my teeth. "They've done nothin' wrong."

"Someone has to be punished." He says it like it's logic.

"Me—I'm the one who disobeyed. Punish me, not them."

Brown narrows his eyes. "You'd take their punishment?" He muses, as if he doesn't believe me. "I have to admit I don't really care who's punished. What I care about is that my new slave learns his lesson. And you don't seem to be learning anything. Listen to you, making demands of your betters. You must learn that you don't demand anything in this house, rat. Or in this city—my city!"

I bite back my sarcasm, dipping my head to the ground. "Please. I beg of you. I'm the one who deserves punishment. Let them go, and I promise I will never disobey you again."

Brown's face is pure satisfaction, and he gestures to Liam and Calvin. They unlock the manacles around Joseph's and Arial's wrists.

"Get out," Brown orders. "And fix yourself up some. You're both a mess."

Arial and John collapse, trembling, and then help each other out the door, throwing glances of worry mixed with gratitude over their shoulders. I watch them go, shrinking toward the ground.

Brown leans over me, a dark grin on his face. "I think I'll make sure you learn your lesson myself," he says, quietly. He takes the barbed whip from Calvin.

I shrink further, and Brown lashes the whip across my back, driving the toe of his shoe into my ribs. I cover my head, resisting the urge to fight back.

Be a good slave. I tell myself. *Be a good slave....*

Rachel

I wake up again to Peter's vacuuming, and I yawn and stretch, sitting up in bed. My jaw drops a little when I see him, startled by his appearance; his expression is haggard, dark circles weighing under his half-lidded eyes, and his movements are slow and stiff. His lip is split, and I swallow. "I buzzed for you last night."

"SorryMissBrown," he mutters, not looking up. His thick Irish accent is slurred, rendering him almost unintelligible. He gets rigidly to his knees and starts vacuuming under my bed.

I lay down on my stomach and hang my head over the edge of the mattress, frowning at him. "Did they let you sleep?"

"Idon'tknowwhatyou'retalkin'about," he mumbles, but I see his body relaxing, and in seconds he's completely lying down, his head resting on his arm and the vacuum cleaner whirring away in his limp hand. I poke his shoulder, and he jumps awake, sucking in a breath.

"Don't lie to me. Whatever my father did to you in the basement, it didn't involve fixing a sewage pipe."

"It did, Miss Brown."

"Let me help you."

Peter drops his head to the floor. "I don't need your help Miss Brown."

"I can get you out of here. It'll take a while, maybe a year or two, but I can do it. I just have to get my pilot's license, then I can take a hovercraft and I can get you home."

"Mmhmm." I can tell that he's drifting off again, and I jab at his back. Peter grunts, jerking his head up and hitting it on the bottom of my bed. He groans and drags his knees under him, rubbing the back of his head as he sits up. He sighs wearily, then reaches for the vacuum, getting slowly to his feet. Whenever Clayton was like this, I'd leave him be after asking him only once or twice what was wrong. He would tell me that he was homesick, but I never believed him. I ignored the signs before, I won't make the same mistake again. I have to help Peter—for Clayton's sake.

Peter leans the vacuum cleaner against the wall and starts wiping down the window, his limp considerably more heavy than before.

I get out of bed, ignoring the fact that I'm still in my pajamas. I catch his arm as he moves a steam-cleaner across the window, and he flinches, wincing. "How bad are you hurt?"

"I'm fine Miss Brown."

"Stop calling me that!"

Peter flinches, swallowing. "I am fine."

I don't believe him. "I don't believe you. Come with me." I lead him down out of my room and down the stairs, hurrying into the foyer. The doorbell rings, and I jump, startled. My mother appears from the dining room, opening the door. Over her shoulder, I see Malcolm standing in the doorway. His smile drops from his face when he sees me with Peter.

"Oh, Malcolm. You probably want to see my daughter, don't you?" I can tell she winks, because Malcolm's face turns bright pink. "She's up in her room, I think she's still asleep." She turns around. She sees me and beams. "Oh—never mind, there she is," she says to Malcolm, then bustles off to the kitchen.

Malcolm stares after my mother with a stunned expression, then looks expectantly at me, his eyes drifting to Peter. "I'll be right with you Malcolm. Peter's sick."

I grimace. Peter's hand is limp in my grasp, and I start pulling him toward the hall. I half lead, half drag Peter into the medical room, making him sit down on the table and wait while I dig around through the cupboards for a TRRD. Time to see how much I learned writing my paper.

I close the cupboards, unable to find a TRRD there. If the TRRDs aren't in the cupboards then where are they? I turn around to see Peter still slumped right where I left him, his eyes darting around the room. He really doesn't look good.

I open a drawer and start looking for a TRRD there, but I've never actually been in this room before Peter showed up—I've had no reason to be. I feel a little guilty at the mess I am making, but I can't leave Peter in his current state, and I am not sure I want to risk alerting my father to what we are doing.

I'm not sure what I expect to find—a few nasty bruises maybe? Or a lot? I don't care. Even if there's just a few small bruises, I have to heal Peter. Then I can talk to Dad, I can tell him to stop. *I'll make him stop, he'll listen to me.* I slam the drawer shut, frustrated that I still haven't found a TRRD. "Where do they keep those stupid things!?"

Peter gets up without a word and starts opening random cabinets. He's still stiff, but his expression is determined—almost desperate.

"What are you doing?" I ask, but he doesn't say anything. I am a little bit relieved to know that he has the energy to help search, but suddenly I get a funny feeling in the pit of my stomach. The way his broad back hides his hands from my sight as he pulls something from one of the cabinets makes me wonder if he is stealing something. I step closer to him and stand on my toes, trying to see over his shoulder, but he's too tall. I drop back onto my heels, crossing my arms. "Peter?"

"I'm fine Miss Brown, this should help," he says, turning around with an Advil in his hand.

I squint my eyes skeptically at him. I hardly think one Advil is all he needs. I don't know what made me think he was stealing something. Why would he? I'm trying to help him.

"Headache," he mumbles, leaning heavily against the counter, as he pops it in his mouth.

"I could get you some water-" I start, but he swallows it without obvious difficulty.

"Peter?" No way it's just a headache.

"Your guest, Miss Brown," he says softly, his Adam's apple bobbing as he swallows again.

I'm about to protest, but he gives me a look of such desperation that I can't speak. His pale green eyes beg me to leave, and I take a step back, pausing in the door frame. Did I make things worse for him by bringing him here to help him? I don't know what to do. I turn and leave him alone in the room.

Malcolm is sitting on the second step of the grand staircase in the foyer, his elbows resting on his knees and his hands clasped in front of him, his head down.

"Hey." I beam, and he looks up quickly, flashing me one of his amazing smiles, but it looks a little strained. I wonder if my expression looks just as strained.

He gets up. "Morning." He grins, holding out his elbow. "Thought we might go for a walk."

"Of course," I say, taking his arm and letting him lead me outside. We stroll down the crystal street, arm in arm until we reach the Greenhouse Gardens, but I don't know what to say. All I can think about is Peter. What did my father do to him? Surely it can't be *too* bad.

"So…. what was wrong with Peter?" Malcolm says casually, but I sense something else is up.

I remember when Malcolm pulled Peter away at dinner the other night, and my walls go up. "Why, are you jealous?"

"No—"

I let out an exasperated sigh. "Dude, can I help my friend without you being suspicious? What kind of girl do you think I am? And—we're not actually dating or anything, so even if I *did* like someone other than you, it would be none of your business," I say, irritated. I am starting to like Malcolm, but now that I am, I'm starting to see some kinks that need to be worked out. "Peter just had a headache or something."

"Ah. Do you know what happened to him?"

I frown. "No, do you?" Malcolm couldn't be like my father, could he?

Malcolm shakes his head. "Nah, only that he's hurt. I was there too when he tried to escape, remember?"

"Yeah, and he whooped your butt." I smirk without thinking.

Malcolm scowls, his nose wrinkling. "I was caught off guard," He growls.

"I'm sure." I wiggle my eyebrows, then nudge his ribs. "You're cute when you're mad." *No, he's not like my father.* I decide.

"Shut up, that's what I'm supposed to say," he tells me, some of the tension leaving his expression. I wish I could relax as well, but my mind is racing. Should I tell him? Maybe he could help me make Dad stop hurting Peter. Or maybe not—I don't want him getting in trouble with his own father: I have no doubt that Mr. Crysis is like Dad. They're like best friends. It's better to not drag Malcolm into this.

Besides, it's obvious that Malcolm doesn't really like Peter. I guess I can't blame him: some hot guy with a sexy accent showed up, kicked his butt, and is now taking up most of my attention. I suppose I've given Malcolm a reason to be jealous. But that doesn't make him the bad guy. Dad's the one hurting Peter. Malcolm's just doing some weird jealous guy thing—which means he might tell my dad about my concern about Peter if I don't obliterate his rivalry now.

I realize that we're outside the door that leads onto the skydeck, where my garden is. "Should we go out?" I gesture toward the door, hoping to distract Malcolm from my concern for Peter.

"We should."

I roll my eyes. "I meant out*side*."

Malcolm smirks. "So did I."

"No you didn't." I stick my tongue out at him. Part of me wants to shut him down, freaked out by the fuzzy feeling in my stomach, but the other part of me welcomes it. At least butterflies aren't as cold as the weights that come with my thoughts of Peter and the basement. And besides, maybe this is a good thing. Not just because it demolishes any reason for Malcolm to be jealous of Peter, but also because I'm slowly getting used to this new Malcolm, and I kinda like the thought of actually having a boyfriend. *Whoa, whoa, hold up.* My mind still shies away from the thought. 'Boyfriend' is such a heavy word. I'm happy just taking it slow, like we are.

We cross the skydeck with some difficulty, as the wind has picked up a little, but the garden is warm and moist. Malcolm stops me. He places his hand on my cheek, the tips of his fingers brushing my hair. "I really like you, Rachel. I've been meaning to tell you, but..." He shrugs, glancing away. "I'm a bit of a coward."

I feel my face burning, but I force myself not to look away, guilt tickling at my mind. "Malcolm...." Before I finish, he kisses me square on the lips. I blink, and he pulls back quickly, his face pink. Stunned, I try to say something, but nothing comes out but the breath I didn't realize I had been holding. *Just when I was getting comfortable with the pace.* I swallow, glance at the ground in case I dropped my brain, and say, "Malcolm, I like you too, but—let's not rush things." I wince, hating myself. "I mean.... I'm kind of.... I don't know, I'm seventeen Malcolm, I'm still thinking things through and it's not like I'm too young or something I just.... ugh, I'm sorry. I just don't know if I'm ready for this. I don't even know what I'd do...." *Now what?*

He shocks me by nodding. "Okay. That's fine with me." He pulls his hand away and grasps my own. "Mind telling me who it is?"

"It's not that, Malcolm. There's no one else, I just—"

"What? Am I too far below your standards?"

I scoff. "Seriously? What's wrong with you? Is it wrong for me to want to take things slow? Everything was fine until you had to go off and kiss me! You did this to yourself!" I feel terrible the second the words leave my mouth, but it's too late to take them back.

Malcolm huffs, looking away. "Whatever."

"Malcolm…. I'm sorry, okay?" I force a smile, feeling guilty. "I just….I can't right now."

"Fine," he says curtly.

We pace around my garden in awkward silence. I struggle to find something to start up a conversation again, but all I can think is *great, now Malcolm is extra jealous of Peter. He'll definitely tell my father now.*

Malcolm saves my life, speaking up about how he wanted to work on the farm for a while, with all the animals. "It could be fun," he says, "I like animals. Especially the cows, even though they stink."

"You would like the cows." I laugh, relieved that I didn't have to fail at starting a conversation. The farm domes on the sides of the city aren't very big; only a few small animals live there, mostly goats, chickens, and rabbits. The rest is dedicated to crops.

"Whatever. They're cute."

"It's cute that you think they're cute," I tell him, grinning even though I feel awkward flirting with him now. Maybe I can pretend everything is still normal, and I won't feel so weird. We can still go back to taking it slow, right?

Malcolm rolls his eyes. "You're making me feel like a girl."

"Wow thanks. You know, not all girls are girly."

"So what, that's how you're making me feel."

I stick my tongue out at him. "Well then good."

He slips his arm around my shoulders and rubs my upper arm. "Aw commere you big baby."

I giggle like the stupid teenage girl I am and push him away, my face turning red. "I should probably get back. My dad was mad at me last time. Wanna stay for lunch?" Now he just seems too relaxed and it's weird.

Malcolm nods. Hand in hand, we cross the skydeck again and head home in an uncomfortable silence. I want to pull my hand away, but I've already friendzoned him hard enough, I don't want to make him feel *too* bad.

When we reach my house, Malcolm stops me on the front porch, taking both my hands in his. "Look, Rachel, I'm sorry."

I stiffen, bracing for another kiss and prepared to slap him if he tries. If he can't play by my rules then I'm gonna make sure it ends now, permanently.

He looks down at our hands, biting his lower lip. "What I did was, a bit rash, and…. I'm sorry. I should've made sure it was okay first."

I nod, totally agreeing with him, then catch what I'm doing and stop. "It's okay Malcolm, I'm not mad at you. I'm just…. uncertain, I guess. I'm not the kind of girl who just jumps into these kind of things, and if you can't figure that out, I'm not sure this'll work." It hurts me to say it to my only friend, but after that kiss, that's all I want him to be right now: my friend.

"Okay. You're right, we should just take it slow." Malcolm looks like he wants to say more, but he shuts his mouth, not looking me in the eye.

"Hey, at least you're being honest." I force smile, and he opens the front door for me. I step over the threshold and freeze.

Peter and my father are standing in the middle of the foyer. Dad looks furious, and Peter's eyes are fixed on the ground.

"Dad?" I ask, and they both jump.

Peter's right eye is swollen shut, and my hands shake. What do I do?

Peter

Just go. I silently will Rachel to leave, to take Malcolm and get out of here. If she starts questioning her father, then I have to pay for it. I've taken my share of punches, I can handle this without her help.

Rachel studies us for a moment, then she looks at me. "Could you make us some lunch, please?" She asks, then turns away. "We'll be in the kitchen."

I release a breath, glance briefly at Brown, then flick my eyes back to the ground.

"You heard her, they're hungry, make them lunch. When you're finished with that, I need you to run an errand for me. Come find me when you're done."

I keep my head down as I hurry into the kitchen. I hate this, I hate pretending to be a good slave, I hate hurting. But after what Liam and Calvin did to Joseph and Arial last night, my fear feels more real than pretend. Before it was just the pain inflicting device, and as much as I hated it, the pain was temporary. But now that other people can get punished for my mistakes….Maybe I don't need to pretend anymore. I thought I could handle this, I thought I could tough it out long enough to get my parachute, but now I'm thinking I'm not as strong as I thought I was. But I can't help it. I'd do anything to avoid another night like that. They didn't just 'teach me a lesson', they beat me within an inch of my life, then healed everything they did, only to beat the crap out of me again. And it wasn't just once, it was *all night*, and they didn't heal anything that wouldn't kill me when they finally left. They healed just enough to keep me alive. When am I going to get my bloody parachute? I can't take this anymore.

Once in the kitchen, I open the fridge—and freeze. What on earth do they even want? Am I allowed to ask? Rachel's hand suddenly appears on my forearm, and she points to the pantry by the door to the laundry room. "Just some soup would be good."

I relax slightly. At least she's not yelling at me. I find soup in the pantry, dumping it in a bowl and taking a second to marvel at its contents. Even the soup has enough seasoning to make it smell better than anything on the Surface, full of vegetables I've never seen before. I set it in the microwave, hesitate, then set the time for two minutes. The whole time my face is throbbing where Brown had hit me, before Rachel and Malcolm walked through the door. My right eye feels swollen, and I can hardly open it.

I spoon some of the soup into two different bowls, then carry them over to the table, setting them down in front of Malcolm and Rachel and turning to leave. "Ah, wait there," Malcolm orders, and I sigh. This little monster isn't the head of this house, and I'm getting a little tired of him acting like he is. I lean against the island, crossing my arms over my chest and trying not to watch them eat.

"Are you hungry?" Rachel asks. I get a strong sense of deja vu, but with Malcolm here, I think it's better to refuse her offers. Brown hasn't given me anything to eat since that nasty gruel yesterday morning. The burns and cuts and broken bones only make me more reluctant to eat.

Be a good.... slave. I shake my head, keeping my eyes on the ground.

"Are you okay?" She gets up to stand in front of me, Malcolm glaring at me from her side.

I nod, instinctively shrinking away from Malcolm, whose blue eyes narrow. Rachel just frowns. "Maybe you should get some rest." She looks more closely at my black eye.

I shake my head again, but then Malcolm says rather darkly, "Yes, he should. I'll take him to his room, you wait here." He takes my arm in a firm grasp, and I wince, his fingers pressing against the bruises covering my biceps.

"Malcolm don't." Rachel catches his arm.

I try to hide how much I hurt.

Malcolm twists away. "No. He's not your *pet* Rachel, this has got to stop," he spits. Rachel takes a step back, shock written all over her face.

Malcolm pulls me out of the kitchen and down the hall, into the basement and to my room. As soon as the door shuts behind us, my legs give out and I let myself collapse on the hard floor, managing to keep my head from hitting the ground. I don't care if Malcolm sees me, I don't need to hide my pain from him, he's the one who causes it. "Didn't I tell you to stay away from her?" Malcolm snarls, kicking my burned back.

I cry out despite myself, rolling away from him, but he just follows me, kicking me again. "Do you listen to no one? With that other guy gone, everything was perfect, but then *you* had to show up. Stay away from her!" He kicks me hard in the stomach, and I double, curling into the fetal position and gasping for breath. Malcolm stomps down hard on my ribs, and I shudder. "You people are *filth*. Hear me? Worthless *filth*. You deserve to starve on the Surface, you deserve to rot in the Atlantic. You are *nothing*." He kicks me again, his shoe cracking my ribs. "Scum like you don't deserve a woman like Rachel. Stay away from her, or so help me God, I'll beat you to *death*." He spits the last word, driving a particularly hard kick at my hip.

"Malcolm," I croak, flinching as he draws back his foot again. He pauses. I convulse on the floor, unable to do much else. Each breath feels like shards of glass are piercing my lungs again and again, but of course I bloody well can't just stop breathing. Even on the Surface, I never hurt this bad. Life was so much easier, and I never appreciated that until now.

"You better not ever touch her again, or I'll kill you," Malcolm snarls, kicking me again. "Now come on."

I groan, unable to get back to my feet. Malcolm's upper lip curls. He stoops, grabbing my arms and pulling me up, but I can't stay standing, and I collapse against him. Malcolm shoves me away in disgust, and I hit the ground hard, moaning as blinding pain tears at my entire body.

"Come on now, get up!" Malcolm spits.

"Can't—breathe." I choke, shuddering. I try to get up, but my arms just twitch, my fingers clenching and unclenching uselessly. Stupid bloody pain. Stupid bloody city. Stupid bloody world.

Malcolm gives me an exasperated sigh, leaving the room. I remain on the floor, struggling to regain my breath, to stay awake, to *move*, but I can't. I just hurt too bad. *Oh God just let me die.* I pray, truly wanting nothing more than to curl up and die. Why can't it just end? Malcolm returns a few minutes later, carrying devices from the medical room. I sigh in relief knowing that they would heal away at least some of the pain.

I have two of those devices too, stashed in my pocket: one from Rachel's room and the other I had stolen when Rachel thought I was getting an Advil. I might have given in and used the healing devices on myself if Malcolm had left me alone long enough—or if I had been able to work my hands at all. I am glad I didn't; these devices are meant for Felix.

Malcolm shoves me onto my back, unbuttoning the front of my overcoat and lifting up my shirt. I can't do anything but shiver, unable to push him away. His eyes grow a little bigger and his lips part slightly as he takes in the bruises and burns and cuts all across my chest and ribs, but all I can do is tremble and breathe, tremble and breathe. He glances up at my face, then picks up one of the devices, pressing a little red button on the handle and moving the device over my chest. My chest grows excruciatingly hot, and I cry out. A few of the burns and cuts on my chest slowly seal over. He heals most of my broken ribs as well.

The process is slow and agonizing and the devices run out of energy long before he has healed all of my wounds. When he's finished, he yanks down my shirt, and the pain is a little less than it was before. I can somewhat breathe again.

"Now get up," Malcolm says with a little less force, looking marginally disturbed.

I exhale slowly, forcing my hands and knees underneath me and dragging myself to my feet, swaying. I don't understand. First the boy's beating me to death, and now he's helping me? *No.* If Malcolm was trying to be kind, he should've bloody killed me.

"Come on now, get moving. I think Brown was looking for you."

I involuntarily groan. I want to cry, to bawl like a baby, but I pull it together and lurch up the stairs, stopping in the hallway when I see Brown.

I jerk my gaze down as Brown stalks down the hall toward me. Malcolm brushes past us, hurrying to get back to Rachel in the kitchen, and leaving me alone with the mayor. I shrink, feeling like a beaten puppy. I'm nineteen. I'm a bloody grown man. I've fought off a Siren. I shouldn't give in like this. But I don't want to hurt anymore. I just can't take it.

"There you are," he says quietly, and I just drop to the floor, landing heavily on my butt and just sitting there, defeated. Nothing I can do or say will help me.

"*Please don't hurt me again,*" I whisper, aching. Not just from the pain, but for my brother, for home. Even for Addy, no matter how irritating she was.

Brown stands over me, his arms folded across his chest. "You know, the young man who worked here before you—Clayton—didn't take so long to break. Perhaps because you're older. Even so, Clayton got too close to Rachel. And Clayton didn't survive his last encounter with Malcolm." Brown shakes his head. "What does it take to get good help out of one of you Surface Rats!"

He nudges me with his foot, and I barely manage to catch myself with my hands to keep from falling backwards on my sore back. "Pathetic. Here I thought all those muscles would make you a better specimen than frail Clayton. I almost miss him now. What a waste."

I remain sitting on the floor with my legs stretched uncomfortably out in front of me, slumped over and leaning way to the right like a puppet without the puppeteer. *Pathetic.* He's right, I should be stronger than this. Maybe Malcolm was right too. I am nothing. I can't even defend myself anymore. My entire body is killing me, but I slowly get to my feet, staggering slightly and catching myself on the wall.

"Now, about that errand." Brown presses a paper into my hand. "You are going on your first trip into town. You will ride with Liam into the city, and he will let you out in front of the store." He hands me some kind of thin card. "You will use that buy everything on the list and bring it back here, do you understand?"

I nod wearily, and Brown turns and stalks off, leaving me alone in the hall. My solitude only lasts a few seconds, though, as Liam is suddenly behind me, clapping a heavy hand on my shoulder. "Let's move," he says gruffly, and he forces me to walk in front of him. I imagine that he has a gun pointed at my back, so I don't feel quite as ashamed of letting him lead me like a child, but he probably doesn't. I wish I had a gun. I could do some real damage with a gun in a city made of glass.

Liam leads me outside and around the corner of the mansion, pushing me into the seat of a small, four door hovercar. He sits in the seat next to me, and the hovertech hums to life. Before he pulls out, though, Malcolm and Rachel run out of the house, waving at Liam to wait. They both climb into the hovercar behind us, and Rachel answers Liam's inquiring look. "I told Dad we were going to the mall."

"Alright then, we'll drop you two off."

"What about Peter? If we buy anything, we'll need someone to carry it," Rachel asks.

Carry it yourself you spoiled brat. I want to snap, but I stay silent. Liam shakes his head, backing out onto the glass street. "Your father gave him a list."

"Oh. Ok." Rachel sounds uncertain, and in the rear-view mirror, I see Malcolm shift awkwardly in his seat.

I rub my black eye gingerly, trying to tell how swollen it is, but touching it makes the whole right side of my face throb. I let my hand drop into my lap. Why didn't I hit Brown back? *Because you're afraid.* I shut my eye. How did I let myself sink this low?

I remain quiet for the entire trip into town. Malcolm and Rachel talk in the back seat, but they sound kind of awkward, their conversation strained. Rachel keeps throwing glances up at me in the mirror, and Malcolm keeps trailing off into an uncomfortable silence, also shifting his eyes toward the front of the car. I ignore them, memorizing the roads and landmarks.

In the center of the Glass City, the bigger buildings reach up toward the dome like upside-down icicles, glimmering in the sun. Up close, they're even bigger than I thought they were. Flashing signs catch my eye, and I struggle to read them with my one good eye; "Bouncing Burgers", "The Glass City Emporium", "The Glass City Wool Factory", and "Designer Shoes". How can there be one entire shop for shoes?

We stop outside a massive, two story building with spinning glass doors, through which I can see silvery aluminum staircases that appear to be moving up and down. Malcolm and Rachel get out of the hovercar, and Rachel taps on the window. Liam rolls it down, and Rachel smiles. "If we're not done shopping by the time you guys are, send Peter in to find us," she tells him, and she and Malcolm turn and head into the building that I assume is the mall.

Liam rolls the window back up, pulling back onto the road. It surprises me that there aren't very many hovercars on the road with us, but the sidewalks are packed with people, a good majority of them wearing green uniforms similar to my own. We stop again outside a large building, the sign screaming "Fred's Fish" in flashing red letters. The thought of seafood makes me homesick, and Liam gives me a look. "Well? Get in there and buy what you need."

I glance at the list; the first items are 'cocktail shrimp' and 'smoked salmon'. Swallowing my pain, I limp into the store alone. The building isn't the fanciest or most amazing in the city, but the size and the structure still stun me. Inside the building, even more amazing than the architecture are the rows of food stretching out before me in massive metal bins full of ice. The room is noticeably chilly compared to outside. It strikes me as odd that up here they would try to keep a room colder rather than warmer. A few other people search through the aisles, all of them dressed in the green servant's uniform.

I have no idea where to start. I approach one of the servants, a young boy black haired boy shoveling tiny shrimp into a clear plastic bag. "Excuse me?" I ask, struggling to keep my voice steady.

The boy jumps, his dark eyes briefly meeting mine before dropping back down to the shrimp. "Yes?"

"Relax, I'm not goin' to hurt you. I haven't been here before, I was just wonderin' if this is the cocktail shrimp?" I've never heard the term before.

He shakes his head, pointing to the bin next to his. "There."

"Thank you." I pause, unsure of where to get a bag, when the boy taps a roll of plastic before peeling a piece off. *Plastic bags?* I've seen sealskin bags, even the occasional clothe bags, but *plastic?* He fumbles with one end of it before opening it into a bag, the same as his. I thank him again as he hands me the bag, and he glances at my wrists.

"Oh." He looks away again.

I frown. "What?"

"You're the mayor's new servant. I—I'm sorry."

"How did you know?"

He points at two gold insignias stitched into the cuff of each of my sleeves; a tiny jumble of shapes that sort of resembles a city. I blink, wondering why I hadn't noticed them before. "Oh."

The boy nods. "The one before you, Clayton, he was nice. He came here as often as I did, and we'd see each other now and then. He'd help me get the things that I couldn't reach, especially in the other stores." I can tell that he's trying not to stare at my black eye.

I scoop shrimp into my bag with the little metal shovel, the cold handle burning my hand. "Is everyone up here like the mayor?"

The boy shakes his head. "No, I don't think so. Just most of them." He sighs, shivering slightly. "And you never know for sure who's who until you do somethin' wrong. The better you behave, though, the less you get hurt."

"Who do you work for?"

"I work with the generators." He holds up his hands, clenching and unclenching his fingers. "I have small hands that fit easily into small places. But I'm also supposed to get food for everyone in the generators once a week. All we get to eat is seafood, because it's the most easily obtained food on this stupid planet, but at least we don't get hurt as often; we have to be able to move to crawl through the tight spaces. Sometimes someone will get electrocuted, or catch themselves on fire, but not too often. I guess it's one of the better jobs we can have."

"How do the generators function?" If I don't get a parachute then I'm taking this whole City down.

The boy hesitates, letting his eyes dart about the room before answering. "Well, in the bottom of each generator—in the main cores—hundreds of thousands of gallons of water, are heated up. The steam turns giant fans, and somehow that generates enough electricity to power the hovertech on the bottom of the city and all the other little luxuries they have here. The steam travels through a pipe on the roof and back down into the pool, so it's recycled."

I'm surprised by how much he knows, and wonder how long he's been here. "What would happen if the fans suddenly stopped turnin'?"

The boy takes in a sharp breath and looks from side to side, but nobody is paying us any attention. "Well—I suppose the hovertech would….stop workin'." His voice shakes with excitement at the idea, obviously he hasn't been here long enough to lose his desire for freedom. "But the fans never stop."

"Could they be made to stop?"

The boy is practically breathless. "I don't know anyone who would do such a thing, but if there was someone who could, they would need weapons to overcome the engineers and then they would have to vent the steam and water from the main chambers. Someone would have to guard the cores until they were completely empty. And then this bloody place would end."

I nod, then make myself look busy with the shrimp as another servant walks past. The fewer people who hear our conversation the better.

"We would all go down with it, but it would be worth it," The boy says after a moment. "They might survive with their parachutes, but they won't last long without their city."

I start. "We don't get parachutes? Not ever?"

He shakes his head and my heart sinks. I brood over this as the boy—Caleb, I discovered—shows me where to find the rest of the items on my list. I'm obviously going to need to adapt my plan. Maybe Caleb is right. Maybe it would be better to bring this entire City down, and go down with it, than keep going the way things are. But I don't know where to get any weapons.

When I have what I need, Caleb shows me where to check out and how, and we part ways. It feels good to have a friend again. And not some spoiled City brat who thinks of me more like a pet than an equal.

Liam is leaning against the car with his arms crossed when I exit the building, drumming his fingers on his biceps. "I was just thinking that I was going to have to go in there and drag you out."

I shake my head. "Where to now?"

"Read the list."

I pull the piece of paper out of my pocket and unfold it; "'carrots', 'peas', 'corn', and 'bread'."

Liam points down the block. "You stop at the bakery before we head to the farm domes. Start walking."

I don't argue; Caleb said that a slave who had been broken didn't get hurt as much, even though they didn't get parachutes. If they think I'm broken, maybe they'll let me recover enough to escape. I hand Liam the fish and shrimp. My hips and back are killing me, but I start walking in the direction he had pointed, struggling to read the signs with my lousy reading skills. It doesn't help that my good eye is swollen shut.

A few blocks down, I see a sign that says "Daisy's Bakery". *At least things are easy to find up here.* The second I step inside, I forget about my pain, my fear, my plans to destroy the Glass City, as my senses are flooded with the overwhelming aroma of baking bread and sweet pastries. I blink in astonishment, having never smelled anything like it—whenever Addy baked rice bread, she always managed to burn it. A small, plump woman bustles around behind the counter, hurriedly moving freshly baked....somethings from the oven to the display case built into the counter.

I approach quietly, waiting for her to finish. When she's sees me at the counter, she sets the rest of her baked goods in the display case and moves to stand in front of me behind the counter. "What can I gitcha?" Her accent is strange. I've never heard anything quite like it. Glass City folk are from all over the world, but most of them have kind of adopted a similar way of speaking. This woman, however, displays her difference from them like a badge.

"I'm supposed to get a loaf of bread." I don't meet her eyes, recovering from the shock of smells and the aching hollowness in my gut.

"Ah, yer Mayor Brown's new servant. Shame really, that Clayton was such a nice fellow. Don't tell Mr. Brown I said this, but I hope ya don't meet the same fate. I'll pray for you, okay hun?"

I blink with my one good eye, stunned. "I—thank you." I try to keep it together and not break down into tears at her kind words. What if she's just pretending?

The woman gives me a sad look, turning and taking a large loaf of bread from a rack pressed against the wall to her right. "Mah name's Daisy, by the way. Daisy Dunham."

"My name's Peter," I say, carefully.

Daisy wraps the bread in plastic. "Well Peter, I have a feelin' God's gotta plan for yer life, so dontcha go and git yerself killed, okay?"

All I can do is nod, feeling slightly uncomfortable but touched all the same. I mean, it would be one thing if my brother said it, but a random stranger? She hands me the loaf of bread in exchange for the card Brown gave me, sliding the card in a strange machine and then giving it back to me. She holds up a finger before I leave, signaling me to wait. She grabs a few things out of the display case and puts them in a small box. "Take these for Mrs. Brown for me, will ya? She's such a kind young lady, she needs a little somethin' extra to keep her goin', ya know? Oh, and this one's for you—ya better eat it quick before someone sees ya." She hands me a basket and a small round pastry, bits of brown stuck in it.

"I don't—"

"It's a cookie darlin', put it in your mouth and start chewin'." She smiles kindly, and I tentatively take a bite. My eyebrows shoot up, and I stare at the rest of the cookie in wonder as I chew, struggling to comprehend how something so small and colorless could taste so good. I've never had anything sweet before.

"Wow." I manage, and Daisy snorts, handing me a napkin.

"Loose the crumbs, hun. We'll let this be our little secret, k?" She wipes my cheek with her thumb and brushes crumbs from the front of my uniform after I cram the rest of the cookie in my mouth.

"Thank you," I say after swallowing, and Daisy's smile gets bigger. Maybe I should think about this plan to crash the Glass City more carefully.

"Don't worry about it hun. Y'all deserve some kindness once in a while. Now hurry along, hun, I don't wantcha to get in trouble because of me." She waves good-bye, and I raise my hand in farewell as well as I push through the front door of the bakery. The car is still just a few blocks down, and Liam leans against the side of it.

I let the smile drop from my face before Liam sees it, and he raises an eyebrow at the box in my right hand.

"What's this?" He asks when I'm close enough to hear.

"The baker told me to bring it to Mrs. Brown."

"Did you pay for it?"

"No, she gave it to me, to give to Mrs. Brown." I suddenly realize that maybe I should have paid Daisy for the box. She hadn't charged me for it….

"Fine, put it in the car," he orders.

Once again I don't argue, obediently placing the box and the loaf of bread in the trunk while wiping my mouth for crumbs self-consciously. The short drive across town to the farm is silent, and I peer out the window in shock as we leave the dome and travel across a skybridge to another dome. This bridge is encased in glass, unlike the one leading to Rachel's garden, but it's also much longer. The second dome is about half the size of the Glass City, and inside are massive fields of crops that I've never seen before, countless servants working away at them.

Liam waits in the car while I go into the barn that has the words "Farmers Market" painted in giant white letters on the front. Inside, the air is cold, but not as cold as it had been in "Fred's Fish". I don't know what any of the vegetables on the list look like, so I approach another Surface Dweller, this one a young woman with shoulder-length brown hair. She starts when I get close to her, and her eyes immediately fall on the cuffs of my sleeves. Curious, I look at hers; a small shape that looks like a doorway is stitched in gold thread on the end of her sleeves.

She hesitates, glancing at my black eye. "Can I help you?" She says in a soft Irish accent.

"It might sound a wee bit stupid, but I don't know what these are." I point to the carrots, corn, and peas on the list.

She smiles, then hides it quickly. "Here—I'll show you." She gestures for me to follow, and she leads me around the store, pointing at each type of vegetable and naming it as we walk by. Some of them I already know, as they can grow on the Surface, but I don't tell her this. I pick up the ones I need, then thank her, allowing a half smile to pull at my lips, the taste of the cookie keeping my mood lighter than it had been in days.

"Where do you work?" I ask before I leave.

The girl drops her gaze to the floor. "I work in the Crypts."

"What?"

"We handle the dead servants. Recycle their uniforms and…" She doesn't finish, and I feel bad for asking.

"You're the ones who leave their names." I realize. Whenever a body showed up in the Atlantic, it always had a name hidden in its mouth—the name of the victim. A small token that helped identify their loved ones, who were thrown away at the end of their usefulness.

She shushes me, glancing around quickly. I hesitate. I guess it makes sense that there are Dead Handlers in the Glass City as well. "Thank you," I say again, more quietly this time. I find the counter on my own this time, pay for the goods, and head back to the hovercar.

The whole trip took barely an hour, and Liam parks outside the mall again, looking at me in the mirror. "Go find them and tell them if they're not here in ten minutes they can walk home."

I get out of the car, stepping cautiously up to the spinning doors. I have no idea which side I'm supposed to enter, but lucky for me, someone exits just before I reach the doors, leaving from the left side of the door. I push through the right side, turning a full circle before I realize how to get out. Can't they just have a normal door with a handle or something? I stop for a moment in the packed space of the main foyer, taking in the sight of all the restaurants surrounding the mostly empty tables in a large room with a vaulted ceiling. Once again my nose is bombarded with a cacophony of smells that I've never smelled before, and I feel my stomach grumble. Where do I look?

I slowly make my way between the tables toward the stairs, catching sight of a few families chowing down on a variety of foods, their servants standing silently behind them. The place is mostly empty, though, giving it an eerie feeling.

The stairs almost kill me. I set my foot on the first step, and instantly I'm carried up, and I catch myself on the railing—only to find that it moves too. At the top. I stumble off, glancing around at the storefronts lining the walls on either side of me, all the way to the back wall. These too, are mostly empty.

I make my way down one side of the mall. About a quarter of the way along, I spot Malcolm and Rachel leaving a store that called "Wishlist", a fluffy brown animal in her arms.

It hurts my ribs, but I hurry to catch up to them. Both of them turn at the sound of my wheezing, and I realize that the animal in Rachel's arms is stuffed. Why she has a stuffed animal, I have no idea, but judging by the big red bow around its neck, I'd say it was from Malcolm—or at least, he bought it for her.

"Oh hey. Check out my new bear." She holds up the stuffed animal.

That is not a bear. "Cute," I say. "Liam's waitin' in the car, says he'll make ya walk if ya take too long."

"Ok." Rachel slides her arm through Malcolm's and hands me two bags. "Then we'd better hurry."

I just want to lie down, to sleep when we get back to the house, but as soon as I enter the foyer, Brown is already there. He shoves a mop into my hand, nearly knocking me over.

I stare after him as he walks away, my right eye still swollen almost completely shut from where he had hit me earlier because I didn't do a good enough job cleaning the living room—even though it was spotless. I have no idea what he wants me to clean, I only know that I better figure it out. There are more high tech ways to clean the floor, so maybe he wants me to clean the foyer, since it's bigger and uses up more energy from the floor steamer. Maybe making me use the mop is his way of saving energy? *Or his way of making me work harder.*

I start mopping up the dirty footprints in the foyer, along with what's left of my good mood. I need to get *out of here.* I'm never going to get a parachute, and I can't quite bring myself to doom people like Mrs. Brown and Daisy. But I have to do something. I can't take another night in the basement if I don't quite mop the floor good enough.

Malcolm leaves, and Rachel sits on the stairs and watches me, a thoughtful expression on her face as she twists the end of her pony tail around her finger. When I'm done, she gets up, lifting the heavy bucket of water before I can. I don't want to object, uncertain if *I* can carry it.

I'm just so bloody exhausted. But I curl my fingers around the handle anyways, giving her a look. She shoots the look right back at me and pulls the bucket from my hand, sloshing dirty water onto the floor.

I sigh, dropping the head of the mop back to the crystal floor. "Please leave," I mumble.

"No. Just let me help you, there's nothing wrong with it."

I groan inwardly. She carries the bucket back to the kitchen, dumping out the water in the sink while I put the mop away. "Wanna go for a walk?" She asks.

No way in hell you bloody rotten little—"No."

"Too bad." She grabs my wrist and pulls, and I almost fall, my knees buckling. I catch myself and follow her to the door, not knowing what else to do. I look around desperately for Brown, so that he can witness my unwillingness, but of course he's nowhere to be seen. She drags me through the park, all the way to the door of her secret garden. I feel like maybe I'm going to hyperventilate. No matter how good of a job I did mopping, I am doomed now. I wonder if it's possible for Brown to hurt me more than he has, but I have no doubt it is and that I will discover these new levels of pain tonight.

"Peter?" She says suddenly as we stop before going out onto the skydeck. She pulls the folded inflatable raft off of the rack next to the door and gets her oxygen mask ready. "You don't have to be afraid out here. This is my place. Nobody can hurt you here."

I don't answer her. In my mind, I am already in the basement, and Liam has the iron red hot again.

"What happened to your brother?"

I don't answer her. I just won't speak to her. That's all I can do.

She pulls me outside into the frigid oxygenless air. She leads me toward her garden, but I stop, leaning on the railing of the skydeck surrounding the little glass dome. I'm just so tired.

"Peter?"

My head feels dizzy, and little black dots float in front of my eyes. The vast sea of clouds rages hundreds of feet below, beckoning me. It's my way out.

I turn to face her; I can't do it, I can't take one more night of pain. "I'm sorry," I mumble.

She pulls me into a hug, which is all I needed.

I take a shallow breath and slip my hand up her shirt. Rachel stiffens, her fingers digging into my burning back. "Peter...." She warns, starting to pull away.

NO! I move faster, forcing my entire arm under the back of her shirt—and under her harness. She jerks away, but I keep her pressed against me, ignoring her screams and fists as I flip backwards over the rail and tumble into the open sky.

Rachel

I scream at the top of my lungs, my voice louder than Peter's as we hurl through the air and plummet toward the Surface. His arm is hooked firmly across my back, still under my shirt and harness. I panic, my stomach doing flips as I pound my fists against any part of him I can reach.

His face twists as he pins my arms to my sides with his other arm, his legs hooking around the back of my knees. We end up with our heads pointed straight down, and the clouds come rushing up to us at full speed. Peter buries his face in my shoulder, and I do the same, giving up on trying to protect my face from the wind with my hands. A cold mist envelops us for about four seconds, and then we break through the clouds and plummet toward the Atlantic Ocean, spinning below.

Terror courses through my veins as I take in the dark water full of ice and snow, the frigid air stinging my face and hands. But as terrifying as falling is, it's sure taking a long time. How am I going to get home—who's even going to find me down there? What will the Surface Dwellers do to me? *What will Peter do to me?* I start struggling again.

"Are you insane!?" I scream when I regain enough control to form words, and Peter winces, opening his mouth to speak. I don't let him. "I trusted you, I was going to help you! Let me go-"

"Rachel the para—" Peter's voice is hoarse, hardly audible above the howling of the wind, but I thrash against him, cutting him off.

"Shut up!" I dig my nails into his sides, and he gasps, his grasp loosening slightly. I struggle to get away from him. I pound my fist against his ribs, and he lets go of me with a sharp cry, twisting in the air to try and grab hold of me again. Fear flashes through his eyes, but I windmill my arms, trying to stay away from him. My eyes fall on the water far below, and fresh panic floods my chest. I clutch on the folded rubber raft as it slips down my arm. What am I going to do if I survive this fall? I can't find my way on my own down there, I'll freeze to death, even with my heat reflective clothes.

Peter angles his body toward me, slamming into me hard and forcing his arm under the back of my harness again. He pries the oxygen mask off my face and presses it over his own mouth and nose. I feel his chest expand as he gasps the air, and I choke as the oxygen is ripped from my lungs. He pulls it away from his mouth, his face twisting again.

"Rachel, what about the-" He starts again, but I bite his shoulder, pushing at his chest. Peter cries out, and—to my utter fury—bites me back until I let go of him, tightening his grasp around my body.

I thrash against him, hollering again even as he presses the oxygen mask back over my mouth and nose. Our altitude is low enough now that it's a little easier to breathe anyway, and I rub it off. "I bet you don't even *have* a brother! You're nothing but a stupid, selfish-"

"*RACHEL THE PARACHUTE!*" Peter screams, his eyes wide. I suddenly realize how close the ocean is, and my anger dissipates almost completely. Peter lets go of me with one arm as I fumble for the strap, and we jolt as the chute explodes behind us, jerking us around. My shirt hikes way up in the back. Peter looks like he's going to pass out. The chute continues to expand, billowing into a full circle and slowing our fall to an easy descent. The silence is deafening compared to the roaring of the wind earlier. Peter's body trembles against mine, his arms wrapped tight around me.

Dad was right this whole time—Surface Dwellers really are just savages that need to be put in line. Whatever my father did to Peter, he probably deserved it—he definitely does now. I can't believe I tried to help him. I start squirming again, trying push him off. "MY FATHER'S GOING TO KILL YOU!"

"Rachel," Peter croaks, his voice sounding weak. "I'm right here, you don't have to scream your bloody head off."

"When we land so help me God I'm going to kill you and find my own way home," I say, low and threatening. Peter doesn't respond, his head resting on my shoulder and both his arms squeezing me tighter, and I realize how difficult it is for him to keep from falling. I start to pry at his arms, but his grasp tightens until it hurts. I stop, panic rising in my chest. This is not what I had in mind for my first trip to the Surface. "Peter you're insane what were you thinking I was going to take you home if you couldn't wait that long you could've just jumped and pulled your own stupid chute-"

"Shut up Rachel," He growls, and I fall silent.

The waves of the Atlantic grow closer. The water looks like an ice cold drink, and I wonder what kind of sea creatures lurk beneath its surface. I have heard stories of sea monsters—ancient dinosaurs that have been hiding in the depths of the ocean for centuries—and I hope they are exaggerations. I clutch the life raft tight in my hands; they're already starting to get numb with the cold, and I don't want to drop our only chance of survival. We're about twenty feet above the surface of the water when the sound of an engine reaches my ears. Peter stiffens, lifting his head off my shoulder as if it weighs a ton, and I give him a smug look.

"That would be my father."

Peter pales, the little color in his face draining. A small unmanned hovercraft whizzes past us, circling around and flying past again.

"You're lucky," I spit, glaring as he flinches. "It's only a drone."

But Peter's eyes are huge.

"Peter, I said it's just a drone." As soon as I say it, a spray of bullets zip into the water. I stare after it, horrified.

Peter's entire body goes rigid, and he looks desperately down at the ocean, but we're still fifteen feet above the surface at least. I panic again, and I follow the drone with my eyes. Why do we even have weaponized drones!

The drone circles back around, shooting at us again, and Peter screams, falling away from me. He swipes at the air frantically, but I'm just out of reach, and his back slams into the water fourteen feet below.

"Peter!" I scream as he sinks beneath the waves. The engine gets louder again, and I play dead as the drone flies past, praying that it won't shoot me. The drone circles a few more times, then buzzes off, soaring across the Atlantic toward the shore.

Once it's gone, I bounce in my harness, trying to fall faster. I don't see Peter anywhere. It seems like ages before I splash into the frigid water. I gasp, goosebumps rising up all over me despite my heat reflective clothes. I squirm out of my parachute harness and dive underwater, straining to see through the darkness. Peter is sinking away from the dim light of the Surface, and I kick toward him. Blood stains the water around him and swirls away as I hook my arm around his chest and struggle upward.

I resurface, gasping and fighting to keep his head above water. The folded rubber square drifts near where I had hit the water, and I paddle to it, hitting the button on the strap and ducking under the water as it explodes into a raft. I splash and kick and struggle to get Peter in the raft. It's impossible. He keeps slipping and he's out cold, so he's no help. I feel like crying or giving up because I don't think he is breathing and I don't think I can do this. But I can't give up. Then suddenly, with a boost from a wave, we're both in the raft. I lay on top of him panting and shivering.

I don't have the luxury of resting. Peter's lips are blue. I can't feel his pulse, and I start pumping his chest, the raft pitching up and down. I start to wonder if I am doing any good when he lurches and rolls onto his stomach choking up blood and water.

He wheezes and his lips turn slightly more pink, but they are still very blue. His eyes roll back up into his head and he passes out again, but his chest is rising and falling.

My eyes fall on three bloody holes across his back, one in his ribs, one on the edge of his left shoulder blade, and one dangerously close to his spine. I swallow hard, trembling, but the blood is only seeping. Whether it's from cold or shock, I have no idea—hopefully that means he won't bleed out before we get to shore. The raft has a medical kit in its supply bag but I want to wait until we are on shore so none of the healing devices get wet. And I don't want to stick around to find out how long it takes to start seeing fins. Or sea dinosaurs. Are they attracted to blood too?

I open the raft's tiny cargo bag and pull out the collapsible propeller. I unfold it and twist the reinforced plastic pieces to catch and hold its form, then hold it over the back of the raft, pressing the button so that the propeller chops through the water.

We slowly push through the waves toward the icy shore, and all the while I feel tears streaming down my face. My eyes dart over the undulating surface of the ocean, alert for danger; a dorsal fin, a head rising out of the water on a long neck.

After the asteroids hit, sea dinosaurs started resurfacing all over the planet. I've always wanted to see one, but now that I'm here, the thought of a mosasaur swimming around underneath us terrifies me. I'm so tense that when the raft jumps beneath me, I scream, yanking the motor out of the water. Peter's blood stains the bottom of the raft, pooling around his body and oozing toward me. Sharks can smell blood in the water from a long ways away, and I don't want to think about how fast they might get here.

Nothing happens. I don't see any fins, so I stick the motor back in the water.

We putt along at such a slow pace that I start to panic again. The shoreline comes into focus, agonizingly slowly.

Peter is bleeding out beside me. There's too much blood. It's everywhere. I reach over with one hand to press against one of the wounds in Peter's back, but I can't cover all of the injuries.

We're almost to the shore when I hear a rumble behind us, and I look quickly over my shoulder. A chill runs up my spine. The head of a sea dinosaur snakes out of the tossing waves, hissing at us.

I scream, barely remembering to hold onto the motor as the waves caused by the beast surfacing pitches the raft, sending us hurling faster toward shore. The beast propels itself toward us, its head continuing to rise out of the water like a Loch Ness monster, rows of sharp teeth lining its upper and lower jaws. Its head must be as big as a hovercraft—big enough to swallow us in one gulp.

Suddenly, it stops, thrashing angrily, its tail whipping up out of the water, its flippers splashing and slapping.

It's too shallow. I realize, relief flooding through my chest.

The dinosaur—a plesiosaurus I think—darts its head forward, but it's much too far behind now, and I slump back against the rubber side of the raft, breathing a sigh of relief. I turn back to shore to see that we're finally there, a solid sheet of ice stretching all the way to the base of a cliff. The raft bumps into the ice, nearly dumping us out into the water. Behind us, the plesiosaurus scoots back from the shallows and slinks back into the sea. *No eating here tonight.*

"Peter? Peter get up, we need to get out." I shake him, but he remains unconscious, shivering and bleeding. A fine trickle of blood oozes from the corner of his mouth and from his nose. "Peter—come on." I'm crying harder now, scared to be alone on the Surface. Chunks of ice float around us, but our heat reflective clothes should keep us from freezing to death right away.

The raft lurches again, and I climb out, stepping onto the ice and sliding my arms under Peter's. Grunting from the effort, I haul him out of the raft, staggering under his dead weight as he slumps against me. Regaining my balance, I stumble away from the edge of the ice, collapsing in the wet snow. Peter sucks in a sharp breath, shuddering awake, and I groan. "Of course you wake up now."

Peter doesn't respond, blinking dazedly at me. His eyes fix on a point somewhere further down the beach, where the cliff rises up from the snowy ice. He points, his hand shaking. "There."

"What are you talking about?"

I don't see anything, but Peter struggles to get his feet under him, only to collapse again. His cry cuts off in a strangled cough, splattering the snow with blood.

"You idiot, you freaking kidnapped me!" I'm angry all over again, wiping my eyes furiously. I stare around at the white and gray world. *How am I going to get home?* "Why on earth would you do something like that?!"

Peter's body convulses and he passes out again, his pale green eyes staring blankly into the distance. Only the shaky rise and fall of his chest tells me that he's still alive. I hate his guts, but I don't want to be alone down here in the middle of nowhere. I take the healing devices and first aid kit out of the raft's bag, shoving them into my pockets. I grab his wrists and start to drag him in the direction he had pointed, but he's so freaking *heavy*. I keep slipping in the snow and losing my grip on his hands and falling backwards.

After I trip for the fifth time, I let him fall. I want to give up, to just leave him here and let him freeze, but I can't bring myself to do something like that—even if he deserves it. And I've got to keep moving, that way I stay warm: my heat reflective clothes won't work if I don't have any heat to reflect. Peter is already shivering a little. I want to heal him now—at least enough so that he's conscious and can help—but now that I think of it, I don't want to be out here long enough for wolves or polar bears to find us. Plus, if I heal Peter enough that he can walk, what will he do to me?

I wipe the tears from my eyes, looking back and forth from him to the cliff face. Now that we're closer, I can sort of see a pile of rocks against its base, and I wonder if there's some kind of cave. Why else would Peter want to go there? But we're still so far away.

I lug him across the beach, drawing slowly closer to the cliff face as Peter grows paler with every step. I try pulling him on my back, his arms over my shoulders, but all that does is force me to stop, his deadweight bringing me to my knees. I thought I was stronger than this. I thought dragging him would be easier, but I'm hardly even doing that. I'm just stumbling on, inch by inch, the deep snow making it all the more difficult to push forward.

I'm not sure what keeps me going—maybe the thought of the warmth and food that might be waiting for me in Peter's cave—but I *finally* reach the pile of rocks, which is much bigger than I thought. I collapse in the snow, sobbing in relief, but I can't stay here. If this is a cave, I need to get inside. I pull myself together, staggering back to my feet. Leaving Peter, I scramble around the pile, searching for some sort of entrance and finding nothing.

"Peter you idiot," I growl, but then my eyes fall on large, heavy looking rock that sits loosely beneath a sort of archway made by two bigger boulders with one long flat one across the top. The rest of the pile is packed tightly, with mud and snow filling the cracks.

I try to pull the loose rock away, then push at it with my shoulder. There's an empty space behind it, revealing a small opening just big enough for someone to crawl through. I hurry back to Peter, hauling him over to the opening and pulling him in behind me. In the dim light from outside, I see a large candle sitting by the entrance, a box of matches at its base.

I strike a match and light the candle, revealing a wide open space that's actually much homier than I had expected. There's a makeshift table pressed against the wall—a dingy, scuffed up chest with two cracked plastic chairs on either side of it. Against the other wall, there's a dirty white plastic cooler that looks like it's been through an explosion—probably something salvaged from a destroyed city after the asteroid struck. Next to it, sitting against another giant chest, are two pair of heavy duty snow boots that look new. It takes me a moment, but I realize that they must've belonged to two Suppliers at one point. I swallow, wondering what happened to them.

I consider leaving, shutting up the cave and trying to find a hovercraft or maybe signal to one, but then I decide against it. I have no idea how to survive down here, and Peter might be my only hope. *If he isn't completely insane....*

I push the heavy boulder back, blocking the entrance again, then look around some more, making sure the cave is empty. There's a tunnel in the back left corner, and, with a worried glance at Peter, I leave him by the entrance, taking the candle and exploring quickly to make sure we're alone.

The tunnel leads to two rooms, the roof getting low before opening to another space with two cots that have chests at the end of them. The other room branches off of this one, through a tunnel that's so low I almost have to crawl to get through it. It's not quite as spacious as the first two, and it's empty except for one giant chest. I quickly find out why this room is empty; it's cold and wet, condensation making the walls slick and shiny, the sand of the floor damp under my shoes.

Convinced there's no one else here, I hurry back to the main cave, dragging Peter into the room with the cots and heaving him onto one—which is difficult to do with only one hand. Glancing around, I set the candle down on the chest at the end of the cot, rolling him onto his back. I pull off his overcoat, and I grimace at his once white shirt, stained red with blood. I swallow hard, turning him back onto his stomach and lifting his shirt, pulling it over his head. I frown; the cloth is supposed to be heat-reflective, but it's as cold as Peter's skin. I fling it away. Something's not right here.

I turn back to Peter and gasp, sickened by what I see. I had been expecting three bullet holes, where the drone had shot him, but there is so much more than that. His back and sides are crisscrossed with burn marks and lash marks—some half healed—and his broken ribs are blackened with bruises. His waist is much narrower than I had expected, and his ribs are clearly visible. I swallow hard, appalled, and some of my anger toward him fades. I can't heal all this with the one device I have.

"What....?" *Happened to you?* I can't even finish the sentence out loud. I pull the healing device from the raft out of my pocket, trying to steady my hands.

The drone's weapon wasn't very powerful; the bullets are lodged in the bone of his shoulder blade and the solid muscle near his spine. I run my fingers over his scarred and bruised ribs to where the lump of the third bullet protrudes. Thankfully it didn't penetrate the wall of his lung;

the projectile's force had not been powerful enough to pierce the membrane. No doubt it left a nasty bruise on his lung, though. That would explain why he kept spitting up blood.

I take a deep breath, swallow back the bile in my throat, then push the tweezers into the bullet wound in his ribs. Peter's face twists in pain and his body shudders, but his eyes remain shut. I turn the tweezers, pressing them in deeper and trying to find the path of the bullet.

When I find it, I follow it until I almost lose the tweezers in his flesh, barely managing to grab the bullet without throwing up. I pull it out, grimacing at the sound it makes when it scrapes against his ribs. I drop the bit of metal onto the sandy floor, kicking it under the cot as I use the healing device to seal the wound and the burns around it.

I dig out the other two bullets, healing those injuries as well. With the little energy left in the device, I heal the worst of the burns on his back and sides. I roll him onto his back and choke back a gasp at the mess that is his chest. Several cuts and bruises mar his skin, and I use the rest of the energy healing as much as I can, until mini TRRD's energy runs out. It's not enough. I throw the useless thing aside and just stare at him, still in shock.

"Who did this to you?" I whisper, terrified of the answer. The wounds are too recent to have happened when he was still on the Surface. I knew my father was hurting him—but Dad couldn't have done all *this*, could he?

I remember the chest in the other room, and I crawl through the little tunnel. Maybe they keep their BRRDs and TRRDs in there.

I open the chest, lifting the candle so I can see inside, and what I see shocks me; heavy duty weapons have been packed into the chest; sniper rifles, military issue machine guns, AR fifteens, semi-automatic pistols—even a few of the Supplier's nanotech weapons.

I cringe. Nanotech weapons are like the reverse of BRRDs: they eat flesh rather than repair it. Only high-ranking Suppliers have these, they are strictly regulated—how did Peter get one? And—what happened to the Suppliers who carried them?

I glance over my shoulder to the tunnel to the other room, where Peter is. Who is this guy? Who am I helping?

I'm tempted to take a gun, but I'm not sure I could bring myself to shoot Peter, even if he attacked me.

I dig through the chest, but that's all there is: weapons and ammunition. No BRRDs or TRRDs, not even a first aid kit.

I slam the lid shut, chewing on my lower lip. I can't just leave Peter the way he is, even if he did kidnap me. There's gotta be a TRRD somewhere. I duck back into the other room.

The other two chests in here have nothing but clothes and blankets in them, and the ones in the entrance room have no tissue or bone repair devices either.

I sit down in the sand next to Peter's cot, frustrated. Don't they have anything useful down here?

My eyes fall on Peter's green uniform.

The overcoat looks a little lumpy, and I pick it up; the fabric is thin—without the layer of heat reflective material lining the inside. But it feels heavier than it should. I feel in the pockets, finding two more healing devices.

"You dirty, thieving, double crossing—" I stop myself.

These TRRDs are a little more powerful than the ones from the rafts medical kit, and I use one of them to heal more of Peter's cuts. I'm about to use all of the second one, but I stop myself before it's empty: I might need it later.

I note where his wounds are still not fully healed, partly to judge the need for more first aid, and partly in case he tries to attack me when he wakes up—I'll know where to hit him to make him hurt. And where's his parachute? Why doesn't he have one? He should have the same harness that I had on under his shirt but it's not there.

I shake myself out of the shock. I can't afford to just stand around staring. If his clothes aren't heat reflective, then I need to get him out of them before he freezes to death—he's already shivering harder. I push him onto his back and undo his belt, silently praying that he doesn't wake up. I leave him in his boxer shorts and hang his wet clothes over one of the chests. I open the other chest, the one with the musty clothes and thick wool blankets.

I drape three of the blankets over Peter, who is now shivering violently. Although I healed most of his wounds, there are still several burns across the small of his back, and judging by the number of bruises I think some of his ribs might be broken. The devices can heal bruises, and there are plenty of those, but I don't heal them—they're not the worst of his injuries. At least he's not as broken as he was before.

I pull two wool blankets around my shoulders and wander with the candle into the other room, opening the chest beside the cooler and finding it filled with firewood and kindling, and I notice the axe propped up against the wall beside the chest. I snatch up the matches from where I left them and pile firewood and kindling into my arms, heading back to the room. I let the wood fall right in the middle of the cave, between the two cots. The sand is blackened and melted, and I see bits of charcoal here and there, so I assume it's safe to build a fire.

I set up the wood and hold the candle close to the kindling, silently praying that it's dry enough to catch fire. The thin twigs flare up, then die out. I grit my teeth, moving the candle to another piece of wood. This time, the kindling catches fire for real, and soon enough, the fire is crackling lively. I go back for more firewood—armfuls of it, until the chest is almost empty.

I glance over to Peter, who's still shivering, his skin pale and his eyes moving back and forth under his eyelids. He probably has a fever, which means he probably needs water. Where can I get water down here? It's not like I can give him saltwater. *Oh.* I slap my forehead. We're surrounded by snow, and I have a fire. *Duh.*

I go back to the entrance with the candle, lifting the lid of the table and finding a large empty ceramic jug, which I snatch up and take with me outside. I quickly fill it with snow, rolling the rock back in place.

I sit in front of the fire, blowing out the candle and setting it on one of the chests. Pulling the wool blankets tighter around me, I watch the flames without really seeing them as I hold the jug of snow near the flames. I want to go home, but all I can think of is Peter buckling under Dad's fist. How could I have been so stupid? How could I let this happen? And why didn't Peter tell me how bad it was? Gosh, how come I'm such an idiot? I should've just been happy with Malcolm, but nooooooo, stupid adventure girl wants to know more about the Surface. Stupid adventure girl wants to find out more about the stupid Surface Dweller with the stupid hot Irish accent. I bang my head against my knees. *Stupid!*

Mom's gonna be worried sick, and so is Dad. Are they looking for me now? Will they even know where to look? Will they *ever* find me? I want to stand out on the beach, so that maybe they'll see me, but I'm afraid. Peter had mentioned wolves and polar bears and those weird Siren things. He could have been lying but I don't want to find out. And what about Peter's brother? There is two of everything here. So he must not have been lying about his injured brother. For a second I hope he is dead, so he doesn't come home and find me here with his half-dead brother. Then fresh tears flow down my cheeks. Am I really the kind of person who would wish someone was dead, just to save my own skin?

Am I the same as the monster who left those scars on Peter's body?

No. I squeeze my eyes shut. I should be dead. This is my fault. I should've stood up for Peter—for Clayton too. If I had just stood up to my father, if I had just opened my eyes, then Clayton would still be here, and Peter never would've been brought up to the Glass City.

And then I had to go and make everything worse with my stupid feelings. I should have just kissed Malcolm back. But no, I had to get caught up in helping stupid Peter. He probably doesn't even care about me—except as a crazy way to escape my father. He probably hates me as much as he hates Dad—and I deserve it. I was probably the cause of most of his pain—why else would Peter try to hide it from me all this time?

Will I ever see Malcolm again? Will he even like me, when he thinks that I ran away with Peter?

The snow in the jug is melted, and I get up, hesitantly sliding my hand behind Peter's head and tilting the mouth of the jug against his lips. I can only get him to drink some of it, though, and the rest dribbles out over his chin. I give up and set the jug on one of the chests. Hopefully he'll wake up tomorrow, and he can drink some then. I can't have him dying of dehydration, I need him to survive down here. I don't know anything about the Surface.

I crawl onto the other cot with two wool blankets, too scared to fall asleep right away, even though it's getting late. What if Peter's brother comes home? What will he do to me? I pull the blankets up higher, as if they can protect me. Maybe he'll have mercy, since I tried to help Peter? Or maybe he won't come home at all.

I watch Peter shiver for a moment, contemplating on whether or not I should use the last healing device on him. Something tells me I shouldn't, though, and an overwhelming guilt suddenly weighs over me like another heavy blanket; those devices hadn't been meant for him.

Peter

The smell of smoke floods my senses.

We're in a cave, with a sandy floor and a fire crackling in between two cots; the one I'm on and another pressed against the opposite wall. I recognize it instantly as the same cave Felix and I had planned to move into.

Felix.

I try to sit up, but my head reels and I fall back. I have to get to him. I'm so bloody close.

Rachel is asleep on Felix's cot, and I watch her for a moment. What am I going to do with her? Her father is no doubt looking for her, I can't have him finding me with her. I can't leave her here either, not with the weapons in the other room—I don't want to come back here and get shot. Or worse, get Felix shot.

Rachel stirs, and I close my eyes. I don't feel like hearing whatever she has to say about my dragging her off the skydeck. Not that I could blame her for being pissed. I lay still, listening to her movements. She scuffs around in the sand a bit, then something cold and damp presses against my forehead. I flinch, my eyes flying open as I smack her hand away.

She squares her jaw. "I can't believe I'm helping you. I should've just left you on the beach. I would've been perfectly fine. I can't freeze to death out there like you can."

But that's not true, even with her special heat reflective clothes. At least, I know that. Scouts' thermal clothing is great in the short term: it holds in body heat, but it doesn't keep the cold out—especially if the wearer isn't moving. She continues her rant, but I tune her out—an art I had learned from years spent with Addy and her children—and look around blearily.

"Don't even think about trying anything, Peter." Rachel scowls at me. "My father will no doubt be looking for me by now, and this will be the first place he looks. I don't doubt that he knows where you live."

I grit my teeth, then realize that the pain isn't anywhere near as bad as it was before, and I'm no longer spitting up blood. I also realize that the only thing I'm wearing is my undershorts…. I pull down the blankets enough so that I can see my chest. There are still countless dark bruises, a few cuts and burns, and pain stabs me in the ribs every time I move but otherwise the majority of the damage done to me by Malcolm and Brown's men is gone.

"No," I mumble, pushing Rachel away from me and ignoring how sick I feel as I lean over the edge of the cot, scanning the room for the rest of my clothes. I see them draped over Felix's chest full of blankets at the end of his cot, and I reach for them..

Rachel holds up a small device. "Don't worry. There's one left."

I stare at it, my befuddled mind not fully comprehending what her words mean, mulling it over and trying to make sense of them. *One left.* I flop back down on the cot, staring at the ceiling of the cave and feeling the breath whoosh out of me. *No….* Those were supposed to be for Felix. He looked barely alive the last time I saw him, one stupid healing device isn't going to save him.

"Why?" I croak, feeling hot and uncomfortable.

"You—were suffering." For a moment she appears confused and guilty. "I—I'm sorry. I didn't think. You took them for your brother?"

I want to cry, to hide under the blankets and will it all away, but I take it like a man. *Grow up you big baby,* my brain orders in Felix's voice. I swallow back the lump in my throat and groan. "How long have I been out?"

"Maybe a day and a half."

"I have to get home," I mumble, leaning out of bed again and pulling the blankets with me.

"You have a fever!" Rachel protests. "You need time to recover…."

"I've recovered enough." My head swims when I stand and stumble over to the chest at the end of my bed. I drop to my knees, pulling out a pair of old ripped jeans and a T-shirt. I pull them on, then put on another pair of pants made of thick, smooth polar bear fur, as well as my father's old wolf fur coat. I shiver, burying my face in the fur collar and breathing in the familiar musty smell. I turn away from the chest, my stomach growling, and make my way through the tunnel to the main room without bothering to look at Rachel.

"HEY!" She yells, hurrying after me. "What are you doing? Where do you think you're going?" Her scowl deepens. "What do you mean you have to get home?! *This* isn't your home?!"

I ignore her, opening the old cooler and pulling out a small strip of smoked polar bear meat, smelling it to make sure it's still good. It's colder out here near the entrance, so the meat was well past frozen while I was gone. The cooler kept it from getting sandy. I open the chest that doubles as a table between the two crappy plastic chairs, and I pull out an old frying pan, a fork, and a knife.

Rachel follows me back to the fire glaring at me as I sit in front of the fire, dropping the meat into the cast-iron frying pan and holding the pan over the flames. For the ridiculous amount Felix and I paid for it, it sure has lasted us a long time.

"How am I going to get home?" Rachel demands.

I ignore her again, waiting patiently for the meat to cook. My stomach, on the other hand, snarls at me to hurry up. One side finishes, and I use the fork to flip it over. The smell is nothing like the rich, heavenly aroma of the foods in the Glass City—it smells rancid and gamey—but to me it smells like home.

"Are you even listening to me?"

"Hmm?"

Rachel throws her arms up and groans in exasperation, stomping around the fire. "Peter I hate you!"

The meat sizzles as I flip it over.

Rachel kicks at the sand. "How could you do this to me?! What did I ever do to *you*?! I was nice to you, Peter, I didn't hurt you!" She grows quiet.

The thin strip of meat is done. I set the frying pan on the ground and scoot a little ways away from the fire, cutting off a piece of meat and shoveling it into my mouth, finally relenting to my stomach's impatience. The flavor of the meat is just as gamey as the smell, nothing like the richness of the little bit of food I had in the Glass City, but I don't care. I'm far too hungry to be bothered about how it tastes.

Rachel yells again, stomping her foot. "What, do you want me for ransom or something?! Why didn't you have your own chute?!"

"Wasn't given one." My answer is muffled by mouthful of meat. I wonder if she's hungry, and I gesture with the pan. "Want some?"

She wrinkles her nose at my offer, but she doesn't answer. "What do you mean you weren't given one?!"

I shake my head, finishing my food much faster than I would've liked. I want more, but I need to get moving. The fork and knife rattle in the frying pan as I set it on the chest at the end of my bed. I point at a large jug on the chest. "Is that water?"

"Yeah, but-"

I snatch the jug off the chest, chugging down every last drop of water. Wiping the back of my sleeve across my mouth and tossing the jug onto my cot, I turn toward the small tunnel leading to the third room.

Rachel spits, "You're a *savage*."

My calm resolve snaps, and I whirl on her, baring my teeth and getting in her face. "*I'm* a savage? I haven't hurt you, I haven't tortured you. You're free to go. If you want to know who the *real* savage is, ask your father. I simply wanted to get home. And *you*." My upper lip curls. "bloody hell you wouldn't leave me *alone*! Every time you dragged me off somewhere, your father or your bloody boyfriend would beat the crap out of me, and I couldn't do anythin' about it because of the stupid device your bloody father stuck in my back!" I stiffen, suddenly remembering it. I hope I'm too far away to be in its range. I must be, otherwise Brown would have turned it on by now.

She looks horrified. "What device? What are you talking about? You're lying, Malcolm wouldn't hurt anyone-"

"I think ya know that's not true. Look, you were just an escape route. I needed your parachute, that's it. I didn't bloody have one. You're free to go."

"To go where?" Rachel exclaims.

"*ANYWHERE!*" I yell back, throwing my arms out to the sides for emphasis. "All ya have to do is tell someone who ya're and you've already got your ticket home. They'll hold ya for ransom, and your father will be there in a flash to blow them all away and take ya back home to your palace in the sky!"

"What is wrong with you?!"

"What's bloody wrong with *me?*"

"Ugh, it's just 'bloody' everything, isn't it? You dragged me off the *bloody* skydeck! Just because you want to go home doesn't mean you can *demand* to go home! We saved your life, Peter! My father could've just found-"

"Stop lyin' to yourself!" I yell, stepping closer to her until her back is pressed against the wall. Fear flashes in her eyes, but I'm too pissed off to care. "It's over Rachel. *Cop on!*" Could she really be this stupid?

"Your Suppliers don't save people on the Surface, they kidnap them! We don't have any *choice*, Rachel! You people take us from our homes and our families and make us your slaves! You torture us! And when we get too old, or when they grow tired of us, they just up and throw us out of the city, whether we're dead or alive! Lucky for those of us down here that some of your slaves find a way to leave a wee little piece of paper in their mouths with their bloody name on it so we have some way to identify the bloody remains of whoever it was they *murdered*!" I'm screaming now, but I don't care. "And if you're wonderin' where your friend Clayton is, why don't ya ask your temperamental boyfriend where he went!? After all, jealousy can be a mighty powerful thing!" I finish, my chest heaving and my upper lip curled in a snarl.

Rachel's eyes are huge, and she's trembling slightly.

I shake my head, guilt cooling my rage, but only a little. She did save my life, which is more than I would've done for someone who abducted me from my home. "You can't shut your eyes anymore. It's time to wake up." I turn away and crawl through the tunnel to the cavern at the back with the single chest pressed against the far wall. I scowl when I see that it's open.

I limp over to the chest and pull out a heavy sniper rifle, my hips still sore from where Malcolm had kicked me. I scope down the barrel, then sling it over my back, as well as a military issue M4. A semi-automatic pistol and one of the Scout's high tech nano-weapons slip into my waistband; I stole the daughter of the mayor of the Glass City, I have no doubt that I'm going to be hunted, even if she's not with me. Normally I would hesitate to carry such a formidable weapon, but after experiencing first-hand what the people of the Glass City do to Surface Dwellers, I don't think I'll mind using one of these flesh eating weapons on a Scout.

I strap on an old tool belt with several pockets, which I fill with ammunition, and I tuck in a knife grenade that my brother and I scored off a Scout a few years ago. I stuff as much ammunition as I can into my pockets before shutting the chest and crawling back into the bedroom.

Rachel is gone, but I don't look for her, picking up the uniform I had been forced to wear in the Glass City and tossing it into the fire, except for the green jacket. With waterproof pockets, this thing could come in handy, no matter how much I hate it. I pull off my wolf fur jacket and put on the green overcoat, snatching up the healing device Rachel had left on the edge of my cot and shoving it into the same pocket that has the picture of my parents in it.

I pull out one of Mum's old polar bear fur coats, something Felix kept, and sling it over my shoulder. Making sure nothing flammable is too close to the flames, I leave the fire to burn out and head into the other room, grumbling under my breath when I discover the entrance is open to the elements.

I pull on a pair of gloves from the table-chest, stuffing an extra pair in my pocket. I push my feet into the Scout boots my brother and I had stolen a few years ago, but Felix's boots are too big for Rachel, so I leave them here. She'll have to survive in her tennis shoes. They're probably heat reflective or something anyway.

I set the matches and the candle by the entrance, glancing around the cave one last time in case I've forgotten something. *Goggles.* I open the table, pulling out a pair of snow goggles. Then I crawl out and push the heavy boulder into place to keep the snow and animals out of our cave.

The wind is brisk and cold, chapping my cheeks instantly. White snow and ice spread from horizon to horizon, bordered by the steely strip of ocean to the west. I breathe in the fresh air, which is much richer than the stuffy Glass City air.

Home. Cold, bloody home. It's good to be back.

I make my way down the beach until the cliff slopes down into the snowy valley, through which a frozen river winds through.

Rachel's footprints precede me in the snow. She's annoying, but she did save my life. I can't just let her wander off into the frozen wasteland alone, she'll freeze to death—even with that thermal clothing. Or get eaten by a polar bear.

Colfer is just across the valley, but her footprints already lead in the wrong direction.

I trudge through the deep snow, my hands deep in my pockets and my face buried in the fluffy white-grey fur of my wolf skin coat, covering all the exposed skin on my face except my eyes, which are covered by the snow goggles.

I follow her tracks for about half an hour, amazed at how far she's gone in so little time, when I hear the first howl. My head snaps up, and I listen intently, wondering if it was just my imagination. But, sure enough, several more howls answer it, rising and falling through the still air.

I break into a dead run, moving as fast as I can through the knee high snow, my sore body killing me. Rachel screams somewhere ahead of me, but I still don't see her. I struggle to pick up my pace, pulling my rifle from my back and cocking it as I go.

I stumble up a small hill and see Rachel backed against a scraggly fir tree, surrounded by a pack of six wolves. She screams again, kicking snow into the face of one of the wolves that lunges forward; it jerks back, snapping at the cloud of white powder.

Four of them are full grown, their backs as tall as my waist, but two appear to be pups, only knee high, tops. I scope down my rifle and fire, shooting the next wolf that jumps at Rachel. The beast collapses in the snow, blood soaking the white-grey fur on the back of its head. Rachel jumps as I fire again, just sending up a puff of snow in front of her feet.

The wolves yelp and flinch back, their tails tucked between their legs. One sees me and starts to run toward me, and I blow it away before it takes more than one bound. I fire another shot just in front of their paws, and they all jump back, turning and racing off across the valley into the snowy remains of the old city. Blackened and broken by bombs dropped by the Glass City decades ago, the ruins are nothing but jagged skeletons of the buildings they used to be.

I slide down the hill, stopping in front of Rachel. Our breath fogs up the space between us. I point. "Colfer is that way you idiot." I backhand her upper arm. "If you want to live through this, don't go wanderin' off by yourself." I pull my mum's coat off of my shoulder and shove it and the extra pair of gloves toward her, then tramp up the other side of the valley, away from the blackened ruins. I pause, glancing over my shoulder when I realize Rachel hasn't moved; she's just staring at the coat in her hands. I gesture with my rifle. "Ya comin' or not?"

Rachel slowly pulls the coat over her shoulders and trips through the snow after me. I wait for her to catch up, then continue my trek up the hill, slinging my gun over my shoulder again and shoving my hands back in my pockets.

"These are Supplier gloves…." Rachel's voice sounds small.

I don't respond.

We crest the hill, stopping at the top and looking down on the sad sight of Colfer, a cluster of rundown buildings with patched up roofs and walls with extra supports on the outsides to hold them up. I lean against a snow covered rock, panting and clutching at my right hip, which hurts the most. Rachel glares at me, but I can see her worry. "Go home," I tell her, still trying to catch my breath.

"What?"

"You heard me," I growl.

"But—I don't know where to go."

"Anywhere. Go to the Dead Handlers, they'll bargain with your father in a heartbeat." Not that I think her father would make any kind of fair trade.

"Dead Handlers?" Rachel swallows.

"They're the ones who go drudge the bodies from the Atlantic. They trade information for food and supplies."

"But…."

"You're not comin' with me," I snarl.

"Peter-"

"No! I can't have your bloody father comin' after me when I'm with my brother."

Rachel is quiet for a moment. "Where did you hear that? I mean what you said before, about Clayton and Malcolm?"

I hesitate. "Ya know what? Don't think about it. Just, go home. Go back to believin' all those bloody lies your father tells you, and maybe you'll grow up to be like your mother. Perhaps ya won't be as harsh as the rest of the world if you remain a wee ignorant little girl."

Rachel's face twists. "You're such a jackass."

"Ah, language," I tell her, pushing off the rock and limping down the hill.

"I don't think I believe you!"

"Good!"

"Malcolm couldn't kill anyone. And nobody throws bodies into the Atlantic. We burn our dead."

"Aye, but Surface Dwellers aren't *your* dead, are we?" I growl. "If they didn't chuck the bodies, the Dead Handlers would have no dead to handle."

"Then they'd have Clayton's body."

I stop, realizing where she's going with this. "Rachel, if they have Clayton's body, then you're not goin' to want to see it."

"Clayton got hit by a bus, Peter. Malcolm didn't kill him." She sounds so smug, so certain, that I suddenly lose all sympathy.

I turn on her. "Ya really want to see him? Fine. Come with me." I lead her down the hill and through town to a large building that used to be some sort of gym, the dingy walls now cracked and crumbling in some places. The rest of the school is a burnt out shell around it. "When did he die?"

Rachel flinches. "Six days ago. The day before you got there."

Part of me is shocked at how short a time I spent in that wretched city, but another part of me cringes—five days is far too long. Felix's wounds were so severe. I push the thoughts away. "The Dead Handlers keep bodies for a week to give family time to claim their dead."

We enter the small foyer outside the main room, and I pull off my goggles. I drop a box of ammunition for a semiautomatic rifle on the scuffed wooden surface of the front desk.

The man at the desk looks up from his stack of papers, which are worn and frail from being written on and erased so many times. "First name?"

"Clayton."

The man ruffles through his papers, squinting through his cracked glasses. "Last name?"

I look to Rachel. "What was his last name?"

"I…. don't know."

"Blast." I grit my teeth. "Don't know it," I tell the man.

The Dead Handler looks up again, then back at his papers. He huffs a sigh, then gets to his feet. He gestures for us to follow as he pushes through the double doors and into the giant room beyond.

Rachel's eyes grow huge when they fall on the rows and rows of broken bodies, stretching from wall to wall. All of them are naked, covered by grimy white sheets; the green servants uniforms must be recycled in the Glass City. A few people stand over loved ones, some leaning against each other and crying softly, others standing in silence.

A few bodies are uncovered, exposing their crushed ribs and bloodless gashes. One of them is riddled with bullet holes, and I wonder if he was still alive when he was thrown off the City, picked off in midair by the drones.

The man moves three rows down, then about thirty bodies back before he stops. "There're only three Clayton's, you're standin' in front of them. I'm sorry for your loss." With that, he turns and leaves.

"Find what you're lookin' for?" I ask impatiently.

Rachel doesn't respond, but her expression tells me she has. She takes a few slow steps forward and drops to her knees beside a man in his early twenties, with blonde hair and green eyes that stare blankly up at the ceiling. There's bruising around his neck, but not because it's broken; the bruises are clearly from a pair of hands. I recognize him instantly as the man Felix and I had pulled out of the Atlantic almost a week ago.

Rachel gently pulls down the sheet enough to reveal the man's broken chest, which has been pounded to the point of caving in, broken bone jutting up from his pale skin. The faint outline of a boot print is evident in the center of the damage. Rachel chokes, covering her mouth with her hand. With trembling fingers, she touches Clayton's face, then falls back, sobbing.

I watch her for a moment, then sigh, stooping and closing the man's eyes and pulling the sheet back up over his face, a custom that lets the Dead Handlers know that they can burn the body.

As I do, I relive the moment Felix and I came to this place, when I was six. My father had been in the Glass City for years. Someone had banged on Addy's door until Felix opened it, and it turned out to be Jimmy with an odd expression on his face. Jimmy's oldest son, Garret, was a Dead Handler, and had recognized our father on sight. It was the first and only time I had ever seen him in person, and Felix had pulled the sheet over his bruised face.

Clayton's blank eyes, the bruises and burns all across his chest and crushed ribs—they are a mirror of my father on that day.

I shake my head, throwing the memory to the back of my mind when my eyes start to burn. "Rachel, I have to leave," I tell her. "Tell the Dead Handler at the desk who ya are, and you'll be home in no time."

But Rachel stands, wiping her eyes and sniffing. "I'm coming with you."

"Like hell you are. Go home," I spit.

"No. And if you leave me, I'll follow you."

I grit my teeth. "And if you follow me, I'll blow your head off." I wouldn't, but she doesn't know that.

Rachel pales, but she squares her jaw and holds my gaze defiantly.

I scoff. "You don't even care! Why do ya want to come with me? Do ya think it'll be an adventure? 'Cause it won't be, I can assure ya that."

"Maybe I can help," She offers, and I roll my eyes.

"I don't need a bunch of Scouts after me, Rachel. Just go home."

"No."

I jerk my hand up, on the verge of slapping her, and she flinches. All she's ever done is cause me pain, and yet she acts as though she's not responsible. I'm so sick of her stubbornness—can't she see she's only putting my brother in danger? She'll lead her psychopathic father right to him!

Rachel is still, her blue eyes wide as if she's certain I'll hit her. But I can't. I'm not like her father.

I screw up my face, throwing my fist down at my side and turning away from her. "Gah! Fine! Come with me! But as soon as I even catch sight of a Scout, I'm ditchin' you and runnin' for the hills." I turn my back on her and storm out, pulling my goggles back on as the wind blasts snow into my face.

I keep to the wide road through the middle of town. It's hard packed enough from constant traffic that a heavy sled and a horse won't sink in the snow. The old shacks of Colfer look just as gray and crappy as they always have. I want to run, to find Addalynn and find out where Felix is, but I'm afraid of the answer. What if I'm too late? What if Felix is already gone? What am I going to do? I could live in our cave, but I'm not sure I could handle being alone in the home we'd created. Maybe I could move to Hearthtown. *No.* I shake my head, blinking back tears. I'd stay with Addy. I'd take care of my family, no matter how much I hate them. It's what Felix would do. And besides, there are Scouts constantly swarming Hearthtown, and with my current status with the Glass City, I think it's better to avoid Scouts at all cost—more so than usual. But I only have one healing device. If Jimmy doesn't have any, then I'll *have* to go to Hearthtown; if Felix is still alive, one device isn't going to help much. Not with his injuries.

Despite my instructions to go home, Rachel follows me all the way to Jimmy's trading shop. I limp up to the counter and pound my fist against it. My ribs and hips are both killing me now, and the small of my back burns like fire.

Jimmy hurries out from the back of the shop, muttering, "I'm comin', I'm comin'." He looks up and his face goes slack.

"Peter?"

I release a breath that was supposed to be a laugh, but sounds more like a wheeze, my cracked ribs making it difficult. "Aye Jimmy, it's me."

Jimmy's mouth drops open. "How....?" He shakes his head in wonder, his short blonde hair falling across his forehead, his blue eyes wide. "Never in all this time since the asteroid struck has any one of us ever come back from the Glass City alive. And yet here ya are."

"Aye, here I am." I drum my fingers on the counter.

Jimmy grins. "Someone shoulda told those city folk that you brothers are known for finishin' your fights!" He looks at Rachel, expecting an introduction.

I ignore good manners. "And…. Felix?"

Jimmy's interest in Rachel dissipates. "He's alive, but…. it's not good, Peter. I helped as much as I could, but I only get so much of the Scout's high tech healin' junk, and it just wasn't enough. Addy and the kids are holed up with Kelly. Felix is there. It's good that you're back before….You can say your goodbyes."

I feel the air whoosh out of me. "Thank you, Jimmy. I appreciate it." I slap a box of ammunition on the table. "Any chance I could get a wool blanket?"

"For Felix? Anythin'. And don't bother with that." He pushes the ammunition back, shaking his head. "No one survives the Glass City. You're a dead man walkin'. I don't barter with the dead."

I stuff the ammunition back into a pocket on my belt as Jimmy hurries to the back of the shop, then returns with a thick wool blanket in his arms. "Thanks," I tell him.

Jimmy nods, then nods to Rachel. "Who's this?"

"My escape route," I mumble, and leave it at that, limping out of the building and down the street. Kelly's tanner shop is just outside the village, beyond what's left of Addy's house. I stop at the blackened remains poking out of the snow. There's a hole in the floor, and snow drifts through, covering the rubble in the cellar with a thick blanket of white.

"What's this?" Rachel asks.

"Home," I mutter. I have always hated living at Addy's, but that doesn't change the fact that this is where I grew up. Whether I like it or not, it was home, once.

"What…. happened?"

I clench my teeth. "Your father blew it up." I keep walking, staggering through the snow until Kelly's tanner shop appears through the falling snowflakes, the rickety old house beside it looming black against the darkening sky. I wobble up to the porch and pound on the door, waiting for it to open. "Don't say anythin'," I mumble.

"Why?" Rachel wants to know.

"You're not from here," I say just as the door opens to a haggard looking Addy, her graying blonde hair frizzy and her green eyes tired. I see Kelly behind her, tending to a fire in the stove. His white hair is disheveled, and he appears more hunched than I remember, even though I haven't been gone for even a week.

Addy's eyes almost pop out of her head, and she does a double take. "Peter? I—how—but—you were taken!"

I push past her, eager to get out of the cold and welcoming the warmth of the fire. "Aye, and now I'm back. Where's Felix?"

Addy swallows, looking worried. Behind her, Kelly looks up, a frown of disbelief pulling at his face.

"Peter?"

"Yes I'm bloody back, now where's my brother?" I pull off my gloves and shove them into my pocket.

Addy startles me by taking my hand and leading me to the back of the small house. She opens a door at the end of a short hall, and the smell of burnt flesh and infection hits me in the face like a blow. I swallow a gag, wrinkling my nose—and then the world grinds to a screeching halt when I see my brother.

Felix is lying on his back on a makeshift cot, the head of it pressed against the middle of the wall to my right. His eyes are closed and his dark red hair plastered to his forehead with sweat. The right side of his face is raw, bloody flesh, as is his right arm from his shoulder to his elbow; he had covered me just before the grenade went off.

I can't find words, can't even remember how to speak, and Addy touches my shoulder lightly.

"His back is worse, but not as bad as it was before. Jimmy helped a bit, and we've removed all the shrapnel, but there's nothin' more we can do. We used half the bottle of medicinal alcohol and almost all the gauze, we don't have enough to cover all the burns. Merry left a few days ago to try and get some supplies from the shop up in Hearthtown, he should be back soon."

Merry was Addy's oldest son, and although he's always been irritating beyond all reason, he's also always been my favorite; he's not nearly as snobbish as the rest of his siblings.

"I can't tell if he's gettin' better. Even Kelly is scared."

Although Kelly is the tanner, he's also sort of a doctor; he had just graduated from college with a degree in doctoring when the asteroids hit.

I want to take a step forward, to move to my brother's side, but my legs buckle and I collapse to my hands and knees, not wanting to believe what my eyes are telling me. I leave the blanket I'd gotten from

Jimmy and crawl over to the edge of Felix's cot, leaning my chest on the edge of it and touching Felix's left shoulder, the one that's closest to me.

My touch is light, but Felix's eyes flicker open all the same, blinking blearily before clearing. I swallow hard, seeing that his right eye is foggy, the blue iris pale and dull. His gaze falls on me, but my face doesn't seem to register right away, his clear left eye moving slowly over my face as he tries to process what he's seeing.

At last he frowns slightly, his lips parting. "P-*Peter?*" He croaks, and I force a smile, blinking back tears and nodding. "Am…. am I dead?"

"No." My voice breaks, but I cover it with a short laugh, placing my hand on the top of his head and resting my forehead against his. "No, you're not dead."

"But…. you…." Felix licks his lips, wincing. "You—came back."

"Course I did, I promised," I tell him, squeezing my eyes shut to keep out the tears. I remember the device, and I unbutton the front of my wolf fur coat, pulling the device out of the pocket of my green overcoat and holding it up so that Felix can see it. "I brought this. I had more, but." I trail off, looking down and to the right, where I can see Rachel's wet, snow clumped tennis shoes. I shake my head. "I don't know how it works," I tell her. There are two red buttons, and I don't know the difference between the two.

Rachel hesitates, then takes the device from my hand. Addy appears to recognize the device. "The worst burns are on his back, I suggest you take care of those," she says, then leaves the room.

I move to the other side of the cot, helping Felix sit up and almost stopping at the horrible sounds he makes. The blanket slides down some, revealing his back, and I want to throw up. The entire right side of his back is charred and bloody, all the way up from his hip to his shoulder, but the left side of the burn is a straight line—evidence that the wound had indeed been worse, and had been healed.

Rachel looks sick, but she has Felix lean forward a bit more, exposing more of his back until she can see as far as she dares, stopping when she can see the bottom of his hip. As far as I can tell, the burn stretches all the way down the back of his right leg, but I'm aware of Rachel's discomfort, so I say nothing of it.

One side of the wound is a straight line, as if someone had taken a healing device and swept it up and down one half of the burn. Instead of using the rest of the energy in the device to heal the burn in the same way, Rachel moves the device over the bottom of the burn, healing all the way across before shifting the device up. When she reaches the small of his back, she stops, repositioning the device at the peak of his shoulder—the top of the burn. From there she continues her work down, until the device stops working and she throws it on the floor with tears in her eyes. The burn is considerably smaller, now stretching from the small of his back to the base of his right shoulder blade. Felix groans as I lay him back down, pulling the blankets up to his chin.

"Don't you dare die on me," I tell him, placing my hand back on the top of his head. I rest my other hand on the left side of his face, my arm across his chest in an awkward hug, and bury my face in his shoulder. "Don't even think about it."

Felix manages to move his hand up to the back of my head, and he huffs a sigh that sounds like it's supposed to be a laugh. "Wouldn't dream of it," He croaks, and I smile through the tears that have finally begun to fall.

Rachel

I watch Peter in silence as he holds his brother, his face hidden. The room is small, but not cramped—it's too empty to be cramped. The floor is covered with thick furs, which is much nicer than the sandy floor of Peter's cave. Even the walls have furs hanging off them—insulation, maybe? I shiver. The people down here don't seem too bad, but they definitely need a hand in home decor.

After a little while, Felix falls limp, and Peter pulls away, his eyes red. He removes his brother's hand from the back of his head and leans back on his knees, rubbing his face.

Behind me, the door bursts open, and Peter and I both jump. A short, dark haired boy, who appears to be maybe eleven, stands in the doorway. He looks at Peter with huge eyes, then races around the cot and slams full force into Peter, hugging him. "Ava's dead. So is Patrick. They were crushed when the roof collapsed."

Peter chokes back a cry as the boy's grasp tightens, looking confused, but after a second he hugs the boy back and buries his face in his shoulder. Tear flow down his cheeks unchecked.

I don't think I have ever seen Peter so vulnerable as this moment—come to think of it I don't think I have ever seen any man so unashamed to show his feelings. Not Malcolm or my father—even Clayton was always careful with his feelings, but that might've been because he was afraid to show them.

My eyes drift to Felix, who's still unconscious. He's got the same hard, chiseled features as Peter, the same dark red-brown hair, but his eyes are blue rather than green. And the entire right half of his face is gone almost all the way to the bone, his right eye clearly blind. I understand now; I see why Peter wanted to get back so bad. My father did this to them. My people. And I let it happen.

I feel my own tears well up for Clayton. I wish he'd had someone who was that devoted to him—obviously it wasn't me. Heartsick, and I wipe away my tears. I don't want to take anything away from Peter's moment with my own self-pity.

The image of Clayton comes back to me. The way his chest was crushed. It couldn't've been Malcolm who did that to Clayton, to my *best* friend. I couldn't even imagine him doing it, let alone why.

Jealousy can be a mighty powerful thing, Peter had said. But why would Malcolm be jealous of Clayton? Clayton had been like a brother. There had never been anything else—that would have been weird.

I tilt my face to hide my tears, blinking them back furiously; I don't want to show these Surface Dwellers any sign of weakness.

Peter finally pulls away, holding the boy at arms-length. "I thought ya hated me?"

"I could say the same about you." The boy wipes his nose on his sleeve. "Why'd ya save me?"

Peter glances at me before saying, "Because I've seen what they do to people like us up there, and ya never would've survived. I almost didn't."

"You don't look too bad." The boy frowns.

"Aye, I had a bit of help."

The boy looks over his shoulder at me curiously. "Who's that?"

"My escape route."

"What?"

"I didn't have a parachute, she did. She was the only way I could get out of the city, and now she won't leave me alone."

I scowl again, and the boy smirks. "She's from the Glass City?"

I stiffen. These people view Glass City folks as monsters—which I guess they're right. My people torture them. But what will the Surface Dwellers do to me?

"Aye, but don't ya tell anyone or I'll cut out your tongue. Cole, meet Rachel." Peter doesn't smile when he gestures to me.

"She's goin' to have a hell of a time gettin' used to it down here."

"She's leavin' as soon as I can get rid of her." Peter glares.

I return his look, crossing my arms over my chest. It's bad enough that I *feel* like an observer, but he doesn't have to talk about me like I'm not here. I'm not even sure I want to go home now, anyway— what is there to go home to? My father the monster and Malcolm the jealous and abusive jerk who still thinks there's hope for the two of us?

Peter turns back to Cole. "I have to leave. Can you promise me you'll take care of my brother?"

"Where are ya goin'?" Cole asks.

Peter sits back on his toes. "To Hearthtown." He points at me. "I need to get rid of her, and I need to get more healin' devices for Felix."

I want to ask why, but I remember that my accent would give me away, so I keep my mouth shut. I thought some guy named Merry already went to Hearthtown for supplies. Why would Peter go there? My blood turns cold. What if by 'get rid of her' he means he's going to kill me? I shake the thought away. *No, if he were going to do that, he wouldn't have saved me from those wolves.*

"Why are you so eager to get rid of her?" Cole wants to know.

"Because she's the daughter of the blasted mayor, and I don't want him showin' up and blastin' the roof off again."

Cole opens his mouth with a sly look in my direction, but Peter cuts him off. "No, ransom will only get us all killed. Her bloody father doesn't play fair, he'd kill us all as soon as she was safe with him. D'ya know where I can get a horse?"

I glare at the little twerp. How does a kid his age instantly thinks of ransom in this place? I suppose it is probably the least hostile reaction to learning who I am, but still. Maybe there's some truth to the word when my father called them savages.

And—I thought Peter had told me I would be held for ransom? Was he lying? Or does he really think my dad wouldn't hold up his end of the bargain? I guess maybe that's true—that my dad would kill whoever was holding me for ransom—but would Peter really damn someone else to that fate, so long as it's not someone he knew? Maybe he didn't think of it before?

Cole answers Peter as though I am not even in the room. "There are a few stallions down at Jimmy's, but I don't know what their condition is. It's hellishly cold for them here in Colfer."

Peter claps the boy on the shoulder. "Good. And watch your language, boy." He stops at the door, looking over his shoulder at Felix for a long moment. Then he shifts his gaze to Cole. "Don't you dare let him die."

Cole nods, also looking down at Peter's brother. "I…. I won't."

I follow Peter out the door. In the other room, a small electric stove squats in the corner, but it's guts have been ripped out so that a fire can be built inside it. A rickety old table stands in the middle of the room with a few rotting stools around it. The shack is lit by candles rather than light bulbs. Don't these people even have bare necessities down here?

"I'm not going back to the Dead Handlers," I tell him, trying not to wonder about their lack of electricity. Peter had said there wasn't any down here before, but I never thought it was this bad. I thought for sure they had some kind of power.

"Well you're not stayin' here," Peter growls.

"You must be starved." An old man's voice sounds before I can retort. I look up at him.

Beside me, Peter shakes his head. "I don't have time for that, Kelly."

"Just sit down, I've already made food." Kelly looks at Peter with stark amazement. "I still can't believe you're alive. None of us come back from the Glass City. You might as well be a ghost."

He makes Peter sit down at the rickety old table, and pulls me over to sit next to him, patting my shoulder. I'm getting sick of everyone going on about how 'nobody survives' in my city. But all those broken bodies in that building earlier makes me question everything I know.

I don't *want* to believe Peter. I don't *want* everything I know to be untrue. I don't *want* to know any of it. I just want to go home, and have everything go back to normal. My face burns as I realize that everything I just thought was exactly what Peter told me to do before he took me to see Clayton. I can't unsee Clayton's body, and I can't let Peter be right. Nothing can ever be the way it was.

Kelly stirs something on the stove; the fire sputters weakly, and beside it, a bucket is full of rotting wood that looks like a chopped up door. He sets plates down in front of us, and I force myself to smile, even though the blobs of pale meat and splatter of thin gravy he scrapes from his pan hardly look appetizing.

Even so, I am really hungry. I haven't eaten in almost two full days. I guess I can choke down whatever this is, I just hope it doesn't make me sick.

Peter eats slowly, but I can tell that he wants to eat it as fast as he can, and it makes me realize how little I saw him eat during his time in my home—and all I kept doing was make him run around after me and carry my bags. How could I let all this happen?

I shove an experimental bite into my mouth as Kelly turns back to the stove. The meat is chewy and rubbery, and I gag, almost spitting it up.

Beside me, Peter mumbles, "Penguin," around a mouthful of food. "And fish." He adds, chewing thoughtfully.

Kelly sets down clay mugs of water for us, before sitting across the table and eating his own food.

I force myself to swallow without throwing up; I don't want to appear ungrateful. Everyone here is so thin. Kelly's coat hangs off of his hunched frame, and the older woman, Addy, takes a plate and sits in the corner. She hugs her own coat to her body, revealing just how narrow her waist is. At her feet seven children sleep in a pile of emaciated bodies. Their hollow features are all similar, obviously related to Addy and each other, but not quite the same either. I suddenly wonder how many different fathers one brood of siblings can have.

Peter is thin as well, but not scrawny like the others. He has a strong, powerful build, broad chest, and thick arms, but even Peter's ribs are visible under his skin. It makes sense if he's a hunter. It's hard to do strenuous, physical activity half-starved.

I glance at Peter, then take another bite, thankful that it's fish this time rather than gross blubbery penguin.

Peter finishes his food and sets down his fork. "Alright. I'm leavin'."

Addy jerks her head up. "What? Where?"

"Hearthtown."

"At least wait until Merry returns," Addy begs, glancing at Kelly for support. "It's night. You're still injured. I can't lose—"

"Lose what, your slave? The only difference between you and the monsters in the Glass City is you don't bloody torture us. Don't pretend that you care," Peter spits. "I know you just need someone to feed you and your brats."

"Peter…." Tears well up in Addy's eyes, and Peter seems genuinely surprised. Addy wipes her eyes quickly. "Just….Stay here. Merry's already gone to Hearthtown, he'll be back soon. At least wait until he's here, if he couldn't find anythin' in Hearthtown then there's no point in you goin' too."

"Merry doesn't know the traders like I do. No trader in his right mind will give up a healin' device to a stranger. There's not enough of them to just hand out to anyone who asks. My brother is dyin', I can't afford to wait," Peter says.

I want to say something to stop him, but I don't know what to do other than follow him toward the door. My heart leaps into my throat at the absolute blackness outside now that night has fallen. Not a single streetlamp lights up the darkness, and there are no glowing sidewalks in the snow. I suddenly want to say I changed my mind and stay with the Dead Handlers. Why did I say I would go? What can I possibly do except watch the polar bears eat him before they come for me?

Kelly stops us at the door and I slump against the wooden frame, letting out a shaky sigh of relief. He presses his wrinkly old hand against Peter's forehead. Peter screws up his face and pulls away, and Kelly looks worried. "You have a fever. At least stay the night here."

"I'll be fine, Kelly, I need to get movin'."

"It's dark out there." Kelly points out.

There's a silence.

"Bloody wolves," Peter growls at length, limping back to the table and sitting down heavily. He shifts his gaze between the front door and the door to Felix's sick room, but he is obviously hurting, and there is a sheen of sweat on his forehead that cannot be from the failing fire.

Addy stands in front of him, almost as if she expects him to make a break for the door. "Look, Peter." She pauses, uncertain. "I'm sorry. For everythin'. I should've been a better aunt."

"Addy don't—" Peter says wearily, but Addalynn cuts him off.

"No. You are still your mother's son, and I—I have failed her. I took advantage of you and your brother, and I'm so sorry." Shame and guilt twist at her face, and she sinks to her knees, leaning her head against Peter's chest. "I don't know what to do, I don't know what I'd do without you. Please don't go." She sobs.

Peter closes his eyes, and I wonder exactly what Addalynn's done. Is she faking it to get Peter to stay? Is she truly that desperate? Or is she genuinely sorry? Either way, I hope it works. It's dark outside, and cold. I don't want to meet wild animals in the dark. That and I want some time to think about going home before the Suppliers find me. The thought of never seeing my mom again makes me sad, but is it enough to make me ignore everything my father has done and go home?

After a while, Peter gently pushes Addy away, not looking at her. "I forgive you."

She sniffs, wiping her eyes. "Your brother's wearin' off on you."

"Don't push it."

Addy smiles briefly, then busies herself with clearing the dishes with Kelly.

I huff a sigh and settle onto an uncomfortable chair as I wait for Peter to make up his mind. Suddenly I miss my cushioned window seat. "I wish I was home."

"Well, now ya know how I felt. If you want to run off again then that's fine with me, but I ain't savin' ya this time." With that he stands up and stomps toward Felix's room.

I follow him into the room at the back of the house, where Felix is still unconscious on the makeshift cot.

Peter raises an eyebrow at me. "What do you want?"

I just don't want to be left alone with these strangers, and although I don't know Peter very well, I know him better than anyone else here. But I am not sure how to say that without sounding weird.

Peter finally grumbles after a silent staring contest between us, but he doesn't kick me out. He moves to a closet, the door creaking and sticking on its rusty hinges as he jerks it open, digging out two wool blankets before shouldering it closed again. He tosses one to me, then lays his on the floor beside Felix's cot.

Once he's settled he looks at me with half lidded eyes. "You should get sleep too. If your father hasn't found you yet, ya might be waitin' for a while."

I pull my wool blanket around my shoulders and sit down where I stand, too cold to fall asleep. Why don't they just turn on the heater?

My are teeth chattering, and he sighs through his nose, cracking an eye at me. He raises one arm and gestures for me to move closer. I scoot forward on my butt until I am sitting beside him.

Peter's hand presses against my upper left arm, pushing me toward the ground until I'm laying down, and then he pulls me closer to him. I lay next to him rigidly. I have had a dream or two about sleeping in his arms—at least I did before he dragged me over that railing—but suddenly it scares me. Instead of his arm, though, he drapes his wool blanket over me and rolls over.

Even though a minute ago I was scared of him putting his arm around me, I scowl at him over my shoulder. But he is already snoring softly, the heat of his fever radiating off his body.

I wake up in the middle of the night to the sound of the door opening, and my eyes fly open. Peter has one arm around my waist, and I scoot away from him quickly, looking up at the stranger who appears in the doorway. A tall man carrying a black duffle bag in one hand and a candle in the other stands over us. He stares at Peter. "How-"

"He's asleep." I interrupt him before I have to hear about how amazing it is that Peter's still alive.

The man narrows his eyes at me. "Who're you?"

My stomach freezes as solid as a glacier, and I try to fake an Irish accent. "I'm Rachel. He saved me."

The man raises an eyebrow, setting down the duffle bag by the end of the cot. "Well I'm Merry. Think you could help me with him? I have fresh bandages—if nothin' else." He gestures toward Felix.

I wrap my blanket around myself and slip around to the other side of the cot, helping Merry sit him up. Felix sucks in a breath, his eyelids flickering, but he doesn't wake up. Merry lifts the duffle bag up beside him and digs through it.

"Blasted wind picked up, started a blizzard. Took extra long to get home. Got lost a few times." He pulls out gauze and tape, gently rubbing ointment into the burns on Felix's arm and face before covering them with the gauze fresh. "Ya managed to find another healin' device?"

I nod slightly, swallowing. Merry shrugs, carefully rubbing the ointment into the wound on Felix's back and laying the gauze over it. I turn away as he tends to the back of his leg, then help him lay Felix back down. Peter's brother still doesn't wake up.

Merry stands, and I struggle to keep my false accent in place as I say, "Wait."

Merry pauses, raising an eyebrow.

I hesitate. "I need some of that for Peter."

Merry frowns, then crouches next to Peter; I scoot off the cot and sit next to both of them, pulling off Peter's blanket and carefully lifting the edge of his coat and shirt so Merry can see the wounds. Merry looks momentarily speechless. Then, "Bloody hell." He pulls the gauze and ointment back out, gently coating the wounds in a layer of the shiny goo, and I grimace.

Peter flinches, his eyes flying open, but I press down on his shoulder before he can get up. Peter shrugs my hands off him, but doesn't stop Merry from pressing gauze over the gashes and burns that I hadn't been able to heal earlier. Peter watches him warily, then his eyes slide closed again.

Merry lifts Peter's shirt further, grimacing at the massive bruises all up his back. "There're no other cuts?"

I shake my head. "I already healed most of them, there just wasn't enough energy in the TR—healing devices to heal all of it."

Merry's eyebrows meet. "'Twas worse than this?"

I don't want to admit it, but I nod anyways. "He could hardly move."

Merry's face twists in disgust, and he shakes his head. "Those people disgust me. What makes them think that just because they have more advanced technology they have the right to haul us off and make us they're slaves? If I ever get my hands on one of them." He gestures with his hands like he's wringing someone's throat.

I stammer for a moment, not sure how to respond—I don't want to agree with him, but I how do I defend what my people have done?

I touch my hand to my throat.

"Can you let go of my shirt now?" Peter says, shivering.

I wonder if he chose to speak up right then to save me from having to think of something to say, or to keep me from revealing who I really am.

Merry scoffs. "Wimp."

At first I am shocked, then I realize the look in Merry's eyes is still dark with concern for Peter.

Merry turns those eyes back to me after Peter rolls over again. "What about you, are you hurt?"

"No. Peter saved me." I don't know what else to say.

Merry covers Peter up again with the blankets. "He's got a fever. It doesn't feel too bad, but you should probably let him rest."

"He's going to leave as soon as he wakes up. Kelly just barely managed to convince him to stay."

Merry shakes his head. "He was always like that. Him and Felix."

Peter

Rachel's back presses against me, and my face is in her hair. It smells faintly sweet, and without thinking, I breathe in deeply. Part of me is repulsed by how close I am to someone from the Glass City, but at the same time, I feel the urge to press closer, to feel the way the curve of her body fits perfectly against mine. I stop myself. *No. Let's not go there.* But I don't pull away just yet.

Despite the way I treated her in the Glass City—and despite the fact that I kidnapped her—she still saved my life. She could've done that just because she was afraid to be alone down here, but she didn't need to heal me. She could've let me hurt, could've used my pain against me the way her father would've, but she didn't. I don't really want to take her with me, but I can't leave her here: if people find out who she is, they'll kill her—or worse. Merry made that pretty clear last night. I have to keep her safe until I can find a way to get her home, I owe her that much.

And it might be better to get her as far away from Felix as possible, and handing her over to the Dead Handlers in Colfer isn't far enough away.

I try stretching my sore muscles. Ugh, I just want to go back to sleep.... No, I've got to get medicine for Felix. I've got to get another healing device—I glance up at the cot, where I can hear Felix's ragged breathing—maybe a couple of them, because they run out of energy and can't be recharged down here. I have no idea how I will convince a trader, even a friend, to sell me two Glass City healing device for a couple boxes of ammo. But I have to try. I can't let him die.

I get slowly to my feet, squeezing my eyes shut to keep out the tears as my broken ribs shift painfully. I feel a little better, but I still dread the journey to come.

"What did they do to you?" My brother's voice startles me.

"You wouldn't want to know." I sit heavily on the edge of his cot. "I had two healin' devices, they were meant for you, but she used one of them and half the other on me."

Felix gives me a wee smile, half his face covered with gauze that Merry must've put on last night. "Good."

"I would've been fine. Those were meant for you, I took them for *you*. Not for me."

"Peter, shut up." Felix closes his visible eye. "You're my brother, I should've done somethin' to keep them from takin' you—I...." He grimaces, shifting.

I sigh, allowing myself the smallest of smiles. "I'm back now. I was only gone for five days. You should focus on gettin' better"

"Five of the worst days of my life. You're the only family I have left, Peter. How can I rest if all I'm doin' is worryin' about you?"

I narrow my eyes. "As if it's my fault I was taken. Don't you start pickin' at me already, I just escaped hell to get to you."

"I'm not pickin' at you ya *fool eejit*, I was just worried."

"Aye, well you have a funny way of showin' it."

"Well sorry if my worry annoys you, next time you're gone I'll try not to lose any sleep."

"You're such a *gobshite*."

"Watch your—"

"Don't you start that!" I snap, rising.

Rachel stirs, startled in her sleep, but she doesn't wake up.

Felix doesn't respond, wincing as he tries to sit up before dropping his head back onto the pillow, the breath whooshing out of him. Some of my anger fades, replaced by worry. I get back on my knees, helping him shift out of the groove in the middle of the cot.

"Merry checked the Dead Handlers every day," Felix says quietly, exhausted.

"Well I'm safe now. I'm not goin' anywhere." I lean over and touch my forehead to his. "Just get some rest. I didn't mean to wake you," I tell him, then I stand, stooping and picking up my coat.

Felix huffs, a sound that's supposed to be a laugh. "We argue over the stupidest things. I know you're leavin', Peter, and I know very well I can't stop you."

I sling my coat over my shoulder. "You're bloody right you can't."

Felix relaxes into the cot, his eyes sliding closed. "Just don't get yourself killed."

I roll my eyes, but resist the urge to answer back. I nudge Rachel with my toe, and she jumps awake. "We're leavin'. There're more Scouts in Hearthtown, and if we make it there alive, then you're most likely to get home from there."

Rachel grumbles, rolling onto her stomach and starting her fifty push-ups.

Felix cracks an eye open, peering down at her curiously until she's done. "What was that?" He asks.

I smirk, and Rachel sighs dramatically.

"Peter asked me the same thing. Don't you guys try to stay in shape down here?"

"Down here?" Felix raises and eyebrow, looking at me.

Rachel pales.

"Aye, she's from the Glass City," I say.

Felix grimaces, but I think it's meant to be a smile. "You've got a lot to learn, little bird."

Rachel sits up, a sad expression on her face.

"Well maybe not. She's goin' home as soon as I can find someone to take her."

"Are you mental?" Felix grips the edges of his cot. "They'll bloody kill you."

I give him an exasperated sigh. "I don't plan on gettin' caught with her."

"Nobody plans for bad things to happen, and that's usually why they happen!"

"What happened to teachin' the City folk to work together?" I remind him.

"If she can help you then take her with you. Teach her how things work down here—just don't get yourself killed by tryin' to get her home!"

Felix looks so desperate that I decide not to yell at him. "I can't let her stay here," I say quietly. "The longer she's down here the more likely her father will come after you to get to me. I can't let that happen. It's better I die than you."

"Peter." But Felix looks too tired to say any more.

"Just go back to sleep." I pick up my guns from under the cot, looking down at Rachel. "Let's go."

Rachel pulls on her boots quickly, then lies on her back, sitting up several times and touching her elbows to her knees.

"Really? More?" I ask as I pull on my gloves.

"Haven't worked out in a while." She grunts.

I shake my head in wonder, then stop her. "You're goin' to get enough of a workout walkin' in the snow ya *eejit*. Don't wear yourself out."

Rachel pulls a face, but I turn away from her, snatching up my guns and two wool blankets and limping to the door as I sling the weapons and blankets over my shoulders. Rachel pushes her arms through the sleeves of my mother's jacket, rushing to keep up.

"I love you Peter." Felix rasps from behind me.

I roll my eyes. "Love you too old man."

Addy is asleep in the other room with the rest of her kids, all of them piled up in a corner with one wool blanket over the top of them. Merry is curled up next to them. I'm glad he made it back from Hearthtown alive. Travel is a dangerous thing down here on the Surface, even with a horse.

Maybe I could make it to Hearthtown without a horse if I didn't have Rachel in tow. She can barely keep her coat fastened properly. I stop her fumbling and align the two sides of the fur coat, pushing the bear-claw buttons through the loops all the way up to her chin.

I open the cracked plastic box next to the stove and grab a few handfuls of polar-bear jerky, stuffing it into a small, fur-lined satchel. I take two water bladders from the hooks above the stove, making sure they're full before slinging one over my shoulder. I hand the other to Rachel, who takes it without looking at me.

I push out the door into the early morning, the icy wind blasting me in the face. *Shoot I forgot my goggles.* I hesitate, but decide not to go back for them. I don't bother to say goodbye, either, not wanting to let Kelly talk me into resting for another day. It isn't snowing, but the wind whips the snow off the ground so that it swirls around us, making it difficult to see even two feet ahead. Snow is packed in front of the door, and it's a bit of a climb to get over it. Once we are out on the plains, Rachel bumps into me, struggling to find her way through the whiteout. I reach out and grab her wrist; It's would be very easy to get lost or separated out here.

We slog through the snow toward Colfer, and I pull my hood up, burying my face into the wolf fur collar of my coat. I pause for a moment to make sure Rachel does the same, pulling her hood down to just above her eyes. Dark clouds loom on the horizon, and I have a feeling that the journey to Hearthtown is going to be a rough one.

When the first rundown buildings appear through the haze of blowing snow, I pick up my pace, dragging Rachel along behind me until we reach Jimmy's shop.

Inside the air is warm again, but the cold has seeped into my bones; either it's a much colder day than I thought, or that blasted Glass City has stripped me of my tolerance for the cold.

"Oi, Jimmy!" I call, leaning on the counter. The man bustles out of the back of the shop in his pajamas, his tired blue eyes lighting up when he sees me.

"Peter. What brings ya back here so soon?"

"Horses. Got any?"

"Where're ya headed?"

"Hearthtown. We'll take Canyon Pass."

Jimmy pales. "It's dangerous out there. Peter, ya just came back from the dead, don't send yourself on a one way trip back to hell. Merry stopped by late last night and said the Scouts are crawlin' all over the place up there, even more so than usual."

Because of me, and Rachel. Her father is looking for her. Though I am surprised they started in Hearthtown and not here. "Aye, well, I can't wait, Felix could die if we don't get him somethin' stronger than ointment. I'm not willin' to take that chance."

"Alright alright, but remember, you're no good to him dead." Jimmy steps around the counter, gesturing for me to follow. "The horses are out back."

We push through the doors and trek back behind the shop, where a sorry construction of wood and corrugated metal leans into a snowdrift. We follow Jimmy into the barn and down the rows of makeshift stalls to four that are occupied by very shaggy, very unhappy looking horses. The horses are already equipped with saddle bags and tack.

Jimmy nods to them. "Take your pick. Normally I'd charge you an arm and a leg, but—since it's for Felix—and since they've been here too long, your gettin' 'em back home is enough payment. They need to be back in a warm place like Hearthtown. They are no good to anybody frozen to death. Just tell Cliona she can pay me back next time she sends supplies."

"Thanks, Jimmy."

"Just shut the doors before ya go," Jimmy says, and leaves us to choose our mounts. No doubt he doesn't want to get caught up in any awkward questions about which horses he thinks are least likely to keel over halfway to Hearthtown. I wonder if the people who brought them here are still alive.

I open the stall of a shaggy dark brown stallion. It's the largest one there—it seems somewhat hardy. I take the one next to it for Rachel; it's a smaller, more stocky mare, with a white mane and extra thick gray fur. I hand the reigns to Rachel, then stuff our supplies into the saddle bags, rolling up the wool blankets and tying them behind the saddles.

"You can ride, right?"

Rachel swallows, looking uncertain. "Can't be too hard, can it?"

I stick my foot in the stirrup and swinging up onto the saddle. I nudge my horse closer to hers, so that she's standing between us. "Put your foot in the stirrup—no, the other foot. Good, now pull yourself up."

Grabbing the horn of the saddle, she jumps, but she can't seem to figure out how to pull herself up.

I sigh through my nose, reaching down to hold out my hand, and give her one of Felix's patented 'you're an idiot' looks.

She glowers at me, but takes my hand.

"Jump," I tell her, and she pushes off with the stirrup. I catch most of her weight on my arm and grunt as pain flares up through my ribs and hips. Gritting my teeth, I lift her up enough so that she can straddle the horse, then let go, letting my breath out all at once.

I turn my horse away from hers and nudge its sides with my heels, urging it into a steady trot and pressing my arm across my stomach to try to ease the jarring in my ribs from the horse's gait.

The heat of Rachel's hand still warms mine, and I clench my fingers to keep it there. Luckily, Rachel's horse follows mine. These horses have traveled back and forth from Hearthtown to Colfer so many times that they know what they're doing and where they're going.

The wind picks up a few hours into the trip, blasting through Canyon Pass, the narrow canyon formed by two glaciers grinding past each other, and the only safe path between Colfer and Hearthtown. I hunch my shoulders and pull my arms close against the cold, silently enduring Rachel's babbling and complaining.

After another half hour, I realize that I've fallen into a sort of half sleep. Rachel still hasn't shut up.

"….ARE YOU EVEN LISTENING?!" She suddenly yells, reaching over and shoving my shoulder.

I crack an eye open, peeking over at her from above my fur collar. "I'm sorry, were you sayin' somethin'?"

She gives me an exasperated groan. "My whole life, nobody ever listens to me. Don't you care about anyone but yourself?"

I stiffen, infuriated. "What the bloody hell do you think I am doin' out here? Not everythin' is about you. If ya just shut your trap for half a minute, maybe people would listen to you!"

"If I'm not talking, then what would you listen to?" Rachel blows polar bear fur from her collar out of her face.

"THE SILENCE!" I roar, and she flinches.

I turn away from her again, nudging my horse's sides to make it go a little faster. Rachel doesn't say anything, and I relax slightly, enjoying the quiet.

I hear a sniff over my shoulder, and I look back.

Rachel's sapphire eyes are glassy as she stares at the canyon wall to her right.

Cool guilt floods through my chest. "Look, Rachel, I'm sorry."

Rachel shifts her gaze to me. "What?"

"I'm sorry I snapped at you. It's just…. you're not the only one with problems." I face forward again, shivering. "I'll get ya home, Rachel."

Rachel wipes her eyes. "I don't even know if I want to go home anymore."

It's my turn to be stunned. "After all this complainin'?"

"I just…." She shifts her shoulders uncertainly. "The City is….as much as I wanted to leave it, it *was* my home. But now…. everything I know is a lie. I didn't want to believe it. For a while I just wanted to go home, to have everything go back to normal, but I know it won't be. It *can't* be normal. Dad lied to me. And Malcolm…." Rachel glances at me. "I can't unlearn what I know, I can't unsee what I've seen."

We ride on in silence for a few minutes, and the canyon widens as one glacier drops away. That side opens up to a wide, flat plain, the blackened remains of an ancient city poking up through the snow in the distance.

I stop before we completely leave the protective walls of the canyon. The path hugs the massive wall of the remaining glacier to the right, and three hundred yards ahead another glacier swells up against it to form another canyon. To the left, the white prairie rises and falls with subtle hills like frozen waves on a sea of snow, devoid of any movement—as far as I can tell.

"Why have we stopped?"

"This is the most dangerous part of Canyon Pass. We're only about a mile and a half from Hearthtown, but it's wide open, so there's no cover if the Scouts fly over."

"You mean Suppliers?"

I roll my eyes. "Aye. And Sirens. This is a spot where a lot of Siren attacks happen." My hand involuntarily goes to my hip, where my pistol rests in its holster.

"You mean you weren't making that up?" Rachel's voice is a tiny whisper, and she glances over her shoulder at the road behind us.

"I'm not a liar."

Rachel shivers. "People travel this way all the time right?"

"I've been through here several times with Felix, we'll be safe again when we reach the other side…." I swallow. Felix and I had been nearly caught several times, both by Scouts and by wolves.

After a moment's hesitation, I nudge my horse out into the open, keeping close to the wall with Rachel right behind me. I keep my eyes peeled, scanning the pure white of the field for anything moving, and watching the gray sky for the black dots of hover crafts and drones.

We're about halfway across when my horse stops, pricking its ears and raising its head. Rachel's does the same, both looking in the same direction. I pull my sniper rifle off my back, peering through the scope.

The sound of a gun going off shatters the muffled silence of the prairie. The glacial wall behind me explodes with a shower of pebbles and ice that sting where they hit unprotected flesh. My horse rears, and I tip over his back and hit the snowy ground hard.

Rachel screams, and I manage to roll onto my stomach, recovering too slowly from having the wind knocked out of me. I force myself to focus, as a figure in Scout snow-camouflage drops his rifle and runs straight for me.

Pulling myself together, I lunge to my feet and tackle the stranger, catching him around the middle, but the world is still spinning. I cling to him more to keep myself standing than to wrestle him into submission.

I stumble as he pushes me off and fumbles for a gun on his belt. I draw my knife grenade, advancing—and stop as the Scout's hood falls back to reveal his face.

Malcolm's eyes go wide, and then his upper lip curls. "Put it down, *slave*."

I grit my teeth, suddenly wanting nothing more than to destroy him.

Rachel has slid down from her horse and run up behind me. Her voice shaking, she says, "Peter? Peter, please don't hurt him."

My scowl deepens, and I bare my teeth, but I lower the knife. "What the bloody hell are you doin' here?"

"I came looking for her, you idiot." Malcolm turns to Rachel. "I took one of the smaller hovercrafts from the resupply hanger, where the security is lighter. It's hidden not too far from here. I can take you home."

"Good," I say before Rachel can respond.

Malcolm narrows his eyes at me. "You think you can hold her for ransom-"

"I'm not holdin' her for ransom, she's followin' me around. She's free to go." I give him a pleasant smile that doesn't reach my eyes, still feeling dizzy from my fall. I wonder if I hit my head. "Go ahead and take your wee little girlfriend home." I ignore the look Rachel gives me.

Malcolm squares his shoulders, lifting his chin. "I'm not going anywhere without Rachel."

I roll my eyes. "I just said she's free to go. Take her home-" I stop, my blood turning to ice. The eerie wail of a Siren drifts over the wind.

"You really think it's just that simple? You took her, you dragged her down to this hell hole, I'm not just going to let you go." Malcolm sneers. "I'm going to make you *suffer*."

"Malcolm get on a horse," I say quietly, taking Rachel by the elbow. "We need to run."

"Get your hands off of her!" He barrels into my chest, sending us both tumbling through the snow.

Malcolm ends up on top of me, aiming a blow at my face. I block it. His fist flies past my head, pounding into the snow.

I close my eyes, as icy snow splatters my face. "Malcolm listen to-"

Malcolm's body is thrown off of me. Snow explodes under the impact of a massive wall of white fur and muscle. I roll onto my side to see a massive Siren as big as Rachel's horse pinning Malcolm to the ground, a few feet away. It's left ear is missing, and so is its tail.

It's *her.*

The horses are screaming. Rachel is screaming. The snarling Siren snaps her teeth at Malcolm's exposed throat, barely held back by Malcolm's hands on her jaws.

I lurch to my feet, my adrenaline spiking, and leap onto the Siren's back. The beast shrieks and bucks. I cling to her fur just behind her shoulders, knowing that if I let go, I'm done for. But the Siren stumbles backwards away from Malcolm, unbalanced from losing her tail to Felix's blade a week ago.

"Run!" I yell. The world blurs as the Siren spins and weaves, snapping at the air, but unable to get me off. I can barely make out Rachel and Malcolm and the horses, but I hope they take the chance to get as far away as possible while the beast is distracted, because there is no way this ends well for me. And once she's done with me, they will be next.

A wild buck flings me sideways, and I realize I could hang on much longer if I wasn't doing this one handed. I need to drop the—*the knife grenade!* My right hand is still wrapped around the hilt in the same death grip that my left hand has on a clump of Siren fur.

I lock my knees around the sinewy muscles of her neck and, with a triumphant cry, I raise the blade high over my head and plunge it straight down into her skull.

The blade pierces flesh, but skids jarringly over the armor-like plate of bone protecting her brain, lodging into the thick muscles of her neck instead.

The Siren wails, stumbling slightly before whipping her head around in a vain attempt to bite me off like a pesky flea.

I hold onto the knife with both hands, flip the cap up with my thumb and jam the button down, knowing I only have a minute or two to get away from it before it explodes.

I let go and another buck sends me hurtling me through the air. I land hard on my side, rolling to a stop face-down in the snow and struggling to pull air into my lungs.

Before I can get up, a massive weight presses me into the snow, and hot breath blasts the back of my neck.

Rachel

I watch in horror as the massive wolf-like beast lowers its slathering jaws toward Peter's neck. *Siren.*

I snap myself out of it and start screaming at the top of my lungs, waving my arms and kicking at the snow. The white wolf looks up at me, its lips peeling back from a row of teeth the size of daggers. The Siren bristles as it stalks toward Malcolm and me, its one ear flattened back against its skull.

"Malcolm run," I whisper, not looking to see if he does or not. I am not sure it would help to run.

The creature prowls closer, bunching up the muscles in its shoulders to pounce. Behind it Peter struggles to his feet, waving his arms wildly. Everything happens in slow-motion.

A soft *click* echoes through the canyon. Then an explosion.

The blast knocks me onto my butt. Peter is closer, and his body is thrown against the stone and ice of the canyon wall behind him. The creature's head is blown halfway off, leaving a gory mess on what's left of its neck. It collapses in the snow, a twitching pile of fur.

I stare at it, shocked and appalled, and then my mind pulls me to my senses; *Peter.* "PETER!" I scream, throwing Malcolm's hand off of my arm as he tries to stop me. I run over to the motionless body in the snow, crouching by Peter's side and digging my fingers into his upper arm. "Peter? Peter can you hear me?"

Peter moans, his breath hitched and uneven, but he remains unconscious. "Malcolm!" I call, but he's already by my side, taking my arm in a firm grasp.

"Let's go, the hovercraft is just over there." He tries to pull me to my feet, but I wrench away.

"What is wrong with you?! He just saved your life!"

"Rachel, he tried to kill you-"

"If he had tried to kill me, I'd be *dead*!"

"He took you-"

"He was just trying to get away from my father—and you!!"

Malcolm draws back for a moment, hesitating. "Rachel, he's not worth it. Just *leave* him."

I narrow my eyes at him, remembering Clayton's body. "*He's* not worth it? I know what you've done. And I know what he's done. He just saved both our lives, which is more than you deserve."

"What are you talking about?" Malcolm asks, but his cheeks burn and I can see the guilt in his eyes.

"And I know what you did to Clayton," I whisper.

Malcolm pales, shaking his head. "I-I don't know what you mean." He reaches out to tug weakly at my arm. "Please, let's go before another of those things come."

"Don't touch me! I saw him, Malcolm! You lied to me! You and Dad and everyone else!"

"Rachel listen, I'm sorry, I don't know what you're talking about. Let's just go home-"

"Not without Peter!"

"Why, because he *told you* that I hurt him? Because he *told you* I killed Clayton? How would he even know? Why would you believe his word over mine?"

"Because I saw it!" I punch him hard in the chest as he tries to get closer to me again. "I saw what you did, all those burns and bruises on Peter's body couldn't have been from injuries on the Surface. He was supposed to have been healed. And, what exactly did you do to him that day at dinner when you suddenly wanted to speak to him in the other room? And Clayton? Why is there a hole in his chest that looks like your boot?"

"What are you talking about? Clayton's body was burned, just like everyone else's in the city-"

"LIAR! I *just* saw him!"

"Look, let's just go home. Your parents are worried sick, especially your mother." Malcolm takes my arms again, and I slap him hard across the face.

"I hate you," I whisper, placing myself between him and Peter's motionless body. "I would rather stay here on the frozen Surface than ever set foot in the City again—or go anywhere with you!"

Malcolm looks hurt, but I don't care anymore.

"Wait. You said the hovercraft was close; we need the medical supplies."

"It's—well it wasn't fully resupplied when I took it. And he doesn't look that hurt," Malcolm says.

"You wouldn't understand. Malcolm please." I choke back tears. "Prove me wrong. Help us."

Malcolm stares at me, his cheek bright red from where I slapped him. He turns away and tears spring to my eyes at the thought of being left alone out here with an unconscious Peter and a dead Siren. But rather than leaving Malcolm picks up the reigns of the horses and yanks them back toward us. They fight their bits, reluctant to be anywhere near the Siren which reeks of blood and the musk of wild beasts.

I look up at him, sniffling.

"We can't carry him the whole way. Let's get him over the saddle."

I laugh, perhaps a little too hard, because Malcolm looks at me sideways as he checks Peter's neck before moving him. We loop a rope under Peter's arms and use the saddle like a pulley to lift his dead weight onto the horse.

When we get to the hovercraft, Malcolm lays him gently on a cot that folds out from the wall of the hovercraft.

It's warm in the craft. Lights blink on and hum as they glow overhead. These simple conveniences, that I have longed for since I splashed down into this frozen world, mean nothing to me. My only thoughts are for Peter.

Peter's injuries are minimal, a lump on his head and a gash on his leg. Nothing that won't heal on its own. Still, I can't stand to see him injured anymore because of Malcolm or anyone in my stupid City. "Where are your healing supplies?" I ask as I pull Peter's weapons from his shoulders, propping them against the wall. I tug my gloves off.

Malcolm checks the cabinets, holding the button of each BRRD and TRRD. He curses when they beep. "They're all out. I told you, this ship hasn't been resupplied yet"

I lay my head on Peter's chest, defeated. "Can't you do anything right, Malcolm?"

Malcolm turns away, and I wonder what he'll do now. He has Peter and I inside his hovercraft, he could fly us back to the City and we couldn't stop him.

But instead he finds some gauze, staples, suture and topical anesthetic from the emergency kit. "This will have to do," He says, dropping them on the foot of Peter's bed. "So you don't want to go home then?" He watches me fumble with suturing and the gauze.

"No."

He's quiet as I replace the bandages on Peter's back, throwing the bloody gauze into the craft's incinerator.

"We need somewhere safe to sleep tonight."

"What's to stop me from flying the ship home with you in it while you sleep?"

"I'd kill you," I say shortly. And I think I mean it. "If I wake up in the Glass City, I'll hunt you down and kill you. And if I can't kill you, I would just hate you even more."

"Fine." Malcolm scowls, turning away again.

I study the back of his head, then say quietly, "Why did you kill him?" Meaning Clayton.

"I didn't," Malcolm says softly, but I can tell he is lying because of the catch in his voice.

My eyes blur. "And why are you lying to me? I already know the truth, or at least some of it. How could you do something like that? To my *best friend*." It's strange that my tone is so calm and even. I don't understand why I am not screaming at him.

Malcolm doesn't answer right away, staring out the windshield as the day fades and snow starts to fall. "Fine. You win. You're right. But that's how life is now, Rachel, ever since the asteroid hit. That's what it's like in the Glass City. *Everybody* is like that up there. The people down here are worthless, stupid, uneducated. They don't deserve to live like us."

I can't believe the words that just came out of his mouth. My heart shrivels in disgust at the vileness of it. "Peter's right. You are a monster."

Malcolm doesn't say anything, pushing past me to sit in the front seat. He reclines back and folds his arms over his chest. I sit down on the floor, unwilling to take the seat next to the guy I used to like.

I look down at the dried blood on my hands and wonder if all my years of willing ignorance makes me a monster too.

"I did what you wanted," Malcolm says. "I helped you bring him here and treat his wound. Doesn't that count for something?"

I don't say anything. I just dig through the cabinets until I find a clean shirt, pulling off Peter's bloodstained jacket and tugging his arms through the sleeves of something clean. I'm about to throw his filthy shirt in the incinerator when I catch myself. Fumbling through the pockets, I find the picture of Peter's parents, looking at it for a second before tucking it into the pocket of Peter's new shirt. I can see Peter's features in his father's face, and they both have the same green eyes. But Peter's eyes are haunted, whereas his parents' are bright and alive, not yet tainted by the horrors of the post-asteroid world.

What happened to us?

I bundle up my fur coat like a pillow and lay down on the floor next to Peter's cot. If Malcolm tries to hurt Peter while he is recovering, he will have to come through me to do it.

Peter

I don't move. The crackle of the furnace sounds all around me, and my chest floods with panic. *No.* I don't want to get up, I don't want to open my eyes and see Liam and Calvin leering down at me, with hot pokers from the fire. Maybe I can escape, maybe I can jump again. I'll take Malcolm this time, he won't be too hard to get rid of. Killing him won't weigh on my conscience.

I crack my eyes open, ready to make a break for the door, but I'm not in Brown's basement. Instead, I'm in a narrow room, little lights blinking on and off in the panels built into the walls. The room is filled with a low hum, the crackle of the furnace having been nothing but the remnants of a nightmare.

I relax slightly, then sit up fast—I'm in a hovercraft. *Malcolm's hovercraft.* There's snow outside the windshield, so I'm not in the Glass City yet. I need to get out of here before Malcolm takes us back. I slip quietly out of the cot, glancing at the healing devices scattered on the ground next to Rachel. My leg hurts, and when I raise my pant-leg, I can see bandages covering a gash in my calf. The healing devices must be empty.

Rachel stirs in her sleep, and I hesitate, not wanting to leave just yet. It's warm in here, and part of me wants to stay and rest. If Malcolm tries to take us to the Glass City, I can just shoot him. I lean against the cot, rubbing the hem of my new shirt between my thumb and forefinger, and my mind jumps to the picture of my parents. Desperate, I fumble through my pockets until I find it, letting out a breath. I pull it out and squint at it in the dim light. It's been too long since I've seen their faces, and now more than ever, I wish they were still here. Traveling through Canyon Pass without Felix, I've never felt more alone—even with Rachel following me

"Whatcha got there?" Malcolm's voice sounds from the front of the room, and I jump. A nail of pain stabs into my skull.

"Nothin'," I say, too tired and sore to sound as snide as he does. I turn away, pulling on my coat, when a soft *click* sounds from behind me. I slump, more annoyed than pissed off.

"I said, what do you have there?"

I turn around, blinking slowly at Malcolm, who has his gun pointed at my chest. I kick one of the empty healing devices, sending it rattling across the floor past Rachel's head. "Guess I can't fix myself if ya shoot me."

"I wouldn't let you even if you could."

"Hmm." I stumble toward him, ignoring his weapon and falling into the seat beside him. My body sinks into the cushion, and I relax into it, too weary to fight.

Outside, the snowy expanse of the break in Canyon Pass stretches out in front of us, dimly glowing in the twilight of the early dawn. The dashboard in front of me blinks with little lights, and heat radiates from the seat of my chair, buttons lining the armrests.

"Well?" Malcolm gestures with his gun.

Reluctantly, I show him the picture of my parents, not saying a word.

Malcolm snatches it from my fingers, looking closer at the old photograph. "Who're they?"

"My parents."

"Where are they now?"

I close my eyes. "They're dead."

Malcolm doesn't respond right away, squinting at the photo as he tries to make out the details. I hold out my hand, wanting it back, but he moves it out of reach,

"You don't need this." He smirks, pinching the top of it with the thumb and forefinger of each hand.

My chest constricts, but I don't say anything, afraid to.

Malcolm studies me, and I hold his gaze, almost pleading with my eyes. That picture is all I have, aside from the memory my father's bruised and bloodless face.

Malcolm rolls his eyes, slapping the picture back into my hand.

I fold it carefully and slide it into my pocket. I lean back slightly, staring out at the ice and snow. After a stretch of silence, Malcolm twists in his seat, looking behind us at Rachel. "She likes you, you know."

I peer over my shoulder at her as well. "You could fool me. She never stops complainin' and she won't leave me alone."

Malcolm smiles a sad sort of smile. "She thinks I'm a monster."

"That's because ya act like a monster, you bloody idiot."

Malcolm drops his gaze to the floor.

I rub the back of my neck. "The world could do with less monsters, ya know? People more like her, and her mother."

Malcolm doesn't reply, and I crack my eyes open again, giving him the most friendly look I can manage, which is much harder than I want it to be. "Ya don't have to be a monster, Malcolm. Just…. don't beat the crap out of people when you don't get what you want." It's weird, talking to Malcolm without yelling at him. Everything I know tells me that I should hate him, but this boy sitting here broken and defeated isn't a monster. At least, not at the moment.

Malcolm's upper lip curls slightly, and he looks away. "You don't know what you're talking about."

"What, torturin' people when they don't do what you want them to? Murderin' someone's best friend because you're jealous?" I shake my head. "You know better than that. Why else would we still be on the Surface right now?" He can't be all bad, or else he would've dragged us back up to the City by now.

Malcolm gives me a black look, but he doesn't deny it. Instead, he stares out the window, where the dark clouds lighten to a dull gray.

"I need to get to Hearthtown. If you want, I'll take the horses and go before she wakes—" I stop, my stomach lurching. "The horses."

"What?"

"Bloody hell you left them outside!" I jump to my feet, snatching up my gun and I shouldering outside.

Right in front of the door, a pack of four wolves are circling Rachel's horse, which is collapsed on her side on the ground, but my horse won't let them near her. Snorting and tossing his head, he rears on his hind legs and pounds the snot out of any wolf that tries to get too close to Rachel's mare. By the look of the wounds on the mare's flanks and the sweat crusting the stallion's fur, the wolves have been at it for a while, lunging and snapping, waiting for the horses to tire.

The wolves pause, pricking their ears toward me, and I raise my arms, yelling at the top of my lungs. They flinch, and my horse rears again, startled. His heavy hooves paw at the air, and one of the wolves lunges at his exposed chest.

The assault proves to be a mistake, for the stallion drops back to all fours and smashes the canine into the snow with his front hooves. The wolf yelps, struggling to get up, but it's too late. My horse crushes its skull.

The other wolves dash backwards, but then stop, standing their ground to raise their heads and howl. They won't be scared off easily, not with the mare's blood on the snow. I raise my rifle and kill the closest wolf.

Rachel tries to run to her horse, screaming when Malcolm catches her around the waist and pulls her back to the hovercraft.

"Keep her inside!" I yell at him.

One of the wolves creeps up behind the mare, but she has some fight in her yet, and kicks out with her hind leg, catching the canine on the jaw with a bone shattering crunch. Squealing, the wolf falls away, pawing at its face and rolling in the snow. I shoot it, putting it out of its misery. Then I turn to the last wolf, only to find that it's not where it was a second ago.

Suddenly, the wolf tackles me to the ground from the side. My gun flies from my hand as I hold the wolf's snapping fangs at bay. I grunt as the weight of the wolf crushes me into the packed snow.

As wiry and strong as this wolf is, it's like child's play compared to wrestling a Siren. Hollering, I use all my strength to shove it off of me, rolling to my feet and stumbling when my weight leans on my bad leg. The wolf wriggles on its back in the snow until it finds its feet again. It lunges at me, but my horse charges between us. He catches the wolf in the chest with his sharp front hooves.

The wolf skids across the snow limply until it stops, blood oozing, eyes glassy.

I stand still, panting. My horse turns toward me, snuffling at my hair and shaking all over. Stroking his nose and resting my forehead against his, I say, breathlessly, "Good boy." Then I crouch beside Rachel's mare and pick up my gun. "Come on girl, get up."

The mare gets shakily to her feet, pressing her broad forehead against my chest and trembling. Her left flank and hind quarters have been torn up by the teeth and claws of the wolves, and when I move closer to examine them, she shies away. I sigh, moving closer again, and the mare hangs her head, murmuring softly. If she can't walk, I'll have to shoot her.

Rachel appears by my side, her eyes huge. "What happened to her?"

"Bloody wolves," I growl, aiming my gun. "I'll have to shoot her."

"What? No!" She pulls the barrel of my gun down, and my finger slips on the trigger, the shot nearly taking out the horse's knee. The mare startles, bolting a few feet, before stumbling. With a high pitched whinny, her hind legs slide out from under her as she collapses in the snow.

I grit my teeth. "*Never* grab my gun like that! *Ever!*" I snap, wrenching my rifle away from her. "Ya could've been killed!"

Rachel swallows, and I turn away from her, gesturing at the horse. "If she can't walk, then I have to kill her, it would be cruel to leave her for the wolves."

"But…." Rachel eyes fill with tears.

I exhale through my nose, gripping her shoulder and making her look at me. "Rachel, I have to shoot her."

"Wait," Malcolm says from behind us, his voice holding no expression. I turn, and he holds up an healing device.

"I thought you said you didn't have anymore?" Rachel frowns.

"I lied," Malcolm grumbles back, bringing the device to me.

Felix. I hesitate, taking the device and studying it. "How much energy does it have?"

"Enough for her wounds, maybe more," Malcolm says, motioning toward the mare. The horse nickers as she tries to get up again, but can't. The stallion nudges the top of her head.

I take a breath, at war between wanting to save Felix and not wanting to shoot the horse. Of course my brother's life is worth far more to me than that of some dumb animal, but with Rachel standing beside me....

"What if nobody has a Healing Device in Hearthtown? Can I take that chance?" I say quietly. Can I really choose between my brother and a horse?

The mare's sides heave, her nostrils flaring with every exhale of breath.

"Peter, please. We'll find another. I promise," Rachel whispers.

"If you go home, I wouldn't need two horses...."

"I'm not going home," Rachel says softly.

I turn to look at her, dumbfounded. "You what?"

"I'm not going with Malcolm," she says again, a note of finality in her voice and a meaningful look at Malcolm. "I'm going to Hearthtown with you."

Malcolm crosses his arms, but doesn't argue.

"Rachel, I think it'd be best if you just went home now," I say. "There's no point goin' all the way to Hearthtown. I have what I need to heal Felix, and you have your way home."

"I can't go back to that, now that I know what a monster my own father is. I can't go back there."

"Rachel, you're father's not goin' to give up lookin' for ya. You put everyone around you in danger if you stay. Malcolm will tell your father where we are, and we'll be caught in no time. You'll be taken home whether ya want to be or not, and anyone in the vicinity includin' me, Felix, and my cousins will be incinerated. You think it's hard livin' with the knowledge that your people are monsters? Try livin' with the deaths of innocent people on your head. Addy's a floozie, aye, but I don't want her dead."

The mare kicks her hooves, whinnying in distress.

Rachel's face crumples. "You can't just leave her."

"She's a horse, Rachel."

"I know, but she carried me all the way here. She did all the work of walking, you can't just shoot her when you could heal her." Rachel sniffs, her eyes pleading.

I study her face, then tip my head back, closing my eyes.

I take a slow breath and trudge past her, coaxing the small mare to stand. Once she's on her feet, she sways dangerously, and I tense, ready to jump away at any time to avoid getting crushed should she fall.

Pressing the healing device against the gashes in her hind quarters, I push the small button, and the mare trembles as the bite marks start to seal over. I continue to move up her side, finishing with her flank and rubbing her neck.

"Good girl," I mumble, resting my head against her flank. She murmurs softly, nuzzling the back of my head. In my hand, the device's "depleted" indicator beeps.

I turn back to Rachel. "Happy now?" I ask as I throw the spent device into the snow.

Rachel looks solemnly at Malcolm. "Tell my father I'm not coming back."

"Rachel, he's not going to listen," Malcolm tells her, almost pleading now. "Just come back with me, everything will go back to normal-"

"You don't get it, do you?" Rachel shakes her head with a look that might be pity on her face. "You're the reason I don't want to go home. I trusted you, maybe even *liked* you, but now…. And Dad? I don't think I can ever look him in the eye. It might be a whole lot harder to live down here, but at least the people are honest and good."

I speak up, impatient. "People are people, Rachel. Go home."

"No," She says firmly, her eyes still on Malcolm.

Malcolm's knees buckle, and tears flow down his face. "Rachel, I'm sorry."

"No you're not." Rachel takes a step backwards from him.

"I won't hurt anyone anymore. I…." He glances at me, then flicks his gaze toward the ground. "You're right. I was a monster. But…. please, just give me a second chance."

But Rachel is already climbing into the mare's saddle, blinking away her own tears. "I'm sorry Malcolm. I'm not going home."

"Rachel-" I start, but I stop at the determined and stubborn look she gives me. Nothing I can say will change her mind. I sigh, feeling sorry for Malcolm. He keeps his eyes on the ground for another moment, then turns without a word toward the hovercraft.

"I won't tell him where you're going," he mutters without looking back, then closes the door. The hovercraft hums, then rises slowly off the ground, spooking the horses as it takes off and soars away. I watch it go, squinting up at the clouds.

After a second, I hand Rachel the reins, giving her a look. "He meant it, ya know. He cares about you enough to change his ways."

Rachel doesn't respond, taking the reins and nudging her horse's sides. I watch her go for a moment, then urge my horse to turn away from her.

"Wait," I call, and swing my leg over the stallion's back.

Rachel stops.

I urge my horse ahead, and he charges through the deep powder, toward an odd shaped lump, covered in a blanket of snow.

Dismounting I kick at the snow with my foot, revealing the frozen carcass of the Siren. I grab a rope from my saddlebags and loop it awkwardly around the hulking, stiff body. I stretch the rope up and tie her to my saddle. I needed some way to afford the healing devices in Hearthtown, and I just found it. The fact that this is the same Siren Felix and I faced about a week ago might get me extra, simply for the story behind her missing tail.

I climb back up into the saddle, and my horse is considerably slower as he hauls the Siren behind him. I hear a soft whine, and frown, looking over my shoulder.

In the space where the Siren had been, a small, furry white form shivers in the snow, huge icy blue eyes staring up at me. It whimpers again, and my throat constricts. The wee little creature crawls out of the hollow in the snow and nudges the mother Siren's hind paw, mewling like a newborn.

Rachel rides up beside me, seeing the reason for my hesitation. She opens her mouth. "Is that-?"

"A Siren pup." I confirm, not believing it. The pup whines, trotting up to the side of my horse and peering up at me with its sad blue eyes. It tips its head back and wails a pitiful melody, nowhere near as eerie and beautiful as that of its dead mother.

"Aw, that's so sad." Rachel looks around. "Shouldn't there be a father Siren or something?"

"It would have come by now if there was."

"What are we going to do?" She is already reaching into her saddlebag to toss it a little piece of dried meat. The pup snaps it up hungrily, her tiny fangs jutting out from her upper and lower jaws.

I lower my face into my palms. First the mare, now this pup? The wee Siren will grow up to be a massive, violent, wolf-like canine just like its mother. But I know how hard it is to live without parents in this place. Rachel doesn't even need to turn her sad eyes on me this time.

I dismount again, taking a few pieces of meat out of my own saddle bags, and crouch in front of the pup. It shies away, whimpering. I pull off one of my gloves and hold out the meat. "Com'ere, ya wee little beastie."

"Won't it grow up to be like that?" Rachel points at the dead Siren, looking incredulous.

"Aye, but I can't just leave it here."

The Siren pup inches forward, not lifting its butt off the ground as it cranes its neck to sniff the dried meat in my fingers. It snaps at it, sharp little teeth almost catching in the fabric of my glove.

Hesitantly, it scoots a bit closer, pressing its furry head into my palm. I rub behind its ears, looking a little closer.

"Good girl." She can't be more than three months old, perhaps she won't remember her mother, perhaps she won't become violent.

The tone of my voice seems to sooth her, and she presses closer, crawling up onto my lap and resting her head on my knee, whimpering. She tucks her tail between her legs, her claws digging into my thigh as she tries to pull herself closer. I stroke the ridge of fur down her spine, and she relaxes.

Grunting, I lift her into my arms, slowly rising to my feet and trying not to put too much weight on my left leg. I struggle into the saddle, my horse murmuring at the excess weight, but I know his strength is enough to hold us. He just won't like it.

"That's kind of adorable." Rachel smirks as I open the front of my fur coat, buttoning it up again after I've wrapped it around the puppy. I pull my glove back on.

The wee little Siren presses her body against my chest, surprisingly warmer than I thought she would be. Though her cold wet nose makes me jump as she shoves it into my armpit.

We ride into the second half of Canyon pass: a dead man, a runaway princess, and a juvenile monster. Things can't get much more screwed up than this.

Rachel

Peter is actually smiling. I realize for the first time, that I haven't seen a real, full smile on his face in the whole time I have known him. I feel the corners of my mouth twitch up.

"Wow."

Peter looks up at me, the smile still in his eyes even though his mouth is grim again. "What?"

"Your smiling."

Peter looks away, fixing his eyes straight ahead. "Life's hard. If you can't smile at a puppy, what else is there?"

"Before it becomes a bloodthirsty man-eater you mean?"

"If you're waitin' for life to be roses and sunshine, you'll be waitin' a long time," Peter says, with a distant look in his eyes. "Felix said—says that."

I swallow. The reality of this world on the Surface is more bitter than I would've liked. Why couldn't the Glass City just share with the people on the surface? "I hate my father."

Peter sighs through his nose. He looks at me at last. "I'm sorry I dragged ya down here, sorry I changed everythin' ya knew. I just…. I saw no other way to escape."

At length, I say, "Don't be. I've always wanted to go to the Surface, I just never realized what it was really like down here." Another question pops into my head, one that's been pestering me since the Siren had attacked.

"….Why did you save Malcolm, even after he'd hurt you so bad?"

Peter looks at me with an odd expression. "Why wouldn't I?"

"Because…. he hurt you. He nearly killed you."

Peter wrinkles his nose, letting go of the reigns with one hand to adjust the strap of his rifle. "Aye, but that doesn't mean he deserves to die."

"He wouldn't've done the same for you."

"I wouldn't say that," Peter objects, looking thoughtfully down the canyon ahead of us as the road starts to slope down slightly. "He did help you bring me back to the ship. And he didn't fly off to the Glass City with us on board, right?"

"Yeah." I'm reluctant to admit it, but I can't deny it happened that way.

"Exactly. Give him a chance, Rachel. Jealousy can make a man stupid."

"Stupid is an understatement."

"Love is rarely understated."

I catch the horn of the saddle as my horse stumbles. "Jealousy is not love."

"Jealousy may not be love, but love is jealous."

"Normal people don't express jealousy with torture and murder."

Peter smirks. "Aye, ya have a point. But it's probably difficult for someone to grow up normal in the Glass City isn't it? I mean, look at you."

I open my mouth, but see that wide smile painted on his lips again. "Shut up," I mutter, and Peter's smile grows. I can't help but smile back.

A few more hours go by, during which the wind picks up and howls through the canyon from behind us. For a while, the Siren pup wails along with it, before it falls asleep again. We keep our heads down against the icy winds, but soon they get a touch warmer.

When I look up again, I can see the foggy silhouettes of buildings through the blowing snow. As soon as we exit the canyon the wind dies and the air is clear, except for snowflakes falling casually around us.

The only sound is that of the wind groaning through the canyon behind us and the crunch of the horses' hooves in the snow. The air is definitely warmer as we draw nearer to the buildings, until the snow around us is sloshy and brown with mud. A rancid smell fills my nose, but I'm not sure where it comes from.

A faint red haze shadows the buildings from behind, lighting up the snowfall and making the blurry outline of a cliff edge just barely visible at the far side of town. The buildings are run down old shacks with shuttered windows, in slightly better condition than the ones in Colfer, and the roads are muddy and wet.

The horses muddle along with their heads down and their ears back, mud splattering up their legs. As we get closer I realize this is a bigger town than Colfer.

Peter stops in front of the second largest building in the town, dismounting and tromping up the stairs onto the porch. He stops outside the door, glancing around as I step up behind him. "Don't say anythin'," he mutters, pulling open the front of my coat. I jerk back, but he catches my shoulder and pulls me closer, dumping the Siren puppy into my arms. The little canine yawns with a tiny squeak, cuddling against my chest, and Peter closes my coat around it. "And keep her hidden."

The Siren pokes her head out and starts to whine at Peter's back. He turns quickly, clamping her mouth shut with his thumb and forefinger. The Siren whimpers, and Peter lets go, stroking the top of her head and pushing her down into my coat.

Peter turns away again, jumping off the porch and untying the ropes connecting the dead Siren to his horse. His limp is considerably more heavy than before, but he slings the ropes over his shoulder and drags the dead Siren up onto the porch, his breath huffing mist into the frigid air. Although it's much warmer in here, I keep my coat bundled.

"Open the door," Peter grunts.

I obey. The pup squirms slightly, then relaxes, her hot breath tickling my collar bone. I can feel her nose twitching as she sniffs curiously.

Peter hauls the Siren carcass through the door, stumbling and catching himself on the counter against the wall opposite the door. He pounds his fist on the counter, and a stout man with shaggy bright red hair and brown eyes hurries out from a door behind the bar, craning his neck to see behind Peter and I. "What've ya got there?" His eyebrows meet. "There's a back entrance for beasts that size!"

Peter pulls the dead Siren closer. "I need everythin' ya can give me for it, particularly as many Healin' Devices as you've got."

The man's jaw goes slack, hanging open as if there's nothing to keep it closed. "Is that-"

"A Siren, yes, and takin' it down nearly cost me my life."

"You're Peter Gerrethson."

Peter nods.

"Jimmy told us all about you and your brother, Felix. You're…. he said you were takin' by the Scouts. How'd ya get back without bein' dead?"

"I found a way out," Peter says, casting a grim look my way. "But right now, I need as many healin' devices as you've got. Ya can keep the Siren, but I want at least some of the meat from it, and I want it known that I was the one who killed it."

"No problem, Gerrethson, you'll be famous. Twice over. There hasn't been a soul who survived a Siren attack in thirty years, and none that I know ever survived the Glass City. Bloody amazin'." The man shakes his head, coming around the counter to examine the dead Siren. He whistles. "She's a beaut. Wouldn't happen to be the same one you and your brother encountered, would it?"

"Aye, the very same."

The man whistles again.

The puppy in my coat shifts, huffing a sigh, and I keep my arms crossed over my chest, keep my head down.

The man stoops, helping Peter haul the carcass onto the counter. Peter clenches his teeth, squeezing his eyes shut and leaning against the bar with all his weight on his right leg, but the man doesn't seem to notice, bustling around behind the counter again. "The name's Cornelius, by the way. Cornelius McNear."

Peter shakes his hand with a brief smile.

Cornelius hurries off into the back of the shop, banging around noisily before returning with an armful of gear, which he plops on the end of the counter opposite the dead Siren. "I only have four devices, each with variable charge left." He displays the devices in his hand, then stuffs them into a ratty old black backpack. "Inside here is also a standard medical kit, and then there's four boxes of ammunition." He pats the boxes next to the pack.

Peter wrinkles his nose, shifting his weight. "Not much compared to what I'm givin' ya."

"Wait," the trader says. He ducks down under the counter and pulls out four knives. "These here explode if ya—"

"I know what they do. It'll hafta do." Peter slings the pack over his shoulder and stuffs the ammo into his pockets. "And I want a share of the meat once it's carved up."

I am ecstatic. I can't believe it was this simple. Now we have everything we could need to heal Felix twice over.

Cornelius bobs his head. "Yes, yes, or maybe the equivalent in caribou. I'm sure ya need some for your baby there." He directs his last words to me.

Peter pauses, his eyebrows going up.

I don't know what to say, praying to God that the little Siren won't move. The Siren puppy must make me look pregnant. "I—that would help," I say quietly, with my fake Irish accent. I catch Peter's smirk out of the corner of my eye.

"Have you decided on a name yet?"

"Um. No. No not yet. But thank you!" I give Peter a meaningful look.

"So is it yours then?" Cornelius asks Peter. "Congratulations."

Peter blushes furiously. "Well, not exactly. More like I've adopted the wee beastie."

Cornelius nods in approval. "Well, take care."

Peter just nods, his jaw clenched hard. "Thank you, Cornelius."

Cornelius grimaces. "Aye, you're welcome. I'm sorry I couldn't give ya more."

"Are you okay?" I ask as Peter limps out the door in front of me.

He nods, but seems relieved when I take the pack from his shoulder and sling it up over his horse.

The puppy in my coat smells Peter, and she starts to squirm. I pull open my coat, and she almost jumps out, lunging toward Peter. "Look who's the favorite." I smile looking up and down the street, but nobody is out at this hour. A few houses down, a gray and white dog watches us warily, its ears straight up.

Peter's folds the Siren pup into his coat again, buttoning it up and holding it close. The puppy relaxes, licking his chin, and Peter's smile becomes more visible.

"Now you can be the one who is expecting." I laugh.

"That was close in there. I don't know what they would do if they found out about this wee beastie...or you for that matter. So try a little harder with that accent next time."

"That bad?" I grimace.

Peter smiles a bit. Without a word, he leads the horses through town. When all the streets and buildings run out, we come to a place where the ground drops away to a wide canyon. Heat comes out of the crevasse in waves. A humid heat. And the stench is like rotten eggs. *So that's where the smell is coming from.* At the bottom of the drop, a glowing river of lava curves like a lazy orange serpent. I blink in amazement, completely awed by the fiery river and the people who are brave enough to live so close. All this time staring at the hotspot from above in my garden, I never imagined it looking like this up close. Or smelling like this.

"Be careful, it's a long drop," Peter says.

I gulp, terrified. Which is ridiculous; for one who's lived forty thousand feet up in the air all my life, I'm sure more scared than I should be.

Then again, with the Surface being nothing but a frozen wasteland, bravery might be trumped by the will to survive. The lava must be what makes the snow melt. I wonder if it is enough to grow crops—how else are they feeding people, and animals like horses?

Peter picks his way along the edge of the cliff until we reach a wide flat muddy field of various stunted crops. It isn't pretty, but it looks like it works. He guides us toward the farm with purpose, and we stop outside the front porch of the farmhouse, which is one of the nicer buildings in Hearthtown.

Peter doesn't even bother to knock. I follow him inside, stepping into a living room like setting with a blackened fire place and some dingy old couches. The scent of something cooking gives the old place a homey atmosphere.

He kicks his boots off at the threshold, and I do the same, not wanting to track mud through the house. We enter a room that looks like an office; it has one desk in front of the back wall and a single file cabinet that looks like it hasn't been opened in ages.

Peter leans against the doorframe, looking drained, and he knocks on the wall. A tall, thin woman looks up from the desk. I realize that, aside from Addy, this is the only woman I've seen on the Surface. Her ginger hair is tied up in a messy bun and her blue eyes look tired, but they fill with something like recognition when they fall on Peter. "Gerrethson?"

"Aye, Cliona, it's me. How's Darragh?"

Cliona just stares at him, her mouth gaping. "You.... were dead."

"Obviously not. But I was taken."

"You escaped," she whispers. It's not a question, but the disbelief in her voice makes my skin crawl, once again reminding me of the horrors my people inflict on theirs.

Peter nods, giving her a faint smile. "Aye. That I did."

Cliona studies him for a moment longer, then shakes her head as if to righten herself. "Darragh is still a mess. Did you see Niall in that awful City?"

Peter takes a breath. "No. I didn't see very many others. Nobody I knew. But I haven't heard he's been found in the water either. He must still be up there"

These people are losing their friends and family members to my home all the time, and I turned a blind eye to it. Maybe I should go back. Maybe I should free the Surface Dwellers in my City, and help them get home.

Cliona's face falls. She takes a deep breath, then straightens in her chair. "What brings ya here, Gerrethson?"

"My brother. He's dyin', and I have what I need, but the horses need rest, and it's gettin' too dark to travel safely."

I vaguely remember Jimmy saying something about leaving the horses here, but I don't say anything. Maybe Peter could make it back to Colfer on foot, but I don't think he wants to risk it with me.

Cliona nod. "Alright, how long?"

"Just for the night. And they need to be fed and watered."

"What d'ya got with ya?"

Peter hesitates, then holds up a finger, leaving me alone and tromping outside. Cliona looks me over curiously. "Haven't seen you around before. Did ya come back with him?"

I falter, not knowing what to say, and Peter limps back into the room. I sigh in relief when he saves me from answering by laying a knife across her table. "Double edged, with a detonator on the top. It's just a small blast, but enough to kill anyone you throw it at. It gives ya a minute to get away, and that's it."

Cliona looks impressed. "Is that a Scout's weapon?"

"Aye, that's the most I have to give."

Cliona studies it for a moment longer, then nods, getting to her feet. "Go ahead and put the horses in the barn, then come on back in for a bite to eat. You must be starved."

"No, really ya don't have to-" Peter's interrupted by a loud growling from his stomach.

I hold back a laugh, pretty sure that was the Siren pup.

Cliona raises an eyebrow at him. "*Starved.*" She translates. "The horses can stay here tonight, and I might as well treat a dead man to dinner." She hurries out of the room.

Peter watches her go, his Adam's apple bobbing as he swallows. "This is bad."

I roll my eyes. "You've got to eat something sometime."

"No, I meant for her." He opens the top of his coat slightly, and the Siren pup pokes her head out, her nose twitching. No doubt she smells whatever's cooking. "She's not goin' to want to sit still for that long. She might try to escape, and then Cliona would see her."

"Maybe we could get it to go?" I wonder out loud, peering at a faded picture on the wall. It shows Cliona and who I assume is her husband, but much younger. It strikes me that no picture I find down here will have been taken after the asteroids struck, as all the digital cameras were wiped out after the EMP.

We head out of the house. Peter leads the horses around the back of the farmhouse and alongside the field, which appears to be growing potatoes. He directs the horses into a large gray barn and into two empty stalls at the far end, the other stalls filled with weary looking horses of all different colors and size, their thick shaggy fur matted with mud—and what looks like blood, on some of them. He removes the saddle bags and slings them over his shoulders, looking pained.

"Here—give me one," I offer, and he lets me slide a saddle bag off his shoulder. It's much heavier than I thought it would be, but I manage to pull it over my own shoulders, letting out a breath. We make our way through the barn and step back outside, and a faint hum vibrates through the air. I think nothing of it, but Peter freezes, jerking his head up and scanning the skies. I'm about to ask what's wrong when he grabs my arm and yanks me back into the barn, shutting the heavy doors and leaning against the wall next to them. The hum gets louder, and I recognize it as the buzz of a hovercraft. I pale, listening to it circle once, twice, three times above Hearthtown before droning off.

Peter relaxes, looking drained of energy, and he heads back outside, limping past the field and into the house. I shut the barn door and hurry to catch up, scanning the skies. Was that hovercraft looking for me? Or was it just a Surface patrol, looking for Surface Dwellers to kidnap?

We stomp back into the house, pulling our boots off again, and Peter leads me into the kitchen. He sits down heavily at a small table, groaning, and Cliona glances over her shoulder from where she's cooking at the small cast iron stove. "You okay?"

"Never been better," Peter lies. Cliona gives him a look that clearly says she doesn't believe him, and she brings over a plate of steaming meat and potatoes, setting it in front of him.

"What've you got in your coat there?" A simple, honest question.

Peter doesn't miss a beat. "Blanket. Stole it from the glass city. Been keepin' me warm all day."

"Is it warmer up in the City?"

"Aye. Not quite as accustomed to the cold as I was."

"I suppose it'll take a while to get used to it again." Cliona looks up at me, gesturing toward the food. "Would you like some too?"

I nod slightly, not sure if it would be rude to eat all her food, but she smiles. She turns away for a second, then sets another plate down in front of the chair next to Peter, motioning for me to sit. "How long have you known each other?"

"Not long," Peter mumbles around a mouthful of food, obviously struggling not to make it clear how hungry he really is. He slows down a bit, taking smaller bites, and I smirk. I'm hungry too, but Peter had given most of the jerky to me on the way here.

"Where'd she come from?"

Peter chokes, setting down his fork and swallowing hard, his eyes watering. "Um…." He thinks for a moment, screwing up his face as he sucks at his teeth. "The Glass City. She happened to be with me at the time of my escape."

"So were you rescued by Gerrethson?"

I nod, keeping my eyes down.

"She's a wee bit shy." Peter clears his throat and takes another bite, relaxing, and I start eating as well. The meat tastes more like fish this time, and there's a bit of rice in it as well. Definitely better than penguin.

Cliona sits down across from me, on Peter's other side, and she too begins to eat.

"What's your name, dear?"

I hesitate, glancing at Peter. Peter doesn't look at me, but I can see the tendons in his neck grow taught. "Rachel," I say, with my fake an accent, hoping Cliona buys it.

"Rachel? Been a long time since I've heard a name like that."

"My mother was American," I say softly.

"Ah, that makes sense." Cliona's eyes smile, then grow sad. "And where are they now? Your parents?"

I suck at lying, so I tell the truth. "They're in the Glass City."

Cliona gives me a depressed look. "I'm so sorry. My son Niall is up there. Perhaps you met him? He has brown hair and blue eyes."

She sounds so hopeful, and I want so badly to tell her that I have, but, "I'm sorry. I might've, but I can't be sure." I should've gone back with Malcolm. I can make a much bigger difference in the Glass City than I can down here on the Surface. *What was I thinking?*

Cliona's face falls, and she gives me a listless shrug. "It's alright sweetie. He was taken two weeks ago, and his brother, Darragh, he's a total mess. See, I lost my husband to them as well, and they helped each other through."

I can barely take another bite of food. I want to apologize. Or do something. I had never realized just how horrible it was for the people left behind on the Surface. They are tortured just as much as the slaves in the City.

Cliona returns her attention to Peter. "So how'd ya kill that Siren?"

Peter pauses with his fork hovering between his mouth and his plate.

"One of those exploding knives in the neck," I say quietly, and Peter looks at me with an expression that clearly says *please don't.*

Cliona looks astounded. "Well I guess those things are useful for more than just a novelty bang."

I continue, leaving out most of the story, but giving a wild demonstration of Peter riding on the Siren's back.

She gives Peter a look. "How on earth....?"

Peter shrugs, taking his time to chew his food. "Adrenaline," he says at length.

Cliona shakes her head, smiling slightly. "Bloody amazin' that's what you are Gerrethson. You and your brother. Promise me you'll make it home in one piece."

"That was the plan." Peter finishes eating before I do, but although he still looks hungry, he turns down Cliona's offer for seconds. "We need to find someplace to stay before it gets dark. Is Conner still runnin' the hotel?"

"Aye, and he's gone cheap. Fewer people have been stayin' there, what with all the Scouts prowlin' the skies. He'll do anythin' for a small amount, as long as it's enough to feed him and his wife."

I grimace, knowing Peter has nothing for food to trade. But Peter just stands, thanking Cliona and heading for the door. Cliona picks up his plate, and I scrape the rest of my food into my hand as she turns around, hiding it in my palm and handing her my plate. "Thank you," I say softly, then follow Peter outside.

I close the door behind me and suck in a sharp breath; Peter's leaning against one of the porch supports, his shoulder's hunched and his eyes squeezed shut, the lower half his face buried in the fur collar of his coat. He cracks his eyes open when I touch his shoulder, worried. "Are you sure you're okay?"

"Aye. I'm fine," he croaks, but I can tell he's lying. He used to be better at hiding his pain—or maybe I have just gotten better at seeing it.

I give him a disapproving look, then pull the front of his coat down enough so that the Siren puppy can poke her head out. I hold the food under her nose, and she sniffs at it, giving it an experimental lick. She snuffles some more, than gobbles it out of my hand, licking her chops.

Peter chuckles, and the Siren licks his chin. "We can't have people seein' ya, girl. Things could get awkward." He starts toward the glacier that makes up one wall of Canyon Pass, where the rest of the buildings squat in the mud.

"She needs a name," I tell him, stroking the top of her head as we walk.

"Then give her one."

I think, rubbing her soft ears. A million names run through my head, but only one seems to fit the little Siren pup. "How 'bout Frosty?"

Peter smiles. "Aye, Frosty is good." He agrees. He gently pushes Frosty's head down his coat, closing off the opening so that she can't get out again. We tromp up the steps to a large, rickety old building with rotting gray walls, and I hope against hope that this isn't where we're staying.

Peter

The hotel is two stories high, propped up against the wall of the glacier behind it. Inside, the floors slope just enough to make a noticeable decline, and I wonder for the umpteenth time how this building remains standing.

I lean on the hardwood of the desk, across the room from the front door. "One night." I croak, and the scrawny old man looks up from his drawing.

Conner's eyes light up. "Peter! I thought you were dead?"

"You have no idea how annoyin' it is to hear that every time someone recognizes me." I growl.

Conner grimaces. "I'm sorry mate." He shakes his head. "Don't blame the people, Gerrethson, they just can't help it. Bloody amazin' it is."

I stare at him hard until he stops talking, and he sighs. "Alright, what've ya got?"

I pull a wool blanket out of the saddle bag slung over my shoulder and drop it on the desk, along with two boxes of ammunition for a sniper rifle. Conner looks like he's about to protest, but I hold up my finger. "I'm only stayin' one night, Conner. One night." But since my being here is probably putting him in danger, I pull out one of the exploding knives, laying carefully it beside the blanket and ammunition. "Just don't push the button, and they'll give ya quite a bit for it down at the trader's shop."

Conner examines it, his face brightening again. "One cot or two?"

I narrow my eyes. "Two," I tell him firmly, and Conner smirks. "Second floor, room seven."

I drag myself upstairs to room seven, using the wall for support. I'm pretty sure my leg is getting worse. The Siren puppy grunts every time I stumble, just her nose sticking out of my collar. *Frosty.* I smile, the warmth of her tiny furry body like a portable heater. I shoulder my way into the room, the rusty hinges resisting my weight for only a second.

Rachel follows me in and shuts the door as I collapse on one of the cots, careful not to crush Frosty.

Frosty squirms free of my grasp, crawling out of the front of my coat and shaking off. She snuffles at my head, shifting her nose through my hair, and I wrinkle my nose. "Frosty, knock it off."

I pull off my gloves, trying to rub the warmth back into my face with my hands.

Rachel breathes a sigh of relief, sitting on the other cot on the opposite wall and dropping her saddle bag to the floor. She shifts uncomfortably, her face reddening as she takes in her surroundings. "That's cute."

"And wet. And cold." I add, rolling onto my stomach. Frosty lifts her little front paws in the air and pounces on my hand, biting it, but not hard enough to draw blood. "Ow," I tell her, pushing her back, but that just encourages her, and she jumps forward again, attacking my hand. I scoot it away as though it were a five-legged creature, and she chases after it with a growl.

I push at her face, catching her lower jaw as she bites my fingers. Frosty growls, opening her mouth and trying to pull away, and I let her. Instantly, she springs forward again, gnawing on my hand like a chew toy. "Commere ya wee little dote." I chuckle, pulling her forward by her front paws as she tries to bite my hands some more. She pulls away, tipping her head back and wailing her song. Immediately I clamp her mouth shut, pressing her head into the cot and jerking my head to look over my shoulder at the door. Rachel watches the entrance as well, both of us listening for footsteps. Frosty mumbles a bark, pushing at my wrist with her fuzzy right paw. I lower my face so I'm at eyelevel with her, my hand still pressed against the top of her head. "Ya gotta be quiet, girl, or you're gonna get yourself killed."

Frosty's playful growl becomes a whimper, and I let her go. She keeps her head on her paws for a wee bit, then gets up and starts tentatively licking my chin, pushing her head beneath my jaw and moving closer until she's squished beneath my head, her own wee little head resting on my shoulder. She huffs, and I smile slightly. "Good girl."

The tone of my voice makes her wag her tail a little, and she licks my ear.

"You really think they'll kill her?"

"Well, she's a Siren. It's possible she'll grow up to be a bloody monster just like her mum." Even though looking at her now all I can see is a playful puppy.

"But…. she also might not. Like, maybe growing up with people could make her more like a dog?" Rachel suggests.

"Most people would say it's not worth the risk."

"Is it really their place to decide?"

I look up at Rachel. She twists her finger in the end of her ponytail.

"Considerin' Sirens kill people, aye, I would say it is," I say.

"And what about the people in the Glass City?" Rachel's blue eyes study my face, waiting for a response. "My father is a monster. Does that mean I'll grow up to be just like him?"

I flick my gaze back down to Frosty. "People aren't animals."

Rachel looks around the room, her expression disapproving. "Is this building even safe?" she asks. I wonder if she's satisfied with my answer or just wanting to change the subject.

"Aye, safe enough. Just a wee bit old."

"I'll say," she mutters. She shifts her gaze to Frosty, reaching over and petting the top of her head. I feel Frosty tense, and she jerks away from Rachel, sniffing at her fingers and licking them experimentally. Satisfied that Rachel is safe, she leans into her hand, a doggy smile pulling up the corners of her mouth. "Maybe she won't turn out like her mother."

I get up stiffly, pulling off the backpack and setting it on the floor next to my saddle bag. I groan, stretching my sore back and shoulders before sitting down on the cot again, carefully pulling off my boots. I tug my left pant-leg up a wee bit, peeling away the bandages and grimacing at the wound. A long, thin gash stretches across my calf, the edges red and puffy. I can feel heat when I hover my hand over it, but I don't dare to touch it.

Rachel crouches next to the edge of my cot for a closer look, gently prodding at the inflamed skin,

I flinch away. "Bloody hell what'd you do that for?"

"Just use one of the TRRDs, Peter."

"The *what?*"

"Healing Device?" She guesses, and I vaguely remember the report she'd given to her mother back in the Glass City, about the Healing Devices. She'd called them birds and turds.

"You have got to call them somethin' else."

"Just use one."

I shake my head. "No, Felix needs them more than I do. And besides it's just a scratch."

"Peter, you're already pretty much starving yourself and depriving yourself of any real sleep. If you heal yourself, you'll still have plenty of energy in the rest of the devices to heal most of Felix's burns, if not all. You have four, your leg would only take up maybe a quarter of the energy in one, possibly a little more. There'll still be enough for Felix, maybe even enough to heal the cuts and burns on your back."

I don't respond, and Rachel sighs, sitting next to me and gripping my sore shoulder. "Stop torturing yourself like this, or you'll never make it back to him."

I let out a breath. "I'll sleep on it," I say, rubbing my face with my hands.

Rachel gives me a look, but she doesn't protest, and instead slides her hand down my arm to my own, squeezing my fingers. "You need to learn to help yourself sometimes. And besides, how are we supposed to get back to Colfer in a decent amount of time if you're hurt?"

"I said I'll sleep on it."

The little sleep that comes to me is tortured with nightmares of whips and red hot pokers and my brother's death. Finally, when my leg begins to throb, I give up. Frosty looks at me curiously as I swing my legs gingerly over the side of my cot, rolling up my pant-leg.

Maybe Rachel's right, and I should just heal it.

Baring my teeth, I slide down to the end of the cot and dig through the backpack, removing one healing device and pressing it against the wound in my leg. I push the button and gasp as the fiery pain intensifies, the healing device slowly repairing the tissue until my leg is fully healed; even the hair grows back.

My jaw relaxes—my whole body relaxes—and I lean back on the cot again. Frosty settles back against me with a satisfied groan, happy to get back to sleep.

In the morning Frosty wakes me by pouncing all her weight onto my chest. I roll over, wheezing, as she wags her whole body and leaps off my cot, bounding across the room and jumping up onto Rachel's cot. Rachel flinches, screwing up her face as a long pink tongue bathes her face in dog spit. I laugh, stretching my back. "Somebody's happy to see you."

Rachel pushes Frosty away and sits up slowly. "Morning," she mumbles over her yawn.

"Mornin'."

Rachel notices the healing device on the floor next to the backpack, but she doesn't say anything. I was at least expecting an 'I told you so.' It's strange, even though I have spent the better part of a week with her, and in some fairly intimate ways, I still don't know very much about her. I guess I was keeping my distance, assuming she would go back to the Glass City the first chance she got.

I watch her pull her hair out of its tie and attempt to comb the long waves with her fingers. She lost everything because of me, and yet she chose to stay. She's got nothing but the clothes on her back. She snags a tangle and her face transforms from barely awake to fully alert as she yelps.

Suppressing a smile I step out of the room, pulling on my jacket as I go. Knowing her, she'll be bumbling around for quite a while before she's ready to go. The building is quiet as I sneak into the washroom, and I spot something on the counter as I splash a little water on my face. I grab it and stuff it in my pocket. I will have to leave Conner a little tip in the room.

I creep down to the kitchen. Conner's wife is already making breakfast, boiling meat in a rusted pot on the stove.

"Try not to burn the buildin' down," I say, snatching two bowls off the lopsided counter.

"Shut it Gerrethson." She slops some of the meat into each of the bowls.

Apparently the fact that I'm still alive doesn't impress her, but I'm grateful that she doesn't comment on it. Back upstairs, I open the door and find Rachel almost ready to go. Her hair is pulled back again but it still looks tangled.

"I would give anything for some coffee right about now," she groans. "Or a—"

I hold up the treasure I'd snagged from the washroom.

"A comb! Thank God!" She takes it from my hand, holding her breath as though it might disappear at any moment.

"Aye, well, I figured since you might be stayin' here a while, a few comforts would be nice. Might stop and get you some clothes if I can." I hand her the bowl of meat, eating my own breakfast quickly.

A smile mingled with a mixture of emotions plays on her face. Regret, maybe? Anxiety? I can't blame her.

"So, when do we leave?" She asks, her face finally settling into a grim determination as she yanks the last of the tangles from her hair. She starts eating her breakfast.

"As soon as possible. We have more than enough tech to heal Felix now. I want to get them back to him before anythin' else goes wrong." The small of my back still burns, but not nearly as badly as it had a few days ago. A cracked mirror leans against the wall, and I turn my back to it, lifting my shirt to see the bloody bandages. I grimace, peeling the bandages away; the cuts and burns on my back are mostly healed, what's left of them starting to scar over. I roll up the gauze and toss it into a small tin by the door, gently pulling my shirt down over my back.

Frosty prances up to me and places her paws on my knees, gazing up at me expectantly. I stoop and lift her into my coat, giving her the last of the meat from my bowl. The Siren puppy licks my chin affectionately, and I rub the top of her head, tucking her into my coat.

"Felix will be okay, Peter. He's been hanging on all this time. If he's as strong and stubborn as you, he'll be fine." Rachel pulls on her gloves.

I do the same, flexing my fingers under the heat reflective fabric. "You're from the Glass City where everythin' is always okay. Down here, anythin' that can go wrong will go wrong. So I'd rather not chance it." I remind her, slinging my guns and backpack over my back, lifting the saddle bag over my shoulder.

Rachel picks up her own saddle bag, grunting under its weight.

"I can take that, if ya need me to."

"I'm fine," she says, even though the strain of carrying the heavy saddle bag shows on her face. My own saddle bag is almost more than my newly healed leg can bear, so I'm sort of glad she didn't give hers to me. I hold the door open for her as she steps out into the hall, and toss an extra case of ammo on the bed next to the empty bowls for Conner's trouble.

After a quick stop at the *jacks* for Rachel, we make our way downstairs. It's still quiet. Something doesn't seem right. I stop, and Rachel runs into my back.

Rachel gives me an inquiring look. "What-"

"Sh," I tell her, listening intently. "Follow me, and keep quiet."

"What's wrong?"

"I don't know. Listen." Conner is nowhere in sight, and everything is quiet, even though the dim light of dawn has brightened to the full gray light of day outside.

As we listen, the shouts of men drift through the walls. Then a horse screams. I feel my blood turn to ice, and I swallow hard.

"What's happening?" Rachel looks panicked.

"Whatever it is, it isn't good." I shove Frosty into her arms, drop my saddle bag, and take off for the door.

"Where are you going?!" Rachel calls after me.

"Stay here!" I yell back without turning around. I shoulder through the door, pulling my machine gun off my back.

A hovercraft soars overhead as I step out into the street; it's bay doors are open and Scouts lean out, held in place by harnesses as they rattle off a spray of bullets. The turrets on the wings are also occupied, blasting fifty caliber round into anything that moves. The residents of Hearthtown are in a panic, screaming and running toward Canyon Pass, where they hope they can gain some sort of advantage. A few of the braver men remain in the streets, firing bullets at the sky. Wolves prowl on the outskirts of the town, waiting for the hail of bullets to cease so they can feast. Already I can see three people dead or wounded, their flesh eaten away by the Scouts nanotech bullets. Closer to me I spot Cornelius grappling with a Scout.

I raise my gun and fire three rapid shots, taking out the Scout, then charge through the mud toward a second Scout. Cornelius, now free, tackles a third to the ground, swinging his fists, pounding the man's face into the mud. I slide to a stop, pressing the butt of my gun to my shoulder and shooting the second Scout before he can plunge a knife into Cornelius's back. Cornelius gets off his Scout, leaving him either dead or unconscious in the street, and gives me a quick nod of thanks, before taking off toward Canyon Pass.

I feel sick, but I follow him, firing at anybody wearing red, and then I hear the low hum of a hovercraft. The entire town seems to pause for a breathless moment. A blood-curdling scream sounds from behind me, and I whirl in time to see Rachel clawing at the face of a Scout, jamming her thumbs into his eyes and forcing him to his knees.

The Scout yells, covering his face. "Miss Brown you have to come home!"

Rachel just kicks him away, scrambling backwards as two more scouts rush to help. My chest constricts and I stop in the slush of the road, turning a circle and scanning the grey clouds for the hovercrafts before sprinting toward Rachel.

"Get off me!" Rachel wrenches away from the taller of the two Scouts, while the other struggles to get the first one on his feet. Frosty falls out of Rachel's coat, cowering on the ground with huge eyes.

I fire three times, hitting each of them in the chest. Rachel shrieks, and Frosty yelps, her tail between her legs.

"I told you to stay inside!"

"No freaking way!" She yells back,

"Then *run!*"

Rachel grabs Frosty, and we take off toward Canyon Pass as a second hovership careens overhead. Rachel puts herself between me and any Scouts that try to confront us, using her body to shield me as I take out those who stand in our way.

"Are you mental?!"

"They won't shoot *me.*" Rachel shoves me aside as a Scout aims his rifle at me. The man hesitates, and I shoot him before he can adjust his aim. We're almost to Canyon Pass when Frosty wails, twisting from Rachel's grasp and racing off in the opposite direction.

"Frosty no!" Rachel shouts, chasing after her.

I make a grab for her arm, but miss, stumbling. "Rachel!"

She ignores me, ducking as a spray of bullets rains down from above. "Bloody hell." I race after them, weaving between buildings and picking off Scouts as I go. "Rachel she'll be fine!"

As soon as I say it, I catch sight of them. Rachel has caught up with Frosty at the edge of the ravine, silhouetted against the glow of the lava flow at its base. She scoops her up and turns into the arms of another Scout. I raise my gun, but the Scout turns Rachel to face me, hiding behind her back. "Don't even try it," he calls over her shoulder.

Rachel struggles, but the Scout squeezes her until she stops, panic flooding her eyes. I could shoot him. Hit him right between his eyes, but I hesitate. His head is right next to Rachel's, and I don't want to do that to her.

"Peter!" Rachel screams, and I whirl around, barely managing to block a blow from a second Scout before it slams into the back of my head. I slip in the mud, and the Scout plants a heavy boot in my chest.

I stagger backwards. My foot comes down on open air and I drop, catching myself on the edge of the cliff. Rachel thrashes against her captor, and the second Scout stands over me. Before I can climb back up, he kicks me hard in the face, and I lose my grip. Fear courses through my veins as I fall backwards six feet through the air before my back crashes against a solid surface, my rifle skittering away.

I blink, stunned, my blood roaring through my ears. It takes me a moment to realize that the sound isn't in my head, and I slowly turn over, still seeing stars; there's nothing underneath me but the river of lava, far below—but I'm definitely lying on something solid.

Then the air beneath me shimmers, and the front of a massive hovercraft suddenly blocks my view of the red orange haze below. I release a breath as I realize I'm not just hanging in midair above a river of lava, but my relief is short lived. I find myself looking through the glass roof of the cockpit down at the pilots. They stare back at me, equally shocked, before angry scowls twist their expressions.

There's an explosion of curses, and I struggle to my feet, ducking behind the dorsal fin of the hovercraft as bullets ricochet off the red and black metal of the sleek spine.

"Get him!" Yells the Scout holding Rachel on the edge of the cliff above. Then he grunts as she bites his forearm.

The second Scout jumps down, landing on the sloped surface of the hovercraft and dropping his gun as he catches himself. He swears violently, lunging toward me, and I leap out of the way. My feet slip on the smooth aluminum and I land hard on my chest. By now, the ship has risen above the edge of the cliff and is continuing to get higher and higher. It needs to land *now*, or I won't be able to get off.

Winded, I barely manage to roll away as the Scout's boot crashes down. I scramble to my feet, barreling into the Scout's chest and sending us both sliding downward, stopping dangerously close to the twin propellers jutting side by side off the rear end. The Scout pins me, pressing my face toward the spinning blades. It takes all my strength to resist, the roar pounding in my ears. Screaming, I shove my knee into the Scout's gut, flipping him up over my head and driving him straight down into the turbines. A spray of blood spirals out from the propeller a second before it stops; the thick bones of the Scout lodge in the propeller, and smoke billows up from where I assume the motor is.

My stomach lurches, and I stagger to my feet as we veer sharply down and to the right. There's a loud whine as the engine sputters and dies. I stumble toward the front where the pilots are in a panic, struggling to right the vehicle as it plummets toward the muddy ground. The ship shudders and I lose my balance, sliding down the windshield toward the ground fifteen feet below. I struggle to catch myself, but the smooth glass has nothing for my hands to grab, and the pilots watch as I slip over the nose of the vehicle and fall.

I hit the ground feet first and roll onto my back, my scream dying to a wheeze, and I just catch a glimpse of the hovercraft crashing in a spray of mud not thirty yards away. The front of it crunches under the impact; glass shatters and steel crumples as the ship skids through the mud before shrieking to a stop. The turbines on its back end whirl to a halt, still smoking and bloody. I tremble all over, crawling toward the fallen mass of twisted steel that no longer looks anything like a hovercraft.

I reach the back of the ship, where the cargo door has been forced open and ripped halfway off its hinges. I try to see through the haze of smoke in the wreckage. On my way to the cockpit, I pass three motionless bodies, all wearing red Scout uniforms and all of them sprawled across the floor near the front, thrown forward by the force of the impact.

I push forward to the pilot's seat, choking on the smoke-filled air and blinking rapidly to clear my vision. Shards of muddy glass prickle under my hands; the crumpled nose of the hovercraft crushes the legs of the pilot in the chair to my immediate right. *So much death.* I stare at the carnage around me, the weight of it all forcing my head down, and my stomach twists. *None of this had to happen.*

The pilot remains motionless, whether unconscious or dead, I don't know. But when I look closer, my heart clenches in panic. *It's Liam.* I want to leave him here, but when I press my fingers under his jaw, I can feel his pulse fluttering faintly.

Part of me wants to let him die, to make sure he can never hurt me again, but I can't do that. No more death. Not because of me. I brace my back against the cabin wall and push my feet at the twisted metal pinning his legs. Then I grab the front of his shirt and haul him out of the chair.

I have no idea where my bags with the healing tech for Felix ended up. My heart flutters briefly, but I hang on to the hope that Rachel has them. Liam isn't going to live without healing.

The hovercraft is a twisted wreck, but I tear through the cabinets, searching desperately for any healing devices I can find. This hovercraft is much bigger than the one Malcolm had. I find the precious cargo in a drawer in one of the compartments. I quickly get back to Liam. Shards of glass stick up from his chest, and I pull them out, one by one, using a healing to stop the bleeding. Then I move to his crushed legs, using a different device to repair the broken bones. I had never noticed it before, but the names of each model are engraved in the black plastic: B-R-R-D and T-R-R-D.

As I finish the major injuries and move to the minor ones, Liam gasps. I jerk back for a moment, checking that my gun is on my hip. Whether he is still in shock from his injuries or recognizes that I am trying to help him, Liam chooses not to fight me. He watches me with a puzzled expression, his blue eyes full of confusion and uncertainty even as he cries out in pain.

I finish just as the device runs out of energy, and collapse back, tired in a way that feels like the device had pulled the energy of its healing directly from my soul.

"Why are you helping me?" Liam whispers, slowly recovering. He spits blood out of his mouth and manages to sit up.

I hesitate. "Just because you'd leave me, doesn't mean I'd do the same. " I hold my gun on him and get to my feet, backing away.

Liam blinks at me, his brow furrowed, but he doesn't try to stop me.

I've done all I can for him. I run outside again, the hum of more engines filling the air. The wolves have advanced on the town, digging into the dead. Above, new hovercrafts are already circling. I panic, wondering if Rachel is on one of them. I suppose that would be a good thing, but now that I think of it, I don't want her to go.

A high pitched voice reaches my ears; "PETER!"

Fifty yards away, and can make out a running figure, weighed down by multiple bags slung over her shoulders.

No, no not in the open! I break into a dead run, charging out across the muddy ground even as my boots slip in the slush.

We close the distance between us quickly and Rachel slams into me, the saddle bags sliding off her shoulders and Frosty squealing indignantly from inside her coat. I catch Rachel before she falls, her feet sliding in the mud, and to my surprise she throws her arms around my neck, trembling.

I can feel her fear radiating from her body like waves of heat. Still stunned, I hold her as she cries, ignoring Frosty's complaints. "Rachel we need to hide. They're still-"

I'm cut off by three more massive hovercrafts rising above the edge of the cliff, and I jerk away from Rachel, stumbling backwards and grabbing her hand. "RUN!" I yell needlessly, and she obeys, racing after me as we make our way as fast as we can toward Canyon Pass.

The few people who are still at the mouth of the canyon point, yelling at us to run faster, but one of the hovercrafts lands in front of us.

Rachel and I slip to a stop, panting and turning a circle as the other two hovercrafts orbit around us. The one on the ground powers down, and a door slides open on the side. Out steps Brown, his blue eyes hard as steel. Two men with guns follow him out, and I recognize Calvin. I stand in front of Rachel protectively.

"Rachel thank God I found you." Brown sounds genuinely relieved, starting forward.

"Stay away from me," Rachel says it quietly, and it stops Brown in his tracks.

"Honey, please—you're mother has been worried sick, I've been looking everywhere for you. It's time to come home."

"She's not goin' home," I say before Rachel can, squaring my shoulders.

Brown's face twists. "You let my daughter go you filthy Surface rat, or I'll blast this little village to hell."

"No." Rachel pushes me behind her, her face etched with rage. "You won't. I'm not going home. I don't want to."

"Rachel, now is not the time to be stubborn. I love you, please just come home."

"Do you really think after everything you've done, you can convince me to go anywhere with you?" Rachel whispers, shaking her head. "Just go. Don't make me hate you more than I already do."

"Come with me, and I'll only kill him," Brown says.

"No way." Rachel shakes her head in disgust. "No—if I go with you, you let them *all* live."

I catch her arm. "Rachel." There's no way I'm letting her sacrifice herself for me.

"Peter I can help you. I can help everyone. On the Surface I can only do so much, but from the Glass City…. I can set the servants free," she says the last part more quietly, so her father doesn't hear.

"Rachel!" Brown snaps, but she ignores him, cupping my face in her hands.

"I'm not going to let him kill you when you haven't done anything wrong. Let me do this. Let me help you."

"Don't."

She ignores me, turning to face her father. "Promise me that if I go with you, you'll let Peter and everyone else go. Promise you'll stop hurting them."

"Absolutely not." Brown looks repulsed. "Rachel, it's time you come home. Let this Surface rat receive the punishment he deserves."

"But he hasn't done *anything* compared to what you've done!" She screams at him, her fury showing in every rigid line of her body.

"Rachel, such is the way of life. He took something that didn't belong to him, and now he has to pay for it. An eye for an eye, right?"

"Don't you *dare* pull that out of context—"

"Why do you want to stay with this rat so badly? You haven't—" Brown stops himself, disgust twisting at his face. "Have you two— ."

Rachel is indignant—and I am too. Before I can say anything, though, Rachel lashes out. "Is that what you think of me? Do you think I'd just sleep around with someone I barely knew?"

My face burns hot, and Rachel continues.

"I guess it makes sense that you'd think that though. After all, we're all just *animals* acting on *natural instinct* and we just don't know any better." She's mocking him now. "Well newsflash, Mom disagrees. Unlike you, she taught me about morality and the value of life. I'm not just some animal, *Dad*, or an object to be fought over."

"Don't make this any harder than it needs to be," Brown growls, his expression darkening. I see his hand start to move toward his pocket, and my blood turns to ice. I had forgotten….

"Rachel, just go home," I whisper, fear coursing through my veins.

"No! Not until he promises to let you go."

"He won't Rachel. No matter what you say, no matter what you do, he's never goin' to let me go. Your father is a monster." A blinding pain suddenly sucks all the breath from my lungs and crumples my knees.

I gasp, and Rachel catches me, keeping me on my feet as I shudder under a massive wave of pain that arcs all the way up and down my spine.

"Peter?!" She calls, and I almost don't hear her, my entire body throbbing and burning horribly as though I've been through a blender.

"I told you not to make this worse." Brown's voice groans, as if this entire encounter is a nuisance, and Rachel screams at him.

"Stop it! Dad stop it please he needs to get home-!"

"Oh, you mean to Colfer?" The way Brown says it makes my heart turn to ice. "To help your brother? What's his name…. ah, Felix. Well, I can't say there's much of a home to go to, now. And Felix? I have him. And he has been fully healed. You see? I am not the monster you think, Rachel. But if you don't come with me." His sneer twists into something more vile. "There will be no Felix."

My heart stops and the breath is suddenly gone from my lungs. "You're lyin'," I breathe.

"No, actually I'm not this time. I'd tell you to see for yourself, but that would require letting you live. Rachel, there is no way I will let this scum live another day, but his brother has not stolen from me, I might let him live if you come with me now ."

"….Dad?" Rachel sounds small and helpless, and I slump against her as the pain intensifies.

I slide down Rachel's back to the ground, unable to remain standing any longer. I curl into the fetal position and just tremble in the mud, gasping for breath as the pain becomes impossibly more intense, until breathing is almost an unachievable action.

Rachel drops to her knees by my side, her mouth forming words but not making any sound.

I stutter in between convulsions, trying to form the words to— what? I want to tell her to save Felix, but I know Brown won't be true to his word. And I don't know what he will do to his own daughter. Will he punish her for defending me? For choosing me over him? I don't know what I want to say to her, but it doesn't matter. I can't speak through the pain. My body is no longer in my control.

Frosty squirms out of Rachel's coat and licks my face, but I can't move, can't breathe, can't do *anything*. I can't stop them as Calvin and the other man grab Rachel's arms and pull her back from me.

Brown slowly approaches. He kicks a snarling Frosty out of his way and holds a small black device in front of my face, turning a wee little dial on it. Fresh hurt explodes all across my body, sucking me rapidly toward unconsciousness.

Brown sits back and hurls the tiny device as far away as he can, then brings his mouth close to my ear. "*Suffer.*" I barely hear him, and then everything is gone except for unbearable agony.

Rachel

"Get off me!" I scream, hitting at Calvin with both my fists and digging my nails into his arms. Calvin grits his teeth, but he doesn't let go; he and another man haul me away from Peter. He's curled on his side in the mud, his entire body convulsing in pain, and his eyes are rolled all the way back in his head so that the whites are showing.

"Peter!"

One of the men lifts me into the hovercraft, pinning me against the wall as Calvin stomps in and my father closes the door behind him. "Dad let me go!"

"No. Your mother's been worried sick about you."

"I'm sure she wouldn't approve of this!"

"Rachel, I don't want to hear it. There's a room in the back, go to it. Wait there until we're back in the Glass City."

"NO!"

My father raises his hand, and I flinch, startled.

"I said go," he growls, and I take a step back, for the first time ever terrified of my father.

I swallow hard, then turn and run to the back of the hovercraft as it continues to rise into the sky. But instead of going to the room, I head to the cargo hold, where rows of escape pods are stored in the walls.

I glance over my shoulder, then hurry over to the nearest escape pod, opening the back and checking to make sure it is fully stocked with survival supplies. I have no idea what my father did to Peter, but whatever it was it looked like it needed a lot of healing. For good measure I grab some extra supplies from another pod and dump them into the back of my chosen escape vehicle.

The escape pod only has enough space to sit two people, enough for me and Peter, if he's still alive when I get back. *He has to be.* Before I get inside, I grab a rifle that is mounted on the wall of the cargo bar for emergencies and I stick it in the back with the medical supplies. Just in case I need to fight my way back to him.

I get in, take a deep breath, then finally work up the nerve to pull the handle in the roof. There's a hissing sound, and then my stomach does flips as the pod drops into a free fall toward the Surface.

"Two-hundred-feet." A robotic female voice buzzes through the small speaker in the dashboard. I swallow, the pod doing a nose dive so that I can see the ground rapidly rising toward me. But if I slow down, it'll be that much easier for my father to catch up, unless he hasn't noticed my absence yet.

Above me, the larger hovercrafts continue on their way, showing no signs that they know of the escape pod's ejection.

"One-hundred-fifty-feet."

"One-hundred-feet."

"Fifty-feet."

I slam the lever next to the steering wheel and the pod hums to life, slowing to an abrupt halt twenty-five feet above the ground. I try to get my bearings. *North.* Hearthtown is to the north. I push the steering wheel forward and the pod zips along the icy surface back toward Hearthtown. I hope.

Eventually I see Canyon Pass, and I know I am on the right track. Soon Hearthtown comes into view.

Below me, several buildings are nothing but smoking, burnt out shells, some not even that. People are streaming through the canyon away from the city, toward whatever safety they hope to find. They move faster when they see my pod coming.

I circle once before I see a small shape in the mud.

I drop the hovercraft to ten feet and then slowly settle it down, opening the top of the pod and jumping out before it's even landed. Thank God the wolves are too busy with the dead to have discovered Peter.

"Peter!" I yell, dropping to my knees and ignoring the wetness that soaks through my fur pants.

Peter doesn't respond, still in the same fetal position he had been in when I had left. All the residents of Hearthtown have evacuated, and the Scouts are gone. The place seems so empty. Nobody is there to help. It's up to me.

But what do I do?

His body is caked in mud, but as far as I can tell, there's no blood. Despite this, his face is twisted in pain and his uneven breath wheezes from his lungs, just the whites of his eyes showing. I reach out to touch his face, but a vicious snarl makes me jerk back.

Frosty's head appears out from under Peter's chin, her fangs bared and her blue eyes fierce. She's managed to wedge herself under Peter's left arm, so that she's pressed against his chest and his body is curled around hers. He's likely squeezing her too hard, but she doesn't seem to care, her muddy white fur bristling.

"Frosty it's me," I tell her, trying to keep the fear and panic out of my voice. "Let me help him." *What's wrong with him, though? How do I fix something I can't see?*

The Siren puppy recognizes my voice, the snarl dropping away and her head tilting to one side. She whines and wiggles, as if she is suddenly certain I will make everything better.

Tears prickle my eyes, because I am not so sure. "Come here girl." I slide my hands behind her front legs, pulling her away from Peter's tight grasp. I give her head a pat, then carefully lift Peter's face out of the mud, pushing him onto his back and pulling open the front of his coats and shirt, but aside from the old bruises, there are no new wounds.

"Peter? Peter can you hear me?"

Peter just rasps, the breath rattling from his lungs. I look around quickly, spotting the saddle bags not too far away, where I had dropped them earlier. I get up and run toward them, hauling them over my shoulders and jogging back to the hovercraft with difficulty.

Should I move him, I wonder when I return to Peter. I don't know. I just want to cry.

Instead I make a decision. I stoop and slide my hands under his arms, grunting as I drag him over to the escape pod and lift him halfway onto the passenger seat. Peter chokes on his pain, his back arching and making it all the more difficult to move him. I gasp, then lift him the rest of the way, letting Frosty jump up on his lap and lick the mud off his face.

I am about to get in my side, when I see something in the snow. It's a small black cube—I recognize it. My father had it in his hands when Peter started screaming for no reason. What could it be?

I pick it up, but it's clearly mangled. There had been a button on top, but it's missing, and a spring sticks out. I poke at the spring with my gloved finger and a spark of electricity fizzles up at me. Peter cries out, shuddering in the passenger seat.

I don't have time to figure it out. I shove it in my pocket and get in the driver seat. We have to get out of here before my father figures out that I am gone.

Peter's cave seems like the best place to hide.

I hurry around to the other side and jump in, closing the glass roof. We ascend quickly, and in no time at all, we're speeding through Canyon Pass, zipping above the few residents of Hearthtown that are still making their way through.

When we reach the break in the pass, where Malcolm had found us, I turn southwest and fly until we reach the Atlantic Ocean.

All the while, Peter trembles in the seat beside me, his arms curled tightly across his stomach and his body bent so that his head is touching his knees. Frosty whimpers, running her wet nose along his face as if she too is trying to find the cause of his pain.

Above us, I can just barely make out the twinkle through the clouds in the sky that is the Glass City, and my hatred for my home grows stronger.

The long stretch of icy beach on which I had first set foot on the Surface comes into view, and I steer into a quick descent, landing near the cliff face with a spray of snow.

Jumping out, I side across the front of the vehicle and pull Peter's right arm away from his stomach and over my shoulders, struggling to keep him on his feet. Peter doubles, slumping heavily and weighing me down, clutching his middle.

I drag him over to the pile of rocks twenty yards in front of us, Frosty dancing around my feet and howling every time Peter screams.

With the one loose rock out of the way I pull Peter inside, then strike a match, lighting the candle and setting it on the table before diving through the entrance and back outside again, Frosty hot on my heels.

I sprint down the beach and take everything from the back of the pod, pulling off my coat and using it as a bag along with the saddle bags, which I sling over my shoulders with difficulty.

Once I have everything, I dash back to the cave, sliding inside and shoving the boulder back into place with my feet as soon as Frosty clears out of the way.

I get up fast and rush into the other room, dropping my coat in the middle of the floor and ducking extra low when I hurry back to the entrance room, because I can't see. Frosty yelps and barks urgently, and I slide my arm around Peter's chest from behind, grabbing the candle and lugging him into the room with the cots.

I drape the blankets over him even as he writhes in pain, slowly moving back to the fetal position with his arms pressed hard against his stomach. His face is contorted with pain, his mouth open as he gasps for breath, but I still don't know what's wrong with him. It has to be something to do with the device in my pocket.

"Peter? Peter I don't know how to fix this. Peter, do you know— can you tell me how—what my father did to you?"

My throat constricts, and my eyes burn, but I swallow back my tears and sniff, pulling out the small black cube again. It doesn't reveal its secrets, looking even more mysterious in the candle light. Obviously I need to fix it somehow, but what if I make Peter worse?

I set the cube down on top of the cooler and lurch to my feet, snatching up the candle and a pitcher from the table as I go. I push the boulder out of the way and scrape up as much snow as I can with the pitcher, then I crawl back inside. I bring it back, almost tripping over Frosty.

"I'm going I'm going," I say, hurrying my steps. I take off my gloves so I can grab a match.

I get the fire going, and then I hold the pitcher full of snow over the top of it, waiting impatiently for it to melt.

As soon as the snow is liquid, I crouch by Peter's cot and use the wet cloth to wipe the mud off of Peter's face and out of his hair, choking back a sob when he flinches away from me.

Maybe it will pass?

I look over at the black cube, terrified of how badly he's hurting. I can almost feel his pain when I pull up his shirt and press my hands against his chest, feeling for anything broken or perhaps damaged in some other way.

But nothing feels unusual to me, no bones broken, he's just in pain—pure pain. I don't even want to imagine how my father could do something like this. But I'm sure this is his fault. How long can Peter stand this level of pain before it kills him?

I sit in front of the dying fire with my arms around my shins and my chin on my knees, gingerly holding the black cube in my fingers, turning it around to look at every side for clues as to how it works.

It's been too long now. Peter seems to be getting weaker with each hour that goes by. His dark red hair is plastered to his forehead by a sheen layer of sweat, and his clothes cling to his body. Maybe if I do something wrong it'll kill him. But If I don't do anything, he'll die anyway.

I take off my gloves and grab a pair of tweezers out of the medical kit from the escape pod. Carefully, I touch them to the spring, testing for that spark again. Nothing happens. I use the tweezers to pull the spring out. It's useless without the missing button.

Inside the device are wires and plastic, and tiny polished plates of metal. I press the tweezers into one of the plates and Peter screams, the blood-curdling cry echoing through the cave. I drop the cube and the tweezers, crying out in horror. I clasp my hand over my mouth, watching as Peter squirms, hoping it will stop. But it doesn't.

"God help me I don't think I can do this!"

Frosty hides in a dark corner, watching me intently with her tail between her legs. I slowly reach down and pick up the cube and the tweezers again. I have to keep trying.

If pressing that way increased it, then maybe…. I try pressing the shiny plate on the other side, and Peter's screams turn to moans again.

My heart leaps.

I press that way again and his suffering seems to ease a little more. I keep doing it, over and over until he is finally still.

Frosty crawls back into the firelight on her belly until she reaches his side and plants her chin firmly on his chest. His breathing becomes regular and even again.

I just stare, not really sure how I did it. The black cube in my hand is a device for pain that my father made to cause Peter suffering.

For no reason other than Peter was born on the Surface. It's disgusting. I throw it in the fire before thinking it through and then dart my wide eyes back to Peter, expecting something to happen.

Nothing happens. The black device melts in the glowing white coals at the heart of the fire.

Peter

I wake up, hot and uncomfortable, to Frosty's wet tongue on my chin. I grimace, groaning softly as I slowly straighten my legs. My stiff muscles scream at me, and I feel my face twist in pain, my entire body throbbing as I stretch out bit by bit. But it's nothing compared to what it was before. I moan, rolling onto my back. Everything that happened is a blur of agony and heat, and my befuddled mind is taking too long to restore itself.

"Peter?" Rachel's voice reaches my ears, and I inhale sharply as the noise hammers at my skull. My eyes have been crusted shut by sweat and tears, but I force them open. Rachel pulls the damp cloth away from my forehead, and I squint up at her blurry face.

She sighs through her nose, gently dabbing at my face again with the cool rag. "Oh, Peter, you're still in there aren't you," she whispers, looking weary. "I thought maybe...."

"Wherearewe?" I mumble, rubbing my face.

"Your cave. I stole one of the escape pods from my father's hovercraft."

"Howlong….?" I can't finish the sentence, my mouth dry and sticky. I wrinkle my nose and take a deep breath; smoke fills my nose and only makes everything worse. I cough heavily.

"Two days. I couldn't figure out what was wrong with you. Then I found this." She holds up a pair of tweezers, which are squeezing a small lump of melted plastic. I frown, and she goes on, "It's some kind of pain inflicting device, or it was. I'm so sorry my father did this to you."

I just tremble and breathe, slowly relaxing for the first time in a long time. *Two days*…. The memories of what happened rush back to my mind.

Brown's voice echoes in my ears; *I can't say there's much of a home to go to, now….there will be no more Felix.*

Panic surges through every raw nerve in my body. I try to sit up, but my muscles are too cramped, and I fall back again, gasping.

"Just go back to sleep," Rachel tells me, sniffing.

"No—I need to get home," I croak.

"Peter, you haven't had anything to eat or drink for two days, and you need rest."

"No. No I need to get home. I need to get to Felix." .

"I don't think that's a good idea right now…." She pushes my hair back from my forehead. "Just wait-"

"No! There's no time!" I struggle to sit up, but only end up rolling off the bed, crushing Frosty beneath my chest. Frosty yelps, startled. I groan, pushing myself onto my hands and knees, and Frosty scurries away. I collapse again, panting, and Rachel's cold hands press against my back, cooling my sweaty skin.

"Just sleep." She sounds on the verge of tears, and she leans forward and rests her forehead on my shoulder, sniffling. "You need it."

I know she's right, but I don't care, even though my entire aching body tells me otherwise. "Home," I manage, crawling toward the exit, but my arms give out again and I fall, exhausted. Rachel pulls at my shoulders, and I flinch away.

"You're going to freeze to death out there or get eaten by a polar bear."

I roll over in the sand, laughing weakly because I think maybe I said the exact same thing to her the last time we were in this cave. I refuse to be coddled though. I have to see if what her father said was true. What's left of my home?

She doesn't fight me anymore, instead she pulls my fur coat out of the saddle bags and hands it to me. I struggle to my feet, fumbling with the coat, nearly losing my balance. I catch myself on the wall of the cave, wheezing like an old man, and Rachel takes my hand, pulling it through the sleeve and sliding the coat over my shoulders. She gives me my gloves, and I put them on with shaking hands.

"At least drink some water," she says quietly, giving me a look as she hands the water jug to me. I don't object, chugging the whole thing and leaning my head against the wall.

Rachel grips my shoulder, her eyes glassy; she stares at me for a long time. "Fine. We'll go."

I nod, still weary, glad she is coming with me. I don't think I could make it on my own.

Frosty prances around our feet as Rachel leads me down the beach to a small, shiny, teardrop shaped hovercraft with a flat bottom, the top of the cockpit made entirely of glass.

I breathe a sigh as I realize I won't have to walk the whole way home.

She tosses some supplies in the back and helps me inside, letting Frosty jump up onto my lap before moving around to the other side and climbing into the pilot's seat and pushing a button. The glass roof descends above us, seals itself tight, and the everything hums to life.

Rachel pushes a lever slowly upwards, and the vehicle rises smoothly into the air, skimming along the beach until the cliff face to our right slopes into the valley. She steers the pod in the direction of Colfer, hovering just a few feet above the snow until we crest the hill that slopes back down to my home.

My heart stops, and the world grinds to a halt.

The hovercraft touches down in front of what used to be Jimmy's trader shop, but now all that's left of it is a charred, burnt out shell. The blackened walls of the Dead Handler's building are the only remains standing that still have parts of the roof, whereas the rest of Colfer is just charcoal and ash and crumbling wood. Even after two days, the remnants still smoke in some places, where the coals are still hot.

An icy wind gusts through the ruined village, carrying with it the leftover scent of gunpowder and burnt flesh. Ash drifts through the air like falling snow, and I take a few stumbling steps down the blackened street, gaping at the scattered remains of houses and shops.

And bodies.

Charred, sullied bodies strewn across the village, bodies of people I knew, people who were friends.

I stagger back, tripping into Jimmy's shop and digging through the debris until I find him and his wife. Their blackened corpses, curled around their youngest son, crumble to dust in my hands.

I choke, falling back and catching myself with one hand, the other covering my mouth to keep from throwing up.

"Peter-"

I don't let Rachel finish, lurching to my feet and forgetting about my fatigue as I take off through the ruins toward the tanner's shop, only one thing on my mind; *Felix.*

I plow through the deep snow, Frosty bounding behind me, squeaking each time she takes another leap through the snow that is deeper than her. I reach the scorched remains of Kelly's house and stop on the threshold, reluctant to search through the ashes and coal.

Rachel comes to a stop behind me, panting.

I don't have to dig in the ruin, I can see the bent and twisted carcasses of Addy and her children, their bodies scattered like refuse.

I drag my feet into the center of what used to be the dining room, dropping to my knees in the soot and the snow. I recognize the scrawny form of Cole, sprawled out beneath the crushed table next to Merry, who is half covering his brother's body. I crawl closer and crumple next to them, blinking back tears. "*No,*" I breathe, the air shuddering from my chest.

Choking, I crawl through the wreckage, brushing each body with my fingers as if my touch can bring them back. But Felix is not here.

I don't know whether to cry in relief or horror at the thought of my brother in Brown's basement room.

My sob finally shatters my resolve into a million pieces. I lower my face to the ashy snow, curling my arms over my head and feeling the tears roll down my face, Frosty's wet nose snuffling at the back of my neck.

No. Is the only word running through my head. Over and over and over. *No no no no no no no.*

I feel Rachel slide her arm beneath my chest, pulling my head and shoulders onto her lap and leaning over me. I curl into a ball and weep, at last crushed by all that has happened in the past week, inundated by the pain and loss and horror of everything that is my miserable life.

After all this, after everything I've gone through to get back, it's all gone. *Everything I knew, everything I loved, just* gone.

"This is all my fault," I rasp, defeat pounding the air out of my lungs in shuddering sobs. "I never should've come back. I should've just stayed up there, then none of this ever would've happened."

"No. No it's my fault. Peter I should've gone with Malcolm, I should've just gone home." Rachel shushes me even as her own tears drip onto the back of my neck.

"It *is* my fault. If I hadn't taken you in the first place, then nobody would be hurt, and Felix would recover on his own. This is my fault. Bloody hell I should've just *died*."

Rachel holds me for a long time, my head on her lap. The air is still, and I shiver, suddenly aware that we need shelter.

I sit up stiffly. Rachel has her eyes closed, and I think maybe she is asleep. Has she slept at all these last two days? Frosty leaps to her feet, gazing at me with her icy blue eyes and whimpering softly.

If we stay out here any longer, we'll freeze to death. Even Rachel's heat reflective clothes can only keep her warm for so long, and my wolf fur coat, no matter how thick, will eventually become sopping wet. Already my legs are freezing, my sealskin pants cold and crackling as I straighten my legs. Although my coat keeps the rest of me warm, I still shiver.

Rachel doesn't open her eyes, and my heart skips a beat.

I am about to shake Rachel's shoulder when a sharp cry comes from the smoking ruins of my home. Hope blossoms in my chest when I see the dark figure slogging through the snow, picking up their pace when they see me. My heart wrenches at the sight of red hair. But it's Jimmy's oldest son, Garret, not Felix.

Garret slides to a stop on the edge of the obliterated house, panting as he realizes who I am. "Peter?"

His tone is vindictive and full of accusation.

I swallow, then nod, discreetly reaching behind me and gripping Rachel's shoulder, trying to wake her up. Garret narrows his eyes, pointing at me. "You were taken."

"Garret…." My throat constricts. All this devastation is because of me. He is an orphan now because of me. What can I say to him?

"This is your fault." Garret shakes his head, his hand trembling. "You came back, you made them mad."

"Garret, I'm sorry-"

"NO!" He screams, charging forward. I scramble backwards, and Rachel jumps awake. "No! You did this! You got them all killed!"

"Garret just listen-"

He doesn't let me finish. I see the madness in his eyes and roll out of the way just as he lunges for me.

He follows me, and I scramble to my feet. Rachel leaps onto his back, struggling to drag him to the ground. Garret shakes her off roughly, kicking at Frosty as the Siren chews on his pant-leg. Rachel falls, and Frosty squeals, scrambling away and cowering.

I raise my fists.

Garret hesitates, knowing of my reputation.

"Garret, I'm sorry. I didn't want this to happen, I didn't know he'd go this far, and I'm sorry, I just wanted to get to Felix, I just wanted to get home. You don't know what it's like up there."

"I don't care!" Garret is beyond deranged. "I was on the beach, and I couldn't do anythin' except hide like a bloody coward! I can *still* hear the screams, Peter. They're all dead and it's all your fault!"

"I know," I croak. "And I'm sorry, but we can avenge them, we can stop this once and for all." I am just saying things to keep him from killing me. But as I say the words, I realize it's what has to be done. It's the only way to get Felix back and stop any of this from happening again. "We have to work together to make them pay."

Rachel freezes on the ground, giving me a terrified look, but Garret speaks before she can.

"You did this, Peter. You're the one who will pay; you're the one who will rot in *HELL*." Garret snarls, lunging at me again and catching me under the jaw with his fist.

I stagger back, pain and stars exploding in my head.

"Peter!" Rachel yells. She grabs for Garret's gun. "Stop it—it's not his fault! My father did this, not Peter!"

Garret wrenches away, backhanding her across the face and knocking her down hard.

Frosty barks, a snarling ball of fur charging in for another attack, but Garret kicks her away again.

He swings a burnt piece of wood at my head. I duck just in time, my legs buckling, and I land on my hands and knees.

"Garret, please."

"No! No they didn't get a chance to explain, they didn't get a bloody chance to talk themselves out of this!" Garret yells at me, gesturing around at the burnt bodies sprawled across the remains. "And neither will you. Now you'll get what you deserve!"

"Garret, let's just talk this through, maybe we can-"

Garret kicks my left side just beneath my arm, and I cry out, half collapsing further into the charcoal. From the holster on his left hip he whips a black nine-millimeter, aiming it at my face, and I flinch, jerking my arms over my head.

Out of the corner of my eye, I see Rachel scooting away, through the snow and burnt debris toward the hovercraft is—where the other guns are. Her hand slips on a piece of wood, making a sharp clattering sound on the coals around it.

Garret turns the pistol on her, his teeth bared and his hard brown eyes crazed. "And you! You filfy Glass City brat!" The gun shakes dangerously in his hand, and I tense. "You're goin' to hell with him!"

Before I can react, he pulls the trigger. The gun erupts with an explosion that echoes across the dead town in all directions. Rachel's body jerks, and blood blooms like a rose from her garden, just beneath her rib cage. She gasps, doubling over in the snow.

"*No!*" I start to get up, but Garret jerks his gun at my head, snarling.

"IT'S MY BLOODY HOME TOO!" I scream at him.

"Not anymore," he growls, his finger tensing on the trigger.

There's a blur behind him, stark white against the blackened remains of Kelly's obliterated house. Frosty materializes out of the debris, fangs bared and ready for a third attack. This time, she hits her mark, tearing at the back of his left heel with her jagged teeth.

The gun goes off, the bullet whistling past my ear.

I gasp, my hand flying up reflexively.

Frosty yelps as Garret kicks her away yet again. He points the gun at her, but I'm already on my feet, barreling into his chest and knocking him to the ground and landing on top of him.

I grab for the gun in his hand, but he jerks it away, pressing it against my side. I catch his wrist and force his hand away just as he pulls the trigger again. Yelling with distorted rage, he rolls, dragging me with him, and the two of us tumble through the charcoal and snow, each struggling to gain the upper hand.

I finally manage to pin him, wrenching the gun from his gloved fingers and flipping it in my hand. Baring my teeth, I pistol whip him hard on the side of the head, and his attempts to get up stop immediately as he gasps, falling limp.

I jump to my feet, hurling the gun into the snow and stumbling away.

Garret tries to stagger to his feet, but he finally gives up, collapsing in the rubble. "I'll kill you," he vows, his voice soft and hoarse. "I'll kill you."

I have to go, I have save Rachel. I take a step toward her, then hesitate. I know he will stop at nothing to carry out the promise, but I can't just leave him here either.

Giving him one last look, I decide bringing him with us is not worth the risk. I scoop Rachel into my arms and whistling for Frosty.

Rachel trembles against my chest, digging her fingers into the fur of my coat.

I run as fast as I can through the deep snow, stumbling and nearly falling just before I reach the hovercraft. Rachel cries out, and I somehow manage to catch myself, my muscles straining as I lurch to the pod and slam against the glass with my shoulder.

"Rachel how do I open it?" I say urgently, glancing back to see Garret shambling through the snow, looking around for his gun.

My eyes fall on a small green button just beneath the edge of the glass. I slam my fist against it, flinching as the sound of a shot fired tears into the quiet of my ruined home. The glass dome raises slowly, and I shove Rachel inside as soon as there's enough space for her to get through.

Another bullet ricochets off the side of the hovercraft. I flinch, sliding under the glass. Frosty jumps onto my lap, and I shove her away.

I press the matching green button on the inside of the cockpit, and recoil as sparks fly across the dashboard, the bullet skipping across the panel and out the other side.

I shove my hand against the lever I had seen Rachel use earlier, and the hovercraft lurches into the air, the top still open wide as we rise off the ground. Rachel screams, barely managing to keep herself from tumbling out of her seat as I veer to the right. Frosty squeals, sliding off of Rachel's lap as I jerk us to the left in compensation. Through a little more dangerous wobbling, I discover that pulling back on it makes us go up, and pushing forward makes us go down.

The glass roof finally seals shut around us and I shakily wrench the craft in the direction of the cave amidst the spray of Garret's bullets. Frosty squeals, sliding off of Rachel's lap as I slur to the right again. Panicking, I wrench the steering wheel to the left, throwing Frosty across the cabin and into my face. The hovercraft turns a wild circle and starts heading back toward Colfer.

Frosty's hind paw kicks the lever as she scrambles to get off of me, jerking it almost all the way down. The pod bucks, diving toward the ground and causing Garret to duck and cover his head as we swoop toward him. Screaming, I push the lever up again, spiraling into the air as I pull back on the wheel.

The glass roof seals around us, and I turn back toward the Atlantic Ocean. "That way!" I yell at the pod, frustrated.

I look over at Rachel; her eyes are half closed, her face pale, and the red stain on her shirt continues to spread. It needs pressure, but Rachel is unconscious and I can't take my hands off the blasted lever.

The beach comes rapidly into view as Colfer disappears behind the hill of the valley, and suddenly I have a new problem. I haven't the slightest idea how to land this bloody thing.

I swallow hard, pulling the lever down and feeling my stomach do flips as we drop toward the ground.

"How do I slow down!?" I holler, as the ground rises to meet us far too quickly. "HOLD ON!"

The bottom scrapes against the beach, plowing through the snow, and then we nose plant at full speed. The pod flips, tumbling over and over. Frosty is thrown into my chest and I grab onto her. The pod seats balloon up around Rachel and I, holding us firmly in place and cushioning the impact. Finally, we grind to a halt, jerked in our seats.

I pant, half terrified, half exhilarated as I try to regain my breath enough to pull myself to my senses. The hovercraft powers down, and I hit the button; the roof slowly rises, and I squeeze out, hurrying around to Rachel and carefully pulling her into my arms. I lift her out of the seat, not bothering to shut the roof again.

Frosty takes care of that for me, slipping off the dashboard and pressing the button with her hind paw as she leaps out and stumbles in the sand, yelping. I charge toward the cave, Frosty limping behind me and squeaking every time she puts weight on her front right paw.

I lean Rachel against my chest to keep her off the ground as I shove the heavy boulder out of the way. Grunting with the effort, I drag us through, keeping her head against my side and out of the snow.

Inside, I can barely see in the light of the dying embers. I stagger to one of the cots and lower her down as gently as I can. My gloves are stiff and I pull them off, whirling and using the kindling and firewood to coax the fire back to life until I have enough light to see by.

I dig through the supplies that Rachel had bundled in the corner until I find a med-kit and a healing device. I rush back to Rachel, dropping heavily to my knees by her side and pulling open her coat. Blood blossoms out across her front, and I grimace, peeling her shirt away from her skin and over her head.

Rachel protests weakly, but I ignore her. I gasp when I see the wound; there's a bloody hole in her stomach. I gently lift her enough to see the exit wound, and I see a slightly larger hole to the left of her spine. I feel Frosty's nose snuffling at my elbow, but I push her away, lifting Rachel just a wee bit more.

Rachel gasps, blood bubbling up from her mouth and nose, and I slide my hand behind her back, applying pressure over the exit wound as I hold the healing device to her stomach and flick the button.

Rachel looks up at me with half lidded eyes, and I can see her strength failing. Maybe she's lost too much blood? Can these devices replace blood?

"Come on, Rachel. Don't die on me. I can't have any more people die because of me!"

Her eyes are open but she doesn't seem to really be looking at me; her gaze is somewhere over my shoulder and her breathing is shallow.

It's hard to tell if the wound on her stomach is sealed over in the mess of blood smeared across her pale skin. I switch the healing device to the wound on her back, when I think it's had long enough on the entrance wound.

I swallow hard, determined to keep her alive. Rachel shudders, and the device heats up in my hand. It has to have enough energy. It can't run out before she is healed. Finally the hum of the device dies away and I grab the kit to look for another.

Rachel chokes on her own blood and slumps forward, her eyes rolling back.

"No!" I shout, finding another device, this one only half full. I roll her onto her side to keep her airway clear and hold the second device over her back again, not really sure if it's even doing anything.

When it runs out too, Rachel is limp, her eyes closed and her skin pale and cold. I toss the device away and pull her off the cot into my lap.

I lower my ear to her lips, but I don't hear nor feel anything.

"*No.*" Not her too. I hunch over her, pulling open the front of my coat and trying to press some of my warmth back into her as Frosty nudges her face with her wet nose, whimpering.

Rachel

The world feels warm and fuzzy, and it takes me a moment to realize that it's still there. That I'm still here. I feel a faint pain in my stomach and bring my hand up to find that I'm not wearing a shirt.

Self-consciously, I cover my bra with my arm, and my hand bumps into someone.

A breath draws in sharply at my touch. "Rachel?"

I pry my eyes open enough to see Peter huddled over me, tears clinging to his eyelashes. He holds me tight against him, and I remember his whispers in my dreams, over and over. *"No. Not her too. Please God not her too. No."*

His fur coat is fuzzy. I don't know why I find that so funny.

Part of me wants to slap him, but mostly I'm just confused. My skin feels crusty. My *mouth* tastes like blood. Colfer….

"Rachel." He turns my face toward his, pushing my hair back from my forehead. He looks relieved. "Don't worry. You're ok now, I think. Just sleep."

I take a shallow breath, grimacing at the sharp pain somewhere deep inside me, and turn my face against Peter's shoulder. Sleep is good. Maybe Mom'll explain everything in the morning.

Peter sighs.

I frown. Sleep can wait. Something isn't right. "What happened?" I mumble, and Peter carefully detaches himself from my side. I shiver as he pulls away, but his green eyes never leave my face.

"You don't remember?"

"I don't…. think so." I struggle to sit up, and he helps me. The crusty feeling on my skin is dried blood. A lot of it. I shiver again, more from the sight of it than the cold. Is it mine? "We were in Colfer."

Peter turns away without a word, opening the chest as the end of the bed and pulling out an old sweat-shirt, which he tosses to me. I accept it gratefully, pulling it over my head.

I try not to feel weird about my shirt being off. He wasn't being a creep, he was just saving my life. When my skin isn't bare to the world anymore, Peter lifts me onto the cot, pulling the blankets up to my chin. "Get some rest," he says quietly; his eyes are haunted by today's events, but whatever it is I can't remember—and that scares me. How long have I been out?

He starts to walk away, but I catch his wrist, sitting up again. "Peter."

Peter pauses, glancing down without expression. His hand is covered in dried blood, too. I swallow. "What happened?"

"You were shot," he says shortly. "I…. I thought you were dead."

I let go of him, trying to remember. I recall bits. Colfer. The charred bodies. A man screaming. I don't remember being shot. "You saved me?"

He shrugs slightly, listlessly. "You're all I have left. And I owe you."

I don't know how to respond to that, hurting for him even as the heat rises to my face, so I gulp and change the subject. "Can I, like, wash up?"

"You might want to just lie down for a while. You've lost a lot of blood."

I shake my head before he's even finished. "I'm covered in blood. I'm going to die of freaked-outedness if I don't wash this stuff off me right now."

A smile almost touches his lips, and he picks something up off the other chest, turning back to me and handing me a cloth and the pitcher full of melted snow.

I raise my eyebrows at him. "A sponge bath?"

Peter sighs. "Unless ya want to bathe with the sharks in the Atlantic. There's no electricity down here, Rachel. No hot water. This is about as good as it gets."

I nod and take the pitcher and the cloth from his hands.

He points to the small tunnel leading to the little empty room. "I'll be in there, if you need me," he says softly, and I can tell by his eyes that his mind is elsewhere.

I set the pitcher and cloth near the fire so the water can warm and stand. My gloves are covered in blood too, and I take them off, dropping them in the sand. I'm unsteady on my feet as I stumble over to him and grip his shoulder, partially to keep from falling, but mostly to try and bring some amount of comfort, no matter how small.

"I'm so sorry." I don't even know what to say. "This is all my fault."

Peter is silent, his arms hanging loosely at his sides. He clenches and unclenches his fingers, a distant look in his green eyes. I slide my hand down his left arm and grasp his fist. "No matter what happens, I'll do everything I can to help you get Felix back. He's in the Glass City, there's got to be a way for us to get to him."

I sigh, resting my forehead against his shoulder for a moment. He pulls away gently before lighting the candle and leaving the room.

There is a squeak and a commotion behind me. Startled, I look in time to see a white blur race toward me, and then Frosty has placed her front paws on my legs, patting my knees and wagging her whole body, her pink tongue lolling out of the side of her mouth.

She seems to be favoring her front right paw. I crouch, rubbing the top of her head and letting her lick my face. "Good girl," I tell her, unsure if she'll understand or not. Frosty's mouth gapes at me in a wide grin, then she turns and limps happily out of the room to find Peter again.

"Is that all I get from almost dying?" I call after her. The pup is undeniably more attached to Peter.

"Huh?" Peter calls back.

"Never mind."

I pull off my shirt and soak the cloth in the water, scrubbing the blood off my stomach and trying to ignore the fact that it's my own.

Frosty squeaks again from the other room, then races through the tunnel to nudge the backs of my knees. I laugh, snatching up my shirt and pulling it back over my head. "Jeez girl, patience."

When I'm finished, I let myself sink to the floor, weary. The cave is silent, and I crawl into the other room—the one with the chest of guns pressed against the back wall.

Peter doesn't look at me as I stand, staring at the flickering flame of the candle on the chest.

"I am goin' to blast that city out of the sky." He looks so fierce, so pissed off all of the sudden that I recoil, shocked.

"Peter—it's still my home."

"Colfer was mine," he spits, his green eyes stormy.

I stare at him, shaking my head. "Peter, that would make you no better than my father. Do you really want to sink to his level?" Because I know it's true. My father is a monster.

Peter flicks his gaze to the wall above my head, taking a slow breath. "But if I don't, then none of this will ever stop. Your people will only continue to kidnap and murder mine, and we won't be able to stop them. This has to end, Rachel. This has to stop."

I know he's right, but, "Peter, there are still people up there that aren't monsters. And your people, too. A lot of Surface Dwellers are stuck up there as well. They don't have parachutes to save them if the city falls."

Peter is quiet for a little while. Then, "This is war, Rachel. I'm not goin' to hide out here while my people continue to get murdered and to lose their homes while your father looks for you."

His words hurt a lot more than they should. I swallow hard, my eyes starting to burn. "And how do you plan to accomplish this, Peter? How do you plan to destroy an entire city when you have only one hovercraft?"

"I'll get more."

"Where? You're *nineteen*, you're too young to hold a grudge!" A second too late I realize I've said the wrong thing and I'm already cursing myself before he snaps.

"Hold a *grudge*!?" He explodes. "They blew up my home! They destroyed everyone I loved and took Felix! And you're complainin' about me holdin' a grudge!?"

Frosty yelps, startled.

"Peter—I'm sorry—it just came out wrong-"

"DAMN RIGHT IT DID!"

"Peter!" I yell at him, getting frustrated. "I'm not trying to hurt you! *I'm not them!* I'll…." I can't believe what I'm about to say. "I'll help you. Alright? Fine. I'll help you, but you have to promise me that you'll save as many people as you can."

Peter studies me, his face pinched and his left eye twitching ever so slightly. Finally, he relaxes. His eyes slide shut and he furrows his brow. "I'm sorry," he whispers.

I step closer to him, gently pulling him into a loose embrace. "So am I."

After a minute, he hugs me back, his arms trembling and his breath coming in shudders. I hold him for a while, knowing that there's no way I could possibly understand what he's going through, and so I say nothing. Until Clayton died, I had never had a taste of real loss and pain.

At last, Peter pulls away, picking up the candle and ducking into the other room. I hesitate a moment before following him. Can I really help him destroy my home?

Peter pulls a new fur coat from the chest at the end of his cot and hands it to me. It's not the one I'd had before. I pull it on gratefully, and Frosty nudges Peter's knees with her nose, whining indignantly.

Peter crouches next to her, rubbing her face with his cold hands. "Yes, you're a good girl," he says quietly, and he kisses the top of her furry head. He pushes Frosty's behind so that she's sitting, and then he lifts her front right paw. Frosty whimpers in protest, licking his hand and nibbling at his fingers when he holds her wrist still as he sweeps it with a BRRD.

"Lucky I found another one. I thought I'd used up all of them on yer mum, wee beastie."

My face grows red at the implication that we're Frosty's mom and dad, but don't say anything.

Peter is quiet as he works, as though suddenly realizing the awkwardness of what he's said.

Frosty yipes, trying to pull away, but Peter holds her paw steady despite her sharp teeth, and when her paw is finished healing, he shoves the device into his pocket and gets to his feet. Frosty sniffs her paw, and then goes bouncing off to a corner to attack a blanket.

"Brimstone. That's where we'll head. Brimstone has hovercrafts, and we're goin' to need them. But first, we're stoppin' at Hearthtown again."

"Why?"

"Can't do this without help."

"What about that guy in Colfer, the one who survived?"

"Who, Garret?" Peter looks so sad all of the sudden that I want to cry. "He's the one who shot you, Rachel. He's broken. He can't help anyone."

My mouth hangs open for a minute, my hand lingering at my stomach. Should I be angry? I decide not to let it distract me. "You're going to take on a high tech city with a few hovercrafts?"

Without a responding, Peter turns away from me and crawls stiffly onto his cot, pulling the blanket around him and drawing his arms close to himself. Frosty jumps onto the cot with him, and I swear she gives me a withering glare.

"First, we need sleep," he says quietly, and I don't argue.

Peter

We lay in the cots until the fire is nothing but dim red coals, but I don't sleep. Every time I close my eyes the image of my obliterated home fills my head. Bodies, burnt husks of those I knew and loved scattered among the ashes. A horrible fury sears through my veins; the need to destroy the Glass City.

I've never felt this much hate and anger before. It scares me, but at the same time, I want it. The Glass City plummeting toward the Surface, crashing into the Atlantic Ocean and shattering into millions of tiny shards. Brown crushed beneath the wreckage, dragged down to the bottom of the sea.

I shift in my cot.

"What was that?" Rachel asks suddenly. She sounds scared.

"Just me." I try to sound reassuring, but I'm not sure I'm convincing.

"I thought there was a monster in the dark." Rachel's words weave through the destruction in my head and drags my mind by the tail back into reality.

Tears fill my eyes, and I am glad the cave is too dark for her to see my face. "I'm not a monster," I whisper.

"No. You're not. "

"How am I goin' to do this, Rachel? I'm not sure I can live with the lives I'll destroy."

"We could just stay here," she says at length.

I look in her direction, confused.

Rachel gets off her cot, crossing the room to sit next to mine. "We could just stay here—no one will find us. We don't have to deal with this world as long as we stay hidden."

"Are you mental?"

Rachel throws her arms up. "There's nothing left, Peter! Your home is gone—and mine is full of monsters! They're *all* monsters out there, and they all want us dead for one reason or another. Let's just stay here, where you can't lose anything and I can't get shot by mad men."

"Listen to yourself," I growl, sitting up. "Do you honestly expect me to cower in here while the Glass City continues to terrorize my people? Colfer might be gone, but Hearthtown isn't—you're still here, do you honestly think your father isn't goin' to come lookin' for you again?"

"You're the one who said you couldn't live with the consequences."

I stop, my throat constricting at the thought. "I have to."

Rachel shakes her head, her eyes pleading. "You don't."

"No, *you* don't. You said you'd help, but if you've changed your mind that's fine. You can stay here, I'm not goin' to ask you to destroy your home, but my brother is up there, Rachel. I can't leave him, I can't….I don't want to be alone." I close my eyes to shut out the tears.

"*I'm* here. I will *always* be here. And I will be with you all the way to the end." She hesitates, studying my face. "Fine. If you're going, then I won't let you do it alone. We can watch the City sink into the Atlantic together."

"Why?"

The corners of her mouth twitch up. "Because we're in this together. We have been since you dragged me off the skydeck—and even before then. I'll always be here for you." Rachel slides onto my cot and presses her palm against my cheek. She gently kisses the corner of my mouth and then, pressing her lips against my ear, whispers, "and don't you forget it."

I bury my face in her hair. I don't know how long we stay like this, me holding onto my last hope and her trying to hold together the pieces of my shattered soul.

The soft scuff of shoes on sand brings me fully alert.

Rachel pulls back. Her mouth opens.

Before she can ask her question, I clamp my hand over her mouth, straining to see through the dark.

The fire is a pile of glowing embers, creating a small circle of orange light in the middle of the room, but other than this there is nothing to see by. Frosty raises her head, hackles prickling. I'm not the only one who hears it.

I slip away from Rachel, pulling my pistol from my belt as I step toward the tunnel.

Frosty brushes against my calf and growls at the darkness in front of us. I fumble through the dark, clamping her muzzle shut with my thumb and forefinger. "Shhh…." I breathe, straining to hear.

The scuffing has grown slightly louder, and a dim light begins to grow as someone draws closer. I press myself against the wall, my left hand pulling back the slide of my pistol as quietly as I can.

The light grows and then bursts onto my vision as the intruder enters the this part cave. His face is shadowed but the small gun in his hands is clearly visible in the light of the flashlight paired with it.

As soon as he passes me, I press my pistol against the back of his head. "Put. It. *Down*."

The man slowly lowers his gun, and I nudge the back of his head. "Drop it."

The man holds the gun between two fingers and drops it, then whirls. In one smooth motion he slams his fist into my ribs and shoves me back.

I stumble, and before I can counterattack the intruder blinds me with his flashlight as he stoops to pick up his gun.

I throw my arms in front of my face, charging forward and slamming into him.

There's a deafening *BANG*.

I stagger back, ears ringing, but I don't have time to stand around stunned as the flashlight swings toward my face.

I dodge, then crouch, scooping up a handful the hot coals of the fire and flinging them at the man's face.

The man cries out, and I use the few seconds I stole to tackle him, sending both of us tumbling through the sand.

I wrench the gun away from his hand and toss it away as he reaches after it. I grit my teeth, using all my strength to lift him off his feet and slam him into the wall, jamming my own gun under his jaw.

He struggles, but I don't let go of him, and his face is suddenly illuminated by his own flashlight as Rachel picks it up and shines it at him from behind me.

"Malcolm?" she says.

He stops fighting and squints into the flashlight beam. Rachel lowers it enough so that he can see her.

"You're alive!" He breathes. He flicks his gaze back to me.

"No thanks to you," I growl. I let go of him, gripping my gun a little too tight. "What are you doin' down here anyway?"

Malcolm doesn't answer right away. Finally, he speaks softly, "Hiding."

I pause, then go to the fire and throw a few logs on to get it going again. "Why?" I ask, once the flames are licking at the fuel hungrily.

He sniffles, touching his face. The burns from the coals I threw are not the only injuries there. "My father. I'm so sorry, I tried not to tell them, but it hurt so freaking bad, worse than he's ever done before..."

"So you told them, even though you swore you wouldn't." I stare at the burns on my hand. I want to slaughter him. To push his face in the fire and watch the flames eat away at him the way they're consuming the logs. "It's not your fault," I say, hardly believing the words as they come out of my mouth.

"I was *weak*. I should've just took it, I shouldn't have said anything."

"But you did," I mutter, handing him a jug of freshly melted snow.

He stares at it, shaking his head. "You don't understand."

"Then help us to understand." Rachel places her hand on his shoulder, and he flinches.

"I don't—" Malcolm's voice breaks, and he seems to shrink into the sand. "I can't...."

"You can't what? Admit that it was too much? That you got people killed because you couldn't keep a secret?" I growl, clenching my fists.

"Back off, Peter!" Rachel snaps.

"No! I think I understand pretty clear. If you'd just kept your bloody mouth shut—"

"It never ends!" Malcolm suddenly screams, his eyes spilling over with tears.

I stop, stunned. Rachel stares at him.

Malcolm shrinks further, dipping his head and yelling into the sand. "No matter how hard I tried to do what he wanted I'd *always* get something wrong! I just—I didn't want to hurt anymore." He sobs, digging his fingers into the sides of his head. "He said he'd stop if I told him, but he didn't. He'd never hurt me like that before—not that bad."

"Malcolm…." Rachel leaves her mouth open, but she doesn't finished, her blue eyes wide.

"I just wanted to get it right," Malcolm whispers. "To be the way my father wanted me to be. But I—wasn't strong enough. I'm not strong enough."

I try to stay angry at him, try to hold onto my blame, but it fizzles out when Rachel gently lifts the back of his shirt, revealing cuts and burns and bruises. Malcolm flinches away, and Rachel covers her mouth with her hand. She looks at me, her eyes glassy.

I don't know what to say. As much as I wanted to beat the crap out of him earlier, seeing him like this now, I hesitate; then grab a healing device from the pile by the end of my cot, handing it to Rachel.

Malcolm's face twists. "I just didn't want to hurt anymore."

"That doesn't justify all you've done," I say, and Rachel gives me a withering look.

"I know. I'm sorry." Malcolm sobs, over and over as Rachel slowly uses up the device on his back. "I'm sorry."

"No one could take this without giving in." Rachel shushes him, blinking rapidly.

"He did," Malcolm spits, glaring at me. "I was supposed to be stronger than some stupid Surface Rat."

I bite back my retort, forcing my breath out through my nose. I did give in, I did submit. But I decide not to tell him that.

Rachel clenches her fists. "Don't start that Malcolm. Do you really want to be like your dad?"

"I'm sorry," Malcolm says again, burying his face in his hands.

"Then start acting like it," Rachel says in a very motherly tone.

"I'm *trying*," Malcolm whispers, sitting up and rubbing his eyes roughly. Frosty approaches him cautiously, sniffing at his shoes and climbing into his lap to snuffle at his face. He pushes her away.

"You can help us," Rachel says quietly.

I stare at her, incredulous.

Malcolm looks up at her. "What?"

"This has to stop Malcolm. All this violence. And murder." Rachel inches closer to him, her eyes pleading. "The City is destroying lives, tearing apart families. We can stop it. We can destroy the Glass City, so they can't hurt anyone ever again."

Malcolm looks dumbfounded, and I grit my teeth. I can forgive him, but inviting him on our crusade to destroy the Glass City? That's taking it a little too far.

"Are you insane?" Malcolm's voice cracks.

"Malcolm please. You've gotten in and out of the City multiple times—you can help us like no one else can."

"That's our home, Rachel!"

"No." Rachel shakes her head. "I don't belong there anymore. I never did. And neither do you."

"You can't be serious."

"Well we are." I speak up, crossing my arms. "If you don't want to help, then fine. I'm goin' to watch that City fall whether you help us or not. We don't need you."

"I can't let you do that."

I set my jaw. "Then stop me."

"Whoa hold up." Rachel stands, glancing worriedly between the two of us. "He's never gonna help us if you keep threatening him, Peter. And Malcolm, I'm sorry, but if you try to stop him, you'll have to go through me."

"Rachel." Malcolm pleads with his eyes, but Rachel stands firmly between us.

He sighs. "I can't just destroy my home."

"After everythin' they've done to you?" I shake my head. "They turned you into a bloody monster Malcolm. Even killin' a man wasn't good enough for them."

Malcolm's face twists, but he doesn't say anything.

"Do you really want to sink to their level?"

"Think of it as a chance to redeem yourself," Rachel tells him.

"By murdering countless innocent people?"

I tense. "Innocent isn't a word I'd use to describe them."

"But not all of them are like my father." Malcolm looks up at Rachel. "What about your mom?"

"We'll save as many people as we can. But this has to end. I don't like it that much either Malcolm, but something has to happen, because the people in the City are never going to change otherwise," Rachel says. She looks sad, but determined, her shoulders back and her blue eyes fierce.

"I don't know." Malcolm stares into the flames, shivering.

I pull a blanket from one of the chests, dropping it in his lap. "Well you'd better figure it out. We're leavin' tomorrow. And we're takin' that hovercraft."

I leave the room before he can protest, ducking through the tunnel into the main cave.

Rachel

I watch Peter leave through the tunnel without a word, shaking all over. Frosty bounds after him, and I know that she can help him a lot more than I can. I swallow hard, my knees buckling, and I sit down in the sand with a dull, heavy *thunk*. Malcolm stares after Peter, and I can see the fury in his blue eyes.

I hug my legs to my chest, resting my chin on my knees and trying to slow my breathing. Standing up wasn't such a good idea.

Malcolm turns his dark gaze to me. "He's going to kill me."

"No. That's something you would do," I say it without thinking and immediately regret it.

"Really? He's the one hell-bent on destroying our home."

"And you're the one who destroyed his." Maybe I'm angrier than I thought.

Malcolm looks at me, stunned. "What are you talking about?"

I shake my head. "It's not your fault."

"Rachel."

"My father-" My voice cracks. "-he destroyed everything, burnt Colfer to the ground. Everyone Peter knew, everything he grew up with. They're all gone."

I see some of the anger leave Malcolm's eyes, see it replaced by horror and even more fear. "I…. I didn't know."

I shake my head. "He already blames himself. Malcolm, the Glass City destroys lives. All it does is bring hurt and suffering to an already broken world. It's time someone did something to start *fixing* it."

Malcolm shivers, his Adam's apple bobbing as he swallows. "I never thought I'd feel sorry for him. I never cared. All I wanted was for everything to go back to normal, all I wanted was to bring you home." He takes a shuddering breath. "You should've let him kill me."

It takes a moment for me to regain my voice. "But then you wouldn't have this chance to redeem yourself. And—I can't let Peter become like my father, killing everyone who pisses him off."

"You seem to care an awful lot about him," Malcolm says quietly.

I exhale slowly through my nose. He's right. I hadn't given it much thought before, but now, I think I've fallen in love with Peter Gerrethson. "I still care about you, too, Malcolm. Just not the same way that I used to. You killed Clayton. You hurt Peter. But…. I forgive you."

Malcolm pulls his blanket tight around his shoulders, covering the lower half of his face and squeezing his eyes shut. "My father tortured the information out of me, it's not fair for Peter to hate me for that."

I wince, my heart twisting. All this time, his father's been hurting him, and all this time, I've been turning a blind eye. Just like with Clayton.

Malcolm goes on. "All my life, if I didn't act the way my father wanted me to, he'd hurt me. I can't help that. I'm not as strong as Peter." He spits the name. "It's not fair for him to blame me."

"You're responsible for your own choices Malcolm. Don't go blaming everyone else." I sigh, snatching up a TRRD from the pile by the cot. "But you can make it right. You can help us fix this world."

"Yeah. All it takes is a little love." Malcolm sneers.

I grit my teeth, pulling his blanket away and lifting his shirt. "You're right. Love is a powerful thing."

"Do you know how you sound?"

"Says the guy who hates everyone. How's that been working out for you?"

Malcolm flinches, whether from my prodding fingers or my words, I'm not sure. "As if 'love' would've made my father stop. You want to destroy the City. Where does love come into that?"

"That's not the point, Malcolm. Look. Not everything is someone else's fault. You beat the crap out of Peter. You killed Clayton." My voice catches, but I push my anger aside. "No one told you to do that."

Malcolm drops his gaze to the fire, his eyes glassy as I slowly heal the lash marks across his back.

"I'm so sorry," I whisper.

Malcolm leans against me, sobbing into my shoulder. I hug him awkwardly, wanting to comfort him but at the same time not wanting to give him any wrong ideas.

He calms down after a while, and I pull away. I get shakily to my feet, staggering over to the tunnel to the entrance cave. The inky blackness in front of me makes me pause. Peter didn't bring the candle.

The darkness is absolute. "Peter?" I call in a whisper.

Silence.

I panic. Did he leave? Did he take the hovercraft and go after the City by himself? "Peter?!"

"I'm not dead yet," he says, so quietly that I almost don't hear him.

I fumble through the dark until my eyes adjust slightly, and I can see his silhouette leaning against the opposite wall. I sit next to him, starting when a sharp snarl sounds from beneath me. Frosty wiggles out from under my legs, growling indignantly.

"Sorry," I tell her, and she climbs onto Peter's lap.

Peter doesn't say anything, and we sit in silence for a long time before I can think of what to say. Should I tell him I love him? Or would that just be weird. "What are you doing?"

He doesn't respond right away. Then, "He's right."

"Who?"

"Malcolm. How does destroyin' the Glass City not make me a monster?"

I'm not sure what to say. Telling him that it's the right thing to do doesn't seem like the right thing to say, but I try anyway. "Because it's what needs to be done."

"You're talkin' about thousands of people Rachel. Half of them are my people." His green eyes glint in the dim light from the other room. "How is murderin' all those people goin' to make me any better than Brown? No matter what the majority has done, I can't just condemn them all. I'm not God."

"Brown murders people just because he can. He takes them and hurts them because he thinks he's above everyone and everything around him. *He* thinks he's God. You're not just killing people for no reason, you're saving hundreds of thousands or maybe even millions of lives. No one knows what the future holds Peter, but one thing we can be sure about is that no one will ever be hurt by the Glass City again."

"So…. doin' somethin' terrible for the right reason makes it okay then?" He tenses.

"No—that's not what I meant."

"Sure sounds like it."

"Peter…." I take a breath. "You're the one who convinced me. Why do I suddenly have to convince you?"

"Because I wasn't thinkin' before."

"And you're not thinking now. This will never end Peter. Ever. Even if I'm not up there, someone will become mayor, and it's not going to be someone like my mom. We've gotta do this—we can find a way to save everyone."

"Why can't you just become the mayor? Why can't you convince them to stop—"

"Because I've been down here. No doubt my father will make sure everyone knows that I've been 'corrupted' by the Surface Dwellers, and I'll be thrown off the City. No one would listen to me. This is the only way Peter."

"Only a little while ago you said you didn't want to."

"No. I said I didn't want to leave here. I wanted to stay where it's safe, not because I don't want to stop the Glass City, but because I'm scared." I hate admitting it, but the thought of charging into the Glass City with guns blazing terrifies me. There will no doubt be resistance, and I don't particularly want to get shot again. "To be honest, I'd rather hide forever, but *you* told me that was cowardly. And you're right. So I'm gonna help."

Peter tips his head back. "You don't know what you're gettin' yourself into," he mutters.

"I do too! I'm putting a stop to what the Glass City once and for all. What are you gonna do? Hide in here?"

"No," he snaps, sitting forward suddenly.

"Then what? After everything you've been through to get to your brother, you're going to let this stop you?"

Frosty stumbles off of Peter's lap, huffing in annoyance as Peter brings his knees up to his chest. He sits like that for a while, and I can almost hear the gears turning in his head. Maybe it's his teeth grinding.

Finally, he says, "I met someone in the City. A boy. He worked in the generators."

"So?"

"So I know how to shut them down. At least, I sort of do."

I stare at him, shocked. "How?"

"You vent the steam, then dump the extra water. Someone has to be there to make sure no one stops it." He looks at me. "The City would lose power, and then it would start to fall."

"Except for the farms."

"What?"

I sit forward as well. "The farms have these kind of backup generators, in case their connection to the main dome is interrupted. Also it's like a precaution—every two years the entire City practices escape drills, dropping everything and running to the farms. If the City falls—when it falls—the farms will disengage and their backup generators will start up. They aren't powerful enough to keep the farms in the air, but they will allow a controlled descent, until they land in the Atlantic."

"We can bring Surface Dwellers there." There's hope in Peter's voice now. "Lead them all from the city to the farms. They'll be safe there."

I nod. "We can shuttle them out with hovercrafts when the farms land in the Atlantic."

"Do they float?"

"I…. have no idea. I hope so. If not, then we'll just have to hurry. We'll save as many people as we can."

Peter considers this. "Aye. Sounds like a plan."

"Good. Then all we need is a way into the City."

He stands. "Already got that."

"You mean Malcolm?"

"Who else?" He pulls me to my feet, but his hand lingers in mine for a second before he turns and leaves the room.

I hesitate, pretty sure my face is glowing. Does he even notice? What if he doesn't feel the same way about me? I push the thoughts away—now is not the time to get all girly.

Malcolm is still where I left him, huddled by the fire with the blanket pulled tight across his back.

"Where's the hovercraft?" Peter asks.

"No."

"Malcolm." I give him a pointed look, and he sighs.

"It's outside. Under active camo."

"Active what?" Peter looks confused.

"Just because you're stupid doesn't mean I have to explain everything for you."

"Watch it you bloody little—"

"Guys!" I hold up my hands, looking back and forth between both of them. "Seriously, you're gonna start already? What are you, kindergartners? Come on. Grow up."

"Kindergartners?"

"See?" Malcolm mutters.

"Can't you two get along?" I plead.

"Not with this stupid *bowsie*," Peter spits.

"What did you call me?" Malcolm gets up, and Peter holds his gaze.

"Who's the stupid one now?"

"ENOUGH!" I stand between them before Malcolm can retort, stopping them with my hands on their chests. "What is wrong with you?!"

"He started it." Peter jabs his finger at Malcolm, who sneers.

"How old are you guys? Am I the only adult in here? Jeez guys." I shake my head. "The past is in the past—"

"A very *recent* past," Peter hisses.

"But still in the past," I growl, trying to tell him with my eyes that he's not helping. "Right now all that matters is what comes next. We're not gonna get anywhere if you two can't figure out how to get along, so shut up and sit down!"

There's a heartbeat where they both remain standing, staring each other down. Then Peter slowly sinks to the ground, sitting in front of the fire. "I'm sorry," he says quietly, but his voice is taught.

Frosty prances up to him and sits as well, sensing his anger and cowering against his side.

Malcolm hesitates, then gets to his knees on the other side of the fire, staring over the flames at the Siren pup. "What is that?"

Peter opens his mouth as if to make some snide remark, then shuts it, glancing at me. "Siren." He pets Frosty, who relaxes and rolls onto her back so he can rub her tummy.

"Like the thing that attacked us a few days ago?"

"Aye."

I watch them as they talk, unsure if it's safe to sit down with them yet.

Malcolm looks up at me. "You gonna stand there forever or are you gonna help us come up with a plan?"

I sit. "So that means you're gonna help us, right?"

"No. It means I'm going to help *you*," Malcolm says, sending Peter a black look.

Peter rolls his eyes, but he doesn't say anything, scratching Frosty's belly. The puppy groans in content, her eyes half closed and her front teeth showing so that it looks like she's grinning. I wish I were a dog. I wouldn't have to worry about anything but food.

"So. We know how to get the City to fall, but the problem is getting in." I cross my legs, leaning forward. "Malcolm, that's what we need you for. You leave the City all the time, right?"

He nods, but he doesn't look at me. "Yeah. To get away from my father. I'd fly as high as I could. Higher than the City. It's…. easier to see the stars up there."

"How'd you get in and out?" Peter asks.

Malcolm hesitates. "The security is lax in the resupply hanger. It's where all the hovercrafts go to get fixed up if they've been damaged, or to replenish any medical supplies that were used. They dump sewage, fill the water tanks. All things that can be done quickly, for the most part, so the men there usually slack off. They'll be sitting around getting drunk or something rather than staying alert."

"Well…. If they're undersupplied, is that going to be a problem for us?" I ask him. If we're going to take on the Glass City, I have a feeling we're going to need all the BRRDs and TRRDs we can get.

"Not for flight. There'll just be fewer supplies on board, and less water for the bathroom. How much less depends on how much was used."

Peter raises his eyebrows.

"Anyway," Malcolm says, "getting in through the resupply doors is also easy. No one expects an attack, so all you have to do is tell them to open the doors."

"Well they won't open the doors for me." Peter glances at me.

"Not for Rachel either." Malcolm looks at me too. "Your father's gone and told everyone that you're dead. Made a whole speech about it and everything."

My heart drops into my stomach, and I feel cold. "Why would he do that?" I whisper.

"To avoid the shame of telling everyone you were corrupted by Surface Dwellers. No offense." Malcolm adds quickly, flicking his eyes to Peter.

Peter doesn't respond, giving Malcolm a sardonic look. Are they trying to be good for me? Did I really get them to shape up?

I shift uncomfortably. "Well the City's going to get a nasty shock."

"Yeah."

Peter leans back on his hands, Frosty snoring away beside him. "I guess that means you're comin' with us," he tells Malcolm. "Don't go messin' up. We don't need another Crysis on our hands."

"Wow."

I smirk. Maybe they have loosened up a bit. "So we have a plan then."

"Not quite," Peter says. "We can't just take on the City alone. We need people. And weapons. The people we can get from Hearthtown and Brimstone, but the weapons…. Well, we've all got weapons down here, it's the ammunition that's hard to find."

"I stole a Supplier's ship this time, they'll have plenty of weapons in there. But yeah, ammunition might be low, depending on how many bullets the Suppliers fired before they came back to the City." Malcolm scratches his chin. "The Surface Dwellers working in the generators might be useful. Give them a few guns and they'll go nuts."

"Just make sure they know you're on their side," Peter warns.

I sit back. "You know, when you two aren't at each other's throats, you're pretty good at using your brains."

They both look at me.

"Wait…. was that a compliment or…." Peter smiles, but furrows his brow.

"Sure." I cross my ankles, grinning. I can't deny that I'm impressed with how well they work together when they're not trying to kill each other. "So *now* we have a plan? We leave tomorrow for Hearthtown and Brimstone."

Peter

Between Rachel, Malcolm, Frosty, and me—we've eaten every scrap of food that Felix and I stashed. But we're fueled up, rested, and we have a plan. Rachel's right. This is going to work, and it's the only way to stop what's happened to Colfer from ever happening again. It isn't murder, it's saving lives and honoring the dead.

Rachel and Malcolm follow me out of the cave, waiting as I push the boulder back in place behind Frosty. "This way." Malcolm says softly, pulling a device from his pocket and pointing it ahead of us, pushing a small button. A large hovercraft materializes in front of us, not twenty yards down the beach.

Malcolm opens the bay door and walks up the ramp and down the hall inside. He sits in the pilot's seat, Rachel in the copilot's. "We'll go in silent, under active-camo. Hopefully we'll be able to get out of the hovercraft before people panic."

I'm not sure what he means by silent, but I don't say anything. I hold onto the back of Rachel's seat as Malcolm gets us under way, pushing the lever slowly so that the vehicle lurches into the air and begins to ascend smoothly. The frozen wasteland zips under us as Malcolm steers the hovercraft toward Hearthtown. As we go, he guides the hovercraft over the remains of Colfer, and I peer through the windshield at the destruction below.

A dark splotch of charcoal blackens a wide swath of snow, stark in contrast to the white world around it. The jagged remains of the Dead Handler's gym reach to the clouds, the only thing left standing in my home. My throat constricts and I turn away from the front window.

I explore the aircraft with Frosty. It's definitely much bigger than I thought; there's a short hall leading back to the cargo hold. Three rooms branch off the hall: a medical room, a cramped bedroom with four bunks, and a bathroom. The cargo hold is about as big as all three rooms combined, taking up the entire back half of the hovercraft. The whole ship is fully equipped with all sorts of high-tech things that we don't have on the Surface: healing devices, nanotech weapons, heat reflective clothes. How much of this will be lost when Glass City falls?

In a matter of minutes the hovercraft touches down on the outskirts of Hearthtown. I knew these things were fast, but I'm still shocked that we arrived in under an hour. Rachel's escape pod had been fast, but this ship was at least ten times faster at full speed.

I find a rope in the cargo hold and tie Frosty to the pilot's seat. She whines indignantly, and I shush her. "I'm sorry girl, but it's probably best for you to stay here for now."

We exit the ship, tramping down the ramp. Behind us, the hovercraft shimmers into sight, no longer under active-camo.

I grimace at the burnt out shells of the buildings of Hearthtown. Not all the buildings are destroyed, but a good section of them are, straight down through the middle of town on either side of the muddy street. Now that the Scouts have been gone for a few days, people are filing out of Canyon Pass, searching through the blackened remains of their homes in search of anything they might be able to salvage.

I make my way with firm strides toward the buildings that are still standing, Rachel and Malcolm trailing behind. Both of them looked horrified, and we stop on the edge of town. A boy picking through the mud for ammunition looks up. He sees us and points, calling to the other people who were digging through the wreckage. Everyone looks up, panic flooding their faces when they see the hovercraft behind us. Apparently they hadn't noticed us land, but the sight of the Scout ship sends them retreating behind cover. The sound of a hundred guns being cocked crackles through the air as everyone points their weapon at us.

I raise my hands, gesturing for Malcolm and Rachel to do the same. "Wait!"

They hesitate, and Cliona rises from cover.

"What makes ya think you can show your face here, Gerrethson?" She calls. She keeps her weapon trained on me.

I swallow hard. Rachel, Malcolm and I are in the open. There's nothing to protect us if the people of Hearthtown decide to open fire. "If I had known," I trail off.

Cliona narrows her eyes, shifting her hold on her gun. "Well, maybe ya should've thought of what would happen to the rest of us when you brought your Glass City brat here with you." She jerks her weapon in Rachel's direction, and I instinctively move to stand in front of Rachel, my hands still raised even though they're shaking now.

"This is not her fault. It's the City's. It's her father's." I lower my hands, rubbing the back of my neck as I shift my gaze over the sea of dirty faces. What do I even say? *God give me the words.* I pray silently, my heart pounding as more people line me up in their sights. I steel my jaw, looking Cliona square in the eye. "We've all been hurt by the Glass City at some point. We've all lost somethin'. Our family. Our homes. I should know. They destroyed Colfer." My voice catches, and some of the people lower their weapons in shock. Cliona's eyes widen, but she keeps her cold gaze locked on mine. "The Glass City needs to be stopped, once and for all," I say.

"And how do you propose we take on somethin' with that much power?" She asks. "The rest of us don't have nine lives."

"Neither do I," I remind them, irritated. "I know how to take the City down. I'm goin' to drag them down to our level and show them the only difference between us is a wee bit of height." I take a few steps forward and clenching my fists. "We're not animals, we're just as human as they are—if not more. We do what we can to help each other, to keep each other alive. We give life, and all they do is take it."

"Ya know why they take it?" Connor stands up from behind the shell of a house. I glance toward Canyon Pass and see the scattered remains of his hotel.

"Because they can!" He snaps. "What are we to them? How can we compare?" He spreads his hands, turning in a circle to take in the destruction around us. "They can do all of this," he yells, "and what can we do? Nothin'! You say you can bring the City down, but how can we believe you? When have we ever had an edge over them?"

"Without their technology, *they* are nothin'," I tell him. "They don't know the first thing about survival down here. Once we've got them on the Surface, and their precious Glass City has been shattered across the Atlantic, they'll be helpless. The Scouts are only a handful of the population up there. The rest are civilians, and Surface Dwellers—"

"And what about them?" Cliona interrupts, her eyes desperate. "What about Niall? If you bring the City down our people go down too."

"We'll get as many Surface Dwellers as we can to the farms. They won't fall." Rachel speaks up, moving from behind me so that she's standing next to me.

A murmur runs through the crowd, and some of the guns shift to her. I step in front of her again, waiting for more interruptions. The people of Hearthtown stare at me with wide eyes, and even Cliona has lowered her gun at the hope of getting her son back.

"The Glass City destroyed my home and took my brother. I know what it's like up there and I can't let this go on. I can't let the City hurt anyone else the way they hurt me. The way they hurt *you*. They've taken too many of us, and it's about bloody time we did somethin' about it. This has to stop. Once and for all, this needs to end."

Nobody moves. They just stare, as if I'm speaking in a completely different language. I suppose it's understandable; no one has ever dared to attack the Glass City, or even planned an attack, for that matter. That kind of idea was reserved for conversations and dreams. After a stretch of silence, Cliona steps forward.

Her head is held high and her eyes are still hard, but she lowers her weapon. "This is bloody insane, but if it means I can get my son back, there's not a person alive who can talk me out of it. Tell me what I need to do." She closes the gap between us and stands by my side.

Someone else stands up from behind the remains of a building; Cornelius shuffles through the wreckage of his shop. He kicks some twisted objects that must've been his ware, sending them skittering across the charred floor. "Ah, what the hell, I'm in." Cornelius pushes through the crowd, stopping in front of me. "Nothin' left for me here anyways. If you can come back from the dead, then maybe the Glass City can crumble." He stands next to Cliona, turning to face the rest of Hearthtown.

About two dozen other people join us, but the rest remain where they are, watching us with uncertainty. Everyone is still for a heartbeat, and then those who remain turn away from us and start rummaging through the wreckage again, I don't blame them.

I turn back to the hovercraft, but the pulsing hum of hovertech echoes from Canyon Pass, freezing me in my tracks.

"Were you expectin' others?" Cliona whispers, staring at Canyon Pass.

"No."

The whole town holds its breath, fearful eyes fixed on the canyon. A tiny hovercraft wobbles above the glaciers, careening toward us at full speed. The hood is slightly crunched, and as it draws closer I can see that the windshield is cracked.

Rachel squints up at it. "Is that my escape pod?"

Before I can respond, the hovercraft drops suddenly, pulling up last minute and skidding through the mud before spinning to a stop about a hundred yards away. The glass roof slowly raises, and someone falls out, staggering to his feet and shaking his head.

"Is that—?"

"Garret," I breathe, cutting Rachel off. The rest of Hearthtown stare at him in confusion. Some of them shrug when they see that he isn't a Scout, going back to what they were doing.

Garret strides toward me with purpose, his head held high and his eyes fiery. As soon as he comes within six feet of me he draws his gun. "You thought you could just leave me there." He pants, pressing the gun to my forehead before anyone can react.

I'm pretty sure my heart stops, but I manage to keep my voice calm. "Garret. Think about it. Think of who's responsible—"

"Shut up!" He yells, and the people around me flinch. "I know bloody well who's responsible, and he's goin' to die right here. Right now."

"No!" Rachel tries to push me out of the way, but Malcolm catches her arm.

"Don't—"

"Get off me!" Rachel tries to wrench away, but I shake my head. "He's right. Just don't."

"No!" Rachel frees herself, tugging at Garret's arm. "Stop this. We're on the same side here!"

"*We* are not on the same side," Garret spits. "*We* will never be the same anythin'!"

"Garret." Cliona inches toward him, resting her hand on his arm. "We're goin' to take down the Glass City. They're the ones who destroyed your home. We can't do that without Gerrethson. Don't you want this all to end?"

Garret doesn't respond, staring me in the eye with the gun still pressed against my head. I keep my hands at my sides, fingers spread. Maybe I can knock the gun out of his hands? *No. Then it might go off and hit someone else.*

"I know you're pissed okay? And rightly so. But you're angry at the wrong person. Why don't you turn it on the ones who deserve it?" Rachel begs. "The Glass City took Colfer. And they'll keep hurting people until we stop it. Help us stop it Garret. Please…."

The gun shakes in his hand, but he finally lowers it, and I release a breath.

"Fine. I'll just have to kill you later then."

"Right." I swallow, trying to relax a wee bit. Everyone else breathes a sigh of relief, but I'm not sure I fully believe him. Garret was completely insane just a second ago—he changed his mind too easily.

"So what's your plan?" Garret doesn't take his eyes off me, his face still at war with itself.

"We head to Brimstone. There are a few more hovercrafts there, and we're goin' to need them."

"And how are we supposed to use them?" Conner crosses his arms. I'm shocked to see that he joined us.

"I'll teach some people how to fly them." Malcolm steps forward. He looks hesitant, but his blue eyes are cold and his jaw is set. "It's not that difficult. Any volunteers?"

"Definitely not Garret. Not after that landin'." I meant it as a joke, but all Garret does is stare daggers at me. I consider telling him to stay here—we don't need his help, really—but that might make him snap again.

Cliona scoffs, moving closer to Malcolm. "Well, I've never flown anythin' before, but I've always dreamed of takin' over a hovercraft and crashin' it into the City. Count me in."

"Okay." Malcolm shifts uncomfortably. "But preferably no crashing please. We kind of need to live a little longer than that."

Rachel nods, wringing her hands. "Yeah. If we're going to help any of the Surface Dwellers in the City, we need to be alive."

"Obviously." A tall, middle-aged man with a thick red beard and a fluffy hood pulled over his forehead speaks up, standing next to Cliona. "I'll keep us alive. Just show me how."

Connor nods his agreement, also stepping forward to volunteer.

"Then what?" Cliona demands.

Rachel looks at me. "Then we vent the steam from the generators. The City will lose power and drop from the sky."

I've never been to Brimstone—it's about two days north on foot—mainly because of the massive fissure that cuts past Hearthtown. If we were walking, we'd have to go around it—or travel east to cross the rickety old suspension bridge—but through the sky, it might take hours, maybe minutes to get there. Malcolm steers the hovercraft easily over the glowing river of lava, and I stare out the windshield in awe.

"What does this do?" Cliona runs her fingers over a giant green button on the wall to the left of Malcolm's chair.

Malcolm turns to look, and his eyes widen. "Hey—get your hands away from that, you stupid Surface Rat!"

Cliona's eyebrows shoot up, and I shove the back of Malcolm's chair.

"Shut up and do your job Malcolm," I say. If he's going to run around insulting Surface Dwellers, things might get difficult.

"That button opens the cargo door—do you want her to send everyone flying out the back?" Malcolm's knuckles turn white as he grips the steering wheel.

"She asked a simple question, stop being a jerk." Rachel gives him a withering look from the copilot's seat.

"Well I'm sorry for being concerned for everyone's safety," Malcolm says with a little less force.

"You can be concerned with people's safety and not be a jerk about it," Rachel says.

"Whatever."

"Malcolm's from the Glass City, isn't he?" Cliona whispers beside me.

I make sure Garret isn't in the cockpit before answering. "Aye." There's no sense hiding it any more. "But they're with us now. You can trust them."

"And what if they turn on us?" Cornelius clenches his fists.

"They won't," I insist, glancing at the back of Malcolm's head. Malcolm shifts uneasily, but he keeps his eyes fixed on the course ahead.

"You seem awful trustin' considerin' what ya said about their home." Cliona clenches her teeth, tightening her grip on her gun.

Rachel turns in the co-pilot's seat. "Not everyone up there is a monster."

"No? Because there's an awful lot of bodies fallin' from the sky. Seems like a lot of monsters to me," Cornelius spits.

"Yes, there are a lot—including my father—but not everyone is bad. My mother never hurt anyone! And neither have I!"

"And what did you do to stop others from hurtin' us?" Cliona casts her accusing glare on Rachel.

"I…. I didn't know that was happening."

"Then what makes you think you're any better than the rest of them?" Cliona's voice is cold.

Rachel shrinks into the copilot's chair. "I don't know."

"Back off Cliona. She's not a monster," I say, gripping the back of Rachel's chair.

Cliona leans against the wall, tracing her finger around the large green button that opens the cargo doors. "Really? Are those the words of a free man or a good slave?"

I slap her hand away from the button, getting in her face. "You watch your bloody mouth woman."

Strong hands grab my arm, and Cornelius pulls me away from her. He shoves me against the back of Malcolm's chair, and the hovercraft lurches.

"Hey! Do you all want to die?" Malcolm yells.

Cornelius opens his mouth to say something, but whatever it was is cut off by a cry as a white blur darts from under the pilot's seat. We both look down to see Frosty tearing at his pant-leg. The rope tying her to the pilot's seat has been chewed to pieces, and I wonder if that's why she's been so quiet until now.

"What the bloody hell is that?" Cornelius breaks away, and Frosty leaps after his shoe.

"A Siren." I catch her mid-pounce, and the pup squirms when I hold her up, kicking her paws and twisting to bite at my fingers. "Look at those wee little fangs."

Cliona and Cornelius look horrified, and Cliona raises her gun.

"Oi—put that gun down!" I hold Frosty closer, and Rachel twists around in the copilot's seat again. Fear flashes across her face when she sees Cliona's gun trained on Frosty.

Frosty licks my chin, then looks back and forth at Cliona and Cornelius, growling uncertainly. "This wee beastie's mum tried to kill me," I tell them, scratching her ears. "But…. well, I suppose there's somethin' to be said about innocence in youth. Would you kill this?"

"Aye, knowin' what it's goin' to become," Cliona growls.

"But ya don't know. Who are you to decide what this puppy will or will not do when she grows up? What makes you think that you have the right to kill somethin' simply because others like it have done terrible things in the past? Only God knows the future." I step back so that I'm standing between Malcolm and Rachel. "But even so, animals are different. Animals act on instinct, they can be unpredictable. These two," I gesture with Frosty toward Rachel and Malcolm, "they aren't animals any more than you or I. They don't act on instinct. They make their own choices. Just because Rachel's father is a monster, doesn't mean she has to be one as well. And just because Malcolm has done some pretty terrible things—"

"Wow, thanks Peter," Malcolm mumbles.

"—doesn't mean he doesn't regret them. People change, Cliona. Not everythin' in this world is set in stone. Even the others in the City can change—all they need is a little push."

"More like a long fall." Cornelius looks at Cliona, crossing his arms.

Cliona doesn't look convinced, but she'll have to deal with it. Behind her, a short woman with dark brown hair rushes down the hall from the cargo hold, her arms full of guns.

"Would ya look at these!" The woman sets the guns on the floor, picking one up to examine it. "There are plenty more where these came from—I think this could actually work!" She looks up at Cliona, her brown eyes sparkling. "We're gettin' your son back."

Cliona stares at her, then at me. Hesitantly, she reaches out and rubs the top of Frosty's head. Frosty leans away, sniffing at her fingers and giving them an experimental lick.

"Fine," Cliona says at last. "But if anythin' goes wrong, I'm blamin' you."

"Right." I look at the other woman.

"Oh—I'm Adara. Cliona is my sister."

I raise my eyebrows at Cliona. "I didn't know you had a sister."

She pulls out her red hair, then ties it up again. "Felix does."

My eyebrows go up further. "Does he?"

"Shut it, Gerrethson."

"Well. All the more reason to get him back then."

Cliona's face turns red, but she doesn't say anything. I smirk.

The floor beneath me rocks as Malcolm touches down on the outskirts of Brimstone.

The ancient castle looks like it's been crumbling for centuries, and the smaller buildings around it huddle against each other. Most of them are shacks, but some of them are larger buildings from the old world—like the Dead Handler's gym in Colfer.

Rachel takes Frosty from my arms, ignoring the puppy's squeaks of protest. "Can't give your Braveheart speech with a puppy. It's a little distracting."

"My what?"

"Never mind." Rachel grins, shaking her head.

Malcolm powers the ship down, standing. Cliona gives him a cold stare, and he inches behind Rachel and I.

"You're scarin' our pilot," I tell Cliona.

Malcolm's fist hits my shoulder, and Cliona smirks. "Good."

I start toward the cargo hold. "Keep in mind he's also the one who's goin' to train you to fly."

The four of us walk down the ramp and stop short as hundreds of guns point in our direction.

Rachel

I squeeze Frosty a little too tight, but Peter appears anything but afraid, and as he steps slowly down the ramp to the ground, hands above his head, a few people lower their weapons, confused at all the Surface Dwellers that file out behind us. The people of Brimstone who aren't pointing weapons at us peer out from doorways and from behind buildings, staring with wide eyes at the Supplier hovercraft.

I inch closer to Peter, but the people in front of us have lowered their weapons, glancing from us to the ship and back again. Are they confused because we don't have red uniforms? *Is that the only thing keeping them from shooting us?* Frosty squirms. I loosen my grasp on her, but I don't relax.

A man shoves through the crowd, squinting at the hovercraft. "Bloody hell. Not sure I can afford it but I'll take it. You have to deal with the Scout pilot though."

"What?" I blurt before I think. He'll take it? Does he think we're selling it? And…. deal with the Scout pilot? I glance at Malcolm, who looks pale.

"It's not for sale," Peter says. "But we'll take yours."

The man looks baffled, and he glances at the people next to him before shaking his head. "Not sure what makes you think I have any. It's not like I collect them or anythin'."

"Cop on, Norman." Garret appears from behind me, and I flinch. "We know you have hovercrafts, so ya might as well hand 'em over. It's not like you can use them anyways."

"Maybe not, but that doesn't mean you get them for free. What the bloody hell are you goin' to do with them anyways?"

"Take down the Glass City," I tell him, moving out from behind Peter a little. A few people give Frosty confused looks, and I look down at her. *Oh yes, I'm so convincing with a puppy in my arms.*

"Take down the City?" Norman says it louder than I did, and a collective gasp ripples through the crowd. "Are you mad? You're only gonna get yourselves killed, and then they'll come down here and wipe us out just to make a point!"

"Only if we fail," Peter calls over the voiced agreements. The crowd quiets down, curious, and Peter goes on. "If we succeed, then they'll never hurt anyone again. But we can't take the City with just one hovercraft." He looks pointedly at Norman.

"Please." I butt in when Norman's face twists. "The Glass City destroyed Colfer and most of Hearthtown. Help us end this. We can return the hovercrafts when we're done."

The crowd erupts in anger, voices shouting over each other as they all throw a million questions at us. Peter gives me a look, and I shrug.

"We had to tell them at some point right?" I say, quiet enough that only he can hear. "And besides, it's not like we're going to lose any hovercrafts. Right?"

Peter doesn't say anything, glancing down before turning back to the crowd. My blood runs cold, and Frosty licks my chin, sensing my fear.

Cornelius speaks up from Peter's other side. "Come on Norman. At least do it for a friend."

Norman runs his fingers through his shaggy red hair. He glances at the raging people around him, chewing on his lip, then gestures for us to follow him. "Come with me. Let's talk somewhere a bit more private."

Peter turns toward an old man from Hearthtown—the owner of the old hotel. "You and everyone else try to convince people to join us. We need all the help we can get."

The man nods, and he and the others from Hearthtown merge with the crowd, struggling to be heard over them. Garret doesn't move.

"I'm comin' with you."

Peter clenches his fists. "Garret—"

"I'm comin', with you," Garret says again. As if saying it slower makes it any less ridiculous.

I press my hand against my stomach, giving him the best death glare I can manage.

"Fine," Peter growls, and I stare at him.

"Fine? It's not fine. Peter he's nuts," I whisper, pressing closer to him so Garret can't hear.

"He'll get worse if he doesn't get what he wants."

"That's not how it works."

"It'll be okay." Peter's voice is assuring, but my heart is still pounding.

"Ya comin' or not?" Norman holds out his hands.

"Go on," Peter tells him.

The man turns and leads us into the city. I glance over my shoulder to see Cliona and Cornelius following us as well, Malcolm and Garret trailing behind. The hovercraft shimmers and vanishes, and I look at Malcolm in time to see him shove the active camo into his pocket.

The makeshift road zigzags through the buildings to the front of a crumbling castle, the old stone damp and covered in patches of rotting moss. The smell is outrageous. Sewage seeps into pools melted into the snow, steam rising off of it and creating a smoggy atmosphere. I don't want to put Frosty down and let her walk through the mess, but my arms are starting to get tired, and if Peter's going to convince anyone to help us, I guess he can't really do it with a puppy. I set her down, and she goes immediately to Peter's side, pressing against his leg.

A few people huddle under doorways, sharing warmth as their breath puffs around them. Their wet, patched up clothes hang off their bony frames, and I wonder if these people have anywhere to go. What do they do at night? Is there a shelter somewhere?

Is this where I'm going to end up when this is all over? Peter still has his man cave, but without Colfer, would he still live in it? And even if he does, Felix will be there too. Where will *I* go? I shiver, suddenly wishing I didn't have to give up my bedroom with my warm blankets and clean floors. Is destroying the Glass City worth it if I have to live like this? I glance over at Malcolm; he looks like he's thinking the same thing, his face greenish.

Cliona and Cornelius, on the other hand, don't look surprised. Is this normal to them? *No, maybe they've just been here before, so none of this is new to them.* I swallow. Not that that's any better. I flick my eyes to Garret, but he stares ahead. I'm not sure he's all there, even now. Maybe I shouldn't have convinced him to come with us back to Hearthtown.

Every now and then, as we make our way through the dilapidated buildings to the castle, I see a body collapsed on the side of the road, or sometimes in the sewage. Whether they're alive or not, I try not to think about it, hurrying to stay next to Peter and grabbing his elbow.

Frosty whines indignantly as I take her place by Peter's side, and grudgingly moves to press against his right leg instead. A few people give her odd glances, but for the most part she remains unnoticed. Maybe she's small enough to be mistaken for a wolf pup. No one's really close enough to see the tiny fangs jutting from her upper and lower jaws, and the ridge of fur on her back could easily be mistaken for unkempt puppy fuzz.

Peter glances down at me, and I lean closer. "Have you ever been here before?"

"No. Don't let anyone touch you."

"Why not?" Malcolm asks.

"The livin' conditions here are worse than places like Hearthtown." I notice he doesn't mention his own town. "Disease is no stranger here, and some of them can be exchanged by just comin' in contact with one of the people carryin' it."

I swallow. "That's unpleasant." I am definitely not living here, that's for sure. But where is there to go? Will I be allowed to live in Hearthtown? Doubt creeps into my mind, and the innocent wish for my plush bed turns into a deep longing.

Peter nods. "People don't live too long in cities like this."

"If one could even call it a city."

"It's as close as you'll get on the Surface." Peter shrugs. "Bigger than any place I've ever been. Aside from the Glass City."

I grimace, knowing what his time in my city was like. *But still.* I look up at the sky, but the Glass City is hidden by the clouds. Do I really want to give up the luxuries of the elevated technologies exclusive to the City? Maybe we can try to get some of those technologies into the farms. Like the hovercars or something. Or heaters. I pull my coat tighter around me. Definitely heaters.

We finally reach the castle, and I trip over a fallen brick that had been buried beneath the snow. I catch myself on Peter's elbow, causing him to slip and grab my shoulder. Frosty prances unhelpfully around our feet. We finally right ourselves and catch up with Norman, who hadn't noticed we'd stopped.

"If you're gonna fall, just fall, don't bring me down with you."

"Well, I really don't want to fall right now, it's gross," I hiss.

Malcolm nudges my ribs. "Smooth."

"Shut up," I grumble, my face burning. I don't bother to look at Cliona and Cornelius, not wanting to see their smirks. No doubt I just convinced them I'm a stupid Glass City girl who can't even handle the snow.

Norman pushes open a pair of massive rotting doors, and we follow him inside, helping him push the doors shut again.

"This way." Norman points down the hall to the right and leads us to this door that opens to a narrow winding staircase that spirals down into the basement. The whole back wall of the basement is collapsed, so I can see the downwards slope of the hill behind it. Four big hovercrafts squat in the middle of the room, lined up in front of the opening as if they're just about to take off, covered in a layer of dust. Frosty snuffles at one, then staggers back, sneezing.

"If you don't know how to fly these things, how'd you get them down here?" I ask, stumped.

"Most people will do anythin' when held at gunpoint. Not that the Scouts' cooperation helped them at all," Norman says with a dry chuckle.

Fear sparks in my chest. If this man finds out I'm from the Glass City, would he kill me too? I say nothing, moving closer to Peter. His broad shoulders make me feel a little safer.

Malcolm runs his hand over one of the hovercrafts, looking over its turbines at the other three. "This one's older. How long have you had it?"

"Now wait just a minute. I never said I was goin' to give 'em to ya." Norman crosses his arms.

"Then why'd you bring us here?" I demand.

"Not sure I like your tone darlin'. I can't afford to look weak in front of everyone. And besides, 'twas gettin' loud."

Cornelius leans against the right turbine. "Why'd ya have to worry about lookin' weak if ya weren't goin' to let us take 'em?"

"You know me. I get nervous under pressure."

"So ya took us all the way over here to say no?" Peter shakes his head. "I'm not buyin' it. What do ya want?"

Norman picks at his teeth nonchalantly. "Well that depends. What do you have to offer?"

I scoff. "Are you kidding me? We're taking on the *Glass City*! Isn't its destruction enough payment? It's not like we're going to keep the hovercrafts forever!"

Frosty barks, startled. She stands in front of me, her eyes fixed behind Peter, Garret, Malcolm, and me.

"Glass City didn't destroy my home. I don't want to piss them off enough to give them a reason to."

Garret's face turns red, but Cliona speaks up before he can explode.

"You know very well you're just as much as a part of this as we are." She gives Norman her steely glare.

"Yeah, we've all lost someone, right?" I ask, looking around. "Even me, and I'm from the Glass City." The fear is back, making my heart pound, but I try to ignore it. Peter won't let him hurt me. "My friend was murdered because he was a Surface Dweller. Who've you lost?"

Out of the corner of my eye, I see Malcolm dip his head.

Norman studies me hard, working his jaw. "My wife. And my son."

"Don't you want to see them again? And not with the Dead Handlers?"

Norman doesn't answer right away. His eyes rove over his hovercrafts, and he finally lets out a breath. "If you can get them back…. I want to be sure that I'll still be here. You can't guarantee I'll come back if I go with you."

"Every person counts," Peter says. "We'll have to split into three teams. One to take out the generators and the other to secure the hangars so the other hovercrafts can land."

"Team three will warn the Surface Dwellers in the Glass City about what's happenin' and get them to the farms." I add. "That's probably the safest task—you could be on that team."

"But how do we get into the Glass City?" A voice behind us asks.

I whirl startled. There's a small crowd of people crammed in the corridor through the doorway, and I let my jaw drop. Have they been here this whole time? How did I not hear them? Peter and the others look equally surprised. Frosty, on the other hand, sits calmly, peering up at me. I have a feeling she saw the Brimstoners a while ago.

"Oi, this is private business!" Norman pushes past me, trying to shut the door.

The same voice protests. "I'd say it involves all of us." A young man shoves through the crowd, stopping the door from shutting. "How do we get in the Glass City?"

"You…. want to help?" I raise my eyebrows.

"We've all lost someone to your city," he says it calmly, but I still feel guilty. "Just like you said. It's time to stop this. How do we get in?"

"That's the tricky part. Only one hovercraft will actually get in, carryin' team one two and three. Malcolm here will be flyin' it," Peter says.

"Why only one?"

"He's the only one who will be allowed back into the city without any questions. They know him, he's come and gone before. They trust him." I look at Malcolm, who shifts uncomfortably. I don't tell the Brimstoners that we're still not sure if Malcolm will even be allowed back in the City, given the circumstances of his departure. I can only pray Mr. Crysis didn't do what my father did and tell everyone that Malcolm is dead.

"If they trust him, then how can we trust him?" Norman narrows his eyes, his hand drifting to his belt, where his gun rests loosely in its holster. I tense, and Frosty barks suddenly, pawing at my leg for attention.

"He's gotten us this far." Peter stops Norman with a hand on his chest. "We can trust him."

"When we get there, the guards will be expecting a pilot, a copilot, and a shipment of slaves," Malcolm says quietly.

"Where do you keep the Surface Dwellers that you kidnap?" Peter asks.

Malcolm narrows his eyes, and I can tell he didn't like the way Peter worded that. "In the cargo hold. They're usually tied up."

Peter looks back at Norman. "We'll have everyone in the cargo hold, holdin' the ropes." He says over the murmurs of the Brimstoners behind us.

I twist my ponytail around the end of my finger, glancing around at all the faces. These people, plus the ones from Hearthtown make what, three dozen? Maybe four? Is that enough to take on the Glass City?

"Once security has been taken care of, the other four hovercrafts can land." Garret's voice is cold, and I flinch.

We discussed the plan on the way over here, but hearing him explain it to everyone else makes me wonder exactly what he expects his role to be in all this. I don't want him in charge of anything, but I guess it's not my call.

"They have a plan, Norman." The man holds out his hands. "And it's a bloody good one. My daughter is up there." His voice cracks. "And if there's any hope of gettin' her back I'm goin' after it. Just give them the hovercrafts."

There are a few voiced agreements as people push into the basement with us. The space gets cramped, and my throat constricts when I'm pressed up against Garret. I half expect him to jab a knife through my ribs or something, but he just shoves me off of him roughly, and I stagger back into Peter. Peter catches me, and we move closer to the hole in the wall to make room as the Brimstoners file in.

Norman gives an exasperated sigh. "Alright, fine. Follow me."

I walk through the hovercrafts with Peter at my side, accessing their panels and activating them to make sure they still work. Some of them are a little low on energy, but should be okay once they get some sunlight. We return to the door of the room. Norman has disappeared, and the crowd stares at us with apt attention.

"We'll leave tomorrow mornin'," Peter tells them. "We should all get some rest. Meet us here, bright and early. And—bring your guns."

The crowd disperses. Malcolm glances around. "I guess I'll start training our new pilots."

Cliona and Cornelius nod, and Malcolm gestures for them to follow him onto the first hovercraft.

Garret grabs Peter's arm. "What happens to me after all this is over? Colfer is gone. Where do I go?"

Peter wrenches away. "What you do is up to you. Colfer isn't the only town on the Surface. There are plenty of places to live."

"My family is dead," Garret spits.

"So is mine," Peter says, holding his gaze.

I stay quiet, waiting for Garret to snap and try to kill Peter. I don't want Peter to get hurt, but maybe if Garret tries to kill him we'll have an excuse to leave him behind.

Garret studies Peter's face, then glances at me. I press closer to Peter's back, but I don't look away.

"The only reason I'm comin' with you," Garret says at length, stepping closer, "is because I want to kill as many of those Glass City bastards as possible."

"If you can't control yourself maybe you should stay here," I say over Peter's shoulder.

Garret stares death at me, and I swallow.

"She's right Garret. We're not goin' up there to kill everyone. If you can't keep the casualties to a minimum then you can't come with us," Peter says.

Garret jabs his finger at me. "These monsters kidnap and torture and murder us, and you want to let them live?"

"Not all of us are monsters," I say, defensively.

"Just because they've done terrible things in the past doesn't mean they can't change. Doesn't mean we should sink to their level." Peter lifts his chin. "You only shoot people who are shootin' at us."

Garret is quiet for a moment. Then, "I'll only shoot people shootin' at us." He turns and boards the hovercraft that Malcolm and the others are in, casting a dark look over his shoulder.

"I don't think we should take him," I whisper.

"If we leave him he might hurt someone." Peter stares after him.

"If we take him he could hurt someone! Peter—all he wants is revenge. He's not coming to help us." I grip Peter's arm, desperate to make him change his mind. "He's insane."

Peter looks down at me. "Maybe bein' there when we take down the City will help him?"

"I don't think so." But I can tell Peter won't change his mind. I silently pray that Garret won't try anything. He wouldn't sabotage the mission, would he? Should we even let him be in the same room as Malcolm?

Peter turns to me, rubbing his eyes with his knuckles, and says, "Right, so we'll let Malcolm teach the others how the controls work, and we'll take these and head off tomorrow."

"You seem to be tired a lot of the time."

"I know." He grimaces. Frosty yawns, sitting down. "I can never sleep."

"How come?"

Peter looks away, shifting his shoulders. "Bloody nightmares," he says it so quietly I almost don't hear him.

"I....I'm sorry." All this is because of my father, my city. And even if I wasn't fully aware of it at the time, I still made things worse for him when we were still in the City.

"Don't be. It's not your fault." He still doesn't look at me. "And besides, haven't had much time for sleep. Too busy runnin' for our lives."

I grimace. That's my fault too. "What time is it?"

"Only about an hour before it gets dark."

It seems a little early to be sleeping, but I guess down here, where there is no electricity, people go to sleep when it starts to get dark. I don't feel tired. My whole body tingles with the anticipation of what we'll do tomorrow.

I tug Peter's sleeve. "I guess we should sleep, but I don't really think I can."

Peter raises an eyebrow.

I shrug. "I know. I'm being selfish. You need your sleep don't you."

"I don't think I could sleep any more than you could right now. There might be an inn somewhere with a bar or somethin'. Felix came here once, a few years ago. Told me all about it." Peter's face falls slightly.

"Well we could find out." I hesitate. "I could do with some music, and dancing."

"Alright. If I remember correctly, the inn is by the castle wall. There's a bar, we can get somethin' to eat. Let's go."

The inn is much nicer than Conner's hotel back in Hearthtown: at least three stories tall, the building looks like it survived from the old world, with sturdy walls and a shingled roof. Granted several shingles are missing and the siding has cracked off in places. It looks like the building used to be four stories high, but the lowest floor has been buried by decades of snow, and a shabby door has been cut into the front wall of the second level.

We step inside, and the air is considerably warmer. A roaring fire crackles against the wall left of the door, and several battered but fairly nice tables are scattered around the room. I stare around in shock. Most of the objects in this room—including a massive chandelier hanging from the center of the ceiling—look to be old world. Some things may have been moved, perhaps from the original first floor, but there are clear signs that someone made an effort to make this place look nice. Compared to the filth outside, this building sparkles. Maybe there is hope for a decent life after all this. All the Surface needs is the touch of a woman with a little time. Some of my anxiety fades a bit, and I relax, breathing in the aroma of cooking meat.

On the right wall, several desks have been pushed together to form a low bar, behind which a short, thin man in green scrubs away at an old glass. Something about his red hair and green clothing reminds me of a leprechaun, but I resist the urge to burst out laughing.

A few other people sit in little chairs at the bar or at the tables, all of them facing an empty platform across from us. A closed door stretches toward the ceiling to the right of the stage. Nobody seems to mind as Frosty trails in after us.

The entire room is dimly lit by the candles on the chandelier and torches on the wall, and when Peter and I step toward the bar, the wooden floor creaks under our feet. The bartender looks up, cleaning a glass with a yellow rag.

"Care for a drink? The show will start in about five minutes."

"We'll have some water, if that's okay," Peter tells him. "And a wee bit of salmon if ya have any."

"Why just water?" I mean, I don't drink, but it's kind of weird not to—we're at a bar!

"My father was an angry drunk. Plus we've got a big day tomorrow, and I don't really want to be hungover."

"Oh," I say. Makes sense I guess. But even so, I kind of want to just lose it for a while. Forget about the world. My mom would be pissed, but….well, maybe just this once.

The bartender shrugs. "Suit yourself. How about one on the house, for the pretty lady?"

I look up, startled at the offer. "Um. Sure."

Peter gives me a look.

"What?"

"Do you know what you're doin?"

"Of course I do, I'm not stupid." I stick my tongue out at him.

"Alright." Peter accepts his glass of water, and I take a chipped stein full of yellow, foamy liquid from the bartender's hand.

"Your salmon will be out in a wee bit," the man tells Peter before we turn away.

Peter sits us down at a table to the left of the stage. I sip at my beer, and the tangy taste fizzes on my tongue. "This is disgusting."

Peter smirks, and I feel my face burn hot. I don't want to admit that he was right though, so I take another drink, determined to finish my glass. I feel slightly guilty, like we should be preparing for tomorrow, or helping Malcolm train the new pilots. But I take another sip and watch the stage with anticipation.

Two men and a woman quietly climb onto the makeshift stage. One man carries an ancient bodhran, while the other has a patched up old bagpipe. The woman has a battered acoustic guitar, and she starts to sing a traditional, Celtic style song. The melody is eerie and beautiful; I find myself clapping loudly with the few other people in the bar when she's done. Maybe too loudly. I take another swig of my beer, wrinkling my nose.

The bartender appears at our table, setting down a cracked plate with a slab of salmon on it. Peter thanks him, pulling out his knife. He holds out a second one for me, but I shake my head.

"I'm not really hungry," I tell him. I think I ate a little too much food on the hovercraft or something, because suddenly the thought of eating makes my stomach churn. Frosty, on the other hand, stares intently at the table, her nose twitching.

Peter shrugs. "More for me then," he says, then digs in.

On stage, the woman switches places with the man on the bagpipe, who puts down his instrument. The drummer pulls a small pipe instrument from his pocket, and they break out into a much livelier song, stomping their feet and clapping their hands. One of the men at the bar starts dancing, and, much to my surprise, Peter gets up and joins him, along with another man and a woman. The four of them sing along to the song, dancing in a circle. Peter draws me up off my chair and we dance as if we weren't suffering from complete exhaustion. I'm unsteady on my feet, but Peter keeps me standing, spinning me and lifting me and turning in a circle.

The song finishes, and we collapse back down in our chairs, laughing. Frosty is still sitting by the table, wagging her whole body with her eyes still fixed on the food.

One of the other men, a tall guy with blonde hair and brown eyes, claps Peter on the shoulder. "You're not from around here, are ya?"

Peter shakes his head. "I'm from down south. Colfer." His voice gives away nothing, but I see his fingers clench as he says the name of his home. Some of the magic of the evening drains away a bit, but everything still glows, the colors around me sort of blurring together. I take another drink.

The man's eyebrows go up. "You're the madman goin' to take on the Glass City tomorrow."

I trade glances with Peter. I open my mouth to suggest we leave.

Peter faces the man squarely and says, "Aye, that's me. News travels fast in Brimstone."

"Well, the name's Kieran. If ya live, and ya happen to end up in Brimstone again, come and join us for another round of fun." Kieran thumps Peter's back, downs the rest of whatever was in his glass, and leaves the bar.

"I didn't know you could sing." I grin over the edge of my mug.

"I can't. Not really."

"Well it wasn't awful."

Peter laughs; the tension has eased from his shoulders again. "It's not good either."

"I wouldn't say that."

Peter looks at me a while, one eye squinted a little and a crooked smile frozen on his face.

"What?" I ask.

"Nothin'."

"If we make it through this, I want this to be our life." I look around at all the people. "Maybe I could live in here."

Peter gives me a funny look. "This is an inn, not a home."

"Well yeah but…." I press my hands into my lap, shrugging my shoulders. "It's so pretty in here. It's got this warm glow. Everything in the Glass City is so cold and sterile. It's all…. glassy, ya know? But in here it's like, fuzzy."

"Fuzzy?"

"Yeah. Like it makes me feel fuzzy."

"I don't think that's the room."

I take another drink of my beer, choking on it as I hiccup at the same time. The hiccup forces out a belch, and I burst out laughing, not caring how loud it is.

Peter raises his eyebrows. "Are you okay?"

"Yeahp. I'm fine." I draw the back of my hand across my mouth and try again, this time swallowing my beer. Peter shakes his head, using the edge of his sleeve to wipe off some of the drips on my chin.

"You're makin' a bloody mess."

I giggle, pushing his hand away. "Peter Gerrethson. I think I'm in love with you."

"I think you're drunk."

"That too." I snort, lifting my glass only to find that it's empty. Disappointed, I check Peter's, taking a sip. I wrinkle my nose. "Why did you have to get water?"

"So I don't make a fool of myself like you are now."

"Hey." I hiccup.

"You've never had alcohol before have you?"

I try to think back, but I can't seem to get my mind out of the present. "Nope," I tell him, pretty sure that I'm right.

"I thought you said you knew what you were doin'."

"I lied," I say sheepishly, pressing my hands into my lap again.

Peter presses his palm against his face, rubbing his eye wearily. "Obviously." He empties his glass, getting to his feet. In the background, the trio is playing another slower, Celtic-style song. "We should probably be headin' back."

"But…. One more song?" I give him my best puppy dog face, but I think Frosty does a better job.

He smiles and shakes his head. "No, I don't think that's a good idea. Come on," he tells me, and he takes what's left of the salmon off the plate, dropping if for Frosty. The Siren pup snatches it out of the air, and I snort.

Peter helps me to my feet. I sway for a second before my knees buckle, and I collapse against him in a fit of laughter. I don't know why everything's so funny.

"This was a bad idea."

"Oh come on. You're no fun." I try to push away from him, but I can't stand on my own. The world spins and I feel really light, like I weigh nothing. Like everything that's happened and everything that's going to happen is all gone, and we're just frozen in this moment. I lean against Peter, wishing I could just stay here forever.

"Don't tell mom I was here." I mumble, knowing that she'll be pissed when she finds out.

"Bloody hell, Rachel." Peter chuckles.

"She always warned me against getting drunk, but I'm not sure why. This has been really fun." I press my face into his fur collar, breathing in his scent. "I feel…. Awesome. And also a little sick. I think I'm gonna throw up."

"Alright. Time to go."

"I don't think I can walk." My knees feel like jelly, but that just makes me giggle. "Jelly is a funny word."

"What?" Peter catches me as my knees buckle again, and before I know it he's lifting into his arms.

The world flips a little, and my stomach lurches. "Whoa. That was weird."

Frosty prances around, whining indignantly. Peter doesn't respond, carrying me outside. As soon as the door to the inn shuts behind us, the cold starts to seep into my bones again, and nothing seems funny anymore. The stench of the streets of Brimstone and the looming terror of what's to come shatter my good mood into a million pieces. I press my face into Peter's shoulder and cry.

Peter

A loud crash startles me from my nightmares, and I jump halfway to my hands and knees, gasping. Frosty barks, already on her feet, her blue eyes wide open and her ears straight up. The blankets slide off my back as I reach for my gun, and I hear Rachel groan.

Confusion replaces fear, and I peer over the edge of the bed to see Rachel on her stomach on the floor. I glance up at the top bunk where she had been sleeping, then back to her. "Did you fall?"

Rachel doesn't respond. She staggers to her feet, catching herself on the doorframe of the bedroom and clamping her hand over her mouth. Heaving, she stumbles out of the room.

On the other bunk bed, Cornelius leans out of the bottom bunk, staring after Rachel. "Is she okay?"

"I think she's hung over." I smirk, petting the top of Frosty's head as I sit up.

Malcolm snores away on the floor, and I wonder how he wasn't woken up. Cliona is sitting up on the top of the other bunk, blinking slowly as she wakes up.

I stretch, trying to rub the sleep from my eyes as I get to my feet. I nudge Malcolm with my toe. "Get up."

Malcolm flinches awake, then sits up slowly, giving me a dark look. Everyone seems so tired. Maybe we should wait a little while?

"So should we go?" Cliona asks now that she's alert.

"I don't know." I look at each of them, finally feeling the fear push against the inside of my chest like a physical being trying to escape, sucking the air out of my lungs. *What if this doesn't work? What if we can't make the Glass City fall? What if I get us all killed? What if....* I rub the back of my neck, glancing at Rachel as she walks into the room. *What if I can't save Felix?* I clench my teeth. I have to save Felix. I have to destroy the Glass City. I have to finish this. *Too late to back out now.*

"You've got that look," Rachel says, startling me from my thoughts. There are dark circles under her eyes, and her skin is still slightly greenish, but she appears to be fully alert.

"What look?"

"Determination," she says it dramatically, and I smile slightly.

"Let's do this."

The main ship was moved inside last night with the other four. Rachel has taken Frosty outside to run off some steam. I watch them through the hole in the basement wall, the sight of Frosty bounding through the deep snow making me relax slightly.

"So what's the plan, Gerrethson?" Cornelius asks. "We've all had practice flyin' now, do we get this over with then?"

"Works for me. Is everyone here?"

"Everyone's here." Garret steps out the side door of one of the hovercrafts, leaning on the railing. "What do *I* do in all of this?"

I turn and study him for a moment. I can't trust him to come with me, and I don't want him anywhere near Rachel—or Malcolm. "You stay in the hangar and defend the hovercrafts."

"That's it?"

"That's it. Lots of Scouts to shoot." I add.

Garret narrows his eyes, but he doesn't argue. Part of me agrees with Rachel—Garret is insane, and encouraging his revenge won't help. But his insanity is my fault, and I want to do everything I can to try and fix him.

I make my way back to the main hovercraft, pushing through people to the front where Malcolm is checking the control panel. A few of the people from Hearthtown hover over his shoulders asking questions. They seem to be catching on fast. I wait for him to finish, then wave him over.

"What?" He asks, coming to my side. He still looks tired, and I wonder if he got as little sleep as I did. He follows me back outside.

The people around us are getting ready, loading boxes of salvaged ammunition and saying goodbye to loved ones. I pray this isn't their last goodbye, but I have the feeling that not all of us will return.

"Are we ready to go?" I ask.

"Ready as we will ever be."

"Good." My nerves are on edge. There's nothing left to do. It's time to go.

"What about you? Are you ready?" Malcolm asks, stepping closer.

I don't answer him. I'm not even sure of the answer myself. "Give them ten minutes, then we'll take off."

"Yes sir." Malcolm gives me a mock salute, then calls everyone to their ships.

The building comes alive with scurrying people, and I walk into the main ship behind Malcolm. Rachel rushes in with Frosty just as Malcolm takes the pilot seat and I take the co-pilot beside him.

"This is it. No turning back now," she says.

I take a deep breath. "I just hope I haven't made a horrible mistake."

"Really? Now you're having second thoughts?" Malcolm rolls his eyes, squinting toward the castle. "You're insane."

"Probably wouldn't work if I wasn't." I half smile.

Malcolm shrugs. "True enough." He pushes a few buttons, and the hovercraft rises slowly off the ground. In front of us, the other four rise out of the castle basement, their noses dipping down as they glide forward like a squad of flying sharks. The turrets on the wings are already occupied. The ships level out and follow us as we gradually ascend straight up.

Malcolm pulls a headset off of a hook on the dash and puts it on his head. "Alright, roll call. Gotta make sure ya'll can hear me."

I just barely hear at least twelve different voices respond, all in turn. "Tell them to stay far enough away from the city to remain undetected or unsuspicious."

"They'll have to go above the city, don't worry, I trained them on it last night." His voice wavers slightly, despite his sure words.

"Will that be a problem?"

Malcolm thinks for a second. "No, they'll be off Glass City radar. The Glass City doesn't expect anything from above." Into the headset, he says, "I want you to head a mile south, then straight up until you're above the Glass City. Once you're above it, stay there until further orders."

The headset buzzes with approvals, and beneath us, the other four hovercrafts peel off toward the south, some moving a little slower or more hesitantly than others. Farther below, the remaining people of Brimstone mass on the hill next to the castle, waving as the hovercrafts roar overhead.

We rise slowly through the clouds, and Malcolm speaks into the intercom. "Alright, everyone in the cargo hold, make it look like you're unconscious or tied up." He sounds like he doesn't want to say those words, but he continues to talk. "If someone comes aboard when we land, don't do anything unless I say so. I will make sure that there are no others nearby who will immediately notice their absence. When we land, stay in your teams and stick to the plan."

"You better get back there too Rachel," I say. Only two could be in the cockpit when we arrived.

Rachel squeezes my shoulder. "We can do this."

"I hope so." Her hand feels hot, and I'm reminded again that I could lose more than just Felix if we fail. I want to give her hand a squeeze, but my own hands are shaking, so I brush my fingers over the handle of my gun instead.

Rachel heads to the cargo hold with everyone else.

We get nearer to the Glass City, but rather than heading toward the dome, Malcolm brings us beneath is, toward the cylindrical structure underneath the City.

"You didn't tell me the dockin' bays were underneath the City," I growl. Although now that I think about it, I remember Rachel mentioning that before—the hangars are all around the outside edges of the City's basement level.

"It won't be a problem." Malcolm assures me. "The hangars are just across from the generators."

"Then how does team three get into the city?"

"The elevators." He shrugs like it's not an issue, but I still feel uneasy.

Frosty bounces onto my lap, wagging her tail. Malcolm's eyes widen. "She's going to be a problem."

Before I can answer, a loud voice booms on the intercom. "Phoenix, state the names of your crew and your mission."

Malcolm glances at me. "Say nothing." He pushes a button on the headset. "Home base this is Malcolm Crysis, my co-pilot is Carl Eamin. I'm bringing in a shipment of Surface rats."

"Eamin? Who's that?"

"New guy. I'm teaching him to fly."

"New guy?" The voice on the intercom sounds suspicious. "That is highly irregular."

Malcolm grits his teeth. "Get over it. I've brought back more than enough Surface Rats to supply everyone with their own pets, so let me land."

There is a long pause.

"Fine. Head to Bay 23. Tell new guy he better be ready for a full inspection.."

I breathe a sigh of relief.

"Are you alone?" Asks Malcolm.

I shoot Malcolm a *you're such an idiot* look, and he turns pale as he realizes how stupid and obvious that sounded.

The voice sounds confused. " Why does that matter?"

"It doesn't. I thought we might need help bringing in the Surface Rats, but they're too weak to cause any trouble," Malcolm says, his voice shaky.

We wait to see if the guy bought it.

"Alright." The guy sounds less suspicious and Malcolm and I both sag in our seats in relief.

Malcolm skillfully steers the hovercraft around the City's basement level and through an opening in the side, where the floor is covered in what seems to be a web of glowing blue electricity.

The net of electricity dissipates, and Malcolm lowers us to the ground, powering down. Lined up on either side of us are countless other hovercrafts, and I imagine that the hangar encircles the entire basement level of the City. Malcolm and I get to our feet. We make our way to the back of the hovercraft, where the cargo door is slowly opening. The Surface Dwellers shift on their feet, some of them lying down with their eyes closed, pretending to be unconscious.

A single man stands outside the door, his hard brown eyes glancing over the Surface Dwellers until they fall on us. He scratches his graying beard with one hand, his other hand near his gun.

"I don't recall your leaving, Crysis."

"I was in a hurry."

"What for? New guy needed training that bad? Or did you guys have an ice skating date planned?" The man guffaws at his own joke.

I stare death at the guy and he finally falls silent.

"Alright then. Let's get these rats out." He stomps up the ramp.

Faster than the man can react, Malcolm lashes out and cold-cocks him with the butt of a gun he'd been concealing.

The man's eyes roll back in his head and he drops like a rock. I clap Malcolm on the shoulder. "Smooth. Ok someone keep him contained, in case he wakes up. Everyone else get into your teams. Team two secure this dock, make sure nobody else is here, and disable the security so the other ships can land. Make sure the other pilots who aren't already flyin' get safely to new hovercrafts. Cliona, you're in charge of this team until we get back. Conner, take team three get as many Surface Dwellers to the farms as possible. The rest of you, let's go with Malcolm to the engines."

The last thing I want is for Rachel to be on the team headed to the engine room. It's the most dangerous part of the mission. But she made her case, saying that the team needed as many people familiar with the City on it as possible, and that she had explored the generators with her father countless times when she was younger. She knew them better than Malcolm. The only thing I could do was put myself on that team to keep an eye on her. I had assigned Felix's rescue to the team in charge of getting Surface Dwellers to the farms. At least that way I don't have to see him if he's dead. I close my eyes to push the thought out of my head, but…. If Brown thinks I'm dead, then why would he keep Felix alive? *No.* Felix will be okay. Brown still needs a servant. He'll have kept Felix alive for that, and maybe to rub it in Felix's face that I'm dead.

All I need to worry about right now is keeping Rachel safe, and that's hard enough with her on the most dangerous part of the mission. She catches me looking and gives me a strained smile. I'm pretty sure it's supposed to make me feel better, but all it does is make my heart pound faster. At least Frosty I could leave behind on the ship.

"Team three, the elevators are over there. They're large enough that all of you should be able to go at once." Malcolm points, and Connor leads his team over to the double doors in a block that juts out from the back wall.

Malcolm hits a button on the back wall adjacent to the elevator, and a massive glass door opens up to a vaulted hallway, dimly lit by red light. A man stands before us, his hand hovering over the other button, and my heart stops.

Calvin's face twists. "You."

I lunge to tackle him, but Calvin dodges, racing into the hangar and staring at the Surface Dwellers still waiting for the elevator. I fire my weapon, but Calvin dives into a room jutting out from the wall to the right of the hallway, slamming the door shut behind him. Through the glass window, I see him pull a lever on the wall, and sirens wail through the hangar.

Bullets explode from hidden automated turrets on the ceiling, and everybody dives for cover. Cliona, Rachel, Malcolm and I duck into the hall with the rest of team one. Fragments of glass spray over our heads.

Malcolm leans out to get a better view and almost has his head blown off. "Team three is pinned."

"If we don't get to the engine rooms, this whole thing is for nothin'," Cliona says, standing up to fire off a few rounds and then ducking back behind the glass wall.

"Our way is clear." Malcolm says, glancing down the long hallway. "At least until the Suppliers show up."

"But team three is in charge of gettin' the Surface Dwellers to the farms!" I remind him. "We need to spread out. There are only three turrets, they can't shoot us all at once."

"But they can shoot some of us!" Rachel looks terrified, and I push her behind me, yelling over the gunfire.

"Teams two and three spread out if you can! Take out those turrets!"

Three men from team two run to our hovercraft, drawing the attention of the turrets. I lean out of cover, managing to take out one turret before the second whirls around to spit lead at me. I flinch back, breathing heavy, and the sound of another turret exploding echoes through the hangar.

The third turret goes up in flames and drops from the ceiling, and all is suddenly quiet.

"Where's Calvin" I pant.

Malcolm shrugs.

There's a small *ping*, and the elevator doors suddenly open. A dozen armed Scouts stand with their weapons raised, and Connor's team scatters as the men open fire. Some of the Surface Dwellers get hit and collapse before they can get to cover, and I yell. How did I let things go so wrong so fast?

"Peter," Rachel whispers, "Take me hostage."

"What?"

"Tell them you have the Mayor's daughter. Hold your gun to my head. They won't shoot me."

"Rachel, no!" Malcolm's face is white. "You're dead remember? There's no guarantee they'll believe it's really you!"

"Malcolm's right," I say.

"All the Suppliers know who I am. They'll recognize me for sure." There is a stubborn set in her jaw.

"Let her do her thing," Cliona says. "We have to do somethin'."

Before I can think it over, bullets ricochet down the hall as more Scouts appear farther down. Everyone covers their heads, and I grab Rachel around the waist. "Stop shootin' or Rachel Brown eats lead!" I scream over the noise.

The gunfire ceases, and I stand, pointing my gun at Rachel's head and pressing closer to her back so that her body shields mine. The Scouts in the hallway are closer now, and some of them inch even closer, peering at Rachel.

"That's right. She's not dead. But she will be if you don't put your weapons down....Now!"

The Scouts flinch, slowly putting their weapons on the ground. I back out of the hallway into the hangar, pulling Rachel with me, and the Scouts follow. Those already in the hangar train their weapons on me, but I duck behind Rachel.

"Don't let him hurt me." Rachel sobs, and the Scouts hesitate.

Where do I go? I have to get the Scouts away from everyone else, but I can't take the elevators and I can't go down the hall—then they would probably block the path to the generators.

"The stairs," Rachel breathes, so quietly that I almost don't hear her. "We can trap them in the stairwell."

I spot a door next to the elevator, and I inch backwards toward it. I catch Malcolm's eye, nodding to the door and hoping he understands that I want him to shut the door once we're through. He nods, but I can't tell if he got it.

The Scouts follow us as I push backwards through the door to the stairwell; I hold Rachel in front of me to block any bullets, though I am ready to shove her out the way if they actually do take a shot. I back up the stairs, making a show of dragging Rachel in front of me, and the Scouts follow us. They keep their weapons trained on me, each looking for a clear shot, but I don't give them one.

The stairway doubles back, and the last Scout squeezes through. As soon as the doorway is clear, Malcolm charges from the hallway and slams into it. There's a *clang* of metal on metal as he bars the door shut, and chaos erupts in the stairwell. The Scouts closest to the door struggle to get out, and the ones closest to us glance behind them in confusion.

As they do, Rachel and I turn and race the rest of the way up the stairs, covering our heads with our arms as the Scouts shout and start shooting at us again.

We burst through the door at the top of the stairs and shove it shut behind us. Rachel presses her palm against a scanner, and the door seals. I pull her away and shoot the scanner, and the two of us stand and listen for a moment to the angry shouts as the Scouts pound against the door.

I turn around. "Great. Where are we now?"

Rachel shakes her head. "The East Gate storage unit. The mayor's mansion isn't too far from here." She looks determined, but I can sense her fear.

Before I can respond the elevator doors open behind us with a *ping*. Rachel and I whirl, pointing our guns at the doors—and lowering them when team three files out.

"Gerrethson." Conner approaches me quickly. "Team two is ready for any other attacks."

"What about team one?" I ask.

"They've already left for the generators. Malcolm said they couldn't wait for you."

"Bloody hell." I push my fingers through my hair, rubbing the back of my neck. "Alright. Stick to the plan. We'll get Felix." My heart clenches at the thought, but there's no point wasting time trying to catch up with Malcolm's team.

"You're in charge." Conner shrugs.

Rachel points to a row of closets on the wall to our left. "We should change into Scout uniforms. It'll draw less attention."

"Scout?" I raise an eyebrow. "Not Supplier?"

Rachel shrugs out of her fur coat. She doesn't look at me, but she's smiling.

I don't push her, shedding my layers as well.

I snatch a coat from the closet for myself, and Rachel and I tug the Scout uniforms over our clothes.

"The way out is through the door at the end of the hall." Rachel calls to everyone else over her shoulder as they grab their own uniforms.

Conner gives her an awkward salute, hitching his new Scout pants up around his waist. None of the clothes fit very well, but at least we look more like a team of Scouts rather than invading Surface Dwellers. Probably won't fool people for long, though.

Rachel leads me down the hall and out the door. I glance back at the building: a single story structure, the long, flat building stretches along the side of the dome. A few hovercars are parked in the garage. I almost suggest taking one, but Rachel is already running down the street.

The blurred, colorful glass of the houses on either side of the street no longer seems as vibrant as before. The clear windows show only the backsides of curtains; it's early in the morning, but sirens are blaring through the city, keeping everyone inside.

Rachel and I creep through the spaces between the houses, picking our way through the vibrant gardens until we reach a point where there is no choice but to cross the street. "How much farther to your house?" I whisper.

"Not far."

We race across the street, but I lag behind a bit. Part of me feels like I never left—like I was just out on a long walk with Rachel, and I know the punishment that awaits me in Brown's basement when we get home. What did the mayor do to my brother? I'm not sure I really want to find out, but I keep running, following Rachel down the street to Brown's mansion.

God don't let him be dead.

Rachel

The City's sirens are blaring now. Multiple ships soar over our heads, on a direct path toward the hangar where the Brimstone hoverships must have landed by now. None of them are going in the direction of the generators—the main elevator leading to them is in the center of the city—so Malcolm's group must have avoided detection so far.

The mayor's mansion looms ahead of us. It's strange that I don't think of it as my home anymore.

Peter opens the door slowly; the house is eerily silent. I follow Peter as he creeps across the foyer, through the dining room and into the main kitchen. My father sits with his back to us at the window booth, but my mother is facing us, her head in her hand as she picks at the breakfast on her plate.

It's been so long since I've seen her, and somehow she looks different now. Older, perhaps. Paler.

I stop in the doorway, but Peter strides across the kitchen and presses the muzzle of his gun against the back of my father's head.

Dad stops chewing, the newspaper folding over the back of his hand. Mom looks up, her eyes widening and her lips parting slightly as her eyes shift from Peter and his gun to me.

"You're supposed to be dead," Dad growls, the newspaper crumpling in his clenched fist.

"Aye, I get that a lot," Peter hisses. "Now, where's my brother?"

"Where do you think he is?"

Peter doesn't respond except to press the mouth of the gun harder against the back of Dad's head. He pulls the slide, cocking the gun. "Is he alive? He better be alive, you worthless *git*."

My father chuckles. "You don't have the guts to pull that trigger."

Peter doesn't miss a beat; he flicks the gun down at the table and fires.

My father screams, jerking his hand back and grasping tightly where his middle and ring fingers had been. Blood gushes from the stumps, splintered bone poking up from raw flesh.

"Don't test me, I'm the one with the gun. This time, you're my slave," Peter snarls, his fury written in every line of his face. If my father isn't afraid, then he is a complete idiot.

"Basement," my father groans through clenched teeth. "He's in the basement."

"Keep an eye on him," Peter says.

I pull out my own gun as he brushes past me.

"Wait-" Mom gets up. "He's hurt. I know what he's done—he needs help."

Peter hesitates, then gives a slight nod, and my mother follows him out of the room.

I keep the gun trained on my father, my hands trembling slightly. Dad holds his injured hand to his chest, now turned sideways in his chair so he can glare at me. Even a healing device won't make his two fingers grow back, but that doesn't bother me as much as it should.

"What did you do to Felix?" I don't really want to know. I just want to keep him talking so that he doesn't make me shoot him.

"Nothing that can't be fixed," he growls.

"You're a monster." I can hardly say the words, my voice catching and my eyes welling with tears. Blood from his fingers soaks his chest, and I inch around the island, snatching a hand towel off the stove and tossing it to him. The cloth hits him in the face before dropping to the table. A week ago, we both would've laughed at him, but now it only makes me cry harder. "Come with us," I beg. "You don't have to be a monster. Daddy please. Come with us."

My father glares at me, slowly wrapping the hand towel around the stumps of his missing fingers. "And sink to your level?" He scoffs. "You're not my daughter. Not anymore. You're nothing but a worthless Surface Rat."

The gun shakes in my hands, and I wipe my tears away furiously. "I'd rather be a Surface rat than the daughter of a monster."

"I never should've let your mother fill your head with her garbage." He says it almost conversationally, taking the last bite of eggs on his plate.

"Garbage? Valuing human life is garbage?" I move around the island to stand in front of him and train my gun on his head.

He doesn't look bothered, reaching for his glass of milk as if I'm not pointing a deadly weapon at his face. I slap the glass out of the way before he can grab it.

"Teaching me to love others and see the best in them is garbage?" I ask with more force.

He shrugs, staring at his spilled milk. "Surface rats are hardly human. I simply meant all her God crap filling your head with nonsense. I should've thought a little harder before I married her."

"You're right. Because you've made her life hell ever since," I spit, infuriated by how calm he is. He still presses his left hand against his chest, but he has regained his composure. I want to blast the smug look off his face, but all I can do is point my gun at him, my finger frozen on the trigger.

"I've ruined her life? She brought her God into this and now look what happened. I've lost my daughter."

"He's a better father than you've ever been," I hiss. Even as I say it, every happy moment I've had with my father plays out like a slideshow in the back of my mind, and I choke back a sob. Was it all a lie? Is he even capable of love? How could he just cast me aside like garbage unless he never really loved me to begin with? How did I never notice how horrible he was? All this time.

My father dabs his mouth with his napkin and rises slowly, giving me a blank stare. Without a word he turns to the doorway.

"Where do you think you're going?" I point my gun at his back, and he stops.

"You can't shoot me," he says, quietly. He glances over his shoulder, and he smirks.

"I will." I pull the slide on my gun, but my hands shake. "I'll do it. Don't move."

My father just shakes his head, walking through the dining room to the foyer. I chase after him, screaming, threatening to shoot him, but he calmly opens the front door and shuts it behind him.

I kick the door, pounding on it with my fists, but I don't open it. I can't open it. I can't shoot him. I turn and press my back against the glass, sinking to the floor and sobbing. I should've shot him. Why couldn't I shoot him? Why was I so weak? *God why didn't I shoot him?*

"Miss Brown?" The voice is soft, but it echoes through the empty foyer.

I jump, wiping my eyes quickly. To my right, the two other servants of the household peer around the edge of the living room entrance. "Arial—Joseph." I sniff, getting to my feet.

They both flinch when I approach, and tears fill my eyes again. "I'm not gonna hurt you, I promise. I'm so sorry I never should've let him hurt you, I never should've turned a blind eye I should've known I should have stopped him—"

Joseph stops me with a hand on my shoulder, and I start crying again.

"I'm so sorry."

Arial hesitates, then pulls me into a loose embrace. "It's okay," she says hesitantly.

"Ja, ve forgive you. You never hurt us." Joseph assures me, but I don't feel any better.

"What are you doing here? We thought you were dead." Arial pushes me back and holds me at arm's length.

I wipe my eyes, trying to calm down, but all I can think about is my father. *I never should've let him go.* "We're taking down the Glass City. You can't stay here."

Both Arial and Joseph are taken aback, their jaws dropping.

"Should ve leave?" Joseph looks terrified.

"Not yet." I sniff. "We have to wait for Peter."

"He's back too?" Arial asks.

I nod. "This was his idea. He's here for his brother."

They both pale, and my heart sinks. *What did the mayor do to him?*

"I knew he looked familiar." Arial looks at Joseph. "He looks like Peter."

I can only nod. I look over at the front door, my arms limp at my sides and my gun hanging from my fingertips. I wonder where the mayor has gone, and my breath catches. How many lives did I just put in danger by letting him live? I never should have let him go.

I should have shot my father.

Peter

Felix swallows hard, grimacing. "I thought you were dead," he breathes. His right eye is still pale and foggy, but the burns on his face are just scars now, as if Brown only halfway healed them. "He told me you were dead."

"You need to stop believin' everythin' you hear," I say, using the rest of the energy in the healing device before taking another one from Rachel's mum and using it to heal the cuts and burns on his legs. Mrs. Brown finishes healing my brother at the same time I do, and we help Felix stand. "Ok, let's get out of here."

"There's no point," Felix says through his teeth. "They'll just find us again."

"We won't be comin' back." I promise. "Not this time."

Felix leans heavily on me, and the three of us head back upstairs. I'm glad to be back in the foyer.

I stop short at the sight of Rachel by the front door, Arial and Joseph standing beside her.

"Good to see you again, Peter." Joseph smiles timidly, but I look past him to Rachel.

Her eyes are red and puffy, and I pull away from Felix. I walk toward her—and stop when I see the tears in her eyes. "Where's Brown?" I ask.

Rachel suddenly rushes toward me. She leans her head against my chest and drops her gun. "I couldn't do it Peter." She sobs. "I couldn't shoot him. I tried but he just got up and left. I just let him go."

I feel cold, but I pull Rachel into an embrace. "It's okay. It'll be okay. I never should've put you in that position, I'm sorry. I wouldn't be able to shoot my father either. Let's just go."

Rachel nods, picking up her gun and trying to stop crying. I return to Felix's side, leaning his weight against me and letting Mrs. Brown run to her daughter. She hugs Rachel, and the two of them sob into each other's shoulders.

"We don't have much time," I say, helping Felix to take a few steps. He's still weak, but at least we won't have to carry him. Joseph appears at Felix's other side, pulling my brother's arm across his shoulders.

"I know," Rachel says, calming down a bit and pulling away from her mother. She rubs her eyes, then sets her jaw, looking at me.

"Before what?" Felix croaks.

"Before this bloody city falls. Malcolm and Cornelius are shuttin' down the hovertech. We need to leave now."

Rachel's mother sighs, as if this was something she had expected. "I'll get some things."

"I'll come with you," Arial offers, and the two women hurry off down the hall toward the medical room.

We make our way back through the city with little trouble, warning everyone we see to get to the farms, even Glass City residents. Many of them don't seem to believe us, but others take off running. We reach the storage building near the East Gate, shoving inside and rushing to the elevator. Arial and Mrs. Brown lag behind a bit, struggling under their heavy backpacks.

"What did you put in there?" I snatch a red Scout coat for Felix as we wait for the elevator. Felix accepts it gratefully, pushing his arms through the sleeves.

"As much as we could fit." Mrs. Brown pants, pushing the button on the elevator and watching the doors slide shut before us. "Mostly BRRDs and TRRDs, but I also grabbed Rachel's baby blanket."

"Are you kidding me?" Rachel bursts out.

"It doesn't take up much space—I made it for you honey, I want to keep some memories."

"Mom you're nuts." Rachel shakes her head, but she's smiling. She pushes a button marked with a down arrow, and the elevator jerks as it starts to lower us to the basement level of the City.

I smile too, and Felix takes some of his weight off me. My smile fades though: this is going too well. It's too easy. We didn't have any resistance going back through town.

I'm starting to wonder where all the Scouts are, but when the elevator doors open again, I get my answer. The Scouts have team two pinned under fire—the team responsible for securing the hangar.

I hear Cliona screaming orders over the noise, off to our right. In front of us, the Scouts are slowly advancing from cover to cover toward the hangar doors.

I don't see Conner, so team three must still be in the City, warning people to get to the farms. They can get to the farms themselves, but for teams one and two, this is the only way out; once the power's been cut, we won't have time to run up the stairs and across the city to the farms.

Dozens of barriers have been set up around the hovercrafts, Scouts hiding behind them and firing at what remains of Cliona's team near the entrance to the hangar. There's a barrier right in front of us, and I shoot the Scouts behind it before diving out of the elevator toward it. Rachel and the others following me, crouching next to me behind the barrier. Felix groans as he leans against it, and I hand him my other gun.

Amidst all the gunfire, my two extra shots hadn't been noticed by anyone else. We have the element of surprise.

"We have to clear the path." Even as I say it, I realize how impossible it is. Every Scout in the City must be here.

"But how?" Rachel twists her ponytail around her finger, tugging so hard I worry she might yank it out.

Mrs. Brown's eyes fill with tears. "We're trapped."

"Shh," I say, trying to calm her before her hysterics give our position away. Too late.

Four Scouts charge toward us from a different barrier in front of ours, their weapons firing. I shoot back at them, then duck for cover again.

Too many bullets are flying around for safe hand-to-hand combat, but the four men leap over our barrier, pointing their guns at us.

I stand and kick one gun away, and Felix wrestles another out of a different Scout's hand. Joseph kicks the shins of a third Scout, and Mrs. Brown forces his gun from his fingers. The fourth Scout loses his weapon to Rachel's teeth, screaming as she bites his hand when he tries to pull her away.

His gun clatters to the floor, and Rachel knees him between the legs. He falls, and Rachel crouches back behind cover.

Two Scouts try to tackle me to the ground. I catch the first man's shoulders and break his nose on my knee before throwing him aside.

The second man hesitates, just slightly, and I draw back my fist and punch him in the jaw, knocking two teeth loose and sending him reeling backwards.

The first man comes at me again, but I dodge his fist and kick him hard in the gut before slamming the butt of my gun against the side of his head.

At the same time, another Scout lunges at my brother. Felix surges to his feet and with a roar, he sends the Scout sprawling.

The last Scout staggers from his knees and grabs Mrs. Brown, who starts screaming.

"Mom!" Rachel shouts, raising her gun. "Don't you touch her!"

The Scout looks confused. Perhaps he recognizes the mayor's wife and daughter, and is confused that they're resisting. It gives me the distraction I need.

I catch the man around the neck, holding him in place as I jam my knee into his kidney and punch him hard three times in the ribs. He tries to twist away, but I kick his legs out from under him and throw him to the ground, grimacing slightly as his head hits the glass floor of the hangar and he goes still.

Felix cries out, and I whirl in time to see him collapse under a blow to his still bruised ribs. I lunge at his attacker—one of the first guys who attacked me—jumping over the body of the other man.

The Scout sees me coming just as I slam into him, sending him flying backwards into the elevator. He lands hard on his back, and I kick him in the face as he tries to get up, knocking him out cold.

I double over, winded, and stagger back to the barrier. Felix is gritting his teeth, and Rachel is hugging her mother. But we can't afford to stop. We took out four, and alerted the dozens of other Scouts in the hangar to our presence. They turn away from Cliona and her team of Surface Dwellers and start shooting at us.

We duck back behind the barrier as bullets start flying our way again. At least now their numbers are split. Hopefully we've taken some of the heat off of team two.

"Maybe we didn't plan this out very well," I say, staring around at the bodies of Cliona's team. They can't hold out much longer like this—they've lost too many. My heart twists. I should've been here. I should have helped. We hadn't anticipated this kind of concentrated defense. We'd relied on the stealth of our mission, but Calvin showing up had ruined that.

"What if you hold me hostage again?" Rachel asks. "I'm the mayor's daughter."

"What? Rachel—" Mrs. Brown gives me a look that says I absolutely will not.

"No, I don't think that will work this time. And besides, that would only get us onto the hovercraft. What about everyone else?"

"Right." Rachel looks puzzled, twisting the end of her ponytail around her finger. "Malcolm's team still needs to get here—where are they?"

"I don't know." I raise my gun over the barrier and squeeze off a few rounds to discourage more Scouts from getting close. "We need to clear the route."

"Perhaps this is vhere ve must part vays," Joseph says quietly. He and Arial are pressed against the barrier, and he looks up at me with wide eyes. "It is every man for himself."

"No." I shake my head. "No that's not how this is goin' to work. We need to work together."

"We could spread out," Felix suggests after shooting a few rounds himself. "I'll draw them off and you can sneak around from the other flank. Those are Surface Dwellers over their by the entrance right? We can split the Scouts' fire three ways."

"No way, I just got you back I'm not goin' to risk losin' you again."

Felix opens his mouth to retort when the lights in the hangar suddenly go out. For a moment it's pitch black: then the pressure holding the hangar doors shut is released and they slide open in front of every hovercraft, letting the afternoon sunlight in and silhouetting the hovercrafts from behind. The four Brimstone hovercrafts circle outside, and I realize team two never had a chance to let them in.

"Malcolm must've cut the power," Rachel whispers.

I take the moment of shock to fire the first few shots, taking out a couple Scouts before gunfire sparks up again. One of the Brimstone hovercrafts smashes through a hanger door before it's fully open, shattering the glass and bending one of its wings. The ship is knocked sideways before skidding across the hangar floor, crushing a row of Scouts as it slides over the barriers.

The turrets on the wings light up, and the remaining Scouts scatter. They struggle to make their way to our right, where they still have space to maneuver, but the Surface Dwellers on the turrets have the high ground, making it difficult for the Scouts to take cover. There's not much I can do but watch as the fifty caliber bullets tear through the red uniforms and metal barriers as the Scouts fall back to a different docking bay, out of sight behind the corner of the elevator block.

"Bloody hell," Felix breathes.

Rachel buries her face in her mother's shoulder, and Mrs. Brown holds her tight. Arial and Joseph just shake, holding each other with their eyes squeezed shut.

There's a sudden crash, and I turn to see the doors to the hallway blast open behind us. Malcolm stumbles out with the rest of team one.

"It's about bloody time!" I yell.

"We got held up." Malcolm looks drained, sagging under the weight of someone on his shoulders. "We need to get out of here. The City is falling."

I don't feel it, but when I look out the hangar doors, the three Brimstone hovercrafts slowly disappear at the top of the hangar doors.

"Then we'd better hurry. We probably have about two minutes before the hovertech has completely failed." Rachel sniffs, standing. Her hands shake as she reaches to help her mother to her feet. We move from barrier to barrier, but with the turrets rattling off every time the Scouts stand to shoot at us, we get to the main hovercraft—the *Phoenix*—without trouble. Malcolm stays behind for now with the rest of team one, giving us extra cover.

The three other Brimstone crafts land briefly, letting off groups of Surface Dwellers who race through the docking bays opposite the ones the Scouts are pinned in. They climb into hovercrafts, and about a dozen more ships rise up and drift out of the hangar, some of them scraping the dorsal fins on the top of the doors as the City starts to fall a wee bit faster.

Mrs. Brown helps Felix onto the *Phoenix*, and Rachel and I follow behind. I'm about to sit in the copilot's seat when she stops me.

"Peter—I'm the mayor's daughter." She gives me a meaningful look, but I'm not sure what she's trying to say.

"So? We need to leave now."

"You don't understand." Her eyes are brimming with tears. "These are my people. I am responsible for them—for their errors and for their safety."

She pushes past me and sits in the copilot's seat.

I grip the back of the chair, worried she is going to do something stupid.

She puts the radio headset on her ears and flips a switch. "Attention, Sco—Suppliers." Her voice booms outside on a loudspeaker. "This is Rachel Brown."

The gunfire ceases on both sides, and I make eye contact with the pilot of the other hovercraft.

"I am the—" She looks to me and takes a breath, "—your new Mayor. My father has abandoned you, he is no longer in charge. The City is about to fall. We have been preparing for this for decades. You know what to do. The Surface Dwellers in the hangar are not your priority, saving the people of the Glass City is your priority. We all need to work together—for the good of everyone."

The silence outside continues. Rachel twists her hair around her finger.

Then, men start shouting orders and the Scouts disperse in all directions, and what's left of team two—including Cliona—run out from cover. Some of them stoop to grab the injured, while others lift the bodies of friends over their shoulders. Felix staggers to my side, catching himself on my shoulder, and we both take in the sight of death in silence.

A lump grows in my throat, but I swallow it back, glancing down at Rachel. She's not looking out the windshield.

Rachel grins from ear to ear, standing to hug me. "I can't believe that worked."

No sooner are the Scouts gone, than Malcolm and Cornelius come racing toward us, hauling someone between them. A horde of people in red trample after them, but they no longer seem to be in pursuit—more like they're running for their lives.

I leave Felix and Rachel and run to the cargo door, waving them inside. Cornelius stumbles up the ramp, carrying the man on his shoulders so that Malcolm can run to the cockpit. Cliona appears at my side, barking directions. I'm glad to see that she's okay. Her team took some losses, but I get the feeling that they would've been much worse if Cliona hadn't been in charge.

When the cargo hold is full Cliona gives me a nod and then takes off toward the cockpit.

The city of glass starts to shake.

"Signal the other ships," I say as I re-enter the cockpit. "Tell them to take off as soon as they have everyone on board." Although it looks like most of them are already gone. Far down the hangar in either direction Scouts are loading civilians and servants alike onto hovercrafts. Some ships are already speeding out the bay doors. I wonder how many people made it to the farms.

I stumble as the ground pitches beneath my feet. Malcolm is already in the pilot's seat, Cliona in the seat next to him. Rachel stands next to my brother. We all brace ourselves as the hovercraft lifts off, the nose tipping down as Malcolm guides the ship toward the exit.

Around us, our other remaining hovercrafts rise into the air and follow us out the door of the hanger. Malcolm steers the ship so that it's facing the City, hovering a few hundred yards away from the dome.

"We sabotaged the converters and killed the generator. The hovertech will take a little bit longer to power down all the way, but there's no way they can turn it back on," Malcolm says over his shoulder. "Cliona, there is someone in the back who is waiting to see you."

Cliona's face turns ashen and she lunges out of the copilots seat, running back through the press of people without a word. Rachel takes her place in the copilot's seat.

I follow Cliona to the back of the ship, not quite believing it could be true. In a city of so many, how did they—

"Niall!" Cliona cries, her arms wrapped around her son, pulling him up into her lap from where he'd been lying on the floor. "My baby." She plants about a thousand kisses on him.

I smile and raise my hand in a half salute to him.

He grits his teeth, blinking back his tears and looks up at me. "Peter Gerrethson. Long time no see," he croaks.

"No kiddin'." I shake my head, pulling a healing device from my pocket and using it to heal his burnt hands.

"I hear I have you to thank for this sorry excuse for a rescue." He coughs, his face streaked with soot and grime that darkens his once bright red hair. Malcolm's team must've found him in the generators.

I shrug. "'Twas a group effort."

He smirks. "'Twas mostly that Glass City kid. Pulled me out of the line of fire."

Cliona looks shocked. "You mean Malcolm?"

Niall shrugs.

Cliona hesitates, then pulls her son back into her lap, cradling him like a baby. "I'm just happy to you're alive."

I grab the wall as the ship rocks again. "It's not over yet. I'm glad you're back. I'll leave you with your mother."

I push my way back to the cockpit. Out the front window I can see that the Glass City has begun to fall, seemingly in slow motion. The farms blast off from either side of the dome, the sky bridges to them crumbling as the two smaller domes spiral away from it. A few more hovercrafts soar out from the cylindrical structure beneath the City.

The massive glass dome shatters into billions of tiny shards that sparkle like snow above the buildings.

Hundreds, maybe thousands of parachutes burst open across the City as the hovertech fails completely and the ground begins to fall away. I guess not all of the people made it to the farms and hovercrafts.

"Malcolm, order our hovercrafts to unload people onto the beach below as quickly as possible and start retrievin' people, startin' with those with parachutes."

Cornelius is behind me all of a sudden. "Why? They're Glass City people, right? Shouldn't we just let them fall?"

"Absolutely not," Rachel says from the copilot's seat. "Malcolm, send the same order out to the hover ships controlled by Scouts, from their mayor."

Cornelius looks at me, obviously still not keen to take the word of a girl from the Glass City over mine.

"It's like she says, Cornelius, we're in this together now." Felix leans against me. "And we're gonna show these people how real human bein's welcome guests into their homes. It's about time we start workin' together."

I smile, hearing the satisfaction in his voice. He's been talking about the City and the Surface Dwellers working together for a long time.

Malcolm relays the message to the other hovercrafts.

"In fact, we need to protect them from sea monsters." I point to the floating parachutes getting closer and closer to the Atlantic. "Fly low over them and start to circle."

"Alright. But they won't hit the water for a while." Malcolm steers the hovercraft to the parachutes.

I nod and help Felix back to the cargo hold, where I go to the right and, after a brief hesitation, he limps to the left. I squeeze past the escape pod furthest from the cargo door and duck into the left wing, climbing the three steps into the turret. A headset rests on the seat, and I put it on, sitting down hard and peering at the weapon in front of me. It's much larger than any machine gun I've ever seen, and there's a lever on the left side of the chair.

"Ello?" Felix's voice sounds loud and clear in the headset, and Malcolm's voice responds.

"There's a lever on the side of your chair. Pull it."

I pull the lever, flinching as the chair and the gun in front of me begin to rise, then slide to the left. For a moment, I'm blasted by cold air and the roar of hovertech, and then a glass dome slides over me, sealing off the wind and the noise. I look around, finding myself on top of the left wing. I swivel my turret so that I can see the vast expanse of ocean below, looking for some hint of sea monsters in the depths.

As I watch, the City tips on its side and starts to shatter across the surface of the Atlantic, and even from way up here I can hear it's final crash. "Bloody hell."

"It's gone," Felix breathes, and I know him well enough that I can hear his awe. "I don't believe it."

Glass skyscrapers explode into countless shards of glass as the City sinks further into the waves, the ocean a glistening rainbow in the dying light shining through the clouds. Rachel's small, circular garden cracks off as the last bit of glass hits the water, it's fall slowed slightly by the impact of the other side of the city. By some miracle it remains relatively intact, floating in the waves. The parachutes float closer and closer to the water.

"Who's that on our left?" Felix says into the mic.

Another ship swoops down on our wing. A new voice sounds in my ears, and I recognize it instantly—the voice of one of the men who tortured me. "Liam Gallowvera, Gerrethson. I'm on your side now."

I grit my teeth. "I find that hard to believe."

"Look, I'm sorry Gerrethson. You saved me, and I owe you. And I am on your side."

"Bloody right you do," I growl. "Now let's keep these people safe."

It took us hours to pick people out of the sky. Only once did a shark show up to attack someone, but Felix and I shot it before it could hurt anyone. Other than the shark, one sea dinosaur showed up, sent back to the sea by a spray of bullets.

The hovercraft is packed, but everyone is finally out of the water. No more parachutes drift from the sky, and Malcolm lands the *Phoenix* on the cliff outside of where Colfer used to be. I climb out of the left wing turret, meeting Felix in the cargo hold as the door slowly drops open.

Rachel jogs in from the cockpit, Frosty blinking sleepily in her arms. I feel terrible for locking the puppy in the bathroom, but I couldn't take her with me into the Glass City, and it wouldn't be safe for her to be running around with so many people crammed on board. She stretches her paws for me, but Rachel doesn't let her go.

"It's finally over." Felix claps my shoulder.

"Just give me a hug you stupid old man." I pull him into a tight embrace.

Felix hugs me back, chuckling. "Watch it kid. I thought you didn't like hugs?"

"Shut up." I blink back tears, finally letting myself believe that he's back for good.

We stand there for a moment longer, then Felix pushes away, grimacing. He ruffles my hair, and I knock his hand away.

He notices Frosty and his eyebrows go up. "Is that a Siren pup?"

"It is. Her name is Frosty." I rub Frosty's head, and she squirms in Rachel's arms.

"Where'd ya find her?"

"Remember that Siren that attacked us? This was her pup."

Felix reaches his hand out to the puppy, letting her lick his fingers. "I suppose she's dead aye? And you bein' the sap you are couldn't bring yourself to shoot her pup?"

Rachel pulls Frosty away, gasping. "She's right here!"

"Would you have shot her?" I challenge.

"Absolutely not. Look at those eyes."

"You're a dork, Felix."

"We should go outside." His good eye is alive with excitement, and he pulls me toward the exit.

Rachel follows us, talking quietly to her mother. Neither of them look as excited as I feel, but I can't blame them; the Glass City was still their home.

The four of us descend the ramp. Rachel sets Frosty down, and the puppy bounds through the snow to my side.

Felix laughs, full and loud. "I never thought I'd be so happy to see this blasted snow!"

I shake my head, grinning. "Just wait. You won't be when your fingers start to freeze."

"They aren't frozen yet." Felix hurls a snowball at me, but it misses by a long shot and hits Rachel in the face.

My jaw drops, and Rachel freezes, her hands hovering on either side of her face.

"I'm so sorry," Felix says, his eyes wide.

At length, Rachel says, "Bloody hell, Felix."

All three of us burst out laughing, and Mrs. Brown allows herself a small smile.

All around us, other hovercrafts are landing, Surface Dwellers spilling out of the cargo holds and onto the beach below, dancing and laughing in the snow. A short ways off to my right, Cornelius's hovercraft touches down on the edge of the cliff. In front of me, the Atlantic glistens with hundreds of millions of tiny shards, waves of glass splashing up against the edge of the ice. The only things still floating are the farms and Rachel's small circle garden, the last remnants of the massive glass palace in the sky.

"It's over," I breathe, hardly believing it. Frosty paws at my leg, whining, but I ignore her.

Felix squeezes my shoulder. "They can't hurt us anymore."

I can sense Rachel's sorrow, and I pull her closer, turning my face to rest my forehead against hers. "I'm sorry."

"Don't be," she says softly, flicking her blue eyes away from the colorful waves to meet mine. "It had to happen sooner or later, and we saved as many people as we could. We still have to find some way to get people out of the farms."

"Well, we should probably get started on that soon." I turn toward her a little more, and there's a resounding *crack*. Pain suddenly explodes across my chest and the air is gone from my lungs.

My legs give out and I collapse, Rachel and Felix catching me before I hit the ground. The metallic taste of blood floods my mouth and I choke on it, feeling it trickle from the corners of my mouth as it bubbles up from my throat. The faces of Rachel and my brother lean over me, their hands pressing against my chest. Frosty is barking somewhere behind me, and Rachel takes my face in her hands, her eyes welling with tears. "Peter? Peter hold on…." Her voice trails off as a loud roar fills my ears.

Felix lifts me off the ground, hauling me back into the hovercraft. Frosty is wailing, Rachel is sobbing, and my brother is praying. A second shot rings out, and Rachel screams. I try to push away from Felix, to see if she's okay, but all I can do is cough, blood splattering across my brother's fur coat.

Felix lays me down in the cargo hold, cradling me on his lap and yelling for help. He turns my face toward his, forcing me to look at him as someone pulls open my coat and lifts my shirt. Something is pressed against my chest, and I scream, the sound coming out as a gurgle as I choke on my own blood.

My brother's face blurs out of focus, and everything goes black.

Rachel

It's been two days since the Glass City shattered across the Atlantic. There are nine of us, seated around a table in a room in Brimstone's inn: Cliona, Cornelius, Liam, Malcolm, Norman, Felix, Peter, my mother, and myself. Peter is still a little pale, but he leans back in his chair with Frosty in his lap, having fully recovered. I still can't believe Garret shot him—and then himself. I feel terrible, like I should've done something, should've tried to help him see that he could be a part of the new world. But part of me knows Garret was too far gone to be saved.

"Any sign of Brown?" Peter asks Liam.

I want to hate that a monster like Liam could be saved while Garret, who had already lost everything, took his own life, but Liam has changed a lot since Peter was in the Glass City. He's no longer cruel and abusive, and has actually been rather helpful in preventing fights—or finishing them. I guess it all winds down to the choices people make.

Liam shakes his head. "He was never on any of the hovercrafts. If he got off the City in a hovercraft of his own, it never showed up on the radar."

My heart sinks a little, and Mom squeezes my hand. I want to be glad my dad is gone forever, but a small part of me still wishes I'd been able to change his heart, no matter how impossible it was.

"What about your father?" I ask Malcolm, wanting to pull the subject away from the mayor.

Malcolm shifts uncomfortably, dropping his eyes to the table. "Oh, he's fine. So is my mom."

"If you need me to kick his arse for you I'll do it," Peter says, giving Malcolm a meaningful look.

"Language," Felix warns.

"Bloody hell, Felix," Peter says, exasperated.

"No." Malcolm smiles sadly. "He hasn't…. done anything. I think he's in shock."

"Well, let me know if that changes. We want *everyone* gettin' along down here."

"Thanks Peter." Malcolm sounds like he means it.

"Speaking of which." I add. "How *is* everyone getting along?"

I had broken the Glass City people into groups, but there are just so many that there was nowhere to put them. The Surface Dweller slaves have already been sent back to their homes—Peter had put Malcolm in charge of a group of pilots, and they spent the past two days flying the Surface Dwellers all over Ireland—and occasionally beyond—returning them to their families. I never realized how many there were.

As for the Glass City people, I had ordered them to stay on the farms. Some of the hovercrafts help with heating—it's not much, but the domes trap the heat. Peter put a few volunteer hunters in charge of feeding them so they don't have to kill the cows, but I had to make sure the City people understood that their rations were much smaller than they used to be—and that the hunters weren't their slaves. The major scientists in the City have already started working on how to get power from the magma vents—they even managed to salvage a steam converter from the depths of the Atlantic.

I sent groups of fifty City people to Hearthtown and Brimstone to help rebuild, using snow or bits of glass from the City that was salvaged from the depths. Once those people are settled, I plan to send two more groups of fifty out, but that all depends on how well that plan is working.

"Fairly well here in Brimstone." Norman answers gruffly. He's only here because he's from Brimstone. "Feedin' them has been difficult, but some of them have actually offered to help hunt. There's still a few brawls here and there. A few Glass City people got their faces shoved in sewage the other day, but so far no deaths. Then again, it has been only two days."

I wrinkle my nose. "What about in Hearthtown?"

Cliona and Cornelius exchange glances.

Cliona leans forward. "Things are pretty rough. It's all the two of us can do to keep people from killin' each other—one of us has to go with the huntin' parties to make sure no one 'accidentally' gets shot. We all in Hearthtown are still pissed about how half our homes were destroyed."

"Maybe it's time they get over it and rebuild," Peter grumbles.

"Come on, Peter." Felix gives him a look. "They have a right to be angry."

Peter scowls. "Aye, I'm pissed too, but ya don't see me shootin' people left and right."

"It hasn't gotten that far." Cornelius crosses his arms. "At least, not yet."

"Maybe Felix could give them one of his 'let's all work together' speeches." Sarcasm drips from Peter's voice, but I detect the humor in it.

"Shut it, kid."

I've never actually seen them together before the city fell, and I'm happy that the brothers are finally reunited—even though they seem to treat each other like crap.

"Hey it might work." Mom speaks up. "Words can be pretty powerful."

Felix shrugs. "Alright. I can give it a shot. But they always seemed to annoy Peter."

"You're my brother, everythin' you do annoys me."

"Very funny."

"Tell everyone we can rebuild. That it'll all be okay if we work together." I reach over and scratch the top of Frosty's head, looking at Felix.

"What are you doin'?" Peter asks suddenly.

I look—then jerk my hand back. The fur I'd been petting was the fur on his coat collar, and I feel my face burn. "I thought that was the dog."

"I'm sure ya did."

"Shut up, Peter." I twist the end of my ponytail around my finger, sucking in my lower lip. Frosty puts her paws up on the table, barking like she wants to be a part of the conversation.

My mother catches my eye. She winks at me, and I feel my face burn impossibly hotter.

"I think it'd be more powerful if you and Peter gave some kind of speech," Felix says, grinning. "Rachel, you're the new mayor. You might not hold any rank here on the Surface, but the people from the Glass City will still listen to you before they listen to one of us. And Peter—you're the bloody face of the revolution. If people see the two of you together—and not tryin' to kill each other—it might help some people get along."

"Unless there are still people who blame me." Peter rubs his chest where Garret's bullet had hit him, grimacing.

I shudder, remembering how his blood had soaked his chest, oozing up from his mouth and nose. I'd looked up in time to see Garret press the mouth of his rifle under his chin and pull the trigger. It had all happened so fast. I shake my head, throwing the memory to the back of my mind.

"I doubt there's anyone in Hearthtown angry enough to try and kill you," Cliona says sadly.

"Definitely no one in Brimstone." Norman shrugs. "Everybody thinks you're a hero. Ya brought back families, Gerrethson."

"Which is what makes it all worth it," I say it mostly for myself, but also for Peter, who still looks sad.

He gives me a reassuring smile, and Frosty sits back down, having come to the conclusion that there's no food on the table. She looks at me, tilting her head and wagging her whole body.

"Alright. We'll give some kind of speech or something." I decide, rubbing the underside of Frosty's chin.

"Sounds good to me." Peter agrees. "But uh, maybe Felix could tell me what to say."

Felix snorts. "You're a grown man, come up with your own speeches."

"I'm not good at talkin'."

"Yes you are," I say.

"Aye." Cliona adds. "You convinced me and dozens of other people to go with you on your suicide mission, I'd say you're pretty good with words."

"Given the circumstances, I think I could've said anythin' and have you convinced, just so long as I said somethin' along the lines of 'the Glass City will fall'."

"He does have a point." Cornelius smirks.

"Fine then, I'll help you." Felix rolls his eyes, kicking his brother under the table.

Frosty jumps, her fur bristling as she stares under the table.

"Then I guess we can all go home." Cliona stands, and I wonder if she's eager to get back to her sons. "So what—should we meet back here next week?"

"Sounds good." Felix nods. "Peter and Rachel can give their speeches in Hearthtown in….three days?" He looks at the two of us.

"I can probably come up with something by then." I agree. Or at least, I hope I can.

Peter shrugs. "Alright."

"Alright." Cornelius bobs his head, getting to his feet. "Then I'm goin' home."

He, Cliona, Norman, and Liam all get up and leave the room. I stand as well, buttoning up my fur coat.

"Do you want to rebuild Colfer?" Peter asks suddenly.

At first I don't realize he's talking to me. I look up and see his eyes fixed on me, and I blink. "Me?"

"Yes you. I don't have to ask Felix."

"Count me in." Felix confirms, lacing his fingers behind his head.

I glance at Mom, but all she does is wink at me, pressing her lips together. *Mom, why do you have to be so obvious?* "I would love to," I tell him, smiling.

"Good." He stands, looking at Malcolm. "What about you?"

"I should get upstairs." Malcolm hunches his shoulders, and my heart aches. His family has been staying at Brimstone's inn for the past two days, while Peter, Felix, my mom and I stayed in the hovercraft. Maybe Malcolm should've stayed with us too.

"Malcolm—if you're father's still hurting you—" I start, but he cuts me off.

"He's not. I already told you, it's like he's in shock," Malcolm says, then sighs. "Maybe I can…. make it better, I don't know. I just…. I want us to be a family, you know? If it doesn't work then I'll meet you guys at Colfer or something."

I let my shoulders droop. "Okay." Maybe he'll have more success with his father than I did with mine.

Malcolm keeps his eyes on the ground. He's about to brush past me when I catch him, giving him a hug. "You're still my friend," I tell him.

He drops his head onto my shoulder, but he doesn't say anything. After a second, he pulls away, opening the door. Music drifts in from the tavern, and he pauses.

"See you guys next week," he says quietly, then leaves.

Felix gets up, holding out his hand for my mother. "I believe I heard your stomach askin' for food earlier. Allow me to treat you to somethin' from the bar," he says.

"I don't drink," she warns him.

Out of the corner of my eye, I see Peter smirk. I feel my chest constrict, and I decide not to tell her that I had a glass of beer the last time I was here. I'll take that secret to my grave.

"That's fine, neither do I." Felix smiles.

Mom's face turns red, and she accepts his hand, also getting to her feet. It's a silly notion, but I wink at her as Felix leads her out of the room. She sticks out her tongue, then shuts the door behind her.

"So…. how are we going to rebuild Colfer? There's not much for wood."

Peter scratches his head. "We'll think of somethin'. Snow houses maybe. We could build somethin' in the farms, right?"

I shrug. I hadn't thought of that. We'd used the hovercrafts to tow the farms to the edge of the water and anchor them to the ice, but it might get too cold inside for the plants and animals to stay alive. The backup batteries had run out of energy on the way down from the sky, and the solar panels on the tops of the barns are not enough to heat the domes. "We could use some of the hovercrafts to help keep the batteries charged. Or build some kind of generator. Or we could just tear down the barns and use them to build houses."

Peter steps closer to me, touching his forehead to mine. "I can't pick a favorite."

I suck in a breath. "W-well. We could do two things. We could build a generator *and* use the glass from the barns to-"

Peter kisses me suddenly, and I pull back, startled.

Peter closes his eyes, grimacing. "Sorry, I-"

I cut him off this time, pressing my lips against his and sliding my arms around his neck. I pull away, and he raises his eyebrows.

"Just caught me a little off guard." I bite my lower lip, and Peter grins, resting his chin on the top of my head.

"Rachel Brown you're the most amazin' person I've ever met."

I rest my head against his chest, but I don't feel awkward like I thought I would. Instead my heart is pounding, and I want to press closer to him. "We should work on our speeches…."

Peter breathes a laugh. "Aye, we should do that."

"And figure out *exactly* how to rebuild Colfer." I add, trying to draw my own attention away from the butterflies in my stomach.

Peter takes my hands from the back of his neck and holds them between us with a crooked smile. "Is that the only thing you wanna build with me?"

I pull away, backhanding his chest. "Hey! At least buy me dinner first!" I laugh. My face feels hot, but after everything we've been through together, Peter's offer doesn't freak me out.

He gives me a funny look, but before he can respond, Frosty barks.

Both of us jump, startled. I had forgotten she was still in here. The puppy whines, pawing at Peter's leg until he scoops her into his arms. She licks his chin, wagging her tail, and I shake my head. "You're still the favorite."

"Hers or yours?"

"Bloody hell, Peter." I give him my best Irish accent.

He grins, slipping his free arm around my shoulders and nudging the door to the tavern open with his toe. "Let's go rebuild our home."

THE END

Barbara Samantha Lucas (sylthuria)

Barbara Samantha Lucas (sylthuria)

Acknowledgments

Thank you to Jan Adams from Whatcom Community College for helping me get started on the publishing process in the first place. I'm glad I was able to talk to you.

Thanks to Chuck Robinson and Village Books for supporting my dream of becoming a published author and introducing me to Brendan Clark, who was willing to mentor me through the publishing process.

Huge thanks to Brendan Clark for spending so much time walking me through the steps of publishing my book—I know I'm annoying sometimes but you managed to be patient with me. Thanks for getting me through this, couldn't have done this without you.

Also a huge thank you to Amanda Haggarty for editing my book. That took a whole lot longer than I thought it would, and I appreciate you sticking with me and answering all my questions—I know I asked a whole lot. You helped me make my ramshackle freshman story into a novel and helped me to improve my writing, I learned a lot from you.

Thank you to my family—my parents and grandparents especially, for their financial help. I know you all have been waiting for my book to actually come out, and here it finally is! Thanks for all your support.

Finally a special thanks to my third grade teacher, Mr. Morrow. You probably don't remember me, but you might remember the 'crazy bird' story I wrote for your class. You encouraged and inspired me to continue writing—plus you were the best teacher I've had.